The Wrong Man

The Wrong Man

David E. Fisher

RANDOM HOUSE
NEW YORK

Library of Congress Cataloging-in-Publication Data

Fisher, David E.
The wrong man / David E. Fisher.
p. cm.
ISBN 0-679-40935-1
1. Spies—United States—Fiction. 2. Spies—Germany—Fiction.
3. Fascism—Fiction. I. Title.
PS3556.I813W75 1993
813'.54—dc20   93-263

Manufactured in the United States of America

24689753

FIRST EDITION

Book design by Carole Lowenstein

This book is for Shaina Emily

The recent reappearance of the Nazis on the world stage has coincided with Germany's reunification, and reflects both a secret fear in the rest of the world that Germany's nightmarish past is on the verge of reasserting itself and a less secret conviction that Germany's reemergence as an economic and political giant in Europe is nothing short of ominous.

—*The New Yorker,* August 31, 1992

Prologue

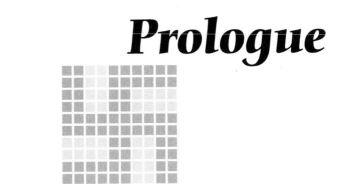

1

FOR SOME REASON Klaus Vorshage thought of the first man he had ever killed. It had been in England, on a lonely country stretch of the Cornish coast; the man had been a member of the Red Brigades whom he had tracked and caught coming out of a small pub just after a misty dawn. Vorshage stopped, looked around, and listened, wondering where the sudden memory had come from. He couldn't have been farther away from those lonely promontories and rocky crags, yet the sound he now heard swept him back to the constant roar of the endless seas crashing against the shore. Then for a moment it ceased, as if the seas had been stilled, and there was total silence; and then a truck ground its gears as it was started with the clutch not fully depressed. It rumbled away, and the only sound left was the swishing of brooms as two women swept the sidewalk's trash and fresh coating of powdery morning snow into the gutter. Aside from the women, and the truck disappearing around the corner, for that one moment the city was empty.

And then he realized what had brought on the memory. It was a triple illusion. First was the sound, the soft roar of traffic from the distant Estonian highways; it mimicked the surf crashing onto the western promontories of England. And there was the smell, borne in on a chilling northerly breeze, bringing a hint of the salty Baltic Sea air into the city. And finally the light: The dull, gray light of the first few moments after dawn on a cloudy northern winter day completed the illusion. There was no sun, no finite source of light, only a faintly growing luminosity that intensified the grayness. It was sad, yet curiously nostalgic; it whisked him back to that lonely morning when he had followed the man from the pub along the winding path until he was sure no one could be watching.

The memory was comforting, and he held on to it as long as he could; but inexorably it began to fade as the city awakened and the distant roar diminished and was lost in new noises, as doors opened and people came out onto the street, as cars came rushing by; finally the last vestige went as a trolley clattered up beside him. He sighed and climbed aboard.

The memory of his first triumph, which had cheered him while it lasted, depressed him now that it was fled—how simple life had seemed then!—and he tried to defeat it with thoughts of today's mission. If life was no longer simple, at least it was interesting. It would be fun to see what was going to happen.

As the trolley rattled away down the avenue, a car grayer than the morning air pulled around the corner and followed.

He rode the trolley through the crooked cobblestoned streets of Tallinn, getting out at Pikk Hermann Square. As the trolley disappeared he stood on the corner, looking around, waiting. The gray car passed by and kept going.

He stamped his feet to knock out the cold in his toes. He stuffed tobacco into his pipe and lit it. He felt better holding it, puffing away, than he had merely standing there with his hands in his pockets. Well, in one way he felt better; in another he was irritated. He didn't worry about cancer enough to stop smoking, but he couldn't help worrying about it enough to annoy him. It was irritating the way they couldn't simply tell you things and then let them alone rather than flogging them to death. His father had lived through the war, and had died of cancer. Oh well.

The car came around the corner again, and again disappeared. Ten minutes went by before it appeared and vanished once more. Five minutes later it came around again and this time pulled up to him and stopped. The door opened and he climbed in. The driver inclined his head in a silent question, and Klaus nodded; the driver returned the sentiment with a grunt, and they both relaxed. It was warm in the car. The driver, a young, large man of Spanish-French parentage, had trailed the trolley watching for anyone who might also be doing so; after getting off at the square, Klaus had watched to see if any other car had been behind the gray sedan the three times it passed. Satisfied that they were alone, they drove sedately through the city and turned to business.

"I read about Haiti," Klaus said, leading into things gradually. "Quite nicely done. I enjoyed especially the *New Yorker*'s description. Did you read it?" When the driver shook his head, Klaus quoted as well as he could from memory: " 'Just past ten on a sunny morning last month in Port-au-Prince'—don't you just adore their style? Quiet, restrained—'a large man carrying an automatic weapon strolled into the garden of the Hotel Santos, where Haiti's Council of State was meeting'—the word 'strolled' sets the tone—'and fired into the lobby, sending people diving to the floor and behind chairs and couches. After emptying his clip, the large man walked out of the garden, got into a car parked across the street, and drove away.' Admirable. Simple, yet efficient."

Jean-Paul Mendoza gave a modest smile, his three gold teeth shining brilliantly in the gloom of the car. "The killing part is always simple. It's the background that counts, the part that no one sees. Finding the proper people to pay to look the other way, without alerting the improper people or— But you are having me on, pulling my leg, as the British say."

"Not at all," Klaus replied. "I myself was never very good at that end of the business. That's why I got out of operations as quickly as I could and moved into administration. Now all I do is give orders and sit back admiringly to see how they will be carried out."

"It sounds simple," Jean-Paul said.

"But, as in your line of work, the real challenge is behind the scenes. The important part of my job is to find the right man for each assignment."

"Well, that part of your job is now done," Jean-Paul said. "How much are you paying?"

"Aren't you interested in who the hit is to be?"

Jean-Paul shook his head. "What interests me is the payment."

"One million deutsche marks."

Involuntarily, Jean-Paul lifted his eyebrows. "*Now* I am curious as to who it is to be. Someone rather important."

Klaus smiled. "Yes. There is also a preliminary hit. To be included in the price." He paused. "Walter Naman."

Jean-Paul said nothing, just kept driving sedately through the city. He stopped at a traffic light and looked across at Klaus. "I thought you and he were friends."

The light changed and the car started forward again. Klaus sighed.

"You are young," he said. "I don't think I was ever quite that young." After a few more moments he said, "Walter and I have worked together from time to time in the past. You and I are working together now. That doesn't make us friends."

Jean-Paul shrugged and extended his right hand. Klaus pulled out a thin envelope and handed it over. Jean-Paul felt its heft without taking his eyes off the road, then glanced inquiringly at Klaus. "Expense money only," Klaus explained, "until you take care of Naman. There is a feeling that we may have to go through several people before we find one who can handle Naman, and we don't want to lose too much money. As soon as he is gone you get half. The rest will be paid into an account you will name when the rest of the job is done."

Jean-Paul nodded and drove another few blocks, pulling up at the next trolley stop. "You understand that our security is quite good," Klaus said, "but there is always the possibility that Walter's contacts may be better. I cannot guarantee that he will not hear about our arrangement."

"He is retired—"

"Yes, he runs his own consulting business these days. All quite legitimate and boring. Don't let that fool you," Klaus warned. "The man is good. He used to be the best. Perhaps he still is." He laid his hand on the door handle. "If I were you, I would get him before he had a chance to decide to get me."

Jean-Paul frowned. "You know your business, I know mine. Yours is now finished. Mine will soon be."

"No questions?"

Jean-Paul shook his head, and Klaus got out of the car and watched it drive away. As he waited by the trolley stop a sudden snow flurry began to coat his head and shoulders, and he hunched his shoulders against the chilling wind. He blinked the snow away from his eyelashes, and thought how simple it was nowadays with these young-sters. Jean-Paul didn't care who was to be killed or why, or even who wanted him dead, any more than he had cared about the Haitians. All he asked was a name, and payment.

Klaus sighed. It would be more difficult with Walter.

2

"MR. CORELLI, SIR."

Walter Naman flashed a smile of welcome as his secretary introduced the tall, rather thin man. He stood up and gestured Mr. Corelli to the comfortable chair anchored to the floor just in front of his desk. "Your letter asking for an appointment carried no letterhead," he said. "May I ask whom you represent?"

Mr. Corelli smiled and nodded, taking it all in. Walter Naman was a good-looking man who appeared to be about fifty-five; Corelli knew he was actually nearly sixty-five. He spoke with a slight German accent, which Corelli knew was genuine but could be put on or off like an old coat. He supposed it was good for business to give off little scents of the Continent. The good Lord knew that nothing else in this office gave off scents of anything that could help business. The Los Angeles sunshine streaming through the windows showed a room shabbily gray, not quite dirty enough to demand cleaning, not quite clean enough to inspire confidence. The office of a business that had never quite prospered, never quite gone down the drain. Sad, really.

Corelli noticed that Naman was sitting quietly, waiting for an answer. "Oh, yes," he said, musically Italian. "Sorry. You may of course ask, but I am not yet at liberty to answer. I am instructed to first ascertain if you are *simpatico*."

"And how are you to do that?"

Corelli waved his hand gently. "I am told I have a way with these things. At least certain people think so, and are good enough to pay me for my gifts, such as they are. I understand you offer a money-back guarantee. It is, of course, worthless."

"As you say," Naman admitted. "It merely indicates a certain level of confidence."

Corelli shrugged. "If we buy your services and you fail, we are dead. To get our money back is not particularly useful under those circumstances."

"On the other hand, if I often failed I would not be able to afford the rent for this office or to pay my secretary. I assume you have been referred to me, and therefore know my reputation and background."

Corelli sniffed. The rent for this office and the salary for that secretary could not be much. But he let it pass without further comment. "You are a German Jew who survived the concentration camps as a child. You have worked for the CIA as well as foreign governments. You are retired, and now advise gentlemen afraid of assassination how to avoid that unhappy end. Presumably your experience with the CIA had to do with such assassinations, so that now you feel competent to guard against them. Much as a successful prosecuting attorney, upon retirement, may make good money advising defense counselors."

"So they say," Naman acknowledged. "And how may I help you?"

Corelli smiled. "I do not move quite so fast as all that. First, there are questions. For example, assuming you once were as good as they say, how is one to know that you have kept up with the times, that your touch has not been lost? What is to prevent me, for example, from pulling out a gun now and killing you?"

Naman returned his smile. "Simple solutions are best. I hope you won't be disappointed to hear that I neither advocate nor use James Bond nonsense. You will not pull out a gun because you don't have one. The doorway through which you entered includes a metal-detector system with a silent alarm. If you were carrying a gun, I'd know it."

Corelli smiled and took off his wig, revealing closely cropped brown hair beneath the long black locks he had worn into the office. Naman was fascinated, leaning forward over his desk and making a steeple of his fingers, resting his chin against them. Corelli bent down and picked up his briefcase. He opened it and dropped his wig in. He reached up and took off his mustache and part of his nose. Naman laughed and called out, "Klaus! For God's sake, Klaus Vorshage! I thought you were dead!"

"*Unmöglich*," "Corelli" said with a smile. "Who told you that?"

Naman shrugged. "Who would tell me such a thing? I'd kill the messenger, wouldn't I? But I haven't heard a word from you for years!"

"Nothing much to say," Klaus said, smiling again. "Nothing much happening."

Naman laughed. "No. Only a total reorganization of the entire world. Germany in control of Europe, Russia a hangdog democracy, the United States afraid of war with a bunch of Arabs. No, nothing happening. Nothing much."

Klaus stripped off the padding from his ears and put it in the briefcase. "Actually, that's what I wanted to talk to you about," he said, his Italian accent fading naturally into a slightly Germanic intonation. He reached again into his briefcase and brought out a small gun. "Plastic," he said. "The bullet casings are also plastic. It carries only a small charge, since a normal one would blow it apart, and so the bullets have low muzzle velocity. They cannot penetrate a bulletproof vest, or even several layers of clothing. But one who is a good shot could, at the range at which we are sitting, split your neck apart."

He raised the gun, still smiling, and began to level it at Naman's neck, when the chair on which he was sitting spun violently around, flinging him across the room. He hit the floor shoulder first and slammed into the wall with enough force to stun him. He was not knocked out, but was unable to move as Naman stood up and walked around his desk, stopped and picked up the pistol, and aimed it directly at his face. "Don't shoot," Klaus stuttered.

Naman stared at him a moment, then asked, "Why not? It's not loaded." He looked hard at Klaus, then put his left hand in front of the muzzle and pulled the trigger. The hammer clicked on the empty chamber.

"Damn it," Klaus said, painfully getting to his feet and checking to be sure nothing was broken, "if you were so sure I wasn't going to kill you, why did you pull that trick with the chair?"

"Why did you pull the gun?" Naman began, but Klaus interrupted: "Don't begin that Talmudic crap, Walter. Answering every question with another question, it drives me crazy."

"Nevertheless, it's the answer to your question. You pulled the gun to see if I was up-to-date. I could have told you about the chair, but it wouldn't have impressed you as the demonstration did, would it? So now let's stop the nonsense, let's sit down and have a drink, and you tell me why you're here." He walked over to the cabinet and opened it. "Still vodka?" he asked over his shoulder.

Klaus sat again in the chair, as a gesture of trust. "I'd like to discuss a situation with you, but first there is another problem," Klaus said. He paused while Walter poured the vodka, and they clinked glasses and drank. "Actually, it's part of the same problem," Klaus said. "You know Jean-Paul Mendoza?"

"I've heard of him, of course. I haven't had the pleasure."

Klaus nodded. "He's going to kill you."

Walter sipped his vodka. "Why would he want to do that?"

"Don't play the ass. He's being paid."

"By whom?"

"Gottfried Waldner."

"You're out of your mind! The chancellor of Germany wants to kill me?" Walter said, and then laughed. "I see. We're still playing tricks, and I fell for it."

"It's true," Klaus said, and they were quiet for a moment.

"Why?" Walter asked.

"Nazi."

"Don't be ridiculous. He was a child during the war."

"His parents—"

"Nobody cares about his parents."

"His parents were Nazis," Klaus continued, "and he fell for the whole line. He's been a closet fascist all his life, and now he's beginning to feel strong enough to come out of the closet. He thinks you may be on to him."

"Me?" Walter shook his head. "I've never come across the slightest hint."

"I don't know the details," Klaus admitted. "But you've spent more time on your obsessive Nazi-hunting than you have on this consulting business lately, haven't you? You've had some successes. Maybe you're closer to him than you think." He shrugged. "Or maybe we're wrong. But if I were you I wouldn't bet my life that we are. Take precautions, Walter."

Walter considered the news. "It's true that one hears stories of a Nazi resurgence in Germany," he admitted.

"They are more than stories. Certain cities—Munich and Nuremberg, for instance—are riddled with Nazi cells, and there are at least a few cells in every city. Such a situation couldn't exist without clandestine help from inside the government."

"Where does that leave you?"

"In a very uncomfortable situation. —Yes," Klaus answered Walter's unspoken question, "I still work for the German security services. It's in connection with all this that I wanted to speak to you, but in checking into your recent activities I came across Jean-Paul. You'd better take care of him first; then we can talk."

"You might take care of him for me," Walter suggested.

"I can't. Sorry, but this warning's as much as I can do for you. There's too much at stake for me to risk my position. Good luck," Klaus added, getting up and carrying his briefcase to the sideboard. He set it down there and, using the mirror, began to put on his wig, mustache, nose, and ears. Walter understood. Klaus hadn't come dressed up for the sake of a joke; it was possible that Mendoza was already scouting around, and Klaus didn't want to be known to be involved. Walter sat silently until he was finished, and then they shook hands and Klaus left.

Walter sat down behind the desk to think. He swiveled around and looked out the window at the bright thrusting spires of Los Angeles. He sighed.

3

VORSHAGE LIKED traveling, not least because it was hard to get bad news on the road. Emergencies could come through at any time, of course, but the run-of-the-mill bad news always waited until he got home. And so he liked traveling, but he hated going home.

The bad news this time was particularly unsettling. No, not *particularly*, he had to admit: It was the sort of thing one got used to in this business. And again he shook his head: No, you never quite got used to it. He leaned back in his chair and closed his eyes.

"You know the Israelis have always been our friends," he said. "We have been one of their staunchest allies since 1948."

The young man seated across from him nodded with a mildly puzzled look in his eyes. What was this all about?

Vorshage also nodded, approvingly. The slightly puzzled look was just right. Why was old man Vorshage blathering on about the Israelis, apropos of nothing?

"Ours is not an altruistic friendship, of course," Vorshage went on. "There are bleeding hearts who would do anything for the Israelis because of our guilt from Hitler's time, but you and I are not among them."

The boy's expression was perfect. Subservient interest in whatever his superior wished to discuss, a slight curiosity as to what it was all about, boredom at an old man's rantings, and just a hint of impatience because he had more important things to do. Karl Friedrichs was a good agent. Vorshage was going to be sorry to lose him.

"We are Israel's best friends," he continued, "because it suits our political scheme to keep Israel alive and well as a pawn in the Mideast, to keep the pot bubbling. For forty years they have helped to keep the Soviets and the Americans on the tongs of a fork, facing each other belligerently, neither daring to allow the other to take over the Mideast—the Russians by getting rid of Israel, and the Americans by making her too strong. And so we help Israel any way we can."

Again Karl Friedrichs nodded, taking advantage of the motion to glance surreptitiously at his wristwatch.

Absolutely perfect, Vorshage thought. What a terrible shame to waste so much time listening to an old man.

"Some of this help is aboveboard," he continued. "We sell them guns and missiles. Some of it is partly under the table: We arrange to have our commercial firms sell them uranium yellowcake. And some is surreptitious: We might, for example, share restricted information with them on an informal basis."

Karl Friedrichs's eyelids flickered with just the right amount of expectation. Finally, here was the point.

And indeed it was. "When I say surreptitious, of course," Vorshage explained, "I mean that the outside world does not know what information we share. But to share information with the Israelis in a manner secret even to us—to *me*—is treason." He shrugged apologetically. "It is even worse than treason. It is a personal betrayal of me."

He kept his hands casually on the desktop. Karl Friedrichs's hands rested, equally casually, in his lap, but his eyes had changed. They understood each other now.

"It's not betrayal," Friedrichs said softly. "I wouldn't want you to think that. My name is not Karl Friedrichs, and I'm not German. I'm an Israeli. I was doing my job."

"Thank you," Vorshage said. "I would not like to have thought it was merely for money—and indeed, I was sure it wasn't."

There was nothing more to be said. It was now only a question of who would make the first move; there was no question at all but that both men could not leave this room alive.

Vorshage leaned back in his chair again and closed his eyes, and the vision disappeared. It hadn't happened like that, of course. He opened his eyes and glanced wearily around the empty room. He would have liked it to have been like that, but it was impossible. A vision out of *High Noon* or any of the other dozens of American Westerns he doted on. The two men, old friends and ancient enemies, steely-eyed and granite-faced, facing each other across a desk or a dusty street or a littered corral, each one waiting for the other's fingers to twitch, to move first toward the gun hanging in the hip holster.

In the real world things were simpler, not so romantic, not so contrived, and much less satisfying. He had received the report when he returned from Los Angeles. They had been aware for some time of the leak, had set a trap, and had caught Karl Friedrichs.

There had been nothing to be said. No explanations of their friendship toward Israel, no recriminations, no explanations or apologies, no regrets. He had simply nodded to the agent who had brought him the report, and two hours later had received the news that Karl Friedrichs was dead. A hit-and-run accident on Goethestrasse. Klaus hoped the boy had never known what hit him. Thankfully the leak had been sealed before anything of great value had gone missing. Karl Friedrichs could not have known more than the vaguest outline of the plan, could not have known that Vorshage himself was involved. He shook it all away and turned back to the routine work of the day. For bad news, he thought, it hadn't really been so terrible.

Part One

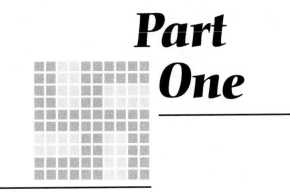

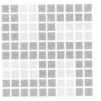

1

1

Lisle Wintre, Mr. Hagan's new assistant, came into the office to conduct her first daily briefing. Determined to make a good first impression, she had been at the office by four-thirty this morning, a good hour earlier than required. Though she had spent that hour, and much of the next two whenever she had a moment free, assiduously rewriting her notes, this activity had served only to make her even more nervous. Now she stood before the deputy assistant secretary of defense for politico-military affairs, her nervousness feeding on the fear that it would be obvious and irritating to the perfectly dressed, cool-looking gentleman who stood up and came out from behind the huge desk to shake her hand. The DASD/PMA was a tall, thin man with perfectly brushed silver-gray hair, a cold smile, and a perfect WASP nose. He made Wintre feel like a child with her five-foot-two-inch frame, conscious of him towering over her, looking down on her paternally. She didn't like tall men, especially those with authority over her. Her father had been a tall man, and though she had loved him dearly she didn't like to be reminded of how it felt to be a child. She said, "Good morning, sir."

William Hagan prided himself on his warm smile and firm handshake, and he gave Wintre the works though he wasn't sure how this young lady was going to work out. He had never hired a woman assistant before, but this girl had fine recommendations, came from a good school, was said to be hard-nosed and a good worker. "This is your first day, Miss Wintre," he said, going back to his desk and sitting down. "Perhaps a ceremonial toast would relax you." He smiled again and swiveled his chair around, opening the door of the cabinet that stood behind his desk.

"No, thank you, sir," Wintre said. She had never had a drink this early in the day in her life. She'd probably throw it up.

"Nonsense," Hagan said, and poured her a good inch of Tennessee whiskey. He handed her the glass, and poured himself a half-inch which he then topped with water. Wintre started to ask for water herself, but Hagan was too quick. Raising his glass, he intoned, "*Prosit,*" as if it were an order, and Wintre dutifully lifted her own glass and gulped half the whiskey down. She spent the next fifteen seconds silently praying and straining to keep it down, while Hagan sipped a bit of his own. Thankfully she saw Hagan then put down his glass, and she followed suit.

"Now then," Hagan said, smiling. "What have we on for today?"

Wintre went through the day's schedule, rattling off her notes. A few hours ago she had been thankful there was nothing unusual or particularly important on the day's agenda; give her just a day or two to get used to things, she thought, and she'd be the best assistant this office had ever seen. But now, on her feet in front of Mr. Hagan, everything in her notes seemed important as she glanced at it but trivial as she talked about it. She was worried about taking too long and boring Mr. Hagan, and about skipping over some vital detail if she went too fast.

Finally she reached the last item without having made a fool of herself. She began to breathe a bit more easily, for this last bit of information was her triumph. Although new at this present job she was not a newcomer to Washington, and she prided herself on an ability to acquire and maintain a diverse suite of contacts. It was gratifying on her first day in office to be able to show off the fruits of this ability. And so with a brief and modest smile, she informed the DASD/PMA that the Israeli government was sending a special envoy with a confidential message for the assistant director of operations of the FBI; he would be flying into Washington National this afternoon at four P.M. and had an appointment set up for five-thirty at Justice.

Instead of being impressed by this information, Hagan simply asked, "What's it all about?"

"It was too confidential to be reported over the wire," Wintre said. "But he'll be here this afternoon. I imagine the ADO will discuss it at tomorrow morning's board meeting." Hagan stared at her, and she continued, beginning to get just a bit nervous. "It's probably nothing important. You know what the Israelis are like these days. They think they've got the answers to all creation, and anything they pick up takes on a tremendous importance. In their own eyes," she concluded lamely.

Ponderously, just a bit pompously—for effect—Hagan said, "Miss Wintre. If you are to be a success here at Defense, you will learn very quickly not to use the phrase 'I imagine.' We are not interested in your imaginings, only in your information. Is that perfectly clear?"

"Yes, sir."

"You will furthermore learn that when somebody comes into this office to talk to me I do not want to have to wait until he opens his mouth to find out what he is going to say. Do you read me?"

"Ah, yes sir. But the envoy is *not* in fact coming to see you. Sir. He has an appointment with the ADO."

"The gentleman does not yet know it, Miss Wintre, nor evidently do you, but he does *in fact* have an appointment with me, this afternoon at five. You will meet him at the airport and bring him directly here, then stand by to take him to Justice for his five-thirty meeting."

The deputy assistant secretary waited. He could see on Wintre's face that there were several questions banging around inside her head. She wanted to ask how she was supposed to find out something that was too secret to be mentioned over the wires, and what she was to do at the airport if, as seemed likely, a representative from the FBI was also waiting to meet the envoy and take him directly to Justice. If she uttered those questions, her career here at Defense would be effectively over and the DASD/PMA would have to embark on the arduous chore of finding another assistant. He didn't want to do that, but it was best to know these things right up front. And so he waited, and was gratified to hear Wintre say nothing except "Yes, sir." Hagan did not, of course, acknowledge by any expression that he was gratified. Instead, he picked up the telephone. "Edna," he said to his secretary, "get me What's-his-name at the company."

He waited with the phone to his ear, staring coldly at Wintre, until the connection was made. "Hello, Henry, this is me. I understand the G-men have a visitor coming in this afternoon from the Holy Land. What the hell is it all about?" He paused, listening, then said, "Perhaps we'd better do lunch today. Johnny Duke's at two? I'll make the reservation." He hung up. "Is there anything else?" he asked Wintre.

"No sir. That covers the day's briefing."

"Yes. Very informative. Thank you, Wintre." When she went he leaned back in his chair and nodded thoughtfully. Wintre was certainly right, he thought: This messenger from Tel Aviv was not likely to be carrying anything of importance. In the ordinary course of things he wouldn't have bothered to talk to him. But it was an opportunity to teach young Wintre a lesson in thoroughness. He glanced at his calendar for the day and frowned briefly. A nuisance, really, wasting half an hour with this man. Still, it was just as well to get these procedural details out of the way early on, and find out if the girl has it on the ball or not. If Wintre couldn't worm out of Edna who his contact was at the CIA, and outbluster whomever the FBI sent to meet this afternoon's messenger, she wasn't the sort of assistant he wanted. We'll see how fast she learns the ropes, Hagan thought, then forgot about her and turned back to the first of the day's business.

2

THE PIT AT the Manhattan 20th Precinct station was crowded, overheated, and dirty; it was a normal day. Under the leaded, wire-meshed windows a detective sat taking the particulars of an apartment break-in from a garrulous fat woman who was clearly enjoying the most exciting thing that would ever happen to her. Further along the wall another detective was filling out the paperwork on a routine mugging. Toward the center of the room were two more desks. One was unattended; on it sprawled two teenagers noisily waiting their turn to be booked by the cop at the next desk, who was writing up their companion.

The holding cell was full: four women and three men in an area built in more optimistic times to hold four men. The wall next to the windows was lined with filing cabinets. Against the third wall stood two more desks, both occupied. At one a uniformed policeman was taking a telephone call, at the other a tired detective was holding a leather briefcase on his lap. It had been taken from the unconscious grasp of a subway mugger who had been shot by a vigilante. Neither of the mugger's known victims had claimed it, but it was a sure bet the mugger hadn't bought it at Bloomie's. The only way to find the owner was to open it and hope there'd be identification inside. But the briefcase was securely locked. So Detective Oliver Robertson took out his Swiss army knife and unfolded the thinnest blade. It was a genuine Swiss army knife; the imitations weren't made strong enough, and their tips broke off in this kind of work. Robertson inserted the blade into the lock and began to jiggle it around.

The fat woman suddenly screeched, laughing at something her detective said. Her detective didn't seem to find it amusing. One of the three teenagers, the one sitting on the empty desk, began to bang his heels noisily against it. The cop told him to stop, and was just turning back to his papers in triplicate when the room exploded.

The events leading to the explosion had begun a few hours previously, in the rain, when Jesus Delgado became exasperated. When the rain had started, right in the middle of rush hour, he told himself not to get upset, to stay calm. After all, in rainy rush hours he didn't have to cruise up and down the city streets searching for a fare; every corner had two or three people waving desperately at him. But within fifteen minutes of the beginning of the rain he had become so infuriated with the sloshing pace of stalled traffic and the impatient idiots who cut in and out of the lanes to gain a few inches at a time that he was no longer able to contemplate the good things in life, and within twenty minutes he had himself joined the lane-crashers and horn-honkers.

The light changed four times while he waited, moving inches at a time, on Fifty-ninth Street between Lex and Madison. As it turned green for the fifth time there were only four cars ahead of him, and he breathed a noisy and sarcastic thank-you to Christ Jesus for this blessing, and then the first idiot in line decided to turn left and there were people crossing Lexington and the idiot stopped and waited for them. The imbecile behind him could either have stayed behind him, leaving enough room on the right for other cars to squeeze by, or could have himself squeezed by and kept traffic flowing. Instead—it was a woman, of course—she pulled to the right, intending to pass, but couldn't decide if there was room enough. And so she, too, stopped, blocking everyone.

Jesus hit his horn, as did everyone in the long line of cars behind him. But the cacophony didn't bother those two idiots, or the people leisurely crossing Lexington. Finally the pedestrian stream ended and the first car made its left turn. As the second car pulled ahead and crossed the avenue, the light changed again from green to red. The unbelievable idiot in front of Jesus put on his brakes. The red lights on the rear of his car flashed into Jesus's eyes like a flag to a bull, and he jammed his fist down hard on the horn. This evidently shocked the driver ahead of him into sensibility, or scared the hell out of him: The red brake lights disappeared and the car shot ahead, zooming across Lexington. Jesus followed, his foot firmly on the gas.

The light changed to red just before the car in front of Jesus hit the intersection, and the car made it across before the Lexington drivers had a chance to start. Jesus himself nearly made it across. He managed to swerve in front of the first car, which—ignoring the cab, because the light had changed and *he* had the right of way—came charging out of the starting block. As he careened in front of the northbound car, Jesus saw open space ahead and dove for it, but a Cadillac limousine in the second line of traffic came just a bit too fast and caught his rear bumper. There was a screech of metal, and both cars stopped.

Jesus jumped out of the car into the rain, screaming blasphemies. His fare got out of the rear door, looked at the bumpers of the two cars locked together, and quietly disappeared into the surrounding crowd. The limousine driver, a small Israeli, inspected the damage and tried to calm Jesus down. "There's hardly a scratch," he said. "You want to make a big deal out of it, or should we just separate the cars and forget it?"

The intersection was totally blocked by now and traffic was already backing up past Madison, but Jesus didn't care about that. He had simply lost control. He was screaming curses at his fare, who had run away with seven dollars on the meter, which was still ticking, and at this idiot limo driver, who didn't know enough to let a man get past a changing light, and at Christ Jesus, who had no sympathy for those cursed to live their lives in this fucking rat-maze.

Finally he calmed down enough to realize that the limo driver was right. He stood on his rear bumper and bounced up and down while the limo driver and two helping passers-by tried to lift the limo bumper free.

They couldn't. It was stuck. The limo driver glanced nervously at his watch. He was already late because of this damn rain and traffic, though he had left early. There was no way he was going to make his pickup. "Why me, God?" he implored. "Why does everything happen to me?" He turned his back on the cab driver, who was screaming into the rain again, and ran across the street toward two telephones on the corner. By a miracle neither phone was in use. As he pulled a quarter out of his pocket he lifted up the headphone of first one and then the other, and discovered the source of all miracles in this city: Nothing was working.

Gerhard Kremble stood waiting on the wet pavement under the green overhanging awning of the residential hotel on West Seventy-first

Street, shifting his briefcase from hand to hand, alternately staring at his watch and leaning out into the rain to look down the street. Crosstown traffic prefers Seventy-second Street, and the people who live on Seventy-first have lived in the city too long to even think about driving a car in Manhattan, so the street was empty even during rush hour.

Finally Mr. Kremble had to acknowledge that the limo was late, and eventually had to decide that he couldn't wait for it and he'd better take a taxi. He stepped inside the lobby and asked the bell captain to get him one.

The bell captain didn't laugh, because this was an aristocratic hotel, but he did explain that on a rainy evening at rush hour there was less chance of finding a taxi cruising Seventy-first Street than there was of Iraq broadcasting Yom Kippur services on their national television. He suggested, instead, the subway. "It's the only way to get anyplace this time of day. Where you going?"

"The Beldenmore Hotel on East Twenty-eighth Street."

"Nothing to it. Everyone'll be going the other way, so it won't even be too crowded. Be there in fifteen minutes, twenty tops." And he told Mr. Kremble how to walk down one block to Central Park West and catch the C train, and advised him to walk to the end of the platform and take either the first or last car in order to get a seat. And indeed Mr. Kremble was able to get a seat, which was fortunate since his briefcase was heavy and he wasn't inclined to put it down on the floor where he couldn't keep a hand on it. Unfortunately, though, he had chosen to walk to the front end of the platform rather than the rear, and so he was in the first car of the subway train when Terry Lee Gaiter opened the door lettered DO NOT OPEN and passed between the cars of the subway train.

Terry Lee looked quickly through the car and decided it looked okay. Nothing special, but okay. There was a bunch of black schoolkids up front, jiving and fussing; they were cool and wouldn't give him no trouble. A bunch of white women near the center; easy, but their shopping bags were cheap and full—they wouldn't have much in their handbags. A few black men, none in suits or jackets: workingmen, who also wouldn't have much. An elderly white man in shabby clothes, tired and swaying with the train motion, staring half-asleep in front of him: looked like a screamer, not worth the trouble.

And then there were about a dozen middle-aged white males who looked as if they might collectively make Terry Lee's time worth something. He walked up to the first, stumbled a bit as the train rounded a curve, and leaned forward into his face. "Give me your wallet, mother-fucker," he said.

He had nothing against the man, but you had to let them know you weren't about to enter into discussions. The man looked up, startled, then swiveled his head toward the other people in the car. Terry Lee leaned forward; you had to stop that kind of stuff right away. He put his finger against the man's nose and firmly turned him back until they were face to face.

Terry Lee was a big man. Most of the bigness was fat, but all of it was ugly. It was his working capital, his stock in trade. "*Now,* man," he said, and the man shifted his eyes toward the other riders but kept his face facing forward. Nobody else said anything. Maybe they hadn't noticed. Maybe they had. If they had, they were probably figuring it was only another thirty seconds until they came to Fifty-ninth Street and the big nigger couldn't hassle more than maybe one more person before then and there were close to a dozen other men in the car so the odds were better than ten to one they could get out without being robbed, and that's pretty good odds for New York these days, whereas if they tried to help the poor schmuck the big nigger would probably pull out a knife and they'd both get cut so what was the point?

The man turned over his wallet, and Terry Lee moved down the line. There were a couple of empty seats and then a white man almost as big as him who wasn't worth the trouble he might be but next to him was a smaller man with a briefcase on his lap. He asked the man for his wallet and the briefcase, but the man refused to give up either so Terry Lee took out his knife and in one quick motion slit the man's right nostril open just as he had seen Jack Nicholson do in some movie. Aside from the artistic aspect, he had found this was a good maneuver because it brought out a lot of blood and everyone looked at the blood and forgot everything else.

It worked just fine. The man screamed and grabbed his nose, and Terry Lee took his briefcase. He would have reached into his jacket and taken his wallet too, but now came a brief episode of pure bad luck. The old white man who had been staring into his own space jerked his head around when the man screamed, and reached deep down into his pocket and took out a gun. He aimed it at Terry Lee just as Terry Lee was reaching into the bleeding man's jacket for his wallet, and he fired twice. The first bullet shattered the window behind the bleeding man, and scared the hell out of Terry Lee, who jumped back just as the second shot came. It hit the bleeding man in the shoulder.

The train came roaring into the station, and Terry Lee tried to hide behind the fat white man until the door opened, and then he made a dash for it. The man with the gun fired again, and the bullet hit Terry Lee as he ran through the door. He fell to the station floor, but then scrambled up and ran again into the crowd.

The man with the gun walked over to the man who was bleeding now from his shoulder as well as from his nose, and who had slumped down unconscious in his seat. "Damn," the man with the gun said, and then he put the gun back in his pocket and walked out of the doors and into the staring crowd and out of this story, just another man with a gun in New York City who had tried to do his duty as God gave him the light to see that duty, and who was now mildly disgusted that he had shot the victim as well as the son-of-a-bitch mugger. Oh well, better luck next time.

It was just pure bad luck that Terry Lee had picked a subway car with a crazy vigilante-type old man with a gun on it, but the next part you couldn't call anything but stupid. Or maybe greedy.

Terry Lee Gaiter thought he was dead when the bullet hit him and he fell sprawling to the dirty cold stone floor of the Fifty-ninth Street subway station, but as soon as he slid to a stop among the scattering feet and felt the pain in his back he knew he wasn't dead yet so he scrambled to his feet and into the crowd and away.

Still holding the briefcase.

What he had in mind was he would get home and smoke a joint and maybe have a cup of tea and lie down until he felt better, but by the time he had run two blocks he was beginning to feel faint and when in the middle of the next block he actually fell down he knew he was in trouble. He would have let go of the briefcase then, but he didn't think of it.

The first few people who came upon him sprawled in the street walked around him and kept going, but after ten minutes the blood leaking out of his back and seeping onto the rain-wet sidewalk had spread out red enough and dark enough that you just couldn't keep on saying the man was probably drunk, and finally someone called the police.

The only unusual aspect of the whole scene, the first cop to arrive said to his partner, was that no one had pried the briefcase out of the poor nigger's fingers and walked away with it.

3

DAVID MELNIK stared out the window, looking down at the clouds, and was sad because the sight didn't make him happy. He remembered lying on his back on the sand as a child, staring up into the bright sky and watching the fluffy clouds scud briskly along, wishing he could see what they looked like on the top side. The bottoms of the clouds were intriguing; they took on the most marvelous shapes. Wouldn't it be wonderful, he thought, to fly up above them and see what they looked like from above? He raised his hands, stretching them forward like Captain Marvel, and wished his body up into the air, concentrated all his mental energies on defeating gravity, on flying and soaring high into the air, arcing his back away from the sand with the effort—

"What are you doing, David?" his mother asked.

"Nothing," he said, and relaxed into the soft sand again.

And now he was flying high above the clouds, looking down at them, seeing them from above, his most cherished dream come true, and of course it was meaningless. He had flown a thousand times over a million clouds and their tops all looked just like the bottoms, with none of the charm and terror and beauty he had imagined; the dreams of a child were more exciting than the reality of a man. He sighed. You get everything you want in this world, he thought, if you just wait long enough. The trouble is, the wait is *too* long, and when you get what you wanted it doesn't mean a damn thing anymore.

It's also never *quite* the same, you don't get *exactly* what you want. Like the story of the man who was given a free wish by a genie and who wished for immense wealth, and soon received a telegram saying his only son had been killed—followed by another from the insurance company paying him a million dollars.

He had wanted to fly by himself, by stretching his arms out; he had wanted the freedom of flight, not the tightness of being confined in a long metal tube burrowing through the air. . . .

He had wanted to be back in the field; it was where he belonged, he argued. But Mazor, his chief, simply shook his head obstinately. Too old, he said. Mustn't tempt fate, he said. You've done that sort of thing long enough. Now stay home and be a *gontser macher,* run the operatives, use your brain, he said. Let the kids take the chances.

"For God's sake, I'm thirty-six years old!" Melnik had protested. "Maybe too old for World Cup soccer, but—"

"There are seven ages in the life of a man, David," Mazor had said, making fun of David's penchant for Shakespeare. "And at your age you stop going out in the field and you start sitting behind a desk, so that we can all take advantage of your experience."

And so they had given Barak the passport that said he was a German named Karl Friedrichs, and had sent him to Berlin. He was a kid, all right, and he had taken his chances. And lost.

The stewardess brought his drink. He sipped it without pleasure, without thought. Barak had been born in Germany and brought up in Israel by parents who insisted on keeping their cultural heritage intact; they had spoken German at home, Hebrew on the streets. Barak had been perfect, he had had as good a chance as anyone else. Just bad luck that they had caught on to him. Melnik wondered what had happened, but after a moment he cut off such thoughts. Unproductive. He would never know what had happened: a moment's carelessness, total stupidity, or simple bad luck. Or just good solid work on the part of the Germans.

He would never know. But he *did* know what the disappearance meant. Friendly nations spy on each other all the time; it's part of the game, and recognized as such. If Barak—or Karl Friedrichs—had been caught delving into the normal diplomatic or even military secrets of a normal German government there would have been diplomatic anger, a note delivered to the Israeli ambassador, an order for Barak to leave the country with perhaps a few other Israeli consulate workers banished as punishment. The Israeli government would have denied in public all accusations of spying, and would have apologized in private, and life would have gone on as before.

But there had been no word of complaint from the German government. Barak had simply disappeared.

They would find him in good time, of course. They would check the hospitals and morgues in Berlin and eventually find the record of a man found dead with no identification, reported missing by no one, killed in a traffic accident or a mugging or a fall from a rooftop; a man about twenty-six years old, with soft blond hair and a slight paunch and a scar, from a childhood accident, behind the right knee. They would find him but would not claim him, and Yitzhak Barak would lie buried in a German cemetery, in the land of his grandparents, and his parents would never know. And Melnik and his superiors at the Mossad would never know how he had been caught. Worse, they would not know any further details of the problem he had been investigating.

Melnik dozed off for a while, and woke feeling sluggish. He got up and walked back to the lav, locked himself in, and took off his hair.

When people first met him they noticed something exotic, almost alien about his appearance, but they usually couldn't quite place it. It was only when he took off his wig—and very few people ever saw him do that—that one realized he was totally hairless: The cheeks were as smooth as a baby's, and there were no eyebrows, the result of *Alopecia universalis*. God knew where in his travels he had picked it up. He glanced casually in the mirror, grimaced as usual—women seemed to be turned on by the effect, but it still bothered him—and splashed his face and head with cold water. The captain began to announce in three languages that they were preparing for their descent into Washington, and he returned to his seat.

It should have been Berlin, he thought. He should have gone there initially instead of Barak, and he should have gone there now instead of to Washington. But Mazor had replied that there wasn't time; they would have to bring to the Americans what they knew and let them take it from there.

Melnik hadn't wanted to go. He didn't dislike Americans, but he disliked America. All that cozy affluence in the midst of a world shaking itself to pieces grated on him. "I'm too old for field work," he told Mazor reasonably. "You said so yourself," he reminded him.

"Too old to sneak down German alleys with a dagger under your cloak," Mazor replied with a smile. "Just the right age to spread yourself out on Miami Beach and look up at the clouds and cooperate over a martini lunch with our American friends. Enjoy yourself, David. It will only be a few weeks."

"Attention, please. Will David Melnik please make himself known? Passenger David Melnik, please contact the head stewardess." The message was announced while they were all standing in the aisle, jammed together waiting for the doors to open. He pressed the call button, and saw the stewardess come edging through the crowd toward him. "Would you come with me, please?" she said. "Do you have all your carry-on luggage?"

He lifted his briefcase in reply and she guided him through the unwilling throng to the doorway, where she pointed to a woman waiting on the ramp. He went to her and she extended her hand, shaking his and introducing herself, telling him that she had arranged his passage through passport control and customs and would be taking him to see the deputy assistant secretary of defense. He followed her up the corridor, nodding pleasurably at her swinging hips and well-shaped legs. Maybe this trip to America wouldn't be so bad after all.

No, he reminded himself. He was too old.

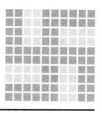

2

1

WILLIAM HAGAN woke up feeling happy, and lay there in bed trying to remember why. He hoped it wasn't just a dream: sometimes he woke up happy when the whole world was shitty, and it turned out that all he had to feel good about was a sexy dream that was already fading away and wasn't worth a damn. This morning he lay with his hands behind his back, staring up at the ceiling, going over yesterday's events slowly, anxious to hold on to this feeling as long as he could.

Nothing terribly awful had happened, but nothing particularly good either, until he came to yesterday's last appointment of the day: the Israeli, David Melnik. "Mr. Secretary," Melnik had greeted him on being ushered into his office. "I wasn't expecting this honor."

He wasn't flustered by it, either, Hagan noticed as they shook hands. A very cool young man. Young to middle thirties, he guessed, trim and neat, not too tall. Hagan generally liked men who were just a bit shorter than he, but there wasn't any obvious reason to like this one. Hard eyes. Expressionless, giving nothing away. Thought he was tough. There was something strange about his face, something exotic which Hagan couldn't place at first, and then he realized what it was: the man had no eyebrows. None at all. And his facial skin was taut and smooth like a baby's. All this scrutiny took less time than the handshake, and as they sat down Hagan asked, "I trust you had a pleasant trip?"—exuding politeness. When Melnik merely nodded he went on: "Everything satisfactory at the airport?"

Melnik nodded again. "Your young lady, Miss Wintre, met me and informed me of the change in plans."

"Yes, it was a last-minute sort of thing," Hagan said. "I wasn't sure we might not have confused the FBI emissary. He knew all about it?"

"I wouldn't know," Melnik said. "Miss Wintre was waiting in the ramp as the airplane doors opened. She managed to sweep me off the airplane and whisk me through customs so quickly we might have missed any FBI attendant."

"Indeed?" Hagan said, congratulating himself. It looked as if his choice of assistant had been made properly after all. "Well, not to worry. I'll have my secretary give a call over to the Justice building and let them know where you are, just in case they've got their agents running around Washington National looking for a kidnapped Israeli emissary. Now then, what's it all about? Can I offer you a glass of whiskey? How would you like it?"

"Neat, please."

Hagan preferred his whiskey mixed with water, but he couldn't very well do that now. They lifted their glasses and sipped, and he asked again, "Well now, what's it all about?" At lunch this afternoon Henderson, his man at the CIA, had been unable to tell him much; Melnik was bringing information from the Yids to the Bureau, and they'd all know what it was about when he arrived and told them.

"We have information that an assassination attempt is to be made on the chancellor of Germany when he visits the United States next month."

Hagan smiled politely. Boring, he thought. If he had ten votes for every rumor of an assassination attempt since he had first come to Washington he'd be president by now. "Who would want to kill such a pleasant man as Gottfried Waldner?" he asked. "Let me guess. The Russians, disturbed at the growing economic strength of the new Germany and afraid of its dominance in the European Community, wish to throw chaos into the Teutonic democracy?"

Melnik smiled.

"A Middle Eastern faction, perhaps," he tried again, "upset with Germany's lack of support for Palestinian terrorism? The Israelis, upset with Germany's support for Palestinian terrorism?"

Melnik glanced at his watch. "Mr. Secretary," he said, "I'm not familiar with your geography, but I believe it's a long drive to FBI headquarters, especially at this time of day. Wouldn't it be quicker if I simply told you what I've come to say?"

Hagan nodded. They had their qualities, the Israelis, but gentle chitchat wasn't one of them. "Yes, please, do tell me."

"You're no doubt aware that there is a neofascist movement in Germany—"

"As indeed there is in every country," Hagan interrupted again. "We ourselves have Patrick Buchanan, who seems to command allegiance among a certain group. And of course, you have Mr. Shamir. . . . Sorry, bad joke. Please go on."

"Because of German history—and perhaps this is false reasoning—one tends to take the German Nazis more seriously. At any rate, there is a movement, which doesn't seem to us to be under any sort of central control."

"And they feel that assassinating the chancellor will give them headlines, coverage, a bit of notoriety if not actual respect?"

"That's our line of reasoning."

"Why should it take place here?"

"We're not sure. But why not? If it's to help the Nazi resurgency at home, surely it's better that it take place on the soil of a country they can call the Fatherland's enemy. Waldner isn't going to Russia or Israel in the near future, but he is coming here."

"You don't seem to know all that much about it."

"We don't, actually. But the visit is coming up next month, so we thought we'd better let you know what we do have."

Hagan had perfected a smile that effectively let the recipient know that, though the smiler was being as polite as possible, privately he thought the smilee beneath contempt. He used it now. "And this information of yours, such as it is—did it arrive in Israel from a mountaintop, carved in stone and accompanied by thunder and lightning?"

Melnik's smile was equally effective. It began and ended with his lips, while the eyes could have frozen the Red Sea. He usually tried not to make instant judgments, but he did not like this man. Still, business was business. "We had an agent in place in the Bundesnachrichtendienst, the German security service. He was able to tell us this much."

"Did it ever occur to you to ask him for more information? For verification? Names and places?"

"It occurred to us. Unfortunately, he disappeared before he could tell us anything else. That's why we thought it necessary to act on the information we have; there won't be any more coming from that particular source.''

Hagan nodded. He understood all too well. His own idea of intelligence-gathering consisted of equipment that sailed five hundred miles above the earth, orbiting continually and looking down with infrared sensors, radar, and telescopic eyes. Of high-powered radios focused on government buildings, and laser listening devices impinging on glass windows. High-tech, sophisticated spying brought home the bacon. Secret agents were another story altogether: They belonged to the gaslit streets and pulp novels of a romantic past. They were as likely to lie as to be mistaken or drunk, and either of those possibilities was infinitely greater than the chance that they might actually penetrate the enemy's security and bring back a story worth listening to. This apocryphal now-disappeared Israeli agent had probably sold his superiors a story concocted in a German beer cellar when he ran out of funds. He had probably pocketed the payment and disappeared because he couldn't think of a few more lies to follow up convincingly. He was probably working for Iraq now; the Arabs were easier to lie to. Well, more power to him.

He himself, Hagan thought, was not quite so credulous as to believe such stories. Satellite photos, that was what he wanted: pictures that one could touch, could pick up and read a license plate on. Spies flitting in and out of dark alleys made for good movies but bad intelligence.

And that was all the Israeli had, a story amounting to no more than a rumor. He had dismissed David Melnik, regretting the time he had wasted. But now as he thought about it he lay in bed and smiled at the ceiling, happy that his waking feeling of joy had not turned out to be an evaporating mirage. If his first reaction on hearing the story had been boredom, his second thoughts during the night had been pleasure. Perhaps the Israelis were right after all; they did seem to have a knack for penetrating subversive organizations and bringing a pearl or two back from the muck, so they just might be right about this. Not likely, but possible. And a Nazi resurgency in Germany, Hagan thought, could be just what he needed. At any rate, he had nothing to lose by following it up. *Good luck to the stupid pricks,* he thought, and glanced at the clock. There was still time for a bit of fun before he had to dress and get to work. He put his hand on his wife's shoulder and began to shake her gently, but when she turned to him in her sleep and opened her lips with a lascivious smile he suddenly turned cold and retreated to the far edge of the bed.

He lay there angrily watching as she fell back into her happy sleep. Who knew whom the bitch was dreaming of?

2

THE POLICE in New York had spent the night sifting through the wreckage left by the bomb, and by morning had found a fragment of leather briefcase singed on the inside and undamaged on the outside, so they knew where the bomb had been. They discovered that Detective Robertson had taken the squeal on a man found unconscious, with a gunshot wound, on Sixty-third Street, clutching the briefcase; he had been rushed to the hospital, but was DOA. He matched the description of a subway mugger shot shortly before the DOA collapsed on the street, so there was little doubt about the connection. The exploding briefcase had therefore not been intended as a bomb attack on the police; it had been brought to headquarters only because the mugger had been caught. Whom *had* it been intended for?

The subway guard at the Columbus Circle station had been too late to stop the fleeing perpetrator or the man who had shot him or any of the eyewitnesses, but had managed to round up the robbery victims and keep them until police arrived. One of them had been no trouble: He lay unconscious on the subway seat where he had been shot. The other was a loud and angry man who kept up a running stream of invective about lack of security and how nobody had cared enough to help and how he had business to get to and couldn't hang around forever waiting for the fucking cops who were probably busy hassling hookers which was a lot easier and safer than protecting citizens on the subways from muggers with knives, goddamn it.

This one—the conscious, angry victim—claimed he knew nothing about a briefcase. But it was hardly likely that the mugger had been walking around carrying it before the attacks. Neither was it likely that he had mugged anyone else after escaping from the subway, since he had been shot during the subway attempt and would obviously not have been in the mood for further hunting.

The other victim was taken unconscious to the hospital; he too was placed under police guard, on suspicion that the briefcase might have been his. By midafternoon he still wasn't available for questioning, but the police had interviewed the survivors of the station bombing. One of them, a black youth sitting on the desk in the middle of the room waiting to be booked, had noticed Robertson trying to jiggle open the lock of a briefcase held on his lap. The boy had turned away to say something to his mate, and then the explosion had occurred.

By late afternoon the police were working on the premise that the bomb had been rigged to go off if anyone tried to break into the brief-case. Their next step was to investigate further the two men who had been robbed on the subway, to ascertain if the first one was lying when he denied ownership of the briefcase or if it was the second man's, and to try to put together from the charred and shattered fragments what had been in it.

3

It HAD BEEN a long day in Los Angeles, and Walter Naman was ready to go home. He turned off the lights in his office, then walked through to the empty receptionist's office and turned out the lights there, too.

He walked to the window and took the videotape out of the small camcorder, glancing out the window as he did so. Everything looked normal out there. He put the tape in the VCR and set it to rewind, glancing at his watch. It had been running since he came back from a late lunch over four hours ago; it would take a couple of minutes to rewind, and he sat down to wait.

He didn't want to bother. Nothing had happened since Klaus Vors-hage had visited him, and though he didn't for a moment doubt Klaus's word, the simple fact that absolutely nothing had happened combined with the lateness of the day to persuade him that checking the tape wasn't necessary. But he had lived this long by being careful, and he wouldn't have felt right leaving the office without looking at it. At fast scan it wouldn't take more than ten minutes. He set the controls with the remote and leaned back in the chair to watch.

It was not the world's most interesting home videotape. It showed a portion of the parking lot outside his window; centered in the frame was his Honda CRX. Minute after minute passed by, but the picture on the screen remained nearly as still as a painting. A few people skimmed across the corner of the video, moving in the fast scan mode like speeded-up Charlie Chaplins, but no one came near the car. Walter's eyes dimmed, his eyelids blinked, he nearly began to doze, and then quite suddenly a man slipped up to the car and opened the door.

Walter woke with a start, snapping his finger down on the *hold*

---

button, and there it was on the screen: someone leaning into the open door of his Honda.

He rewound a few seconds, and then watched in normal mode. The man walked directly to the door of the Honda as if it were his own. In his left hand he carried a small package, in his right hand he held a key. Without hesitation he bent to the door of the Honda and opened it. No one passing by would have noticed anything unusual. He leaned in and put the package under the driver's seat. Then he closed the door and locked it and walked away.

The whole operation hadn't taken five seconds. No one noticing him would have actually noticed him: a perfectly ordinary man going to his car and putting in a package. He hadn't fumbled with the key at all, he hadn't been picking at the lock or manipulating it, and Walter thought about that for a moment: How had he known exactly what key would open the car? And then he noticed on the screen the rear of the car, and shook his head sadly. *Sloppy, sloppy,* he thought; *I'm getting too old for this business.* On the rear of the car in small chrome letters was the name "Packer Honda," the dealer from whom he had bought the car. All Jean-Paul had had to do—Walter stopped at that thought, rewound the tape for a couple of seconds, and zoomed in on the figure now once again leaning into his car; yes, it was Mendoza—all Jean-Paul had had to do was call the dealership, tell them his name was Walter Naman and he had lost the keys to the new CRX he had bought from them, and could they please give him the code number so he could buy another? He would have been told the code was listed in the car's manual, and he would have replied that he hadn't bothered to keep the manual. He would have been told to come in and bring identification, and he would have replied irritably that he was calling long distance from halfway up the damn state and he was stuck in a roadside restaurant and he had dropped the damn key and he had been looking for a goddamn hour and couldn't find it and what the hell did they want, for him to take a goddamn taxi all the way back to LA? In a few minutes he would have been given the code number, and could then have bought a replacement key at any Honda dealer.

Walter rewound and ran through the scene again, with the zoom tightly on Jean-Paul. His movements were easy and casual, but he held the package in his left hand with a definite firmness, keeping it always carefully level. Walter noticed that even when Jean-Paul leaned into the car, the package remained perfectly level.

Jean-Paul was good, but not great. He had taken the trouble to scout

out Walter's car from a distance so that no one had noticed him. He had seen that Walter didn't have an alarm system on the car, which wouldn't have surprised him: There isn't an alarm made that could slow down a pro for an instant. He would have seen, further, that Walter never bothered to check under the seat when he got into the car, and obviously had come to the conclusion that this behavior meant that Walter was not aware of any danger; he had not considered the possibility of an unobtrusive and continuous electronic surveillance of the car. This was a reasonable mistake to make, but a great man would not have made it.

Walter called a taxicab, grabbed an overnight bag he kept in the office, and walked down the three flights of stairs. He never took the elevator; one of the few lasting scars from his childhood in Auschwitz was a terrible fear of enclosed spaces. When the cab came he gave directions to a chemical-supply house, and when they arrived there he gave instructions for it to wait. He went in, made a quick purchase, and got back into the cab. "The airport," he said.

On the way he tried to pick out a tail, but wasn't able to. This didn't surprise him; Jean-Paul, although perhaps not great, was certainly good, and Walter purposely didn't make the cab take any evasive action which would have pinpointed a car trailing them. Everything nice and easy, he thought: Keep Jean-Paul's scenario intact; he didn't suspect anything, Walter just happened to be going out of town instead of home in his car tonight.

He paid off the driver at the airport and walked inside leisurely, obviously not late, obviously not rushing. Until he passed completely inside and out of sight of anyone outside, and then he turned suddenly to his right and dashed down the corridor to the next aisle. He took the escalator down to the arrivals level and ducked through the crowd and outside. He hopped into a cab and gave his office address. This time, as the cab pulled away, he looked around very carefully. On the way to his office he twice changed instructions to the cabbie at the last moment, so that they veered off the thruway without notice. No one was following. Jean-Paul would still be in the airport, searching a bit anxiously; he would soon give up and return to the office building.

Walter had the cab pull into the parking lot in the rear. He paid the driver and waited till he left, then carefully opened the door of his car. He reached in and *very* carefully took out the package. He laid it on the hood of the car. It was an unsealed manila envelope with a cigar box inside. He slid the box out of the envelope and opened it. Then he took out of his pocket the small bottle of mercury he had bought in the chemical-supply house.

Mendoza's obvious effort to keep the package level when he placed it in the car had been definitive: The bomb in the cigar box was a simple and effective one. It had a nearly complete electric circuit connecting the detonator to the charge; the circuit was broken only because the mercury connector wasn't quite full. Thus, when the bomb was held carefully horizontal the connection wasn't quite made. If the package tipped to the side, or was shaken at all—as by the motion of a car accelerating—the mercury would slosh around and touch the detonator connection, completing the cycle—and *whoosh!*

Walter added a bit more mercury, drop by drop. Not enough to close the circuit, of course; but more than before, leaving the barest fraction of a centimeter unconnected. Then he shut the box again, slid it inch by inch back into the envelope, and with painstaking slowness put it carefully back under the seat. He closed the car door infinitely carefully, subconsciously holding his breath as it quietly clicked into place. And then he took a long breath, looked at his watch, and went back into the building and up the stairs to his office to watch.

Jean-Paul, having lost him at the airport, would return to the car. He couldn't take the chance that someone might bump into the Honda or try to break into it while Walter was away, and set off the bomb. That would, of course, warn Walter that he was in danger, and a warning was to be avoided at all costs. A man with Walter's reputation, warned of danger, would be impossible to kill. So Jean-Paul would have to return and remove the bomb.

It was half an hour before he turned up. It was dark by now, but the parking lot lights were bright and Jean-Paul made no effort to slink in. He walked boldly up to the car as he had done before, unlocked the door as casually as any real owner might, and reached in. He took hold of the box and began to take it out of the car, holding it as carefully as he had before—which was no longer carefully enough.

The explosion was sudden, and though he had been expecting it Walter jerked back from the window. The sound was partially deadened by the closed window but it was loud enough, and the sight was truly spectacular. The Honda's gas tank exploded with the mercury bomb, and flames shot nearly as high as Walter's window.

Walter turned away and carried his overnight case to the cabinet on the opposite wall. Putting it down, he opened a drawer and took out a single change of underwear, a pair of socks, and a shirt. He left the rest of his clothes in the drawer, together with his toothbrush, comb, and shaving equipment: It would seem to anyone who checked that nothing was missing. He opened another drawer and leafed through the several passports and charge cards he kept there, all in different names. It would be useful to have them all with him, but Norma, his secretary, would surely notice their absence and begin to wonder.

He paused, thinking of her. She would be upset at his death. Then he shook his head. Couldn't be helped. He'd make it up to her when he came back. He selected one passport only, and hoped she wouldn't notice. He went to the door and paused, looking around the room. He noticed the camcorder by the window, and went back to it. He opened it and took out the tape. He put it in his pocket and looked once more around the quiet room, then walked down the stairs and out the front door. He took a crosstown bus, walked several blocks after getting off before hailing a cab, and then, once again, he went to the airport.

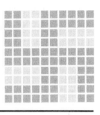

3

1

William Hagan cut the car's engine as he came around the corner at the top of the road and coasted quietly the rest of the way. He turned smoothly into his driveway and, finding it empty and the garage door open, slid ahead into the empty garage. He got out of the car and walked silently into the house, hung his hat and coat in the hall closet, and tiptoed through to the kitchen and back again, although with no car in the driveway or the garage it wasn't likely that anyone was here. He walked quietly up the carpeted stairs and poked his head suddenly into each of the bedrooms before he was satisfied. Then he came back downstairs and poured himself a stiff drink of whiskey, diluted it half with water, and swallowed it whole. *Bitch,* he thought.

A hell of a thing, he thought, *when a man's afraid to walk into his own home at night.* Of course, it wasn't night yet; that was the whole point. He had told his wife he wouldn't be home until late tonight, and then had purposely come home early. He hadn't *wanted* to find her in bed with someone, but—

Well, never mind. She wasn't even home. Of course, that didn't mean she *wasn't* in bed with someone, somewhere. He put down his empty glass and went over to the telephone. The red light on the answering machine wasn't blinking; there were no messages. Well, maybe. He took out the cassette and carried it into his den. He slipped it into his tape deck and hit the *play* button.

"Charlotte?" a woman's voice screeched. "Are you there? Don't be an absolute bitch, darling, pick up the phone. I'm dying to—"

"Hello? Melanie?"

"So tell me, darling: How did it go last night?"

"Melanie! Don't talk on the phone—"

"If he's there, all you have to do is say something noncommittal."

"It's not that, he's not here. I just never know when this damn thing is recording. I think if I pick it up before the beep goes off it records everything we say."

"It doesn't matter, just erase it when we finish."

"Yes, alright, I can do that. But just a minute, let me see if I push the button now—"

And the line went dead. Last night she had started her new jujitsu class; was Melanie really that interested in how the class had gone? He could stop in at the dojo tomorrow, he thought, and casually ask how his wife was faring. He could visualize the puzzled expression on the sensei's face. "Mrs. Hagan? We have no Mrs. Hagan in our classes."

He shook himself like a wet puppy. No, he couldn't do that. She might destroy their marriage but she hadn't the power to destroy his dignity, unless he surrendered it himself. And he would never do that.

He rewound the tape and put it back in the answering machine. He poured himself another whiskey and water. *Stupid women,* he thought. Charlotte would never learn anything about machines. Still couldn't operate the CD or VCR, and didn't understand that pushing the erase button on the answering machine only rewound the tape to its beginning so that the next incoming message would be recorded over the old ones, thus erasing them. But if there were no new messages, the old ones were still there. *Stupid, stupid.*

What was he going to do now? He didn't know. He shook his head. He didn't feel so bright himself.

It had been one hell of a day, he thought, sitting in his favorite chair, sipping whiskey, sighing, almost enjoying, with masochistic perversity, his anguishes. Almost.

It was the goddamn Constitution that was the problem. Well, it was Congress, really, but it was the fucking Constitution that gave those pricks the power to spend the government's money, and what the hell did they know about it? People who use every waking moment thinking about how to get reelected don't have time to think about what's good for the country. All they know is what their constituents complain to them about.

The euphoria over the Iraqi war had lasted a while, but now the reaction was setting in. At first everyone was walking around clapping themselves on the back for being Americans, congratulating themselves for developing laser-guided missiles that could fly down a street, stop at a red light, turn the corner, and wipe out a protected bunker ten feet underground while the soldiers who fired the missile were safely opening beer cans two hundred miles away. Everyone had been ecstatic about the practically negligible American casualties as the soldiers sat back and let their smart weapons fight the war, but now the people were beginning to realize just how much those smart weapons cost. One hundred million dollars in Tomahawk missiles alone on just the first day of the war, and more and more each and every day.

And now the bill was coming due: Congress had to appropriate money to replace those weapons—and to pay the engineers to develop new and smarter ones, since every country in the world had seen what they could do and was busy researching ways to counter them in the next conflict. And Congress didn't want to pay.

"We just can't afford another generation of intelligent weapons, that's the long and the short of it," Representative John Clifford (D-Mass.) said, summing up the feeling of the committee. "Not when we're already developing another generation of dumb ghetto kids who are going to be more explosive than any bomb in our arsenal. We've got to get them off the streets, educate them—"

"And leave the country defenseless?" Hagan had asked.

"No one's suggesting that," Chairman Edward Falsner (R-Wisc.) had replied testily. "But in tight economic times we have to kill two birds with every stone. Instead of weapons, we spend the money to develop the army and marines, the ground forces. This gives the ghetto kids jobs, educates them, and maintains our defense posture at the same time."

"It's not as if we're fighting the Soviets anymore," someone else had chimed in. "The only wars anyone can see in the coming years will be against the great unwashed—mobs of Arabs or Latins—and a marine with a bayonet is the best defense we've got."

Stupid pricks. Hagan sighed again and refilled his glass. What could you say to them?

"Goddamn it, you better think of *something* to say," Harry Grodin, president of Ameresearch International, had told him angrily at lunch. "I've got payrolls to meet, and with those bastards passing laws that say I can't sell technology outside the country *and* cutting our own government contracts, where's the money coming from?"

Grodin had been the first, and by no means the most vociferous. As the afternoon wore on and the word of the committee's deliberations got around town, Hagan's phone began to ring off the hook. PAC spokesmen and lobbyists and "concerned individuals," among whom Grodin liked to place himself, called to remind Hagan of favors done and obligations due. "*Do* something, goddamn it!" was the general tenor of the conversations, with someone occasionally being crass enough to mutter, "What the hell you think we're paying you for?" as he hung up the phone.

They *weren't* paying him, of course; not in the legal sense, *sensu stricto.* But in any man's climb up the political ladder, the rungs are made of rolled-up dollar bills; and if the rungs begin to give way . . . Hagan had found his constituency in the sophisticated technology industries of defense, and if he failed to keep his constituents happy he would plummet down the ladder more rapidly than he had risen. He had no illusions on that score, no comforting political philosophy to fall back on. He was a pragmatist, and when reality scorched the eyeballs he couldn't even blink.

He could, however, take a drink or two to ease the pain. He was on his third whiskey when the front doorbell rang. He wondered who it could be. He thought of the philosophers of the Middle Ages who argued about the number of teeth in a horse's mouth, and the apprentice who suggested they get up and go outside and simply *look.* They had thrown him out the window. The fool hadn't understood it was more fun to think about such things than actually to get the answer. Hagan thought he'd sit here like a Middle Aged philosopher and sip his whiskey and wonder who could be ringing the bell, instead of getting up to see.

It couldn't be his wife: She had her key. Unless she had lost it, had dropped it among the bedclothes and never been able to find it again, like her virtue. A good metaphor, that. A damn good metaphor. Pity he'd never be able to use it in a speech.

The bell rang again. Couldn't be the cleaning woman, she had her key too. Unless she had lost it in the bedclothes . . . No, he was rambling. He waited. A long time went by. Must have given up and left. Seventh-Day Adventists, he thought, going house to house looking for converts. Not in this neighborhood, lads.

And then the bell rang again, and he remembered that he had asked Wintre to stop by on her way home. That's how he had put it, "on your way home," although of course Silver Spring couldn't possibly be on the girl's way home. He laughed, and got up and answered the door.

"Good of you to come," he said, ushering her into the house. "I do appreciate it, I assure you. Not too far out of your way, I hope? Let me pour you a drink."

Wintre had learned a lot these first couple of days on the job. She had thought seriously about quitting and looking for other work, but decided that if she was going to restrict her employers to people she could admire and enjoy on a personal level she'd be limiting her future considerably. Hagan was a force in Washington—and, even more important, was *known* to be a force. This meant he was a comer. A position as his personal assistant was too important to be thrown away simply because the man was a shit.

She was determined to move up the ladder, which meant making a success of this job. She just wasn't sure how much she was expected to take. Should she have told Hagan straight out that Silver Spring was nowhere near like being "on her way home," that she lived in downtown Washington, or was this simply the standard sort of iron order within a velvet glove that kept relationships polite in the Washington hierarchy? She didn't know, but she was determined to make a start. "I'll have some water in mine if you don't mind, sir."

Hagan lifted his eyebrows and nodded cheerfully. The girl was learning. He didn't trust an assistant he could push around too easily; if he could do it, perhaps others might be able to do the same. On the other hand, he did want someone he could push around when the occasion demanded it. He splashed some water into Wintre's glass and handed it to her, raised his own glass to his lips, and they each sipped. Yes, that was much better, he thought, as he gestured Wintre to a seat and took his own. "Where do we stand?" he asked.

"The Israeli—David Melnik—is going to stay on temporary duty in Washington, working on this German thing with the FBI."

"They haven't a clue, have they?" Hagan interrupted.

"Sir?"

"The FBI, the CIA, the Mossad, the whole damn bunch of them. They get information, you see, but they have no understanding. The strategic concepts, that's what we need. An understanding of what all the bits of information really mean, do you see? A means of putting it in context. What is all this nonsense about killing the German chancellor?"

"Nonsense, sir?"

"Rubbish, nonsense, a big hoo-ra about what? What's the *context*?

Who's going to kill the man? Why? What does who stand to gain? Where do *we* come into it? They haven't the faintest idea," he complained.

"As a matter of fact, they do have at least an idea or two," Wintre said.

Hagan was leaning back in his chair, his head bent forward, staring into his glass. He lifted his eyes, moving nothing else but his eyebrows, to get them out of the way. "I'm all ears," he growled.

"There's evidently been an active Nazi underground ever since Hitler's day, but it's been *far* underground. Now, with democracy and unification opening the door to all sorts of political parties, it's been resurging. With the political pressures of the European Community, the ECGS, and NATO all claiming the dominant position in Europe, and with different German parties pushing for dominance in each of these, they figure that to assassinate the chancellor—and blame it on someone else—will open the gates of confusion and let them come plowing through."

"An interesting simile," Hagan said. "Hardly accurate, though. One doesn't use a plow to drive through an open gate."

"No, sir. But the idea is to spread confusion and allow the party prepared to take advantage of the others' hesitancy to gain an advantage. In fact, to take over the government."

Hagan snorted. "Nonsense."

"It *did* work before," Wintre suggested. "The burning of the Reichstag was the excuse for Hitler to become dictator in 1933. And when they needed more power they took advantage of a Jew's assassination of a Nazi diplomat in Paris; that led to Kristallnacht in 1938, and when it was over no one dared stand up to them."

Hagan shook his head wearily. "This isn't the 1930s, Wintre. This world is not that world. You know the old saying: Those who remember history too well are doomed to repeat it." He chuckled, then suddenly began to talk solemnly, as if he were lecturing a class of undergraduates. "What Germany seeks today is not Hitler's concept of lebensraum, but economic and political dominance. Anyone who studies history seriously has to realize that the richest, most successful nations are not necessarily the biggest and most powerful militarily—look at Japan and Germany after the war, Britain before it. Not one decent-sized army among the lot of them. Instead, what they had—what is needed—is strength of will and character, as the Vietnamese demonstrated. What is needed is *ein Volk, ein Führer*. The other nations of Europe are wasted relics of what they once were. Spain, France, Italy,

Austria, even England are ready to be dominated by a strong Germany. The idea should be not so much to conquer them as to take over the idea of a United States of Europe, a European 'house'—and perhaps America and Russia can even rent rooms in that house. But the one who holds the mortgage will be Germany!'' He stopped, confused. He seemed to have gotten his argument turned around. He blinked and looked up at Wintre, who nodded seriously and said, ''Exactly.''

Hagan closed his eyes and leaned back again in his chair. ''Pour us each another drink, child,'' he said, holding out his glass without opening his eyes. He felt Wintre take the glass from his fingers, and he fell into a reverie. Germany was not the problem today, that was what people didn't understand. The Jews, especially, could never understand that. But Germany has *never* been the problem. The problem today is, and has always been, France.

They had screwed up everything since the 1870s. Since the *1770s,* come to that. But forget the pissant kings, the Revolution, the Terror, Napoleon, all that crap. Just look at this century. A quarrel between the Austrians and the Serbs wasn't any business of the French, and if the French hadn't started the saber-rattling there never would have been a First World War. Then they had screamed all through the twenties and thirties about how wonderful they were: *''Elan! Elan! Toujours élan!''* And then they had gone and built the silly Maginot Line, which was more a fortress to keep them *in* than the Germans *out*—and of course Hitler had recognized that. It had given him the freedom to start the war all over again.

''What? I didn't quite get that?''

He was talking out loud, he realized. He smiled cunningly, and kept his thoughts to himself, because he felt the beginnings of an idea now.

The French were the problem still today, he went on without making a sound. *They* were the problem, he thought as he sipped his whiskey. They were ready to back down and let Germany take over all of Europe, convincing themselves that their superior sense of civilization would counteract the uncouth German aggressiveness. Oh yes, certainly; it had worked for the Romans against the Goths, had it not? As it had worked for the Greeks against the Romans and for the Chinese against the Mongol hordes, and for the French themselves against Hitler. Why is it no one ever learns the lessons of history?

The French were currently frustrating all the efforts of the United States to rework NATO into the dominant European multicommunity forum. They thought the European Community would be better for them since it would keep the United States from dominance. But they didn't realize that the absence of the United States would open the door for German dominance, and by the time they realized it would be too late. But a coup in Germany, a takeover by the right wing, perhaps even by a group that could be labeled neo-Nazi . . . that would shake them up. That would bring them into line. And not only them: It would snap those pansies in Congress to attention, all right. If the bogeyman over the horizon was German, if people again began to worry about German efficiency, German technology, German guided missiles and jet aircraft . . .

Not that it was likely. The story the Israelis were peddling was not likely to be true. On the other hand, who knew? Anything was possible in this confused and confusing world.

"Sir?"

He was smiling. He felt his lips smiling, and pulled them back into a thoughtful frown as he sipped his drink. He was having the beginnings of an idea, of a very good idea. He opened his eyes. "You'll have to get used to me, Wintre. When I start to think a thing through, nothing stops me. I did that to the President once. Now listen here. I have some orders for you."

2

"I'M NOT going to tell you," the man said.

Detective Paul Horner looked at his partner blankly. These were the first words the mugging victim had said to the police, and they were in answer to the simplest of questions. Horner and Blank had come to the hospital as soon as they received word that the man was conscious and could be interviewed. They had entered the room and introduced themselves politely and asked his name, and that was his answer. Horner sighed. It looked like being a long interview. Horner was a large man, topping six foot two, with a good two hundred and twenty pounds of flesh that was still largely muscle after nearly twenty-five years with the New York City police. And yet he projected an appearance of gentleness; he was always cast as the good cop in good/bad interrogations. His nickname was Jolly G., short for Jolly Green Giant, partly as a joke about his color, which was a deep, shiny black, partly for his gentle nature, and partly for his personality—the way they might name a hyper, nervous guy Cool Hand Luke: Horner always looked a little bit sad. But this gentle, sad appearance could prove deceptive. They still tell the story of how, one night before he made detective, he was on

---

uniformed patrol and stopped a suspected stolen vehicle; the driver pulled out a gun and shot him. The bullet hit Horner in the shoulder; he dropped his gun, and somehow as he staggered back he accidentally kicked it under the car. The driver hit the gas, but he let out the clutch too fast and the car stalled. Jolly G. lost his cool; enraged, he reached out with his left hand and—while the driver was pumping the gas and flooding the carburetor in an attempt to get the car restarted—he ripped the car door right off its hinges, yanked the driver out, and slammed him against a brick wall. Of course, it was an old car. . . .

Funny, he thought of that incident now as he leaned over the hospital bed and felt a sudden twinge in his back, forcing him to straighten up. It hadn't bothered him for years afterward, but lately these short, sharp pains were getting worse. He had wrenched his back not when he ripped the car door off but when he yanked the driver out and slammed him against the wall. Served him right, Horner thought, twisting and trying to stretch his back out, and turning his attention back to the man in the bed. "I thought it was a reasonable question," he said. "Would you mind telling me why you won't answer it?"

The man turned a fraction of an inch away, toward the wall, but grimaced with pain at the motion and stopped. He was trapped there. He closed his eyes.

"Man won't answer a simple question like what's his name, I gotta start to think the man feels guilty about something."

He waited. The man—Gerhard Kremble—lay in bed with his eyes shut, wishing they'd go away, wondering what they knew. He had come back to consciousness in this room a few hours ago, and had tried to find out what had happened. He had been cut and shot in a subway mugging, he was told, didn't he remember? Yes, he remembered that, but what then?

He had been brought to the hospital and the bullet had been taken out and his nose and shoulder stitched up, and he was going to be just fine. He nodded. He couldn't ask what he really wanted to know, so he had just asked if he could see a newspaper. Sure, they said, they'd try to find one for him. He had asked several times and had repeatedly been told, Sure, right away, but nobody brought him one.

He didn't know if they had caught the mugger or not, or if they had the briefcase. He didn't know if anyone on the subway had told them he had been robbed of a briefcase. He knew the police would be coming to talk to him, and he had decided he'd better say nothing, just in case. But now he realized how it sounded. It would only make them suspicious. "I can't tell you my name," he said finally.

"Why not?" Horner asked, friendly enough.

"My wife thinks I'm in Philadelphia on business."

His voice was slightly guttural, hard on the consonants. Horner wondered if that was a result of the wound and the drugs, or if it was a foreign element. The man's English came fluently enough. "And where are you?" he asked.

"I'm here, aren't I?"

"Doing what?"

"Lying in this bed!"

"I mean, what are you doing here in New York instead of being in Philadelphia on business?"

Kremble opened his eyes. "I have a girlfriend," he said.

Horner studied him. "I haff a girlfriend" was what he had said. "That's where you were going? On the subway? To see your girlfriend?"

Kremble nodded.

"What's her name?"

"If I don't tell you my name, you think I tell you hers?"

"What kind of business you got, that you should be in Philadelphia?"

"Look, I'll be honest with you—"

"Oh, good."

"—no matter what you say, I don't tell you a thing, and that's the honest truth. I done nothing wrong, it's not a crime to get mugged, is it? Because if it is, half the people in this city would be in jail. So I don't have to tell you nothing, and that's exactly what I *do* tell you. Nothing."

"Your wife must be pretty worried. She hasn't heard from you since Monday."

"She doesn't worry. I never call her when I'm out of town. I'll be back before she misses me."

"She might notice the bullet hole in your chest, or even your new nose."

"So I'll tell her what happened. I'll say it was in Philadelphia. They have muggers there, too. You think you guys have a monopoly?" He tried a smile, just for effect.

No effect. Horner stared at him, thinking. "I can't exactly put my finger on it," he said. "You talk a good English, idiomatic and all, but I don't know." He turned to his partner. "What do you think? We got an accent here, or what?"

"A definite accent," Blank said. "Foreign. Jersey, maybe? Newark?"

"Brando," Horner said, zeroing in on it. "Marlon Brando in *The*

Young Lions. I just saw it on TV." He turned back to the man on the bed. "What are you, German?"

Kremble didn't like that. He was proud of his English; he thought he spoke without any accent at all. He nodded briefly.

"Been in this country a long time, though, huh? Brought up here?"

Kremble closed his eyes again. He thought his story sounded convincing, and his accent had nothing to do with it. People with accents can screw around too.

"Your wallet has two hundred dollars in it. Nothing else."

"You shouldn't have looked in it!" Kremble said angrily. "It's private property."

Horner shrugged. "Wasn't me. Hospital wants to know if they're going to be paid."

"I'll pay them! They don't have to worry."

"In this city? You kidding, man? How come you got money but no ID in your wallet, no credit cards? A fine, upstanding citizen like you?"

"I told you. I'm incognito." He closed his eyes firmly.

"That's a fine word," Horner said. "We don't hear words like that much on the street nowadays. How come no driver's license?"

"I'm not driving a fucking car, am I!"

Horner nodded. "Yeah, that's the kinda words we hear more of. Well, it's been good talking to you. I gotta run now, unless there's anything else you want to chat about?" The man in the bed closed his eyes again, and Horner and Blank left the room. They closed the door, nodded to the cop on duty beside the door, and left the hospital.

On the sidewalk outside, Horner took out of his pocket a small, rectangular green-and-white plastic card and stood looking at it thoughtfully.

"What do you think, J.G.?" Blank asked. He was a younger man of normal size, who looked small beside Horner. He had a boyish grin, and when he flashed it people said he looked remarkably like Robert Redford. They worked well together: Blank laughed a lot, and although Horner didn't, he liked the sound.

Horner stood silently, thinking. He had been given the plastic card when he stopped by to talk to the doctor before going into John Doe's room. The doctor had said, "I might have something for you," and had fumbled in his desk drawer and brought out the card. "This might be his," he said. "It's—"

"Yeah, I know what it is," Horner had said. "What do you mean, it might be his?"

"They found it in the emergency room Monday night."

"And we get it *now?*"

"What can I tell you? I didn't know anything about it till half an hour ago. You know what it's like down there. They've been asking around, the people who came in then, you know? Haven't come up with anyone who claimed it, but of course there's a lot of people they saw that night that they couldn't reach. In-and-out, walking wounded, dead, you name it. So anyhow, it *might* be his."

"Where'd it turn up?"

"On the floor. The first thing they did with him was cut his clothes off. I mean, it wasn't all that clear he was going to make it, they weren't worried about maybe something'd fall out of his pockets, you know what I mean? So anyhow, if you want it, it's yours."

Now Horner stood outside the hospital looking at it. The card was a magnetic room key, with the name of the Hotel Dorset on it. This was a small, classy hotel on the Upper West Side, not far from the subway John Doe had taken. He could have booked a room in it while telling his wife he was in Philly . . . or the card could belong to someone else.

"So what do you think?" Blank asked again.

Horner sighed. "Worth a try," he said.

At the hotel they ran into problems. The manager was very polite—it really was a classy hotel—but without a search warrant he really didn't see what he could do.

"We can get a search warrant," Horner assured him. "But you could save us a bit of aggravation if you'd just—"

"Actually, even with a search warrant," the manager said, "I'm not sure what we could do for you. I don't know what room it's for. The card has the hotel's name on it, but not the room number. You understand that precaution, of course."

"Can't you just run it through your machine and tell what room it's to?"

The manager shook his head; it didn't work like that.

Horner changed tactics and asked if the manager could tell him which of his guests had not returned to the hotel Monday night. It took a few minutes to check the records, which showed three men who had paid for their rooms in advance and hadn't bothered to check out, had simply left. "No rooms where baggage or clothing was left behind?" Horner asked.

No, there were none. Which meant that the card wasn't John Doe's, or he hadn't anything with him in the way of luggage or a change of clothes, or he had shared the room with someone else who had checked out.

Horner thanked the manager and they left his office. In the lobby they paused to talk. "There's one other possibility," Blank said.

"Yeah. He was with someone who doesn't know what happened and hasn't checked out yet."

"Not likely."

"No."

"But possible."

"Yeah. How many rooms you figure this place has?"

"Twelve floors. Maybe ten rooms on a floor."

"Hundred and twenty rooms. Less than a minute a room, that's two hours tops."

"Worth it."

Horner blew out his breath in a long sigh. His back was bothering him now, and standing around hotel corridors for two hours was not going to help it one little bit. He stretched, tried to reach behind himself to knead it, and nodded his okay to Blank. They turned back into the lobby. The manager had disappeared back into his den and the people behind the front desk ignored them. They took the elevator to the second floor and began. Horner waited by the elevator as lookout while Blank walked down the corridor, pausing to insert the card silently in each lock. In a few minutes he was back at the elevator. "All red lights," he reported, and they took the elevator to the next floor.

Horner was up for promotion to a new job that would take him off investigative detail, give him a nice desk to sit at all day. He'd get one of those good chairs with a high back and lumbar support, pay for it himself. Or maybe a rocking chair, like Jack Kennedy had on account of his bad back. Yeah, he thought, a good, sturdy rocking chair, sit in his new office all day, give the goddamn back a chance to heal. . . .

On the seventh floor Blank got a green light indicator. He nodded to Horner, who came quickly down the corridor to join him. They took out their revolvers; Blank inserted the card again, got the blinking green light again, and Horner turned the handle and shoved the door open.

A naked man was sitting on the edge of the bed, and kneeling on the carpet between his legs was a naked young lady. The man gasped in astonishment; the woman probably would have, too, but her mouth was full.

3

SHE CHEWED QUIETLY, looking down at her food or around the room more often than directly at David Melnik. Truth to tell, Lisle Wintre was embarrassed at being with him; embarrassed with herself for lying to him. Which was silly, she told herself, forcing herself to look up at him and smile. He couldn't know of her lies, and it wasn't her fault, anyway: She was only doing her job. There was nothing to be embarrassed about. And yet, she thought as she glanced away, unable to hold his eyes with her own, she simply couldn't be comfortable when she knew she was lying.

In the usual course of events she would have been enjoying herself. He was a good-looking man with a quiet but exotic manner. He had an unidentifiable touch of the East about him, and ordinarily she would have been interested in him in a social way. Quite unbidden the thought occurred to her that she was using "social" in the sense that people used to speak of "social diseases," and she smiled at the thought.

"The duck is amusing?" he asked.

"I'm sorry," she said, swallowing her food. "A thought suddenly occurred to me. Private joke." She was being rude now, which was unforgivable. If you're going to break bread with a man and look him directly in the face and lie to him, you must at least be polite.

But it wasn't her fault, she screamed silently. And he smiled in return and asked if she had lived in Washington long. She shook her head. "New York. My father was a cop. I was always frightened," she said, and stopped, realizing that she had been trying to apologize for the lies he didn't know he had been told with a personal truth he wasn't interested in.

"Of your father?" he asked.

"No. Of his work. The violence, the killing. I'm sorry, I didn't mean to say anything about it. It's not really a suitable dinner-table topic, is it?"

"It's hard to talk about anything real these days without getting into violence. But of course there have been few times in history when that wasn't the case. You said he *was* a cop; is he dead?"

"Yes." And then she added, "I saw him die," and immediately wished she hadn't. "Let's talk about something else."

"Our plans," he suggested. That was, after all, why they were having dinner together.

Oh dear, she thought. She had tried to put it off as long as possible, but it was time to get into some heavy lying now. "You've reported what you know to the FBI . . ."

Oh yes, he thought. He had done that. After speaking to the assistant secretary of defense he had been taken to the Justice Building and seen the personal assistant to an assistant director. His information had been taken down and he had been told they would be in touch. A hotel had been recommended.

He had checked in, showered, and had a meal sent up to his room. He found a movie on television and fell asleep watching it, waking when the credits came on. He turned out the lights and lay down, but found he couldn't sleep. Jet lag. He lay in bed a while longer while the clock clicked around nearly to midnight. Finally he got up and dressed and walked the two flights down to the ground floor.

The lobby was deserted except for the desk clerk and a policeman leaning on his elbow, casually talking to him. Melnik walked across the lobby toward the front door, but before he reached it he was stopped by a shout. He stopped and turned around. The cop and the clerk were looking at him.

There was no one else in the lobby. He said, "Did you call me?"

"Yeah," the cop said, coming toward him. "Where you going?"

"Out."

"Yeah? Where exactly?"

"Nowhere exactly," he said. "Just out. For a walk."

By now the cop had reached him. He stood in front of Melnik, hands on hips, toothpick in mouth, holster on hip. He shook his head. "Uh-uh," he said.

Melnik didn't know what he meant. "Are you telling me I can't go outside?"

"Not *can't. Shouldn't.* Not a good idea, not out there."

"But why not? What's out there?"

"Washington, buddy. Downtown Washington. You don't take a walk in downtown Washington at midnight."

Melnik considered that. "It's not against the law?"

"It's just not a good idea."

Melnik nodded and thanked him, but said he thought he'd take just a quick stroll. He'd be sure to stay on well-lit streets. The cop shrugged and watched him go. He had done what he could.

By the time he had turned the corner, Melnik felt as if he had stepped out of reality and into a Hieronymus Bosch painting. There was no one else walking, but on every street corner there was a gathering of macabre figures gesturing lewdly to the few cars traveling by. There were girls in harem outfits with see-through pants, girls in short tight leather skirts, fat girls and skinny girls, tall and short, old and young. There were boys in tight slacks, with waving arms and ludicrously swerving hips. And there were creatures who were not identifiably male or female. Nearly all were black. When a car came by they lurched out into the street with waves and cries; when it passed they subsided onto the sidewalk. Most of them ignored Melnik as he walked by; a few propositioned him without much interest, turning away from him even before he said no: It was clear that their business was car-oriented. Pedestrians were either voyeurs or lost and frightened tourists, not worth bothering with.

He was so fascinated and repelled by the swirling chiaroscuro—*this* was the capital of the Western world?—that he didn't notice the dark space between two buildings, and he passed too close to it. As he did a pair of huge arms swung out and grabbed him from behind in a bear hug, lifting him from the ground and pulling him off the sidewalk into the darkness.

He was held tight there, and another figure materialized from the shadows and came toward him. In the half light from the street he saw a knife glistening in the boy's hand. The boy didn't say anything; he just giggled and came toward Melnik, reaching out with the knife.

Melnik ignored the monster that held him with his arms pinned to his sides. He concentrated on the one with the knife, waiting until he came closer, waiting until the knife was almost touching his face, the point almost at his right eye, and then he kicked out hard. His toe caught the boy in the groin, and the force of the kick smashed through his scrotum, driving it up into his gut. The boy's eyes popped and the knife dropped.

As his foot came back he accelerated it, kicking backward now with his heel against the shin of the man who held him. The man grunted and his bear hug relaxed just a bit, just enough for Melnik to be able to drop his right shoulder below the man's arms. He bent his knees and drove his shoulder up into the man's armpit, reached up with his left hand over his right shoulder to grab the man's shirt, pulled down with his arm and shoved up with his legs and shoulder, and lifted the man off his feet and pulled him forward through the air over his shoulder and down onto the boy who had fallen to his knees. As the big man landed heavily Melnik caught his wrist and elbow and twisted until he felt a pop.

The boy was knocked over to one side. He began to scramble to his feet but Melnik kicked him again; this time the point of Melnik's shoe caught him just under the chin and snapped his head back. The boy fell like a sack of coal to the pavement and didn't move again.

The other one tried to get up but Melnik kicked again, hitting him on the cheek. He felt the cheekbone snap and the man screamed and fell backward, then pulled himself up again and ran away.

And it was all very quiet. Out on the lit pavement a couple of figures peered over to see what was going on, but they quickly moved away again. Melnik looked at the figure on the ground. He bent down and felt his neck for a pulse. There wasn't one. The neck had been broken.

He started to straighten up and suddenly noticed, with an involuntary shudder of revulsion, something lying on the ground, dark and soft and hairy; he thought it was a rat. But it didn't move, and he leaned forward to look more closely. It was his wig. Oh great. He hadn't even noticed it fall. If he hadn't happened to see it just now, if he had returned to the hotel without it and the police had found it along with the dead body, he could have been in for some embarrassing questioning. It was made in England, and the police lab would probably spot its foreign origin. The police would then check with Interpol, and his name would surface as a foreign counterterrorist agent who was known to use deadly force.

That sort of thing would not do. He picked it up and brushed it off and replaced it carefully on his totally bald head. It would not do at all, he thought. Perhaps Mazor was right. He was getting old and, worse, careless. That was not tolerable.

He straightened up, and found that he was trembling. He held his hand out in front of him and saw the fingers twitching. No wonder he had been careless enough to nearly forget his wig: He had been frightened. He was still scared. He could have been killed here in this Washington alley, and for what? What was he doing here? Mazor was definitely right: He was too old for this.

But how could he be old? He wasn't even grown up yet: He didn't have a wife, he didn't have children. He was still running around the world playing games, he hadn't yet grown up and begun to live a real life. And yet he stood here in this alley shaking like an old man after a little exertion. He stared at his twitching fingers, willing them to stop, but they ignored him. His body was growing old, he thought, before the rest of him really grew up.

He thought of taking the knife, of throwing it down a sewer so it wouldn't be taken and used by another of these creatures, but decided it wasn't worth the bother. It didn't look as if there was a shortage of weapons on these streets. He stepped shakily out onto the pavement. Everyone was looking the other way.

He went back to the hotel. The cop had been right; going for a walk had not been a good idea.

The next morning the streets were different, full of people hurrying along, noisy with shouts and assorted sounds from cars, taxis, and buses. He walked down Pennsylvania Avenue toward the Mall, enjoying the crowds. On H Street an old man lay stretched out full length on the sidewalk, his clothes tattered and skimpy, his eyes welded shut with coprous black sores. As David approached he saw a young woman come out of the furniture shop a few doors down, carrying a bundled blanket. She put it over the old man. He opened his eyes a crack, as far as they would go, smiled at the girl, and pulled the blanket around him. She turned and went back into her shop. A young man in a dark-gray pin-striped suit stepped nimbly around David, pirouetting neatly to avoid actually stepping over the old man, and said over his shoulder to the girl hurrying after him, "Set that up right away. I want to see him as soon as I can."

"I'll take care of it," she said as he waved good-bye without looking back.

David passed them by and continued on his way. What was the point, he wondered. Why bother? And then he thought, not for the pin-striped prig or the sycophant following him, but perhaps for the young girl with the blanket. Perhaps.

He visited the museums and came back to the hotel to wait. So far his visit to the FBI had followed normal procedures. His message had not been urgent—the German chancellor was not due for another six weeks—and he could be expected to be called back to see the assistant director personally within a day or two. At that time a team would be assigned and they would get to work.

Instead, the phone had rung in the late afternoon and he had been invited to dinner by Miss Lisle Wintre. Curious. The assistant secretary of defense for politico-military affairs could be expected to be interested in the proposed assassination of the German chancellor—and so Melnik had not been terribly surprised upon being taken to see him upon arriving in Washington—but surely his interest should be proprietary and transitory. He had hoped at first that Miss Wintre's dinner invitation had been her own idea—she was a slim, pretty little thing with a light touch of sensuality hanging about her shoulders, and could have made his visit here pleasant—but when she picked him up in the lobby she had disappointed these hopes by her businesslike attitude and by informing him that she was to be his liaison with the FBI. She, in effect, was to be his team. Together they would investigate and prevent the assassination. He smiled at the thought as she rambled on with a benign and totally irrelevant discussion of how they might accomplish that end, speaking with the earnest demeanor of the untrained liar. He sliced his duck and chewed it. It wasn't bad, and the vegetables were excellent, but something was definitely rotten in the state of Denmark.

She had taken him to a small country-style French restaurant in Georgetown, and after eating they wandered around the neighborhood together, looking in store windows, picking through paperbacks in used-book stores. He picked up an old Ed McBain 87th Precinct mystery to save "for the flight home," he said; she found an Agatha Christie she hadn't read.

She should have said good night and left him when they left the restaurant. She had done what she had been told to do, and whether he suspected or even knew that she was lying to him didn't matter: This was the way it was going to be, and no amount of browsing through old bookstores was going to change it. But she hated to leave him like that, with the lie lying between them on the tablecloth, so to speak, and so they wandered on into and out of bookstores and up toward the Kennedy Center.

It was a lovely evening, cold but clear and crisp. The people wandering the streets in Georgetown were college students or faculty, or looked as if they were. Up here on the grounds of the center they all looked like what society people in a democracy are supposed to look like: rich and bright and energetic and happy. Melnik thought about the grotesque figures inhabiting "downtown Washington," as the cop in the lobby had called it last night, and found it hard to believe they were only a few blocks away.

They stood looking across the Potomac toward the Roosevelt Memorial, with the traffic noise from the parkway reverberating peculiarly pleasantly, like the sound of surf. "How did you get to be doing this?" she asked into the breeze.

"What?"

"Chasing assassins." She turned away from the river and looked at him as if to ask, What's a nice girl like you doing in a place like this?

"It's a living," he said. After a while he asked, "What should I be doing?"

"I don't know. You don't look tough enough. If I met you at a party I'd think you were a dentist. Or no, maybe an actor. Or a doctor."

He laughed. "Or any profession where you don't have to be tough?"

"I didn't mean it as an insult," she said. "I meant, you don't look like the type of man who would choose a violent profession."

He nodded. "My father was a doctor," he said. "He was also a tank commander in the Israeli army reserve. He was killed in his tank in the Yom Kippur War. I don't know . . ." he added, and drifted off into silence.

"I know what you mean," she said after a while. "My father . . ."

He waited, leaning next to her on the white balustrade, looking off across the river, and she told him about her father. "He was disappointed when I was born. He had wanted a boy, a son." She thought about it. "I don't think he ever noticed I was a girl."

"Hard to miss," Melnik said.

She smiled. "Thank you. I meant when I was little. He just never paid attention to the fact I was a girl. We played ball together, which was fun, and he took me hunting, which was all right except for when you actually had to shoot something. And he wanted me to be a cop like him." She shook her head. "I couldn't. I was afraid. Shooting a rabbit was bad enough, but shooting a person—and one who could shoot back . . ."

"It's not pleasant," Melnik agreed. "Is that what happened to him?"

"Worse," she said. He thought she wasn't going to say any more, but after a while she continued, not looking at him, staring out over the river. "I was sixteen. The day after my big party. Daddy and his partner took me along on patrol. They weren't allowed to do that and I told them I really didn't want to go, but Daddy said it was my Sweet Sixteen present."

A bell began to chime inside the center, and the last few of the people standing around went inside. Melnik and Wintre stayed where they were, and in a few minutes it was completely quiet.

She had sat in the back seat as they cruised the city streets. She remained there as they pulled a speeder to the curb. Her father had gone to collect the driver's license and registration while his partner waited beside the patrol car, alert for any problem.

She had seen the problem first: a glint of movement behind the darkened windows of the car, a glint that might have been light reflected from a gun, and in the next moment—the longest moment of her life—she saw a flash of light and heard the explosion and saw her father lifted off his feet, spun around in the air, and smashed to the ground. The car took off and disappeared as her father's partner emptied his gun after it and then ran to his friend lying bleeding in the street.

She sat paralyzed with terror in the patrol car until he came running back to her, yanked open the door, and shouted at her to get the hell out of there. He called in for help on the police radio, and when he finished was startled to see her still huddled in the back seat. ''Get the hell *out* of here!'' he shouted, yanking the door wide, then ran back to her father's body. She wanted to help, wanted to throw herself over her father and stop the bleeding, to fly down the street like Superman and catch the escaping car. But she couldn't fly like Superman, and she was afraid to approach her father. She turned and ran off down the street, she ran all the way home.

She came to realize that he had yelled her away from the scene because they had had no right to take her cruising with them. She understood that it had all happened in the fraction of a second. She understood all that, but in her dreams it was different. For years, in her dreams, the moment between the first glint of light she had seen behind those darkened windows and the eruption of the blast stretched into long minutes—long minutes in which she sat huddled and frightened in the patrol car, unable and unwilling to risk her life by jumping out and warning her father. In the dreams her father's partner turned to her staring and wondering what she was blubbering about while the gun in the car was slowly raised, and slowly aimed, and finally, finally fired to kill her father. In her terrible dreams her father died because she had been afraid.

''But that isn't true,'' Melnik said.

''No,'' she replied. ''I suppose not.''

He shook his head. ''Try that again,'' he insisted.

She took a deep breath. ''It isn't true,'' she said. ''He didn't die because of me. Still . . .''

''I know. My father died because he wanted to protect my mother and me. I'm still trying to pay him back.'' He shook his head, dispelling the mood. ''But I like what I'm doing,'' he said. ''So it's not so bad.''

''And what is it that you do, besides flying to America to warn us about problems?''

''I kill people,'' he said. He stared down into her eyes, his own clear and blue like glass, holding her pinioned there. Then he broke the spell and looked away. ''I kill people,'' he repeated. ''Or at least I used to. People who kill other people. People who plant bombs in airplanes, who ambush schoolbuses, who organize ambushes of tourists and kibbutzim. I find them, and I kill them.''

She didn't know whether to believe him or not. ''You arrest them?''

He shook his head. ''You can't play civilized games with people like that. You arrest one of them, and his friends hijack an airplane and kill the passengers one at a time until you release him. Arresting them only makes things worse."

She *couldn't* believe him. "If there's no trial," she asked, "how can you be sure you always have the right person?"

"We are very careful."

It was horrible, she thought. He was standing there, a pleasant man who could be a dentist or an actor, telling her he was a murderer. "You're not perfect," she argued, "no one is. At least once in a while you must kill the wrong man."

"Or woman," Melnik said. "But it's never happened."

"Without a trial, you'd never know."

He nodded. "You cut right to the heart of things," he admitted. "Well, you told me about your nightmare; that is mine: that someday it might be the wrong man. However"—he straightened up and smiled bitterly—"it's all over. At least for me. I should have said, 'I *used to* kill people.' Now I just deliver messages. I am too old for anything else."

4

"*Grüss Gott,* Vorshage," Helmut Schlanger said. "You have some news for me?"

"*Jawohl, Herr Minister,*" Vorshage said, coming into the room and taking a seat as indicated. "It's not what I hoped, but . . ." He shrugged, and handed a faxed sheet across the desk.

Schlanger took it and leaned back in his huge chair to read it. "From our man in Los Angeles," Vorshage explained, and Schlanger nodded. The fax consisted simply of a clipping from the *Los Angeles Times,* reporting that a bomb had exploded in a car in a downtown parking lot; the driver had been killed instantly, the corpse burnt to a crisp. Ironically, the *Times* reported, the victim was the owner of a company well known in international circles for expertise and advice in counterassassination work, advising clients around the world how to live safely in countries where terrorism was rampant. Walter Naman, the article continued, had been born in Germany and survived the camp at Auschwitz, escaping the very day he had been consigned to the gas chambers. . . .

"*Also,*" Schlanger said, returning the piece of paper. He was a slim, cultured man of fifty-five, with hair slicked back in a compromise between the old Teutonic fashion and the newest style, graying perfectly at the temples. His mustache was neatly trimmed, his grooming casual but absolutely perfect. "So Jean-Paul Mendoza is our man."

"It would appear so," Vorshage admitted.

Schlanger gave a quick laugh. "I told you so. Youth must be served, as they say. Better all around: I much prefer the mercenary to the idealist. More dependable. Everything straightforward, cards on the table." Suddenly he sighed, as if a great load of weariness had settled on his shoulders. He kneaded the ridge of his nose with his fingers, rubbed his eyes, and sighed again. "*We* must be the idealists, Klaus, you and I. For the rest of the operation, better to have men who will simply take orders in return for payment." He smiled sadly. "Are we really going through with it, then?"

Vorshage was as surprised by the question as by the use of his Christian name. "Everything is in place. All we were waiting for was the choice of the right man. It's necessary—"

"Yes," Schlanger interrupted. "It *is* necessary, isn't it? We can't let things go on without direction any longer, we can't let our government settle into decay, can we? It's a terrible thing to do, but I suppose it must be done, *nicht wahr?*"

Vorshage had been about to say that it was necessary to move fast now that all was in place; he took it for granted that the necessity of the action itself had been settled long ago, when they first embarked on this course. It had been Schlanger's idea from the beginning, after all. Or, at least, Vorshage had presented the facts in such a manner that Schlanger thought it was his idea. As vice-chancellor of the Federal Republic of Germany, Schlanger knew better than anyone the risks and the rewards—and, as he said, the necessity. It had even been Schlanger's idea, though Vorshage had been ready to suggest it, that they hire an outsider for the job rather than use one of their own agents. Failure was a possibility that must be faced, in which case it was imperative that the perpetrator not be linked to themselves in any obvious or provable manner. Even more important, success must be planned for—and success was more probable with an outsider, given the inevitable leaks and infiltrations in an organization as large as Vorshage's.

Karl Friedrichs bore witness to that. There might be others like him, and there surely were supposedly well-trained men in their organization whose tongues loosened over drinks or in bed. Facts like these had to be faced, no matter how proud one was of one's subordinates. But once an outsider was launched on his mission he would be independent of such problems; though the strategy might be discovered by alien agents, the tactics would be held in one man's mind and therefore would be impenetrable.

"It is a time to try men's souls," Schlanger said, getting up and terminating the meeting. "Do you know who said that? One of the original American revolutionaries, I believe. Let us hope we have the success they did."

"I have every confidence, *Herr Minister*—" Vorshage began, but Schlanger cut him off by merely nodding, dismissing the pedantries and routine responses. "You are disappointed that Mendoza won his little battle with Naman," Schlanger said as he walked him to the door. "That is to be expected: No one likes to be proven wrong." He gave his famous smile of sympathy, as if he too knew the feeling; but Vorshage knew that he couldn't even visualize what it meant to be wrong. The smile clicked off; it was time to move on. "The Romans who removed Caligula with their knives were heroes," he said. He nodded, as if to himself. "You will proceed with Mendoza,"

The words were dismissal. Vorshage nodded, pocketed the fax sheet, and left the room without another word. He stopped at the supermarket and bought a pair of lamb cutlets for dinner. He paid extra for New Zealand lamb; he still didn't eat lamb from Eastern Europe because of Chernobyl. He didn't like to take chances.

He smiled as he let himself into the apartment. Distaste for risk was an unusual characteristic for someone in his line of work, one might have thought, but it was precisely because of this trait that he was still alive and working after thirty years in the business. The thought sobered him, bringing poor Naman to mind, and the smile faded.

He hadn't expected Mendoza to succeed; he had never expected that. He had thought he'd be reading in the papers of Mendoza's end instead of Naman's. Well, it had to happen to each of us sooner or later. He nodded; that was the really depressing thought. If Naman could be had, so could they all. He put down the cutlets and took out once again the faxed newspaper article. He spread it out on the table and read it again. "Ode upon intimations of mortality," he thought. His own mortality was spelled out in Naman's death.

They had first met, he and Walter, more than twenty years before. Though Naman was an American citizen and worked for the CIA, he had been born and lived the first twelve years of his life in Germany and so had been assigned to the European scene. They had first worked together against a Libyan hit squad that had come to West Berlin to attack the American chargé, and had impressed each other with the quiet efficiency with which they had eliminated the threat. There had been no arrests; the Libyans had simply disappeared.

Naman and Vorshage had subsequently cooperated against the East

German Stasi, the Russians, and several terrorist groups, and never a bitter word had passed between them. They had celebrated Walter's retirement together at the Hotel Adler in Berlin, and then Walter had gone to Los Angeles to set up his private company and live safely into old age. Of course he hadn't stuck to that; it had quickly become too boring. He had kept the company operating, but had spent most of his time searching for, finding, and killing the old Nazis. Quietly, efficiently, without fuss.

Klaus sighed. He had never thought it would come to this, never thought he would be standing here reading Naman's obituary. When this job had come up and the ape Mendoza had been recommended, Klaus had argued instead that Naman was the only man to carry it off as they wanted. When the suggestion was made that they pit the two against each other and go with the winner, he had never thought the winner might be Mendoza. Well, perhaps it was all for the best.

"Guten Tag, Klaus."

Really good training takes over, like a knee-jerk when the nerve below the patella is struck, and so though Klaus froze at the unexpected voice he didn't betray his astonishment. His first thought was dismay that he had been so preoccupied with Naman's death that he hadn't noticed any sign of entry into his apartment; he really was getting old, he thought. Perhaps it was time for *him* to retire. "I bought two lamb cutlets for my dinner," he said. "Will you join me?"

"What wine?"

"Wine? What's happened to you since you went to Los Angeles? *Weissbier!"*

Walter laughed and got up from the chair deep in the shadows. "Sounds good. And what were you reading that made you so oblivious? You were a thousand miles away. Is life so easy here now that you can afford such behavior?"

"I'm truly ashamed of myself," Klaus said. "I was reading of a man's death in Los Angeles. It seems that a car exploded. . . . Was it Mendoza?"

Walter nodded, leaning over his shoulder, reading the article.

"You're sure?"

"I'm sure. And while everyone thinks I'm dead, perhaps you could tell me the whole story?"

"Yes," Klaus agreed. "I'd like to tell you everything. In fact, I'll do better than that: I'll show you. We'll have our lamb and beer, and then I'll take you somewhere tonight."

• • •

It was like watching an old World War II movie. First of all, it was in black-and-white: The cellar they were crowded into was lit only by a single bulb hanging from a wire cord, throwing shadows in wild arcs as it was jostled by the excited people. And then there were the faces of the crowd: caricatures rather than portraits, rough and crudely drawn, with violent emotions spilling out of the eyes and mouths. And the sounds, the words: Walter had never thought he would ever again hear such words spoken aloud, although he knew there had always been and always would be people who thought the thoughts the words expressed.

He half expected Erich von Stroheim to stride up to the front of the room, decked out in a Nazi *Gauleiter*'s uniform, or Paul Muni to stand up in the rear and begin an anti-Nazi speech, and be clubbed and trampled by the crowd.

It wasn't much of a crowd, actually: hardly more than a dozen people, all men, mostly middle-aged. But in the small, dimly lit cellar it took on the proportions of a surging hysterical mass as the speaker ranted on.

They had arrived at the house by ones and twos, walking down a long, dark alley, and had been admitted only after careful examination by a large man who answered the door. He had opened the door only a crack when Klaus knocked, had looked suspiciously at Walter's face and asked what he wanted, but Klaus had leaned forward and said, ''It's all right, he's with me.'' The guard opened the door wider, reached out and pulled Klaus forward into the light, recognized him, changed expression into what was meant to be a smile, and waved them in.

''Remember after the war?'' Klaus whispered as they took their seats. ''We were afraid that the Nazis had done such a good job of indoctrinating their youth that we'd never be able to wipe the movement out of the nation, that all the children would grow up into good Nazis. But it didn't seem to happen. At least, we didn't *think* it happened. We just didn't give it enough time,'' he said bitterly.

In front of them there was a simple wooden desk. A bright lamp standing on it floodlit the dim room as a rough, large-bellied man stood up and began to talk about God and Right and Freedom for Germany and the Traitors and the Jews and the Destiny of Germany. . . . Naman looked at the ugliness and power of the man, and thought of Yeats's lines: ''And what rough beast, its hour come round at last, / Slouches toward Bethlehem to be born?''

''They did their work well, better than we thought,'' Vorshage said, still talking about the Nazis. ''What we didn't realize was that the children born during the Third Reich were just five or ten years old when the war ended. They grew up in the devastation that followed; they were more concerned with building their own lives, in trying to put food on the table, than in building a new Reich. But now they're in their early fifties, ready to burst out and take over. Unification came so suddenly it took everyone by surprise, but now they're looking around and seeing that anyone can take the power, can take it all. There are hundreds of cells like this," he whispered. "All kept small, no strangers admitted unless vouched for."

"And nobody in the government knows what's going on?"

"Of course they know what's going on," Klaus snapped. "That's the whole point."

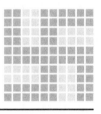

4

1

WILLIAM HAGAN indulged himself in irritation as he twisted around in the interior of the large black car and extracted his wallet while the guard at the southwest gate waited patiently. Hagan took out his ID card and handed it through the window. The guard made a show of looking at the picture on the card, then leaned in the window to stare at Hagan's face. *He knows damn well who I am,* Hagan thought, but he said nothing. The guard punched his name into the computer, reading it letter by letter from the ID, and finally returned the card. "Meeting's in the Situation Room, Mr. Hagan," he said.

Hagan nodded, and the chauffeur moved the car gently forward as the iron gates opened. Hagan loved and hated the protocol; loved the tourists on Pennsylvania Avenue craning their necks around trying to catch a glimpse of who it was entering the White House, hated having to submit to a formal identification instead of being waved in on sight. He smiled grimly. One day the guard would neglect to check his ID, would smile and wave him in . . . and Hagan would have his job for it. The thought satisfied him. *Serve him right.*

This pleasant thought disappeared in the first few minutes of the meeting, and things got worse as the meeting progressed. The National Security Planning Group was discussing Germany and the problems unification had brought to the American presence in Europe. The CIA representative reported that, despite the spate of stories in newspapers around the world, there was actually no indication that the neo-Nazi movement in Germany was any stronger than in other countries.

"Oh dear," Hagan said, and they all turned to him. "Sorry," he said, "didn't mean to interrupt. But you know, you people really did say the same about the ayatollah's underground movement, telling Carter that the shah was in control. And you told Kennedy that the Cuba Libre forces would find a wave of hysterical sentiment when they strode ashore at the Bay of Pigs—not mentioning that the bay was on the other side of a swamp and a few mountains away from Havana."

"Yes," the President said, "but no point going into ancient history now."

"Just pointing out that there *are* a few uncertainties attached to that position. And if Germany does swell up and burst at the seams, oughtn't we to be prepared?"

"Can we afford to be prepared," the State Department representative asked, "when we are faced with much more probable problems elsewhere? The state of our economy mandates a ranking of priorities. As I understand it, continuing troubles with the Arab countries are more likely to be our immediate source of concern."

This brought a wave of approbation from around the table, and Hagan shut up. They spent the next two hours discussing the funding needs for low-tech versus high-tech, sophisticated weapons. The consensus of the group was clearly that the sadly insufficient military funds must go to strengthening ground troops. Hagan tried to argue for the smart weapons. "Don't forget 1991 and Iraq: We found that although a sophisticated nation like the French could 'see' the F-117A 'Stealth' fighter-bomber, the Iraqis could not. If we hadn't been developing it for use against the Soviets, it wouldn't have been good enough to use against the Iraqis. You have to overdevelop weapons." But in the face of a tight budget this argument didn't have much weight, and Hagan soon saw the odds stacked against him and dropped it. He sat back and let the talk swirl around him. He was a realist, and realistically, taking account of politics in a democracy, the only way to fund high-tech weapons is to have a high-tech adversary in the wings.

Germany, he thought. He needed Germany as a high-tech villain. If there really was a Nazi-organized assassination planned, how lovely it could be. A powerful Nazi Germany would scare the hell out of the French, make them turn to the United States for "friendship," let the

U.S. move into a position of authority in Europe—but only if America had the sophisticated weaponry available to impress them all. Oh, what a lovely world that would be.

He reflected on his orders to Wintre, and how clever he had been. He had told her to tell the FBI that the Israelis were nuts; that he, Hagan, had confidential information that what the Israelis thought of as a serious plot was actually nothing but talk from a group of neurotics. Then, if the killing didn't take place, he would get credit for having his finger in the right pie. And if it did, even better—that would shake up the French, strengthen the case for complex weapons systems, and provide the funding for his friends. And he could always claim he had never told Wintre anything. He would fire her for misrepresenting him to the FBI. Too bad to lose a good assistant, but that's life.

Hagan didn't say anything for the rest of the meeting. He knew when to hold his tongue. That was a crucial skill for getting on in Washington, as it was in personal life. He never said a word to his wife about his concerns, about his suspicions. Let her think he knew nothing, give her enough line, feed it out carefully, until she bit off too large a chunk. . . .

Damn. He was getting himself upset. He tried to refocus on the arguments spinning around the table, but he couldn't help wondering where she was at this precise moment.

2

WHEN CARLOS GRASS's date hadn't shown up two days earlier, he wasn't terribly upset. Actually, the man wasn't Grass's date; Grass was cast more in the role of chaperon. And like a good chaperon he had shown up early.

He was a large, heavily muscled man who would ordinarily stand out in a crowd, but he had learned to disguise his physique with a casual stoop and a soft way of walking, which also hid the limp he had acquired in a knife fight in Buenos Aires. So no heads turned when he wandered into the Beldenmore Hotel lobby at four o'clock, bought a *Times* at the newsstand, and found a comfortable seat. Promptly at five he spotted the contact coming in, a young, bulky, red-haired man who looked something like Boris Becker. For a moment Grass had a twinge of disgust, the man was so easy to make; and then he realized that this wasn't fair: He had a description and the time of the appointment. The man glanced at his watch, checked it against the lobby clock, and took a seat.

And then nothing happened for two hours. Grass struck up a conversation with a young lady who sat beside him, and when her husband arrived a half hour later she gave a what-might-have-been shrug and left Grass sitting there. The redheaded idiot didn't have the sense to do anything similar; he simply sat there like a wart on a frog. Anyone checking the place would surely notice him.

But no one was checking the place. Grass would have spotted any surveillance. No one was looking, and evidently no one was coming. He watched the hand of the lobby clock move slowly around toward seven. Well, this sort of thing happened sometimes. It was likely to be due to no more than the rain and an inexperienced courier who hadn't allowed enough time to get across town. But he himself was experienced; he took a quiet pride in doing things right. So he waited under the clock at the Beldenmore till seven o'clock, and saw Mr. Boris Becker get up and leave; though the odds were better than even that the courier might simply show up late, Mr. Becker's instructions were to wait two hours and no more.

He himself waited another half hour, just to be sure, and then he, too, left. He had dinner and went home, planning to return the following night at seven, following the plan for staggered hours in case of an aborted rendezvous. He would again wait two hours, and if no one showed up he would initiate the routine to let the people at the other end know. That was what he planned to do when he went to bed that night; when he awoke in the morning everything was different.

The front page of the *Post* that was delivered to his hotel door told of a bomb attack on a Manhattan police station, and on the third page of a subway mugging that ended in a vigilante shooting. The suspected mugger had been found two blocks from the subway station, bleeding to death on the pavement, clutching a briefcase. He was dead on arrival at Bellevue, where one of his victims, shot by mistake by the unknown vigilante, was in serious condition.

These various pieces were not necessarily all part of the same puzzle, but Grass began to plan in case they were. He walked down to the medical uniforms store off Thirty-third Street and bought a male nurse's uniform, a clipboard, and white walking shoes. That evening, carrying a briefcase that held the uniform, clipboard, and shoes, and a 9mm automatic fitted with a silencer, he waited again in the Beldenmore lobby, this time not under the clock but across the lobby where he could keep an eye on anyone who might come by. The Becker man was there again, promptly on time, but the courier once again did not show, and at nine o'clock Mr. Becker left.

Grass walked to the registration desk and booked in, paying cash in advance. In the room he changed into the nurse's uniform and shoes, strapped the gun under his shoulder, put his suit and jacket in the briefcase, mussed the bed, and left. He took the subway to Astor Place, leaving the briefcase by his seat when he stood up and got off the train. The man sitting next to him noticed, but said nothing. As the train started up again the man happily and casually draped his own hand over the handle. Grass hoped he could use the suit.

He waited across the street from the staff entrance to the hospital as group after group of workers left, until finally a male nurse left without company. Grass followed him up the block. A hundred yards before the subway station a basement entrance into a brownstone offered refuge. A quick chop to the neck and a spin move, and the man tumbled silently down the stairs. Grass dropped down beside him, took his wallet and pin-on ID card, and was back on the sidewalk, heading toward the hospital, within thirty seconds. He took the cash out of the wallet as he walked—waste not, want not—and dropped the wallet in the corner trash receptacle. He pinned on the ID and walked into the staff entrance. He never even bothered to look to see if the photo on the ID was a close match; if he was lucky no one else would look, if he wasn't lucky he would think of something. Having a 9mm strapped under one's shoulder gives confidence.

He was familiar enough with the hospital to know where seriously injured gunshot victims would be kept, and if he was right he wouldn't have to know anything more. As he walked briskly down the halls he passed several rooms with hospital papers stuck into the envelopes attached to the doors; he whipped off several of these and clipped them to his board.

As he finished one corridor and turned right to go down the next, he saw that he had indeed been right. By the door at the end of the corridor sat a uniformed policeman. Grass walked straight up to the door, nodded at the cop, and turned the handle. The cop stood up quickly. "You're supposed—" he began.

"Just giving him a suppository," Grass responded cheerfully. "You're welcome to come in and watch. Wouldn't mind giving *you* one when you're off duty, ducky," he added. That approach usually either made you a friend or scared them off, but the cop stood his ground.

"You gotta have authorization to go in there," he said.

"Well, I've got *that*," Grass said, still in character, and shoved the clipboard under the cop's nose. As it reached eye level, blocking his view, Grass reached under his white jacket and pulled out the automatic.

"I don't see—" the cop began, pushing the clipboard away, but by that time Grass had brought the gun up under the clipboard and against the cop's lower jaw, its muzzle slanting upward. He pulled the trigger and there was a soft pop, a sudden jerk of the cop's head, and a sharp splattering of blood against the wall.

Grass caught the falling body easily under the armpits and swung him around facing outward, his own back against the door. The corridor was empty, except for a patient hobbling down the hall away from them. Grass pushed the door open and pulled the cop in. He dropped him beside the door, shut it behind him, glanced quickly around the room and walked to the bed, making his first mistake: He didn't notice the small television camera perched high on a shelf in the corner, surveying the room.

In the nurses' service station Patrolman Richard Jensen was fooling around with the small blond nurse everyone called Bitsy. He was fascinated with how such a little woman could have such large breasts. He could hardly keep his hands off her. He glanced up from time to time at the television screen he was supposed to be watching, but nothing ever changed on it; all he saw was a room empty except for a man in bed with tubes stuck in his arm.

All day long there were people coming in and out of the station, so all he could do was look at Bitsy's chest and joke around with her a little. She didn't seem to like it, exactly, but at least she didn't get mad, so who knew? Jensen had been waiting all day for them to get a little time alone together, and finally without warning there was no one else in the room. Just all of a sudden everyone else seemed to have something else to do, and there he was sitting in front of the television screen and there Bitsy was with her back to him, fiddling around in a drawer and humming to herself.

He took one last look at the screen, one last look around, and got up from his seat and walked over to Bitsy and put his arms around her and grasped her breasts. Not hard, but tightly; not viciously, but firm. For a moment he didn't know how she was going to react, and then she sort of leaned softly back against him and he grinned and began to rub her lasciviously and she reached one hand behind her and brought it down over his belt and down to his testicles and took hold of them and his thoughts soared to heaven and she grabbed them tightly and began to squeeze hard. At first he thought she was just passionate, but then she squeezed so hard that his eyes bulged and he screamed and let go of her breasts but she just twisted around, still holding him in her grip, twisting him with the motion of her own twisting around and he sank to his knees in pain before she let him go. Then she turned back to the drawer she was rummaging around in and ignored him, humming quietly again.

Patrolman Jensen hobbled back to his chair and sat down gently, very gently. He didn't think to turn around and look at the television for quite a while.

The man lying on the bed had his eyes closed. He seemed about the right length and build, his hair was the right color, but it was hard to tell; people looked different lying down, especially with their eyes closed. "Did you have a good flight?" Grass asked.

The man's eyes shot open, and Grass saw that they were brown. Good. The man blinked nervously, but didn't answer.

"We don't have time to fool around," Grass said. He pointed to the dying cop, whose blood was running across the floor. "Did you have a good flight?"

The man blinked twice, and Grass slapped him hard across the face. "I've got to get you out of here before someone comes in," he hissed. *"Did you have a good flight?"*

"It—it was stormy over the Azores," the man replied.

"You didn't come through Paris?"

"I was too tired," the man said, finishing the litany, and Grass congratulated himself: This was his lost courier. Most people would have waited for instructions; there were few who could think on their feet. "What happened to the briefcase?"

"I lost it in the subway. It wasn't my fault, I was robbed—"

"I know, don't worry. What did you tell them?"

"Who?"

"Who? The police, idiot! What do they know?"

"Nothing. I didn't say—"

"Then why do they have a police guard on you? Come on, what did you tell them?"

"I swear! All they know is I was robbed!"

He had the look of truth about him, so Grass killed him with a quick shot into the ear. He took one last quick look around the room, and with a shock saw the small video camera staring at him from its perch high on a ledge in the far corner. He couldn't tell if it was on, or if anyone was monitoring it. And then he realized that someone would have come in already if they had seen him on it. So it was probably okay; at any rate, what was done was done. He stepped quickly out the door and turned down the corridor. A nurse was walking toward him. As he came up to her he smiled; if she had returned his smile he would have had to kill her, but she walked past him without noticing. She wouldn't be able to describe him. At the end of the corridor he turned left, went down the steps, and in two minutes was out the staff entrance and on his way back to the subway.

3

MRS. ADAMS had said it was just a job like any other job, the only difference being that it paid better and you didn't pay taxes except on the actual twenty-five dollars an hour for the escort work, which was nothing. But Julie had known deep down that nothing goes unpunished in this world. She wished she had never come to this terrible city. People back in Omaha didn't go breaking into hotel rooms waving guns, and if they did they wouldn't find a nice girl like Julie naked on her knees doing *that* to a man— Oh God.

Her first thought when they broke in was that she was going to be raped and killed, and then when she saw the men holding out their wallets with badges dangling and heard them shout "Freeze! Police!" she felt even worse. She was going to be arrested for *prostitution* and her picture would be in the papers and— Oh *God!*

But none of that actually happened. They let her and poor Mr. Johnson get dressed—she almost had to smile when she remembered the expression on his face; he was even more frightened than she—and then one of the policemen, the big black one, had taken him out in the hall and probably asked him the same questions as the one who looked like Robert Redford but kept smirking all the time was asking her. She told him the truth, that she had come here on a job—"to see a friend" was what she said at first, but talking to a cop was like talking to a used-car salesman: No matter what story you made up at the beginning you ended up telling the truth, that you were prepared to spend more money on the car than you were saying, that you were *dying* for a red convertible and didn't care *what* you paid, that you didn't really expect much on your trade-in, and that you were actually a prostitute.

She told him that Mr. August had called the Dreamgirl Escort Service and Mrs. Adams had given her the assignment. She had come here four nights ago expecting to escort him out to dinner and maybe a show, she tried again to explain, but the policeman said "Cut the crap," which wasn't as polite as "Just the facts, ma'am," but meant the same thing. So she told him they had dinner sent up to the room and stayed there all that night and all the next day. Mr. August—

"The guy you were sucking off when we busted in?"

She closed her eyes involuntarily. She hated gross people, and now she decided she hated gross New York City cops more than anyone. It was torture to have to explain to someone like this. But she had to, didn't she? "No," she said. "That's Mr. Johnson. You want to hear about him or Mr. August?"

The big black cop had come in then, alone, and nodded for her to continue.

"Mr. August is the guy rented this room?" the small cop asked her.

"That's what I'm telling you. Mr. Johnson just came today."

"What's Mr. August look like?"

She described him as well as she could, and the detectives nodded. "Okay, go on."

"I'm trying to," she said with dignity. Mr. August had left the room, she said, about five-thirty the next day, this past Monday, and had told her to wait for him. "He didn't say when he'd be back, he just said 'Wait for me.' But he never came back that night."

She ordered room-service breakfast the next morning and watched television all day; they had cable with HBO at the hotel. She had a room-service dinner that night, and watched a movie and fell asleep. By this morning he *still* hadn't come. At eleven o'clock this morning the phone rang and she had thought it would be him but it was the desk downstairs. They asked if Mr. August would be vacating the room, and she had thought what the hell, she might as well enjoy this life so she said no, they were planning to stay for another week. She didn't know why she said that, but she knew that to check in at a hotel like this you had to leave your credit-card imprint and so it would all be paid, and she had nothing to do anyhow. He had paid her in advance for that first night—that was Mrs. Adams's rule, get the cash out of the way first— but he *had* said to wait and so she thought when he finally came back she might be able to get him to pay for all the time she had waited, and anyhow she had nothing better to do and she thought she might as well live good for a few days in this snobby hotel.

Then this afternoon her beeper had gone off. She called in to the office and Mrs. Adams said that Mr. Johnson, whom she had met before, had called and specially asked for her, and was she free? She didn't tell Mrs. Adams she was still at Mr. August's hotel room; after the first night she figured it was none of Mrs. Adams's business. She said she was free, and Mrs. Adams gave her Mr. Johnson's number at work which was where he was, and when she called him he said he could take a couple of hours off this afternoon and how about it? So she invited him over, because she wasn't going to give up any income-producing dates waiting for a guy who God knew when he was coming back or if he'd even want to see her when he did, right?

In the car on the way back to headquarters Horner received a radio call telling him to check in at the hospital, but since they were nearly at the precinct by then he decided to call from there. He stopped at his desk to check on any other messages that might have come in, hoping to have heard from the assistant commissioner, Ronald Waxman, about his promotion. But there was only a note from Ted Kuzlewski, the lab man. Horner decided to talk to him first. He left Blank regaling everyone with how the hooker had almost swallowed the guy in her shock as they burst into the hotel room. "I thought we were gonna have to use the Heimlich crunch to get her to cough it up," he was saying to an appreciative crowd as Horner slipped out of the room and down the hall.

Kuzlewski was a fat, pompous man who did his work well but was always telling everyone else how to do *their* work, which did not make him too popular around the place. Horner kind of liked him, at least he *tried* to like him, thinking that Fat K just felt inferior because he was locked in a lab and not allowed out on the street. So he listened patiently as Fat K started in on him. "In the ordinary course of events," Kuzlewski said, leaning back in his chair with his hands folded over his belly, "you couldn't have expected much from us. The fire that followed the briefcase explosion would have burned everything in the case, as it was obviously intended to do. But since it took place in a police station, this didn't quite happen. Not completely. The boys were on it quickly and put it out. Not before everything in the briefcase was destroyed, but before it was *totally* destroyed, if you take my point. A few scraps of things here and there were left, and I can tell you I spent a few long hours on my hands and knees in that place scraping up bits of particles and dust, separating them from what was undoubtedly in the room before the briefcase exploded, and— Well, you get the picture."

Kuzlewski went on from there, lecturing about all the technical details like sulfide tests and electron microscopy which Horner didn't give a damn about, until finally Horner couldn't take it anymore and rather innocently said he was confused. "Didn't you send everything over to the FBI lab? Because you don't have the equipment to handle this kind of job? Weren't *they* the ones who did the analysis?"

"Well, yes," Fat K admitted. "What I'm trying to do here is explain it to you. What they did."

"Why don't you just tell me what the results are?"

Fat K snorted to himself: What could you expect? He leaned forward and picked up a sheet of paper and glanced at it. "The technical terms wouldn't mean much to you," he announced, "but it's basically money."

"Money?"

"In the briefcase. Lots of money. This man was carrying probably something like over a hundred thousand in cash. Plus some ceramic." He looked up. "Psychoceramic."

Horner was confused. "What's that?"

"Psychoceramic," Fat K said again. "Cracked pot. Get it?" he laughed. "*Crackpot.* Psychoceramic!" He began to wheeze from the laughter and wiped tears out of his eyes.

Horner smiled weakly. "Funny," he said.

"What the hell," Fat K said, "you gotta laugh in this job or you go nuts. Anyhow, the ceramic in this briefcase wasn't for any pots. High-grade carbon-impregnated aluminum oxide. The kind of stuff you can build a fighter plane out of, a Stealth fighter. Nonmagnetic, but strong. Wouldn't be picked up by a metal detector, or probably even X rays or neutron activation. They found enough little chunks to suggest a tube with an inside diameter of half an inch, which suggests to you what?"

"How long a tube?"

"Impossible to say. At least six inches, but short enough to fit in the briefcase. So what do you think?"

"A gun barrel?"

"Bingo! I always said you were the only smart guy in this shop. And get this: Not many people know it yet, but the Israelis have designed themselves a new gun, the Uzi RKS, nonmagnetic ceramic alloy, quiet, long-range, accurate. For snipers, assassinations, or just good all-around fun. Now put it all together, what do you get?"

"You tell me."

"South American drugs. This guy's carrying around money like this, you gotta figure it's drug money. And they buy every new weapon comes on the market, it's like designer jeans, they got to be first with it, you know what I mean? I double guarantee you, you make this guy he'll turn out to be Colombian, Chilean, Mex, one of those. Mark my words."

"Name's Kremble," Horner said. "Gerhard Kremble."

Fat K looked crestfallen, but only for a moment. "German," he said. "Lots of Germans went to South America after World War II. Argentina, Bolivia. How do you know his name, anyhow?"

"Found his hotel room. Lady he was with graciously gave us written permission to look around. You're right, he's German. Found his airline ticket and passport. German passport. Flew in from Frankfurt. No South American visa stamps in the passport."

Fat K sat back sadly. "Not drugs, then." He had been so happy with his deduction.

Horner felt for him. "They got drugs in Germany, too. Could be anything, at this stage."

Kuzlewski smiled weakly and nodded. That was the problem with this business. Everything was so complicated. "What are you gonna do next?" he asked.

"Got a call from the hospital," Horner said. "Maybe Mr. Kremble's ready to talk."

5

1

WALTER NAMAN woke up smiling. He held on to the memories gently; he had learned that if he tried to grasp them too tightly they dissolved and faded away, leaving him alone in a terribly real world. The sunlight streamed in through the curtains and flickered on the ceiling, and the images flickered with it, and Lise was twelve years old again and lovely as a sunbeam, and she was the devil incarnate.

She laughed. Even as a child, she never giggled. He couldn't hear—couldn't remember—what she was laughing about, but he thought of that story Noël Coward told about the first time he had met Gertie Lawrence when he was twelve years old, and she a year older: "She carried a handbag and a powder puff, and she gave me an orange and told me a few mildly dirty stories and I loved her from that moment onwards."

He closed his eyes, and the years went back along with the room, and without opening his eyes he saw again the long dark flight of stairs to the attic.

"Lise's in the attic, playing with some old clothes," Mrs. Berthold said. It didn't sound like much fun to an eleven-year-old boy, and he would have decided to go back outside but Mrs. Berthold said, "Go on up, you know the way," and he hadn't known how to refuse without being impolite. Funny: It had begun so dully, and had since become one of those few days one remembered clearly across the eons of time.

In the few minutes it took to reach the top of the attic stairs he decided to make the most of an unpromising situation by at least surprising and frightening her. He crept up those last few stairs and inched open the door. When he peered through the crack he didn't recognize her; if he hadn't known it was Lise he would have slunk back downstairs without going farther. As it was, he stared fascinated. She was dressed in her mother's clothes, wearing a wide-brimmed hat with a tremendous feather that curved up out of her head and back over her shoulder, coming nearly as low on her back as the long, straight, black hair. The gown came to the floor and curled there around her bare feet. It was red and glittering, as if made of magic diamonds. Her left hand disappeared into a large fur muff, while her right hung languidly by her side, trailing a silk scarf to the floor. She was unaware of him. She was studying herself in a full-length mirror, turning her body slowly from side to side without moving her feet, bending her knees and hips gracefully to accommodate the movement.

He didn't know why, but he was embarrassed, as if he had caught her doing something shameful. And so he had: She was growing up, leaving him behind, and though he didn't understand it he was both frightened and shamed by it. He banged the door open and burst through, shouting "Holla!" as loudly as he could. But she only glanced up at him in the mirror and smiled condescendingly without even bothering to turn and face him. "What *are* you doing, Walter?" she asked, as if she were his mother, though she was only a year older. "Playing games?"

Somehow she was so far above him that his shame and fright left him, and only awe remained. "What are *you* doing?" he asked, coming quietly into the room.

"Shut the door," she said, and when he did she turned from the mirror and looked at him directly, and it was like one of those moments when he came suddenly into a room and his parents stopped talking, and he knew that something he didn't understand had been happening.

"Do you want to see my breasts?" she asked.

He was confused and frightened; he didn't understand. He knew about women's breasts. But Lise—?

She was holding herself quite straight, and for the first time he realized that she was a couple of centimeters taller than he. He didn't at all like the look on her face, but he was fascinated by it. He couldn't take his eyes off her. He remembered the picture in his encyclopedia of the mongoose staring at the snake, and this frightened him out of his wits, but he could as soon have jumped over the moon as walked out of that attic room.

She shrugged her shoulders in a casual-seeming motion, and then she stood there and frowned, and then she shrugged them again and waited another moment, and then she pouted and reached up and moved the line of her red gown slightly off her shoulders, and when she shrugged again in that casual way the gown began to slip down. She stood there without moving, tall and straight, with that mysterious expression on her face, as the gown slid slowly down over her shoulders as if it were alive, like a snake slithering down her skin. It stopped for a moment, hanging there, caught on the protuberance of her nipples, and then suddenly it fell to her waist, catching on her hips.

Her breasts were exposed, and Walter stood there until the gown stopped quivering and hung still on her body. Then, despite himself, he took two small steps forward to look more closely. It was dark in the attic. The only light, coming in through a side window, bounced around the room among the myriad objects, picking up from each of them its color and leaving with each a bit of its own intensity. In that dark, richly colored light her skin was a ghostly, translucent white, fascinatingly pale above the rich scarlet of the gown. The breasts pushed up out of her thin, flat chest as if they didn't yet know they belonged there. In the center of each breast a small dark red nipple protruded like a half-buried stone.

"You can touch them if you like," she said, speaking from a great height somewhere above him.

Oh no, he couldn't. Not in ten thousand years. He thought surely he must be stepping backward, walking away from her, running down the stairs and out to play with his friends, but his legs weren't moving. Instead, his hands moved forward and out, touching her on a bare shoulder, moving down across her collarbone, across her chest, until his fingers touched a breast.

He didn't believe this. He didn't understand anything that was happening. He felt the swelling in his groin and he thought he would die of embarrassment. He didn't dare look to see if it showed.

He knew about sex. He had talked about it with the other boys, and he knew that someday he would touch a woman as he was now touching Lise. They had all talked about what they would do when that day came. But he couldn't possibly do that now, today, and certainly never with Lise.

And yet instead of laughing at her, instead of joking and teasing her for being seen half naked, he stood where he was and touched her breast.

Her arm swung loosely forward and her hand brushed across the front of his pants, bouncing against his swollen penis. He jumped back in anguish, his face flushing. He wished frantically he could explode and disappear in a gigantic puff of smoke and never be heard from again.

"You can touch me there, too, if you like," she said. She pushed the red gown down over her hips and it fell to the floor. She stood there naked, totally naked in front of him. He couldn't move. She lifted one small foot and stepped daintily out of the folds of the garment. With the other foot she kicked it gracefully behind her. She stepped forward on her naked feet, and now she was so close their bodies nearly touched.

He couldn't look her in the face; he was frightened of that serious smile on her lips. He couldn't raise his eyes anyhow: He was gazing down fascinated at the little tuft of black hair that blemished and set off her otherwise white body.

"Do you have any hair there?" she asked.

Dumbly, he nodded. It had started to sprout just a few months ago, and he had been disappointed as he watched it grow blond and nearly invisible, as blond as the hair on his head.

"Let me see," she commanded.

He couldn't move. He felt he couldn't breathe.

"Let me see," she said again, and in desperation—unable to resist her—he began to undo his short pants. They dropped from his fumbling fingers and fell to his knees, then to his ankles, and he was terribly aware of how childish he looked in his underpants. *She* had been naked under her red gown.

"Let me see," she said again, softly but insistently, and he hooked his fingers into his pants and pulled them down, and his penis sprang out like rubber and she gave a little girl's gasp. Then she reached out and touched it.

He was going to fall down. He was going to faint. The light streaming in the solitary window was picking up all the colors of the rainbow and flinging them around the room in a whirling maelstrom. He wanted to run away but his legs were chained to the floor by his pants clinging to his ankles, and he stood there while she touched him.

"You can touch me there, too," she said.

But he couldn't, he couldn't. And then he saw his hand, attached somehow to his arm, beginning to move forward toward her—

Footsteps! Footsteps coming up the attic stairs!

He stood there paralyzed as Lise turned away and stooped and slid her hands into the tumbled gown and pulled it up over her shoulders and in one moment was perfectly dressed again. He stood there paralyzed as the footsteps came clacking up the attic stairs toward the door.

"Put your pants on!" she hissed angrily.

He couldn't move, and then finally he broke loose and bent and tried to pull up his pants but his underwear was tangled with his shorts around his ankles and his fingers wouldn't work properly, they fumbled ineffectually over the woolen cloth, and then the footsteps reached the top of the stairs and the door opened.

Lise pushed him roughly, and he tripped over his pants and fell into the corner. The shock revived him, and as he pulled his pants up he saw Lise turning majestically to the door as her mother came in. She arched her arms wide, like a swan, and pirouetted slowly. "How do I look, Mama?" she asked.

Her mother, squinting to adjust her eyes to the dark room, laughed. "You're the image of your grandmother, God bless her, in that gown," she said. "Isn't Walter here?"

Lise gestured languidly, and Walter stood up in the corner, some-how—with the grace of God—with his pants back on. "I'm over here, Frau Berthold," he said.

"I've just taken the cookies out of the oven," Frau Berthold said. "Come down and have them with some milk."

And so they did. The next morning Walter was jostled awake by his father and told to dress quickly and pick out one toy to take with him. They had to be at the train station in an hour. They were being relocated to the East.

At the station they were politely but firmly directed into lines by soldiers. The Berthold family was there too, but when Walter stepped out of line to get to Lise he was pushed back by a soldier, and his mother grabbed his hand and held him tight.

And the next time he saw Lise she was the Germans' whore.

Angrily he got out of bed. He had lost it again, and the day was no longer beautiful. Why couldn't he learn to control it, hold on to it? It was all he had left. . . .

No, that wasn't true either. It hadn't been the next time he had seen her, and it wasn't all he had left. But there was no point going on. He had lost it again. He washed and began to dress. He had work to do today, and miles to go before he slept. Thousands of miles.

Last night he had been summoned back to Vorshage's apartment. It was bourgeois to the point of dullness: an unobtrusive entrance between two stores on a commercial street, a dark staircase leading up two flights, and then a door opening to a pleasant old-fashioned roomy place. Inside a man was waiting for him, and the dullness disappeared. Naman recognized him immediately when he leaned forward briefly out of the corner shadows, and the old hooded lamp on the table cast a dim light across his face. But the man never took off his coat or wide-brimmed hat, though the apartment was excessively warm, and when he settled back into the corner again his face returned to the shadows.

"Darf ich ihnen Herrn Naman vorstellen?" Vorshage said formally, and the man extended his hand and they shook.

The man himself was not introduced, his name never mentioned. Walter understood that. Total deniability at all times. If the question should ever come up, Helmut Schlanger, vice-chancellor of the Federal Republic of Germany, had never been in this apartment at all.

"Well," Vorshage said, rubbing his hands, "I'll put on some coffee. A friend brought me some real Sacher torte this morning. If you'll excuse me."

He left the room. For a moment there was silence. Then, without preamble, Schlanger said, "A nasty business." He shook his head sadly. "A very nasty business."

"I don't yet know what the business is," Naman prodded.

Schlanger shook his head. "Treason, I'm afraid. Damned and damnable treason. Vorshage will explain after I've left. I am here only to assure you that he speaks for the *real* German government. He has my support in this nasty business." He seemed fond of the phrase, and repeated it, shaking his head sadly. Then he stood up. "You will understand the necessity of secrecy," he said. "There are those who would call what *we* are engaged in, treason. Indeed, the vast majority—not knowing the strength of the filthy minority—would undoubtedly classify it so. I myself am very unhappy. But you are one of those who suffered at the hands of the Third Reich, and you are, I am told, a student of history. You will understand how it all could have been avoided if a few strong and resolute men had not been afraid of the label of treason, and had struck down the monster before September of 1939." He moved to the door. "It is always hard to predict the reaction of history, but I know in my heart we are such men: strong, resolute, and absolutely right. And today is such a time."

Vorshage stuck his head back in, breaking the mood. He smiled warmly and said the Sacher torte looked delicious and the coffee would be ready in a moment, and then he disappeared again. Schlanger smiled and said, "It's been quite a while since I had real Sacher torte. Of course, it's not as good as it used to be. But I mustn't keep you; you'll want to wash the filth of the streets off before you eat."

Naman took the hint and left the room. When Vorshage came back in he found Schlanger gazing thoughtfully out the window. "What do you think?" he asked.

Schlanger shrugged. He prided himself on being able to size people up face to face within a few moments, but Naman had eluded him. He clicked on the radio and Beethoven swelled into the room, drowning their conversation. He took Vorshage to the opposite side of the room. "I would have preferred Mendoza. But"—he smiled bleakly—"this man is either better than Mendoza or luckier, so how can we lose?" He paused. "You're sure you can handle him?"

"He won't need much handling; he's done this sort of thing before, remember. He's very good at it. You remember when the Stasi penetrated our security? It could have been a political embarrassment if the man had been arrested. But the CIA would have been even more embarrassed, and so while we were discussing what to do about it they sent Walter to Tübingen and the problem simply disappeared."

"That was a long time ago. He's retired now, he's an American—"

"He was in Auschwitz. His parents died there, all his family died there. The only girl he ever—"

"I know, I know."

"The point is he hates Nazis with the only passion he knows. His business is a failure because instead of putting his profits back into it he spends them hunting old Nazis on his own. He hunts old men who are no longer any danger to anyone, because he *hates*." Vorshage paused. "Oh, yes, he will do this job. And he will spend eternity blessing us to his God for giving him the chance."

Schlanger nodded. They had discussed all this before; he knew about Tübingen and a dozen other cases Naman had handled with dispatch; he knew about the Nazi-hunting and about Auschwitz. Still, they were about to place a lot of trust in the man. It was a worrisome decision. "You have full confidence in him?"

"I do. And what is just as important, he trusts me." He paused. "When you come right down to it, trust is a precious commodity in our business."

"So is money. Offer him the same amount we would have paid Mendoza."

"Naman is not that kind of man."

Schlanger smiled again. "And they say Germans have no sense of humor! I shall bring up your remark the next time someone tries to tell me that." He walked to the door, paused, and turned around. "We are all that kind of man," he said. "You think I'm wrong? Well, pay him the money anyway. As our Jewish friends put it, how could it hurt?" And he was gone.

Walter came back and looked around the empty room. "He didn't stay? Not even for the Sacher torte?"

They had it on the bare, wooden table in the kitchen, with steaming mugs of coffee and fresh cream. "So what are we talking about?" he asked Klaus.

"We would like to hire you for a little job."

Naman swallowed a bite of the Sacher torte. "Good," he said, nodding appreciatively. "Better than I expected." He glanced at Vorshage. "Now that Mendoza's out of the way, you mean?"

"I wouldn't lie to you. There are those in our group who didn't think you'd be able to handle him. They thought you were as good as dead and weren't worth bothering with. They wanted us to avoid any possible compromise of our sources. I went as far as I possibly could in telling you about him, further than I should have. I couldn't do more."

Naman nodded, and Vorshage smiled. "And after all," he added, "I myself was sure that more wouldn't be necessary. Luckily, I was right." He wiped a streak of chocolate from his mouth, laid his napkin down, pushed his cup and plate away, and leaned forward over his elbows. "We've known about the neo-Nazi movement for some time. We didn't worry about it. You have people like that in every country in the world; you'll never get rid of them. Like cockroaches. You can't wipe them out, but you keep them under control and try not to think about them scooting around the house while you sleep."

He gestured angrily. "But it has slowly become apparent that they're becoming hard to keep under control. They begin to grow, to reproduce, to gather strength. Today they are on the verge of becoming more than disgusting: They are becoming frightening. They are nearly ready to break out. Why? Someone is protecting them, organizing them, preparing to use them. The question is who."

Vorshage scratched his cheek, inspected his finger, stared into the distance. "The question was a difficult one to answer. Everything was being done surreptitiously, you understand. Nothing overt. And yet the pattern was clear. Our people find hints of a munitions cache. We finally get a lead where it might be; we raid the place . . . it is empty."

"Perhaps your information was wrong."

Vorshage shook his head. "We dusted the place and found traces of everything from gunpowder to plastic explosive. No, it had all been there, and recently too. But there had been a leak."

"Leaks can occur at all levels."

"This leak, it turned out, was at the highest level. Government is a very complex thing, you understand, and in a multiparty system like ours it is even worse than in the United States. Decisions are made that affect many different processes and situations, so that to any one given decision—by any one given official—a variety of motives may be imputed. For quite some time now this has been our number one priority. We have gathered information, computerized it, analyzed it, and finally the pattern becomes clear. And it all points to one man. Gottfried Waldner, the chancellor of Germany."

He pushed back from the table, leaned back in his chair. "Now I have to admit to you that he is chancellor because he is the cleverest politician in Germany. He is smarter than Schlanger, smarter than me even." Vorshage smiled briefly. "The point is that we have been able to gather sufficient evidence to know what he is doing, but not enough to convict him of any crime."

"You don't have to. Just go public with what you have and he'll be voted out of office."

This time Vorshage gave a long and loud laugh, really enjoying himself; he was truly amused. "The German sense of humor is nothing compared to your acquired American one! Of course he'll be voted out of office—just as Reagan was when the facts of the deficit became clear, when it was proved that his administration was illegally selling weapons to Iran and supplying weapons to the Contras, when he violated the laws of the land. *Nicht wahr?* America went in a few years from being the greatest creditor nation on earth to being its greatest debtor. And of course the American voters rose up and threw Reagan out of office! I must have misread the results of the 1984 election. But never mind. The people were smart enough, of course, to vote against a continuation of his policies with Bush in 1988. Yes, of course they were!" He stopped laughing. "Let's be serious, let's act like grown men. Waldner is a master of politics. He makes Reagan look like a cowboy and Bush like a clown. He has a genius that hasn't been seen in Germany since Hitler. Every day he gets stronger and stronger; there is *no way* to destroy him at the polls. Because, you see, in addition to his genius at fooling people he has below him the strength of the tentacles of the Nazi movement. It's like an underlayering of concrete that gives him a stronger footing than anyone else," he said, mixing a metaphor. "No, Walter, I'm afraid there is only one way to bring him down . . . just as there was only one way to bring Hitler down once he became chancellor."

He sighed and reached out for the pot of coffee, poured another cup for Walter and for himself. "We are a fragile people, after all. We have in our history the terrible consequences of a nation shattered into small competing states, over and over again. We lived as a disunited people until 1870, when Bismarck showed us how strong we could be if we stood together. And the hundred and some years since then have seen a terrible struggle between the natural forces of Europe, which seek to keep us shattered, and the dream of what could be if we draw together. It becomes an overwhelming siren call to the masses: a strong leader whispering *'Ein Volk, ein Führer.'* We are on the verge of finally rising above it, of finally showing the world and ourselves that we can exist as a normal nation without threatening anybody, and by the labor of our own hands become economically successful. If we can get beyond this one last madman, we have a chance. But we must get rid of him; there is no other choice. Will you help us?"

"I don't know. I'll think about it."

"No, there's no time left for thought. He is traveling to America next month. This must be done before he feels strong enough to come out as leader of the Nazi party, and before his death would make him a martyr. It can't be done in Germany because he is always surrounded by these people. His security is phenomenal. In addition to the normal government security, his hoods are always with him, in the crowd, surrounding him. I can show you pictures. No, it must be done on his American trip. He wouldn't dare take his Nazi mobsters with him, and a man who knows his business—you—can deal with the official security precautions. Preparations are all in place."

"Preparations?" Naman shook his head. "If I do this, I do it alone."

"Of course," Vorshage agreed quickly. "That's the whole point, that's why we want you. History has shown us that one doesn't"—he paused—"*remove* a national leader by committee. The American CIA tried for years to get Castro, the French OAS tried to get De Gaulle, the German generals tried to get Hitler. They all failed. And who succeeds? Lee Harvey Oswald. Sirhan Sirhan. James Earl Ray. Each time, one man; and each time in America."

"Then don't tell me about 'preparations.' "

"Nothing complicated. We have simply set up a few stations in America with money and an excellent new gun. You know about the Uzi RKS?"

"I've heard."

"Nearly recoilless, reasonably quiet, with repeating motion and outstanding accuracy. All we intend is to have the gun in place with operating money, so you don't have to worry about the logistics. Unfortunately," Vorshage admitted, "there was a slight problem with one of the couriers."

"He was caught?"

"Not so bad as that. But he was mugged in the New York subway. The money and gun were stolen."

He paused. Naman stared at him, waiting.

"The mugger was shot and caught."

"So the police have the stuff he was carrying!" Naman said angrily. "That's the result of your 'preparations'!"

"Not quite so bad as that. The briefcase was rigged against tampering, and when the police tried to open it the whole thing exploded. They have nothing."

"They must have the man who was robbed, the courier."

Vorshage hesitated a second, then shook his head. "He was killed in the hospital, before the police had a chance to talk to him." He smiled confidently.

But Naman had seen the moment's hesitation. "Klaus, Klaus," he said sadly, "never try to con an old con man. What happened?"

Vorshage would rather have skipped this part of the conversation, but it was too late. "I don't know," he admitted.

Naman stared at him wide-eyed. In an operation like this, to "not know" something that had happened was disgraceful. Vorshage shrugged apologetically. "Someone killed him."

"Not one of your men?"

Vorshage shook his head. "Someone walked into his hospital room and shot him. It's probably just the sort of thing that happens in New York all the time."

"The police took no precautions? After the bomb in the briefcase exploded in a police station?"

"They had a guard at the door. He was killed too."

Naman also shook his head. "So it was not 'just the sort of thing that happens in New York all the time,' eh? Someone looked for him, found him, and silenced him. And you don't know who?" He got up and put on his coat.

"Where are you going?" Vorshage asked.

"If you were me, where would you be going? Away, that's where! What would it look like to you? In an operation like this, such things do not happen. If they do happen, someone who thinks he is in control is *not* in control."

"Don't overreact. Some operational mistake, that's all; a lack of communication. I'll find out what happened, don't worry. And after all, what's the result? The money and gun are gone, blown to smithereens, and the courier is dead. The trail ends there. No harm done beyond the loss of the gun and money, and we'll replace them both."

"I would like to do you this favor, Klaus. And I would like to prevent a Nazi insurgency if I could. But—"

Vorshage stood up and walked to the window. It was an unimpressive view: a typical city street, the shops closed, the sidewalks lit by streetlights and the glow from a few windows. "I still get a kick looking out this window at night," he said. "Isn't that silly? Childish. But it's the simple pleasures that are most important. It's been almost fifty years since the city was blacked out, but that was so frightening that it still gives me a flush of pleasure to look out and see the streetlights lit at night." He turned back to Naman. "What simple pleasures would you indulge in with a million deutsche marks?"

Naman gave that some serious thought. "One point four million, plus expenses," he said finally.

Vorshage laughed. "I told Schlanger money meant nothing to you, that it would be an insult to offer it, and here you are holding me up for an extra point four million and expenses."

"You're right about the simple pleasures," Naman said. "I've been thinking about retiring lately. Buy a house near the sea, forget a world well forgotten, eh? I've been thinking that if I could sell the business for a million dollars I could do it. But of course the business isn't worth anything without me; I couldn't sell it. So I've been dreaming of a business proposition that would bring in a million, and here it is. One point four million deutsche marks, one million dollars American, tax free, and I can retire."

"Done!" Vorshage said.

Naman sighed. "I'll think about it. And if I do it, I do it alone."

"As you wish, of course. But there will be expenses. You'll need money, identities, passports—"

"Money," Naman said. "One hundred thousand dollars for expenses; I'll take it in cash. The 1.4 million to be deposited immediately in a numbered Bahamian account."

"Bahamian?"

"The Swiss are becoming too dependent on the EC, too subject to pressure from curious governments. The Bahamas are preferable. And I'll supply my own passports.''

"We have people who can provide them with no risk.''

"Except that the people who provide them will know about them. Just as someone knew about your courier in New York. No, thank you; just the money, please.''

"The expense money I understand. But why the rest of it? If you fail, you're dead. So what good would it be to you?''

Naman just smiled softly, and Vorshage shrugged and said, "As you wish. If I need to contact you, if any new information comes in about Waldner's itinerary or any precautions he is taking, I will place a personal in the New York and London *Times*. You will read these papers every day.''

Naman nodded.

"If you need to contact me—'' Vorshage continued, but Naman interrupted him: "I will read the *Times* to please you. But do not look for any communications from me. You will not hear from me again until the work is done.''

"As you wish,'' Vorshage repeated.

It just went to show you, Naman thought, how little anyone really knew anyone. He and Vorshage had worked together, had been friends, for more than thirty years; and yet the man believed him when he said he wanted to retire.

A house near the sea? Morning walks along the sand, evening drinks while the sun set? A world well forgotten . . .

No. This world had burnt itself into his flesh too deeply to be forgotten. This was not what he wanted the money for. And if he failed, if he died, at least she would have the million dollars.

2

AT ELEVEN O'CLOCK in the morning David Melnik left his hotel and walked to the corner of Twelfth and Eye. A woman was using the phone booth, so he waited. The appointed time came and went, and still she chattered on as he glanced irritably at his watch. It didn't really matter, they would simply keep calling until the line was clear, but he didn't like standing around waiting.

Finally she finished and he took over the phone. The noise from passing cars was loud, and he squeezed a lump of cotton into his right ear. When the phone rang he picked it up and held it to his left. "Shalom," he said.

"Good morning, David." Mazor's voice rang through loud and clear, speaking in English.

"So what's going on in Tel Aviv?"

"Over here life is beautiful," Mazor said. "The corn is as high as an elephant's eye."

"Here the corn is always green," David answered. This exchange didn't mean anything; Mazor always liked to play games on the phone in case anyone was listening. Let them think coded messages were being passed; Mazor got a kick out of imagining scores of weary CIA agents poring over their words trying to extract a meaning. But it was merely habit. There was no way anyone could have tapped into this conversation; to ensure this, Mazor had had someone from the Israeli consulate walk to Melnik's hotel and tell him to come to the telephone on this corner at noon.

"Making progress, are you?" Mazor asked.

"Not much," Melnik said. "Something is not exactly kosher."

"That's why I'm calling. Our man in the FBI tells me that they have received instructions from a Mr. William Hagan, who is evidently some kind of deputy assistant secretary—"

"I know who he is. He interviewed me upon my arrival here."

"Ah. Well, you don't seem to have impressed him terribly much. He has told the FBI that to his own secure and personal knowledge this story of an attempted assassination is pure Israeli poppycock. He used a more vulgar word than poppycock, you understand."

Melnik's eyebrow muscles contracted; if he had had eyebrows, they would have risen. "Why would he do a thing like that?"

"No idea. But he did, and so the FBI is not taking anything you say seriously. You probably have already noticed a certain lack of action on their part."

"I took it for the usual American get-up-and-go, which got up and went shortly after Vietnam."

"Don't be so intolerant," Mazor said. "Look what they did to Iraq."

"This call's too expensive for a discussion of political philosophies. How did he tell the FBI?"

"What do you mean, how? You mean what? Or why?"

"No. *How*. Who brought the message?"

"Ah, just a minute, I have it right here." There was the sound of shuffled papers, and then Mazor's voice again. "His personal assistant, a Miss Lisle Wintre."

"Thanks," Melnik said. "Thanks a lot."

"Don't hang up, I have more for you."

"I wasn't going to hang up on you, don't worry."

"You sounded perturbed. Is Miss Wintre what they call a looker?"

"She is that."

"They're always the worst. Don't trust the girl just because she has big blue eyes, or big whatevers. But I'm teaching my grandmother to suck eggs, as they say."

"You said you had more. More facts or more homilies?"

"Facts, laddy, facts. There was some kind of police bombing attack in New York. They've traced it to a man named Kremble."

"Do we know him?"

"Low-level courier. Mercenary. Will carry anything for anybody."

"So we don't know if it has anything to do with Waldner."

"We don't *know* much of anything, old boy." Mazor had trained at various times with most of the NATO nations, and a few Arab ones as well, and he had the annoying habit of picking up expressions from each language. They fell into his conversation obtrusively. "But we do know that he has worked in the past for a man named Vorshage—"

"I know of Vorshage. Bundesnachrichtendienst. Is he part of this?"

Melnik could hear Mazor's shrug across the four thousand miles. "Go know. But as long as you're spinning your wheels there in Washington you might as well check it out, as they say in your part of the world."

"This is not my part of the world," Melnik said. "I'm here under your orders."

"Good. I'm glad you remember that. So here are my orders: Follow up on this bombing. The man in charge is a New York detective, Paul Horner. Incidentally, this information was received separately from that about your reception by the FBI. Although the bombing was reported—routinely—to them, they have made no connection to your story."

As Melnik walked back to the hotel his initial reaction was to take care of this on his own. Why should he tell Wintre anything? He was angry. But the anger was unreasonable—that was his second reaction. People who worked for people had to follow orders; it wasn't anything personal. By the time he reached the hotel he had acknowledged that he wouldn't have been so angry if Wintre were a man. It was those big whatevers and the poorly disguised innocent eyes that got to him, and he was a chauvinist sexist pig, he told himself. He went up to his room and called Wintre, but she was out to lunch.

She was not eating, however. She was reconstructing the scene of the crime. She had walked to the Kennedy Center and now stood on the patio, looking out over the canyon. This was where they had been when he told her. It had been such an ordinary evening. No, not really ordinary, for she had spoken to him of her father's death and of her own part in it, real or imaginary, and she had never spoken to anyone of such things before. But she had felt a closeness somehow, a feeling of sympathy she had never experienced with anyone else. Which was what had made the evening extraordinary, really. And then he had spoken those words—she would never forget them: "I kill people," he had said. "I find them, and I kill them."

She hadn't believed him at first, but those cold blue eyes admitted of no evasion. She stood there at the same spot now, and forced herself to admit it: He was a paid killer. He had said it with no emotion beyond a certain shyness, as if he were confessing to being a shoemaker or a street peddler. "I kill people."

Which made him no better, in essence, than the man who had shot her father. She shuddered and turned away from the canyon. She walked back to the office. What was wrong with her, she wondered? She works for a bastard and falls for a killer.

"Oh no," she said aloud, so that the people she passed on Eye Street turned to look. Oh no, she said again, but this time silently. I may have no choice in whom I work for, but I can most definitely choose whom I fall for.

She was concentrating on that thought as she came back into her office and he was standing there, waiting for her. "Clear your desk and pack a bag," he said. "We're going to New York."

3

PATROLMAN RICHARD JENSEN had been in a state of controlled panic for the past two days, ever since he sat groaning in the chair at the nurses' station waiting for the pain in his testicles to subside, and had glanced up at the television screen and noticed the blood dripping out of Mr. Kremble's left ear.

He had stared at the screen for about thirty seconds, not believing his eyes. Christ, he had stared at that damn screen for about six hours already that day and not a damn thing had moved! Not a fly or mosquito, and he had stepped away from it for less than a minute to grope

Bitsy— He couldn't believe his eyes. He jumped to his feet, grimaced for a second when the pain and nausea shot from his groin up through his stomach, and then shook it off and raced down the corridor to Kremble's room.

As he turned the corner he could see the guard was gone. *Where is the son of a bitch?* he thought. *I'll have his ass fried*—and at the same time, as if in contrapuntal stereo, he was also saying, *Horner's gonna have my ass on a platter.*

He burst into the room and stopped short. The guard was crumpled in a corner beyond the angle of the television camera, soaked in his own blood. Kremble was lying on the bed, his head tossed to one side from the impact of the bullet, blood gently oozing out of a hole in what had been his ear. Jensen crossed quickly to him and took his pulse, then dashed across the room to take the guard's pulse: it was totally useless, his hand was shaking so much he couldn't have felt a tidal wave in their veins, but there was nothing to feel. The cold death in the two bodies was evident. There was only one person living in that room, and when Horner got through with him he'd wish he weren't.

He ran back to the nurses' station and called in to headquarters, then rounded up the nursing staff, and by the time Horner showed up he had his witness ready.

"Okay, let's go over it again," Horner said wearily, taking off his hat but not bothering with his coat, flopping down on one of the chairs in the nursing lounge. His back was acting up again, and he squirmed around to find a comfortable position. "You left your station for thirty seconds to take a piss, is that it?"

"He asked me to keep an eye on the set," Bitsy spoke up from the corner. "But then a patient rang and I had to leave."

Thank you, Jensen breathed fervently to himself. *I will always love you, forever and ever.*

"How long were you actually gone?" Horner asked Jensen. "No exaggerations now. Make it as accurate as you can."

"I had to go down the hall there," Jensen said out loud, mentally trying to account for the time it had taken for him to get up and walk across to Bitsy and put his hands on her breasts and have her practically destroy him, and then to stagger back and fall on the chair and groan for a while. How long had it actually been before he had looked up at the set again? "It could have been as long as two minutes," he said. "Two minutes at the outside."

"Lousy luck," Horner said. "When you came back you saw he was dead?"

"Well, what I saw was his head was at a crazy angle and what looked like blood on his ear," Jensen said, "so I ran down to see, and yeah, he was dead. Him and the guard."

"Nobody saw anything?"

"While I was waiting for you to come I checked with the other nurses, and Nurse Angstrom here was walking down the corridor past Kremble's room just about then."

"What did you see, Miss Angstrom?" Horner said, turning to the young nurse.

"Well, not much. There was a male nurse walking down the corridor, that's all."

"Somebody you know?"

"No, I didn't recognize him. I mean, that's why I mentioned it to Mr. Jensen. Patrolman Jensen. But there's a lot of people here I don't know. It's like a big place, you know?"

"Could he have been coming from Kremble's room?"

"Well, he could have. I mean, I didn't see him come out of there but, like, that's where he *could* have been coming from. When he passed me, you know?"

"Can you describe him?"

She shrugged helplessly. "He was a *big* man, about your size but— well, younger and—"

"Looked more like muscle than fat?"

"I think so, but I didn't really take any notice. There wasn't any reason to. At the time, I mean."

"Hair? Age? Race?"

"Oh, he was white," she said. "Maybe, what, thirty years old? I mean, I'm just like guessing, really. He wasn't a kid, and he wasn't *old*, you know, he wasn't *forty* or anything like that."

Horner kept his thoughts to himself on that one. "Hair?" he asked again.

"Sort of average." She smiled helplessly.

"What color is average hair? Red?"

"Oh no, not red, not blond, just sort of . . . brownish."

"Could it have been black?"

She thought for a moment. "I don't think so. No, he was all so *average*. Brown hair, I think."

"Cut long, short?"

She grimaced, and before she could say "average" again he cut in and said, "Well, thanks very much. We'll see what we can do with that."

She turned away, then stopped and turned back. "There *was* this other thing," she said. "He limped."

"What do you mean? He was injured, hurt?"

"No, not that bad. The kind of limp where he's disguising it, you know what I mean? Like if somebody has something chronic wrong with them and they don't like to admit it so they walk upright, but they're still not walking exactly right. Most people might not even notice it, he probably himself doesn't even know he walks funny, but we're sort of trained to see things, I guess."

"Which leg?"

She thought for a moment. "Like he was sort of leaning on his right a bit more than normal. It wouldn't be all that noticeable," she cautioned. "I mean, don't go looking for Quasimodo or anyone like that."

Horner nodded his thanks. It was better than nothing, but not much. He congratulated Patrolman Jensen on being so efficient in rounding her up as a witness, since if he hadn't acted that quickly she wouldn't have remembered precisely when she had been passing down that corridor. Jensen was embarrassed, flustered at the praise, and Horner guessed he had probably been fooling around with one of the nurses instead of taking a leak, probably the short one with big boobs who had tried to corroborate his alibi, but you couldn't really expect a man to sit and stare at a TV without blinking for eight hours. They hadn't thought it important enough to put two men on the screen. The screen itself was only a backup for the guard on the door, whom they had been relying on. Horner supposed they should have had two men there, but even in retrospect he couldn't justify two men taken from a police force so undermanned that the city was sinking in ooze around their feet.

The next day Horner brought Nurse Angstrom down to the station and had her spend several hours combing through mug shots, but she didn't come up with an identification. Or rather, she came up with about thirty-five people, all of whom "could have been the one." From their records, none of these would have had the skill to take out the guard so smoothly.

Horner wondered what was going down. He thought it might be drugs or Mafia, or it might be quote international terrorism unquote, so he notified the FBI and said the hell with it; he had nowhere else to go. He went home to his apartment, unlocked the three locks with three separate keys, and opened the door. He called out "Anybody home?" as he did every night. One night he thought she was going to answer, and then he would know for sure that he had gone crazy.

His wife, Florence, had been dead for nearly fifteen years now, and

Sara had left him and gone to Florida with her husband almost twenty years ago, and he had loved them both and loved them still. Sometimes, like when he came home to his empty apartment, it hurt so much he wanted to just lie down and die.

> I loved her in the summertime,
> And in the winter, too . . .
> And the only only thing I ever did wrong
> Was to save her from the foggy foggy dew.

He stomped across the room to the stereo and put on a Stones record to shake the nonsense out of his mind. He poured himself a drink because of the guilt, even though he knew it never helped.

When he was young, when he was actually doing it, he had never felt any guilt. He never had any choice in the matter, so how could he feel guilty about it? The passion was absolutely overwhelming; he couldn't have resisted it with a suit of armor and a pocketful of rosary beads. But now all the passion was spent, and the guilt he had thought beneath him came in the night to overwhelm him. You'd think with Florence dead and Sara reconciled to her husband, he told himself, you could live and let live.

He had thought no one would ever get hurt because they would never talk about it. He and Sara had decided they would never let anyone suffer because of their passion; they wouldn't get divorces, they wouldn't run off together. But they simply couldn't help going to bed together.

When Sara got pregnant he fumbled for months with the words to ask the question, and finally blurted it out: "Is it mine?" And she had laughed that glorious laugh and tousled his hair and said How could I know? "You think a bell rings when the connection is made?" she asked, giggling. "Or do you think that somehow women just *know* these things? It doesn't work like that, love."

"I thought you being a Catholic and all, you could just ask God."

She smiled sadly and asked, "If I weren't Catholic, would we get divorces and marry each other?"

"No," he said. "You know we couldn't."

"No," she said, and pulled his head down to her breast. "We love Frank and Florence too much to do that to them. Does that make us better people or worse?"

"I don't know. It's just the way it is. It's *our* passion, and if anyone is going to suffer for it, it's got to be you and me."

"But we're not suffering, are we? We're indulging ourselves and having a wonderfully dirty time." She sighed. "It's not as if you don't love Florence—"

He nodded and kissed her breast. "I do love her," he said. "I really do."

"I know," she said. "I don't understand, but I know."

"What can't you understand? You love Frank, too, don't you?" he asked, raising his head.

"Oh yes. I love him very much, and I don't understand that either. I guess it's just the way it is."

"Yes," he said.

"And we'll go on forever like this," she said. "And no one will ever know."

But they didn't go on forever, and everyone did know. Florence was the first, she knew as soon as the baby was born. She looked just like Sara, everyone said, except for the mouth. Even on the day Florence first saw her, when she was just hours old, Florence gasped and started to say something but choked it down. On their way home from the hospital she had said it: "She's a beautiful baby. She looks just like Sara."

"I wouldn't know," Paul said. "I can never see those things."

"Oh yes. She looks just like Sara," Florence said quietly. "But she has your mouth."

He had been so shocked that he hadn't even been able to deny it. It wouldn't have done him any good, because even if you couldn't really tell for sure in a baby only a few hours old, as she grew older, as she became two and three and four, as she grew into a lovely child with Sara's big eyes, a loving child who hugged him and called him Uncle Paul, it became absolutely clear that Florence was right. Eventually even Frank, the girl's "father," Sara's husband and Paul's partner, realized the truth.

Frank never said anything to anybody. He just went quieter and quieter, until finally he wasn't talking to Paul, not a word. He wouldn't even look at him. One day he said simply that he was quitting the force. He had found a job in Florida.

Paul and Sara were no longer sleeping together by then. They had stopped when she was pregnant, and after the baby was born it had never been the same again. They were both embarrassed by the child's looks. Paul never stopped loving Sara; he was just a patient man: He was waiting for them to get used to the situation, to gradually get together again. Instead he heard Frank tell him about the new job in

Florida. When he tried to talk to Sara she evaded him, until suddenly they were just gone.

"Oh Jesus," Paul said now, finishing off his drink and sitting alone in his apartment staring at the dead television screen. He groaned aloud. "How could you ever do such a son-of-a-bitching thing like that to your own partner, you bastard?"

And then he remembered dimly the passion that had driven him, that had seemed so overwhelming at the time and now was only a vague memory, and he wondered at it and, wondering, finally fell asleep.

The next morning he made his report to Captain Hanrahan and suggested that the case go in the dead-letter box. "We don't know who Kremble was or why he was carrying the briefcase. We don't know who he was taking it to and we don't know why he was killed. We've got no ID on the killer and no leads." He spread his hands helplessly. "We've got nowhere to go."

"Maybe something will turn up," Hanrahan said.

"Sure," Horner agreed. "Maybe." Hanrahan nodded, and Horner got up and left. When he got his new job he wouldn't be aggravated with crap like this, he thought. He wouldn't be working individual cases; he'd be initiating new programs, working out the strategies rather than aching over the details. He was looking forward to it; he was getting too old for this shit.

He was sitting at his desk an hour later when the sergeant on desk duty stuck his head around the door and said, "Couple of people here to see you, J.G." He looked up to see a young woman come through the door, followed by a man of distinctive appearance: He had no eyebrows and his skin was hairless as a baby's. *Alopecia universalis,* Horner thought, not fooled by the perfectly fitting wig.

"Like to take a moment of your time," the man said, taking out his wallet and showing him an Israeli intelligence identity card. "Understand you had a little bombing here."

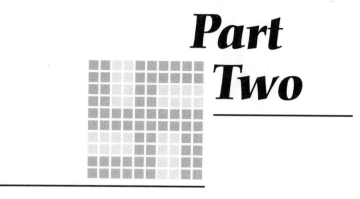

Part Two

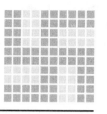

6

1

GERHARD HAUPTMANN is not a Nazi, though the left-leaning German Green party has occasionally described him as such. He has also been described as a Communist by the conservative Christian Democrat party. He takes comfort in the fact that they both can't be right, and describes himself simply as a capitalist. If his motives are mistaken by others, that can't be his concern.

Gerhard Hauptmann's department, he says, is sales. And who buys the stuff and for what purposes—well, that's not his department. He is actually being modest when he says his department is sales: He owns the whole company. What he means is, his *interest* in sales. As he is fond of pointing out, ours is a market-driven economy; the firm that prospers is the one that finds the market. And his firm, Deutschmeister Gesellschaft, has certainly prospered.

"A tribute to Thomas Jefferson, Adam Smith, and laissez-faire," he likes to say. It is also a tribute to his own single-minded drive and purpose, which is simply to make money.

A dozen years ago he invested his firm's entire capital in uranium yellowcake, at a time when France's Phénix breeder reactor was the talk of the international industrial complex. The Phénix was about to prove to the world the viability of the breeder: a nuclear reactor that turns its waste—nonfissionable U-238—into fissionable Pu-239, thus producing (or breeding) fuel more quickly than it consumes its original U-235 fuel. The breeder can produce one hundred times as much Pu-239 as the U-235 it starts with, and so the worldwide price of uranium had plummeted. Hauptmann's board of directors protested: What madman would use all the firm's capital to buy yellowcake at a time like this?

What Hauptmann had realized was that there was another world market for yellowcake that was independent of the demand for reactor fuel. A Third World market, one might say. When he offered the uranium to Israel at the pre-Phénix price, they protested. When he pointed out the advantages of doing business with his firm, no matter what the price, the Israelis acquiesced. And so, once the yellowcake was mined in Africa by a Belgian company it was sold to a firm registered in Switzerland and shipped to Argentina. It was *shipped* there, but it never arrived there. Though the paperwork showed the yellowcake had been sold to a Swedish firm while en route to Argentina, it never seemed to arrive anywhere. The International Atomic Energy Agency lost track of it, and while they were chasing the paperwork a nondescript freighter docked in Tel Aviv, and two years later when the Syrians began making noises about mounting a unified Arab invasion of Israel to avenge the Yom Kippur debacle, they were told by Egyptian, Iraqi, Saudi, and Jordanian intelligence services to back off and shut up: Israel had the bomb.

By then Iraq was already dickering with Deutschmeister Gesellschaft for its own shipment of uranium. Since Israel had a head start Saddam Hussein meant to catch up fast, which meant he wanted enriched fuel—uranium with a higher-than-normal proportion of U-235—and Hauptmann had to explain to him that enriched fuel was not necessary for a reactor. Hussein nodded and lifted his lidded eyes and repeated that he wanted enriched fuel. Hauptmann had to explain that the international atomic community paid much more attention to shipments of enriched fuel because it was more easily converted into weapons material. Hussein nodded. The price of oil was climbing steadily at the time, and his pockets were deep. And so they came to an agreement.

The enriched fuel was harder to come by, but not much. The French shipped a slab of it to India. The U.S. Congress had voted not to provide India with enriched fuel because of the danger that India might put together a bomb to use against Pakistan; but when India threatened to cut off diplomatic relations and turn to the Soviet Union for aid, the United States worked out a deal whereby the French would provide the Indians weapons-grade uranium, no questions asked—and so when one more French order was processed through Deutschmeister Gesellschaft for shipment to India no one paid attention. The French were happy with the business, India was happy to get its cut, and once again the shipment changed destinations en route and the paperwork became so complex that the IAEA gave up.

The money rolled in without limit. In addition to the high price paid for the uranium itself, Deutschmeister Gesellschaft tacked on enormous shipping and handling costs. Since the shipping and handling were the key to the whole affair, the Iraqis didn't haggle about price. And after the Israelis bombed their Tammuz 17 reactor in 1985, the whole process simply started all over again, doubling Deutschmeister Gesellschaft's profits.

The key to all this financial skulduggery was Germany's adherence to the political philosophy of Thomas Jefferson and Adam Smith, which the French called laissez-faire, a political philosophy that the United States, Britain, and France seemed to have forgotten during the last few decades. President Reagan had tried to bring it back into the American political system, but even a man with Reagan's popularity could not overcome all the watchdogs of Congress; and though several American firms tried to emulate Deutschmeister Gesellschaft's success in selling uranium and weapons-grade fuel to whoever wanted it and could pay, they were crippled by the American insistence on abiding by IAEA regulations. So much of their potential profit went into bribes and political contributions that they were unable to pose much of a threat to Deutschmeister Gesellschaft's dominance of the international nuclear-weapons trade. The British Parliament served much the same purpose, and the French simply hadn't the organizational skills to compete.

It was at this point in history that Gerhard Hauptmann informed his board of directors that Deutschmeister Gesellschaft was investing a significant portion of its profits in setting up an institute for pharmaceutical research.

The explosion heard 'round the board table was reminiscent of Hiroshima, but Hauptmann explained that there was a tremendous need and market in the Third World for new pharmaceuticals. For example, nearly four hundred million people there suffer terribly from schistosomiasis, he informed them.

''What?'' they asked. Some African rivers, he explained, harbor a fluke that penetrates the skin of swimmers and waders, subsequently making its way through the veins until it reaches the liver, where it sets up residence, lays millions of eggs, that form cysts, and results in debilitation and ultimately death. "I am informed that within ten years we can reasonably expect both a cure and a vaccine for this terrible disease. The market will be tremendous."

"The market is nonexistent," he was told scornfully. "The four hundred million people who have schistosomiasis are black savages living in tribal huts in the wilderness. They do not own condominiums on the Champs Elysées, town houses in London, or summer homes on Martha's Vineyard. They do not pay taxes or buy automobiles. And when they are sick they do not buy medicine. They just crawl off into the jungle and die. They have no money."

Others around the table agreed. "There may be a market for schistosomiasis pharmaceuticals, but there is no money to pay for them."

"One has an obligation," Hauptmann replied, "when one makes an obscene amount of money, to send some of that money back into research capabilities that may benefit mankind. Even though the profit margin may be vanishingly small."

The statement looked good in the minutes of the board meeting; it looked impressive in the official report of the meeting that was circulated to the stockholders and the press. What was neither reported in the minutes nor circulated to the press was Hauptmann's wink and smile as he said it.

Three years later Deutschmeister Gesellschaft was making profits which made its previously "obscene" nuclear-sales figures look paltry, building "pharmaceutical" factories in Iraq and Libya. In fact, pharmaceuticals were indeed produced—in the ten percent of the floor space opened to visiting journalists. The remaining ninety percent fabricated nerve gases and distilled mycotoxins for delivery by Scud rocket, artillery shell, or bomb. Since the biochemical technology of pharmaceutical research is identical to that involved in chemical-warfare technology—with the additional advantage that in the field of chemical-weapons surveillance there is no overseeing international body like the IAEA to be a nuisance—and since the cost of producing poisonous gases is much less than that required to put together nuclear weapons, while the terror effect is nearly as great, the result was that Libya and Iraq were willing to pay just as much for the capability, while Deutschmeister Gesellschaft's costs were much less. Profits soared.

"Wie geht's?" Vorshage asked, taking off his hat and sitting down.

"Ganz gut," Hauptmann replied. He liked Vorshage. He liked the way the man behaved: Vorshage was a no-nonsense sort of person. He was the only man Hauptmann knew who came into this office without behaving as if he were entering the Holy Cathedral of St. Paul for a private audience with the pope. He liked the way Vorshage walked in and took off his hat and sat down without being asked, and without fawning or asking about the health of Mrs. Hauptmann and all the little *Hauptmänner;* he liked the way Vorshage got right down to business. And he liked thinking of him as *my secret agent.*

Vorshage did not like Hauptmann. He thought he looked like a George Grosz caricature of what he actually was: a loathsome, greedy capitalist growing fat on the world's misery. He was a pudgy little man who tried to hide his baldness by growing his last few strands of hair long and brushing them across his shiny pate. He wore a small black mustache and smoked thick black cigars, brandishing them in his visitors' faces in the most obvious and pathetic phallic substitution Vorshage had ever seen. In his mannerisms he gave the impression of a bad actor trying to decide whether to imitate Sydney Greenstreet or Peter Lorre. But to go with all this he had a complete lack of scruples—and enormous wealth. He paid well for what he wanted. And Vorshage had no intention of ending up like poor old Walter Naman, spending the last years of his life trying to live on a government pension and trying to sell his services in a market flooded with similar people, old intelligence agents trying to turn a dollar by selling their knowledge of assassination techniques. He was doing Naman a favor, getting him enough money to retire comfortably with one last job, and he himself was collecting enough to pay for an even more comfortable retirement in a few years. "We have our man," he told Hauptmann. "Walter Naman, the one I told you about."

Hauptmann pursed his lips, looking thoughtfully at Vorshage. He reached into his desk and pulled out a newspaper clipping, the one from the *Los Angeles Times,* and slid it across the desk. Vorshage shook his head. "I told you, the man is good. It was Mendoza, the other one, who died. Naman is signed on and ready to go. Do you want to meet him?"

"Don't be impertinent. I meet nobody, nobody meets me. That is our arrangement."

Vorshage nodded. "Naman will need a hundred forty thousand marks for expenses," he told Hauptmann. "And 1.4 million as payment when the job is completed."

Hauptmann smiled. *"Billig wie Borscht."*

"The 1.4 million should be deposited into a Bahamian account within the next few weeks. He will need the hundred and forty thousand in cash as soon as possible."

"Of course."

"Can I come for it tomorrow?"

"No."

"The next day? We don't want to keep him hanging around uselessly in Germany."

"Tomorrow is fine, but you're not to receive it. I want Schlanger to ask for it."

Vorshage nodded. He understood. Not only was Hauptmann getting Schlanger to do his dirty work for him, he was putting Schlanger in his political debt at the same time. Schlanger would pay a visit—politician to industrial leader—and would ask for a political contribution for necessary but unreportable expenses. Hauptmann would understand; this sort of thing happened all the time in a democracy. One passed laws to keep the government honest, and then one circumvented the laws to keep the government operating. Hauptmann would not ask what the money was for; he would simply hand it over. And Schlanger would leave the office with the money in one pocket and a political debt in the other. Hauptmann was a fat, ugly, greedy little man, but no one ever said he wasn't smart.

"And there are no problems?" Hauptmann asked. "Everything is going smoothly?"

Vorshage nodded. "Right on schedule. Naman thinks he's working for Schlanger, and Schlanger thinks he's stopping Hitler. We had a slight problem with one of our caches, the one in New York. But you don't want to hear about operational details."

"Not if it's all cleared up. But if anything has gone wrong—?"

"Nothing has gone wrong. It's all under control."

Hauptmann nodded happily. "You're a good man, Vorshage. That's my secret: I always choose good men."

Vorshage rose and left the room on that note, and Hauptmann watched him go, waited until the door had shut behind him, and then began to laugh in a high, dry cackle. "Nothing has gone wrong," he repeated out loud. "Everything is under control." He laughed so hard his eyes began to run. Vorshage was a good man after all; Hauptmann was happy to see how well he could look one in the eye and lie. After the good laugh, he wiped his eyes dry and settled down, then pressed the buzzer on his desk. Immediately the door behind him opened and Carlos Grass walked through. "You heard?" Hauptmann asked.

Grass smiled and nodded. "You'd think he had planned it himself," he said.

"I'm pleased with your work," Hauptmann said. "I want you to continue. Stay in touch with everything and keep me informed. And as soon as Naman carries out his assignment—''

''I understand,'' Grass said.

''No, I don't think you do. I'm putting you in charge of the whole operation.''

''I'm going to be Vorshage's boss?''

Hauptmann nodded. ''But he won't know it. Sit down. We have a lot to talk about.''

That evening Grass sent a telegram to Los Angeles, to a woman named Norma Middler. He asked her to obtain a tape of a speech Gottfried Waldner had given in English a few months ago to the British Houses of Parliament. He asked her to keep one copy of the tape in the office vault and to send another copy to a New York laboratory called Audio Technology Associates, which did computer analysis of voice patterns. Their digitized analysis was to be held for pickup by a man named Henry Larkinson.

He signed the telegram Walter.

2

VORSHAGE ENCOUNTERED the man who looked like Boris Becker eating peanuts in the zoo. It was a cold windy day and no one was around, but these days there are so many devices for spying on conversations from a distance that it had become habit for him not to trust open spaces. He walked past the man without a glance and entered the long tunnel leading to the snake house.

The man followed, and halfway down Vorshage stopped and leaned against the wall. The man came up to him; Vorshage held his hand out, palm upward and fingers curved. The man poured peanuts into it. Vorshage cracked one, extracted the kernel, and popped it into his mouth. *''Also, sprech','*' he said.

''Where do I begin? I don't know how much you know already.''

''Don't worry about wasting my time; it's paid for by the taxpayers. Start at the beginning and go on to the end.''

The man thought a second, then said, ''I was to meet the courier in the Beldenmore Hotel lobby at six o'clock last Wednesday. I was to take the briefcase he would bring and return home. I was to keep it until someone asked for it with the proper procedure. I was not to attempt to open it; it had been rigged against tampering.''

Vorshage cracked another peanut, nodding encouragingly.

"I waited the planned two hours, but he did not show up."

"Did anyone else?"

"Pardon?"

"Did you notice anyone else who seemed to be waiting?"

The man laughed. "Everyone in a hotel lobby at six P.M. is waiting for someone." He stopped laughing. "I didn't notice anyone watching me, or acting suspicious in any manner. But I must be honest: I don't see how such a person might have been recognized in such a place."

Vorshage took another peanut and nodded. "Continue, please."

"I returned the next night, two hours later, as arranged. Same result. I read in the newspaper about a briefcase exploding in a police station, and that the briefcase had been taken there from a mugging victim. I reported all this to my contact. I was told to return to the hotel each night at the same time. No one ever showed up. Yesterday I was ordered to report to Berlin, to meet you here." He paused. "That's it, from beginning to end."

"You did not attempt to contact the mugging victim?"

"I didn't know where he was. The paper reported he was taken to the hospital, but there are many hospitals in New York and I'm not familiar with them. At any rate, I had no such orders."

"Of course not," Vorshage said. "You'll forgive my asking. Do you know anything else? Any rumors, tidbits, ideas?"

The man shook his head, and Vorshage held out his palm to be filled with peanuts again. "Enjoy the snake house," he said, and walked alone out of the tunnel, nibbling on the nuts.

3

WALTER NAMAN wandered down to Berlin's *Strich*. He walked up and down and was approached by an endless stream of streetwalkers, most of whom were so doped up they couldn't mumble coherently enough to ask *"Fucken Sie mir?"* They were garishly appealing from about fifteen feet away; up close they were so dirty and disgusting it was hard to imagine anyone going to bed with them. And then one came up beside him and slipped her hand through his and asked, "What's a nice guy like you doing in a dump like this?"

She was slim and blond, and she spoke English with a German accent in a manner reminiscent of Dietrich: cultured, husky, sexy, civilized. She was clean and quietly effervescent and she smiled at him and steered him around the corner. "My place is just a few blocks away," she explained. "Away from the riffraff."

He went with her quietly down the street and in through the heavy door and up the stairs and into the apartment. He sat down on the bed while she took off her clothes, and when she stood naked in front of him he waited, looking at her, wondering if perhaps . . .

But of course nothing happened inside of him, because there was nothing inside; he was empty. What they had taken out of him at Auschwitz would never be replaced. He sat there on the bed and looked away from the naked whore, his eyes roaming the walls of this small room, seeing other rooms in other years.

His own room; the small cot in the corner under the dormer window, which he couldn't see out of unless he stood on the cot on tiptoe and hung on to the windowsill with his pudgy fingers; the sun streaming in; his eyes fluttering open with the dawning day; and suddenly the door slamming open and his father rushing in.

He had flown into a panic that day when his father told him to get up quickly and get dressed, they were being relocated to the East. He had tried to protest—how would he ever find Lise again?—but his father wouldn't listen, simply rushed around the room taking his clothes out of drawers and throwing them at him, shouting at him to get dressed quickly.

It had been the night after his first experience with the naked Lise, and he had slept turbulently all night, tossed by thoughts as if he were one of his toy sailboats on the pond in a raging wind. He had fallen asleep grasping through his pillow at her soft white body, and to be roughly wakened from such dreams to be told they were leaving immediately and forever was impossible to accept.

But accept it or not, away he went. There was no time to protest, no time for tantrums or arguments. Though he had grown from childhood into a barely aware adolescence in a world frightening and insecure, he had never seen his parents like this. They would not talk to him except to tell him to hurry, they would not listen to his entreaties. They didn't argue with him, they simply didn't listen to him; they ran busily from room to room while he wailed uncomprehendingly and unheard, and within the hour they were at the train station, huddled in their compartment, waiting.

All the Jewish families in the quarter had gone together, had packed up as much as each person could hold in one suitcase and carried it down to the train depot and sat in the unmoving train for hours. His mother had been the first to complain to the guards that they needed food and water. His father had pulled at her arm, shushing her, but she yanked away and told the soldiers the children were hungry and thirsty. The guards smiled and were polite, apologizing for the inefficiency of the operation, assuring them they would soon be on their way and that everything was in readiness for their arrival.

Those guards remained in the station when the train finally pulled out that evening. The very different guards on their arrival three days later in the East were not polite, and had dogs.

They traveled for three days and two nights, and when finally they got off the train they were separated into four groups. His father went with the men, his mother with the women, the luggage they had so hurriedly and carefully packed went with all the other luggage, and he went with the boys. He never saw his small suitcase with the one toy he had been allowed to bring—or his mother or father—ever again.

During the three-day train ride from Munich his thoughts had alternated between physical fear and sex, between the unknown future and Lise. For the rest of his life he would remember those few moments in the attic with Lise, but the three days on the train merged into a cacophony of fear and sexual longing, and of the following years he remembered almost nothing at all except that by the end of them his concern with sex had somehow disappeared and he was left with nothing but fear.

Today he remembered nothing, in his conscious mind, of those first few weeks except that he was taken from his family and given a bucket and a pair of pliers. He was shoved with other small boys, each with a bucket and pliers, into a huge dark room filled with the overpowering stench of excrement. The large doors slammed shut behind them and he stood paralyzed with fear, nauseated by the smell. Then by the dim light of the overhead lamps he saw the other boys move forward, crawling over—over piles of huddled, intertwined, naked dead bodies. Crawling over them, pulling their mouths open, reaching with the pliers into their dead mouths . . .

Shamzl the shoemaker probably saved his life by getting him assigned to work for him. Still in shock from those first few days, Walter began to live with Shamzl in the small cobbling shop, sleeping behind the bench and eating occasional scraps, his skin gradually turning dark from the tannic-acid fumes, until the day the blond lieutenant stopped him as he was crossing the front square on his way to deliver a pair of boots to the camp commandant. He was scuffling along as usual, huddled over, trying to attract as little attention as possible, when for some reason the lieutenant grabbed him by the collar and yanked him to a halt. He knocked the dirty cap off his head and laughed. "A little blond Jew," he cried delightedly, rumpling his hand through Walter's thick, straight hair. "There must be a drop or two of Aryan blood in there. What do you say, boy? Did your mother fuck Germans?" He laughed again and asked, not unkindly, "What are you doing, boy?"

Walter tried to explain that he was delivering these boots to the commandant, but the lieutenant simply plucked them out of his hand and tossed them casually over his shoulder into the mud. "You are too pretty for such duties, my little friend," he said. "Come along with me, we'll find something better for you to do."

He pulled Walter away by the collar of his jacket, the boy's feet flailing furiously in order to follow quickly enough to avoid falling down. He was sure that if he fell the lieutenant would simply pull out his Luger and shoot him on the spot. And he might not have been wrong. Years later he wondered if Shamzl had been shot in just that way when the boots had failed to show up at the commandant's office. He wondered if Shamzl had died believing that Walter had carelessly failed him.

They put him to work in the brothel. The handsome blond lieutenant liked the idea of the pretty blond Jew bringing in the towels to wipe the German sperm from the Jewesses' beds.

Walter didn't mind. It was easier work than shoemaking, the stench of sweat and secretions was no worse than that of the tannic acid, and in the brothel the German guards were always happy. Not always pleasant, but at least happy.

None of it, in Walter's mind, had anything to do with sex. Or rather, nothing in Walter's mind had anything to do with sex anymore. The concept had simply vanished from his consciousness. He did not remember Lise or that day in the attic, and if he had he would not have remembered his feelings at the time. All the embarrassment was gone, all the longing, all the anguish, all the mysterious questions. Neither feelings nor time had any meaning in the life he now led. There was only the present, and there was only action: Eat, sleep, don't attract attention. Survive.

And so time, unacknowledged, passed; and feelings, unacknowledged, died; and Walter lived as a rat lives, scrounging among scraps of garbage for food, hiding in the dark from footsteps, existing within a circle whose radius was hardly larger than the reach of his outstretched fingers as he scuttled in and out of thin rooms separated by wooden partitions, each just large enough to encompass a small cot, wiping down the mattresses with grimy towels, scuttling like a crab through polluted seas.

Time, as unaware of him as he was of it, continued to move along. And 1943 faded into 1944 and 1945. In the spring the snows melted and the mud unfroze, but nothing else changed. The thick black smoke poured out of the furnaces by day and night, the stench held darkly over the ground, and Walter carried his towels from room to room.

The girls in the brothel didn't bother to dress or to clean themselves beyond an occasional swipe with the towel Walter brought them. Their nakedness did not excite him or even interest him; through no conscious process he had discovered that the secret of survival was to retreat from consciousness. The horrors to be seen in that place if one were careless enough to look would have turned the strongest of men to stone. So, like Perseus with Medusa, he did not look; unlike Perseus, he also did not see, did not care.

It was a large camp and the girls, like all the other inmates, came and went without end. To a survivor they were all alike, all the same, with no individuality, no characteristic features to be recognized any more than one of the chickens served on his mother's dining room table in those days before Hitler. Until one day in that spring of 1945 he entered one of the wood-partitioned rooms in the brothel barracks and leaned around the girl sitting on the edge of the bed, to wipe down the mattress. He stumbled as he straightened and made the mistake of looking up to catch at her to keep from falling, and he saw that the girl was Lise.

She hadn't recognized him when he entered, hadn't looked at him or seen him until he gasped. She was nearly two years older than when he had last seen her, nearly fourteen now, skinnier than ever, but surely a prize in that brothel for her breasts had not yet begun to sag.

At that moment it all ended. The wall that he had so carefully built crumbled, and he saw everything he had kept hidden behind that wall. He knew how a girl like Lise would be prized in that brothel, and how such a prize would be used, and used, and used. He tried to say her name, but she stared at him with such intensity from such a distance that he couldn't speak. Nor could he, despite the training of that past two years, lower his eyes. It was all he could manage to back out of that little room, staring at her face all the while.

Afterward he realized the source of the intensity of her gaze. The instant it had changed from blank numbness to pain was the instant she recognized him, and he realized what she had been doing as he backed out of the room. She had been trying to cry, but could not.

He stared at the naked whore sadly. In some sense he knew what he was missing; in another it was all a foreign scene to him. At any rate, there was nothing to be done. He leaned down and took the knife out of his ankle sheath. He laid it beside him on the bed, where it glinted brightly in the feeble light.

"Erich," she said, *"er hat ein Messer."*

There was a slight movement behind him, and Walter said in German, "Come in, Erich. But don't be hasty. There's no problem." He looked slowly over his shoulder as the closet door opened and a short, muscular man came out. "Get dressed," Walter said to the girl. "It's Erich I want to talk to."

"Do I know you?" Erich asked.

"No, but I know you," Walter replied. "Oh, not *you*, but I knew there'd be someone like you waiting here."

"How did you know?"

"She's too pretty," he said, watching her as she hurriedly dressed. "Too clean, too cultured to be walking those streets. She can make more money in a better setup, so I knew she was making even more money bringing suckers home for Papa. Elderly men, rich men who are walking those streets looking for something they're not going to find there, men who are repelled by the filthy sluts who proposition them. Men who see this clean, young, lovely woman as an image from their fantasies, who come here with her thankfully, and who give up their money easily because they always knew it was too good to be true. Do you let them screw her first?"

"Why not?" Erich replied. "It's easier that way. Usually they fall asleep and Triki takes the money and leaves without any fuss. When they wake up they look around and leave."

"And you're here in case they don't."

Erich nodded. He came carefully around from behind Walter, his eyes on the knife on the bed.

"You take their papers as well," Walter said.

"Why should I do that?"

"Because papers are worth money." He nodded to the girl, who was now dressed. "Good-bye," he said.

She looked at Erich, who nodded, and she left.

"I want to buy a passport," Walter said.

"I don't know if I have any."

"If you don't, I'll have to look elsewhere. If you do, I'll pay three hundred deutsche marks. So let's not play games."

Erich walked across the room and opened a drawer.

"Stop," Walter said. "I'll look myself." He gestured with his head, and Erich walked to the opposite corner. Walter got up, taking his knife with him, and began to leaf through the papers in the drawer. There were quite a few passports; he had struck it rich. One of them was perfect: A Canadian born sixty years ago, a couple of inches taller and thirty pounds heavier but with brown eyes like Walter. A pair of lift-heels would take care of the height, and people often lose weight.

He took the money out of his pocket and laid it down on the bureau. He had been careful to take exactly that much with him, carried loose in his pocket, so that he wouldn't have to take out a wallet and tempt the man with the thought of more money available for the taking. But he could see the look in the man's eyes: stupid, greedy. Walter had to consider how he should go about getting out of here alive. He knew he'd be safe once he left this room, because there wouldn't be anything the other man could do. He couldn't report the loss of the passport even if he wanted to because he wouldn't know what name was on it; it was hardly likely that a man like Erich would keep a written record of his holdings, so he wouldn't know what was missing from the drawer.

"I'm sure you have a gun," he said, "and you would like to see if I'm carrying any more money. I assure you I'm not. You may feel reluctant to accept my word on that, but I hope you at least will believe that this knife is a sharp one, and is balanced for throwing. If you're very fast you'll get off one shot. If you don't hit me with it, you'll find this sticking out of your ribs before you can fire a second. Believe me, it's not worth the risk." He put the passport in his pocket. "I'm going to have to ask you to stand there absolutely still. Don't make a move while I leave."

He turned toward the door. Just as he reached it he heard a soft swishing sound. He spun around, dove to his left and threw the knife in the same motion. Erich had the gun out of his pocket by then, but the knife caught him in the ribs before he could pull the trigger. He wasn't very fast after all. He fell backward, and the gun dropped out of his fingers when he hit the floor.

Walter jumped over to it and kicked it across the room before he turned to the man. "Why do you all have to be so greedy?" he asked quietly. He bent down and pulled the knife out of the man's ribs: He had to give a hard jerk to free it, and Eric gasped with pain. Walter wiped the blade on Erich's shirt and replaced it in his ankle sheath. "You're bleeding badly," he said. "Don't move, and I'll phone for help once I'm away from here."

Erich didn't answer; he lay on his back, gasping for breath, trying to hold his hand against his side tightly enough to stop the flow of blood. It was a useless effort. Walter left the room and walked down the stairs. If they saved Erich's life, he realized, they'd ask him about the man who stabbed him, and Erich would have no reason to lie. He shook his head sadly; Erich's life wasn't worth the risk of his own. He turned the corner, passing a telephone kiosk without stopping, and walked back to his hotel.

4

". . . SO THIS is an unofficial visit," the young man, Melnik, was saying.

"And why is that?" Horner asked.

"I came to America to work with the FBI." Melnik spread his hands. "The FBI doesn't seem to want to work with me. I heard about the bombing from my own sources, and rather than go to the Bureau and try to get them to set up a meeting with you I thought we'd just come along ourselves."

Horner nodded toward Wintre. "I thought you said the young lady had connections in Washington. She couldn't help you?"

"I don't work for the FBI," Wintre said. "I'm not a policeman in any sense. I work for the deputy assistant secretary of defense for politico-military affairs."

She stood up and looked out the window. She hated this place. It was still the same; all police stations, she guessed, were the same. It was like being sixteen years old again, taken down here by her father, trying to hide her boredom and hide herself from her fear as he showed her around, introduced her to his friends, showed her what his life was all about. She didn't *want* to be a policeman, she almost shouted, she didn't want to carry a *gun*— She looked around suddenly, but Horner and Melnik were talking together, ignoring her. She had been afraid for a moment that she *had* shouted.

But she hadn't, she never had. She used to smile and try to look interested and pretend she wasn't afraid, even when Daddy took her down to the firing range. She didn't like guns, but she really hated the targets they shot at: cutouts that looked like people, men and women jumping up out of the dark shadows at you and you had to decide if they were friendly or hostile and whether to shoot at them or not. Half the time Daddy would pat her on the shoulder and say, "Too late. You reacted too late. You'd be a dead policewoman by now if this were real."

And then finally one night it *was* real, and she *had* reacted too late and totally wrong. She had sat in the car and squealed like a baby and babbled like an idiot while the man in the car raised his gun and aimed it at her father, she had babbled unintelligibly while his partner had turned to her and asked over and over again what was wrong, and so instead of watching her father and protecting him he had been taking care of her as her father was shot dead.

She took a deep breath. No, that wasn't true. It had been a second—a *fraction* of a second—that she had gasped and pointed, and it *couldn't* have distracted his attention. He must have seen the shadow behind the glass moving just as she had; it had just all been too fast for anyone to react. It wasn't her fault. Really, it wasn't.

"Kremble was a low-level courier for anyone with money," Melnik was saying. "So we can't be sure he's tied to the assassination. But he has worked in the past for Klaus Vorshage, who runs the Gestapo—"

"The *what?*" Horner asked.

Melnik laughed. "Sorry. That's what we like to call the German security services. Israeli sense of humor."

"Macabre," Wintre said from the window, then turned away again as they turned to look at her.

"We don't know for sure that Vorshage's in on it, but someone in the Gestapo certainly is. And Vorshage's the kind of guy who knows pretty well what his men are up to. Of course, he's getting old, so who knows?"

Horner nodded. "I get two kinds of people coming in here on 'unofficial visits,' looking for help," he said. "One kind, they know all sorts of things they aren't supposed to know. The other kind . . ." He shrugged.

Melnik waited.

"The other kind," Horner went on, "they don't know nothing. They got maybe hints, they got ideas, they got *theories,* but they don't *know* nothing."

Melnik nodded. "I don't know nothing," he agreed.

5

GERHARD HAUPTMANN, on the other hand, knew exactly what he had to know and what he had to do. He knew, as did anyone who read the back pages of American newspapers, that the President of the United States was pushing Congress to appropriate a larger American contribution to the International Atomic Energy Agency in order to stop the proliferation of nuclear weapons.

Hauptmann knew also that the American secretary of state was pushing the other nuclear nations hard for matching increases in their contributions, and that the American ambassador to the United Nations was lobbying behind the scenes for increased investigative powers for the IAEA. He was also aware of the American initiative for creation of an analogous agency to investigate and possibly even control international shipments of industrial and research tools related to biochemical warfare.

He wasn't terribly worried about all of this. He was, in fact, amused by the efforts expended on atomic-weapons control; he had moved beyond that field in the past few years and couldn't care less how strong the IAEA now became. And he wasn't worried about the possibility of an international biochemical-weapons agency because of the close tie-in between biochemical weapons and pharmaceuticals. The IAEA could manage a showcase control of atomic weapons, since to build these you had to build factories on the size of Oak Ridge or Hanford. These could be seen on satellite photos, and a suitable fuss would be raised in the UN. But for the production of nerve gases, of mycotoxins, of anthrax and bubonic-plague germs, and of delivery systems for all these, nothing more was needed than small, routine pharmaceutical-production centers. With a few days' advance warning, such as the IAEA was required to give, the sludges could be dumped and the pumps reprimed and nothing but malaria and leishmaniasis medicines would be seen by the investigating teams.

The IAEA had slowed down the production of nuclear weapons in Third World countries, but hadn't been able to stop it. A similar agency would be even more helpless against biochemical weapons.

So none of the American initiatives worried him. What *did* bother him was the German problem.

The wind blew in a sharp gust out of the northeast, and the lake waters began to roil a bit. Hauptmann sat calmly at the helm of the thirty-foot sailboat, skimming the surface of the Wannsee, and thought about himself thinking about his problems. Albert Einstein used to come out on this same lake to sail, alone as Hauptmann was now, working out problems no less complicated than those he himself was expounding.

The chancellor, Gottfried Waldner, was making noises about the German contributions to undeveloped nations' weapons research. Which was not necessarily bad: The proper noises, made to the proper forums, would serve to quiet the Greens—those environmental fanatics who were against everything nuclear and everything artificial, even to the point of wanting to ban DDT, food flavorings, and colorants. These people were arguing vociferously about the dangers to German citizens of unauthorized and uninspected shipments of nerve gases and such through German ports and over German highways. All nonsense, of course, but anything the chancellor could say to shut them up would be worthwhile.

The problem was that Waldner was making his noises in inappropriate forums. Instead of giving loud emotional speeches to screaming hordes of the unwashed, he was speaking quietly and behind the scenes to lawmakers and law enforcers. He was talking of doing more than talking, of taking action, of stopping the leaks of technical information and sophisticated machinery and even of scientific knowledge; he was threatening to close down the whole German "pharmaceutical"-export industry.

He was serious and he was dangerous, and he had to be stopped.

Stopping someone was never difficult; stopping the subsequent investigation, or misdirecting it, was the problem to which one had to give creative thought. The more important the person stopped, the more momentum the investigation into his death would have. The elimination of the chancellor of Germany would give rise to a multitude of investigations, just as the fertilization of a tuber leads to sprouts: The sprouts and investigations would spring from the buried body, reaching up into the light of day and searching with eager fingers for something to grasp. The elimination must be cloaked in as deep a misdirection as was the Kennedy assassination, which remained to this day a model of deception.

And so Hauptmann had visited with Vorshage, and together the two of them had decided on the method. Make use of the national phobia: fear of a rise of Nazism. From that basic idea it had all grown, and had gotten better and better along the way. Schlanger had been easy to fool and had joined eagerly, anxious to show his resolve to stomp out the beastly Nazis. He had continual second thoughts, of course—the man was a nerve-wracked weakling, irresolute and wavering—but the thought of his destiny as Waldner's successor helped steel him to the necessary design. He thought that he was the instigator, the leader of the brave revolutionaries, and that Vorshage was working for him. He thought that Hauptmann knew nothing of the plot, and was bankrolling it only on Schlanger's word that an expensive operation, necessary for the republic, was in hand.

And Vorshage thought that *he* was in control of the whole operation. To an extent he was—he had hired Naman—but Hauptmann was not satisfied that it would all end with Naman. So he had brought in Grass to keep an eye on things, and Grass was working out so well he had put him in charge of finishing matters up. There was no reason for Vorshage to know this. In fact, if he did know he would undoubtedly object, for Grass was in fact a minor employee of Vorshage's Bundesnachrichtendienst. But he had moonlighted for Hauptmann before and had always given satisfaction, and Hauptmann was a great man for letting the youngsters have their chance. Besides, he liked the idea that neither Schlanger nor even Vorshage knew the entire plan.

The sail luffed and Hauptmann adjusted the tiller automatically, tacking into the wind in more ways than one, and smiling happily to himself.

6

HORNER DROVE THEM to Bellevue and parked in one of the spaces marked "Doctors Only." As they walked away from the unmarked car Melnik turned to look back at it, then asked him, "Aren't you afraid they'll tow it away?"

"One of the advantages of life in the NYPD," Horner said. "They don't have money to buy us new cars every year, or even every five years, so after a while every street cop and tow truck in town gets so they recognize our cars. Of course, so does every street punk and perp in town, which kind of negates the whole idea behind having an unmarked car, but so it goes."

As they took the stairs to the third floor rather than wait for the elevator Horner waved them ahead, and as they climbed he asked Melnik about his leg. "War injury?"

"More of a skirmish," Melnik said. "Rocket shrapnel."

Wintre glanced back at him; she hadn't noticed him limping before.

"Hardly noticeable, I'm told." He smiled at her. "And even then, only when it rains."

"It's not raining."

"It will," he said. "Never fails."

Horner led them down the third floor to the nurses' station, where the nurses who had been on duty the day of the murder were waiting for them. "Sorry to bother you again," Horner said to them. "Like to go over what happened one more time."

"We already told you, and dictated our statements—"

"Sorry," Horner apologized again. "Gentleman here wants to hear for himself." He nodded at Melnik. "Very important man," he said softly, leaning forward confidentially. "Israeli. And this here"—indicating Lisle Wintre—"is the personal representative of the United States secretary of state."

"Defense," she corrected him. "Deputy assistant secretary of defense for—"

"Whatever," Horner said, still talking to the nurses. "So if you wouldn't mind going over your stories just this one more time . . . ?"

Although Horner had already told him their stories in exact detail, Melnik listened attentively as they told him again what had happened. Nurse Angstrom described the male nurse she had seen walking down the corridor near the death room. This was the story they were counting on, since they knew someone had jumped a male nurse a few blocks away just minutes before the shooting, and had taken his ID. Melnik didn't say a word until Nurse Angstrom was nearly finished and said what he had been waiting to hear.

"A limp?" he interrupted as soon as she mentioned it, as if Horner had never told him about it. "A limp is good. If it's real. Unfortunately"—he shrugged apologetically—"a limp is also the sort of thing an accomplished assassin would know how to imitate, to leave behind as false spoor."

She shook her head. "I don't think he was even aware he was doing it," she said.

Melnik looked skeptical, but she was adamant. "It was a real limp," she said. "Not like yours."

"What do you mean?"

She sighed. "Do you know how many people we get in here every day with fake injuries? They're in a cab that stops suddenly at a red light or they go into a grocery store and slip on the wet floor, and all of a sudden they've got backlash neck injuries that are worth a half-million-dollar suit, or a wrenched knee that will spoil an athletic career and is worth a couple of million easily. They come in here limping and groaning and holding their heads to one side and dragging their bad foot, and believe me if you don't get so you can spot a phony injury within ten seconds you're going to waste a hell of a lot of time as a nurse in this place."

Melnik smiled at her. "That's all I wanted to know," he said. He turned to Horner. "We can go now."

"You didn't have to make up a big story about rocket shrapnel and only hurting when it rains," Lisle said as they got back to the car, which had not been towed away. "You could have told us."

"Then if she had spotted it, I wouldn't know if maybe you had given it away with a look or a smile. This way we know for sure: That nurse is one smart cookie, and our killer limps."

"So he limps. Is that such a big deal?"

"No," Melnik admitted. "But it's the only deal we've been dolt."

7

1

"WHAT DO YOU THINK of this fellow Melnik?" Hagan asked without preamble.

"About as expected," Wintre answered. "He's charming, affable, bright, and arrogant. He doesn't have any respect for my office, although I sometimes catch him looking at my legs."

"You're not becoming particularly fond of him, I gather?"

"Not particularly. He's pleasant to be with, but there's an inner hostility. I don't know why." *Since he doesn't know I'm lying to him,* she added to herself, wanting to say it out loud but not daring.

"Well, they're like that, aren't they?" Hagan said. "Those people. Actually, I'm glad you two haven't got too friendly. There are things I may ask you to do that he shouldn't know about."

"Of course," she answered, only mildly astonished that he seemed to have forgotten that on his instructions her entire relationship with the man was built on a lie.

"In fact, I think I—"

The buzzer sounded in mid-sentence, and Hagan glanced at it coldly before leaning over to press the intercom switch. He did not like being interrupted. It had damn well better be at least the President, he thought.

"Sorry to interrupt you, sir," his secretary's voice came through, slightly metallic sounding. "Mrs. Hagan's here to see you. She says it's not important if you're busy—"

"Never too busy for her," he said. "Ask her to come right in."

He got up from his desk and kissed her warmly on the cheek, introduced her to Lisle Wintre, and expressed surprise that she was in town. "You didn't say anything about it this morning at breakfast," he reminded her.

"Just a whim," she said, her smile blasting his into oblivion. "The *Post* had an ad for a sale at Macy's, and that's always such fun."

"Hardly worth the trip in," he suggested.

She laughed. "It's not exactly like booking a trip on the *Lusitania*. You come in every day," she reminded him, "and you don't make a fuss about that."

"I wasn't making a fuss. I just hate to see you bothering yourself to save a few dollars, when you can get the same item at the mall near us—"

"You don't understand the thrill of the hunt," she told him, smiling conspiratorially over at Lisle. "Men have a genetic deficiency that way. Something to do with the Y chromosome, I think. Scientists have proven it with experiments on rats. There isn't that much of a difference, you know."

"Between the X and the Y?" Lisle asked, confused.

"Between men and rats." She turned back to her husband. "Only joking, dear. And I'm sorry to have interrupted you with Miss Wintre, I know how you hate that. I told Miss Pherson not to buzz you if you were busy. I just thought as long as I'm in town, perhaps we could have lunch together?"

Hagan hesitated only a fraction of a second. "Yes," he said. "I'd like that."

"Excuse me, Mr. Hagan," Lisle interrupted, "but you have a luncheon appointment with Senator McMahon at one."

"Oh, I'm so sorry," Mrs. Hagan said. "I *knew* you'd be busy. I just thought perhaps, on the off chance . . ."

Hagan smiled brightly. "Well, it's the thought that counts." He wondered what thoughts were actually running through her conniving head. "Maybe," he said, "I could break that date with McMahon. What do you think, Wintre? Could we fit it in later?"

"I don't see where, sir. Your day is full, and his secretary made a thing about finding time for you, so it might be difficult on his side."

"Well, it was just an idea," Mrs. Hagan said. "I knew you'd be busy. I'll see you for dinner, then?"

Hagan nodded, kissed her again, and she left. To go where, God only knew. The worst part of it was not knowing whether she was really sleeping with someone or not. But then he corrected himself; he was too honest to let that lie pass. The worst part was the doing of it, not the lying about it. Because while he thought she *might* be doing it he continued to torment himself, but if ever he found out that it was true, that she was fucking some other man, he would kill them both.

He felt the heat rising in his hands and at the back of his neck, and he knew that this was true: He would kill them. He forced a cold calmness down. He swallowed it deep down into his gut, until the hot tingling left him. Then he smiled and shook his head, in control once more. The little bitch. He laughed.

"Sir?" Lisle asked, wondering what he was laughing at.

"Ah, Miss Wintre." He remembered that he was not alone, and turned to her with that tone of voice she had already learned to dread. He walked across the room and sat down again at his desk. "As my wife quite properly pointed out, I hate to be interrupted."

"Sir?" she asked again, confused.

"When I tell someone—particularly my wife, but including *anyone*—that I will meet them for lunch, I do not expect you to—"

"I'm sorry. I only thought—"

"I *detest* being interrupted, even for apologies!" He paused, and this time Wintre only nodded. He was bristling with anger, but managed to control it. He knew he had the McMahon appointment, but he had wanted to see that bitch's face when he told her he'd meet her for lunch. If only Wintre hadn't interrupted him at that moment— No, he thought, recovering himself. His wife was too clever to betray anything, anyway. When he had gone on to say he'd break his appointment and meet her, she hadn't batted an eyelash. What did she care, after all? If she had to break her luncheon date, she'd simply meet the man afterward. Of course, it *was* possible that she had come in merely for a Macy's sale. . . . He glanced over at the *Post* lying on the coffee table to the left of his desk. As soon as Wintre left he'd check to see if there really was such an ad. But there would be, just as he was sure she wouldn't have flinched if he had said he'd meet her for lunch. He had to give his wife full marks for efficiency. You couldn't trick her. Without realizing it, he took a certain pleasure—a kind of masochistic, paternal pride—in her cleverness.

He waved it all away with a careless flick of his fingers. He was back in control. "You were saying, before we were interrupted? This business about your New York trip?"

"Yes, sir. Mr. Melnik came to me and told me about this police-station bombing in New York—"

"How did he find out?"

"He didn't actually say. But it was written up in the papers. There was a decent-sized article in *The New York Times,* and he could have seen it there."

"How does he connect it to his supposed German assassination?"

She smiled apologetically on Melnik's behalf, deciding on the spur of the moment that Hagan didn't deserve to be told everything. "I haven't the faintest idea. Pure imagination, probably. It did turn out after we'd got there that the man killed in the hospital was a German tourist, but that's all there is to connect it."

"He's the one who brought in the briefcase with the bomb?"

"They're not even sure about that. The man was mugged, and the mugger had the briefcase, but nobody knows for sure that he took it from this man."

"And that's it?" Hagan asked.

She nodded, and he leaned back to think it over. "Pretty slim pickings," he said.

"Yes, sir, I think so too. That's why I didn't think it worthwhile to try to talk him out of going there to investigate."

Hagan nodded. "Keep him busy, eh? Very good." He smiled his bleak smile and turned to the paperwork on his desk. "Thank you, Wintre. You'd better take the first train back, see what he's up to, keep an eye on him. That'll be all for the moment."

As she stood up to leave she saw that he had already forgotten her.

2

HELMUT SCHLANGER came out of Gerhard Hauptmann's office carrying a small valise he had not gone in with. He took the elevator down to the lobby and walked out, got into his limousine, and moved off down the street. Carlos Grass started the car engine and moved slowly a couple of blocks behind him. This part of the tail was easy enough. No one was going to suddenly take the large, stately limousine on a wrenching series of turns against traffic to lose a possible follower. No one in the limousine would even suspect the presence of one.

Schlanger was driven back to his government office building, got out of the limousine, walked up the wide stone steps, and disappeared inside. Grass parked across the street and waited.

Less than an hour later Klaus Vorshage appeared and went inside. Within fifteen minutes he came out again, carrying the small valise. He set off on foot, and Grass locked his car and followed him. This part was a little trickier: Vorshage was a trained man, and it would be difficult to follow him if he didn't want to be followed. But there was no reason he should even think of the possibility, and as it turned out he did not. Without any effort to evade or look for a follower he went straight to the Tiergarten, and there beside the pool he met Walter Naman.

"Here's your expense money," Vorshage said, handing over the valise. "But I don't know what you're going to do with it."

"Spend it, of course."

"I meant, how are you going to get it into the States? Why not let me simply pack it up and mail it to one of our men there? It'll never get opened going through customs, and all you have to do is pick it up."

Naman shook his head. "That's where the danger is, picking it up. I want no contact with any of your people there. No, thank you." He took the valise and hefted it to feel its weight. "I'll take it in myself."

"That's dangerous. If they find it at customs—"

"If it's confiscated I may have to ask you for more. I assume that's not a problem."

"If they confiscate it," Vorshage said irritably, "they'll confiscate *you* as well."

Naman smiled. "Don't worry so much. Your part is done now. You have nothing to do but relax."

"Do you know how you're going to do it?"

"So soon? I haven't had time to think."

Vorshage nodded. "Well, be careful."

"That's what it's all about," Naman agreed. "Not just to do the job, but to do it safely. I will, I promise you."

"*Wiedersehen.*" Vorshage shook his hand, and they parted.

Grass put the photo that Hauptmann had given him back in his pocket. That was Naman, all right. So far it had been easy enough. Now came the hard part. From all he had heard about Naman the man would be likely to take all precautions. Grass would have to be on the alert every moment.

What he hoped to do eventually was to establish a link with Naman, become part of his team. Until he could figure out some way to do that, he had to follow him. Once the trail was lost, Naman could disappear and go anywhere in the world until he surfaced to make the hit, and that would be too late.

As Naman walked briskly out of the Tiergarten, Grass sauntered along behind him, moving unobtrusively but equally fast.

Naman sat in his hotel room, staring morosely at the money spread out on the bed. Despite his assurances to Vorshage, he knew that money was a nuisance, almost as bad as a gun. He didn't dare carry it through customs. If they happened to open the valise and find it, he would still be in jail when Waldner made his American trip.

The safest way would be to do what Vorshage had suggested and mail it into America. But if he sent it to a dead wait, to himself at a hotel to be picked up when he arrived, and customs happened to check on it and find the money, they would be waiting for him. Better to send it to someone to hold for him. But it had to be someone he could trust, someone he could call and explain why he wasn't dead, someone he could be sure wouldn't open the package or tell anyone.

There was nobody. And that was what was making him so sad as he sat there in his hotel room. He had spent more than sixty years on this earth, and he had no one. Of all the people he knew there was no one he loved, and only one he really trusted: Klaus Vorshage.

He wondered if perhaps he should turn the money over to Klaus and let him mail it to one of his agents as he suggested. But no; trusting Klaus was not the same as trusting his entire organization. Somewhere in it there were bound to be leaks; there always were. No, Naman decided, getting to his feet, no, it was better to be alone. Loneliness was not a weakness, but a strength.

He felt better now, his momentary reverie over. He was strong again, alone again.

Grass activated his team. There were two entrances to Naman's hotel and twenty-four hours to the day; no one person could keep an eye on both entrances all the time. As it happened, however, when Naman left his hotel at nine the following morning, carrying the valise, it was Grass who was on duty outside the front entrance.

He took a taxi and Grass followed, alerting his team by mobile telephone. Since such calls are not immune to interception they used a simple code, transposing the names of streets and adding forty-five degrees to directions. And so Naman's taxi sped northwest out of the city with Grass following, and with two other cars spread out at two-mile intervals ready to pick up the chase if there was a problem.

There were no problems. The taxi drove at a reasonable speed over well-used roads, and finally pulled in at a private airport on the outskirts of Berlin. Naman entered one of the several small buildings as Grass slid into a parking spot, wondering what was happening.

What was happening was simple enough. Naman had called ahead, and his chartered aircraft was waiting. They filed a flight plan for Bonn and he and the pilot walked out together, got into the small single-engine plane, and took off.

Grass got out of the car, cursing. He ran into the building and paused to regain his composure. He was in a small room with a counter running the length of one side. There were airplane pictures on the walls, aircraft magazines on the one table. He thought at first the place was empty, but then saw the young woman busily reading a woman's magazine behind the counter. She looked up at him and he nodded. *"Morgen."*

She returned his greeting brightly and asked if she could help him.

"I was wondering about taking an airplane ride," he said. "A plane just took off as I came in. One of yours?" When she said that it was, he said that was the sort of ride he had in mind. "Will he be back soon?" he asked.

"No, he's off on a charter trip to Bonn," she said. "But we have several aircraft. I could arrange a ride for you in one of them."

Grass said he'd think about it, and left. He hurried to his car and drove through the parking lot to another of the buildings on the other side of the airfield. "Do you have charter services?" he asked immediately.

The young man said they did.

"How fast can you get me to Bonn?"

"We've got a twin-engine that can put you there in less than an hour."

Grass nodded. Naman had left in a single-engine plane. By the time it landed he could be waiting there with a taxi all rented. He relaxed for the first time in ten minutes. "Let's go," he said.

As they walked out to the plane he was working things out in his head. Naman was going to be tougher than he thought. At this stage he should have no suspicion that he might be followed, and yet he was taking no chances. Grass didn't think that when Naman landed in Bonn he would bother to check on all the other charter services in the airport to see if anyone had followed him, but in any event he would naturally become more and more careful as they got closer to the assassination. If he was this suspicious this early in the game, it would be hard to keep him in sight all the time and yet remain invisible.

This was not going to be easy, Grass thought. But he would do it. He would stay with Naman all the way through, and as soon as Waldner was dead he would—

Well, as Hauptmann said, when someone establishes a classic pattern it doesn't make sense to fool with it. The 1963 assassination provided a perfect model: Find someone capable of doing the job, give him a reason to do it, and as soon as it is done kill him to cut off the investigation at the knees.

When they were well out of sight of the airport, Naman turned to the pilot and asked if they could please fly to Munich instead of Bonn. The pilot looked at him curiously, but his not to reason why: He radioed in to sector control to change his flight plan, and the airplane tilted thirty degrees to the left, came around on the new course, and flew on.

Grass landed at Bonn within the hour and hurried outside to line up a taxi. He had the man pull into a spot near the exit of the parking lot and he waited there, scanning the sky carefully, looking for Naman's plane.

3

> "Keeping time, time, time
> In a sort of Runic rhyme,
> To the throbbing of the bells—
> Of the bells, bells, bells—
> To the chiming and the rhyming of the bells,
> Bells, bells, bells, bells . . ."

Melnik's voice trailed off into a whisper and then stopped, and it was quiet in the room.

"This is the dumbest damn thing I've ever heard of," Horner's voice rasped. "What are you going to do now, take her back into a previous life?"

Melnik leaned back and relaxed. Horner liked to talk tough, but he had been careful not to speak until Miss Angstrom was totally out and the spell couldn't be broken. "We shall see what we shall see," Melnik said.

"Undoubtedly," Horner agreed. "But what will that be?"

"Let's find out." Melnik turned back to the nurse. "Do you know what day this is?"

"Wednesday," she said.

"No, no, no. It's Thursday." He waited; there was no reaction. "Do you know what day this is?" he asked again.

"Thursday," she replied.

"You know this is all bullshit," Horner said.

Melnik agreed. "People try to do too much with it. They think it's a science."

"It's bullshit," Horner insisted.

"It's somewhere between the two."

"Most states no longer accept evidence given under hypnosis," Wintre put in from the corner where she sat.

"Damn right, too," Horner said. "You can make some people remember anything you want them to remember, whether it happened or not. I bet you could make her"—he nodded at Angstrom—"pick John Wilkes Booth out of a lineup as the killer."

"I could make her stand on her head and spit wooden nickels while whistling 'Hatikvah,' " Melnik agreed. "But that isn't what I'm trying to do. I just want to make sure she doesn't identify someone she saw some other day."

Horner shrugged. "I guess we got nothing to lose." He glanced at his watch. "Except maybe an hour or two."

"Thirty minutes, tops," Melnik promised, "or we give up. Where are you working this evening?" he asked Miss Angstrom.

"Emergency," she said.

"Is that your permanent assignment?"

"Yes."

"Find it interesting?"

"Yes."

"What are you doing now?"

She opened her mouth, searching for words, but none came.

"You're walking down the hall," he told her. "Dr. Livingstone told you to check on the patient in 375 every half hour. Do you remember he told you that?"

"Yes."

"What's wrong with the man in 375?"

"Pneumonia."

"You're walking down the hall now. You're passing room 353, 355, 357 . . ."

"Yes."

"Are you alone?"

"Yes."

"No one else in the corridor?"

"There's someone . . . a male nurse is coming toward me."

"What's happening now?"

"I'm still walking down the hall. We just passed each other. No one else in the hallway."

"What door are you passing now?"

"363 . . . 365 . . ."

"You're at the end of the corridor now?"

"Yes."

"Where is 375?"

"I have to turn left at the end."

"Is there a door at the end? On your right?"

"Yes."

"What's the number?"

"369."

"Is anyone else there?"

"No."

"Is anything on the door?"

"No."

Melnik stopped and leaned back in his chair. After a moment he said, "Let's try it again. This time I want you to tell me everything you see."

He started her again down the corridor, but she gave no additional details beyond counting out the room numbers by herself as she passed them. When she finished Melnik told her to rest for a moment.

"What's the point of all this?" Horner asked.

"She walks down that hall every day of her life. Sometimes the corridor is empty, sometimes it's crowded, but there have to have been more times than just that once when there happened to be exactly one man in the hall. How do we know she's remembering the right day and the right person?"

"I don't know. We take our chances, is all."

"If we have to," Melnik agreed. He glanced at his watch. "I've still got ten minutes before the half hour is up. Let's try it again."

Forty-five minutes later he was saying, "You can't rush these things. She's a good subject, I think we'll get somewhere if we stick to it. You could go out for coffee if you want."

"I guess I'll wait around," Horner said resignedly. Wintre had her eyes closed, sitting patiently on her chair in the corner.

They went down the corridor again. This time he asked her to say out loud what she was thinking, and she rambled on about her mother and her sister, and a young intern who kept going out of his way to find her and who might ask her out, and the trouble she was having with her landlord and the people downstairs, and the roaches in her apartment. Now he asked her to describe everything she saw, and she interspersed her comments about her family and her aggravations and her hopes with the numbers of the rooms she was passing, and which of them had papers tacked to the door. When she passed room 369, just as she began to turn left down the corridor, she mentioned that there was a splattering of dark spots on the wall beside the door—

"That's it," Melnik said quietly, letting her ramble on but turning away now, smiling at Horner and Wintre. "Those are the blood spots from the murdered guard. She's at the right day. Now let's show her the pictures."

He took her slowly and carefully out of the trance, coming without transition back to consciousness. "How do you feel?" he asked.

She blinked several times and took a couple of deep breaths. "Fine. How was I?"

"Just great. Now we'd like you to look at these photos and see if you recognize any of them."

Two days ago, after talking to Horner the first time, Melnik had called FBI headquarters and asked for a file search of anyone who might have carried out such a hit and who also had a limp. They said they'd get back to him. He still hadn't heard a word, but on the same day he had called Mazor in Israel with the same request. This morning he had received an international telephone call, telling him to go to the Speedy Quick Copying Center a few blocks from his hotel. He arrived there just as a long fax was coming through. The seven photos had lost some quality in the transmission but were still clearly recognizable.

Except to Miss Angstrom. She looked at them carefully, one at a time, and put them into two piles. The pile of four she handed back to Melnik. "It's none of these," she said.

"You're sure?"

"Never saw them in my life." She tapped the other pile on the table. "But these, I just don't know."

Melnik glanced at them. They were all the same type of man: large physique, pleasant face, light brown hair, no distinguishing characteristics. He looked through the four rejected photos: One man was really ugly; another had a large nose; the third had a bad scar; the fourth was much older.

"Would you like to try again?" Wintre asked her. "Look at these three one more time?"

"No," Melnik said, pocketing the photos. "Thanks," he told Miss Angstrom. "You've been a big help."

As they left he explained: He preferred to chase a couple of innocent men rather than take a chance on losing the real one because the witness felt pressured to narrow down the field. "First impressions are best. We'll have to work with that."

Horner said glumly, "It could still be none of the above. She didn't give us a positive make on any of them. There could be another guy out there limping around the world killing people."

"I'm betting on two things," Melnik said. "One, this was a good hit, which means the guy is experienced. You don't learn how to find and kill people by reading books, you learn by doing it. Which means there's a good chance our intelligence has him on file, which means he's one of these three men. That's point number one."

He hesitated, grinding his teeth. "To be absolutely honest with you, I have to admit that point number one is not so great. There's always the possibility that someone good enough to kill this guy in the hospital is so good that he's out there and we don't know about him."

Horner nodded. Wintre asked, "So what's point number two?"

"Number two is a much better point. Number two is, we don't have anything else. So we might as well find these guys."

They looked at each other and shrugged. "Any other questions?" Melnik asked.

"Just one," Horner said. "What the hell is 'a sort of Runic rhyme'?"

4

WALTER NAMAN took a taxi from the airport in Munich to the train station. He booked a ticket on the night train to Paris, checked the phone book and found a downtown athletic club, and walked the three blocks though the weather threatened rain. On the way he stopped in a hardware store and bought the best combination padlock they had. At the athletic club he signed up for a six-month membership, was shown through the facilities, given a magnetic card key, and assigned a locker. Alone in the locker room he opened the valise he was carrying and removed the top layer of underwear, socks, and shirts. Beneath it was the money Vorshage had given him. He took it out and put it in the locker, put on the padlock and spun the dial several times, yanked at it to be sure it was locked, and left.

He killed the rest of the time till his train left with a meal and a movie at the theater in the station. Arriving in Paris early the next morning, he immediately took a taxi to the Gare du Nord, bought a ticket to Le Havre, went out for coffee and brioche, and just barely caught the train.

It wouldn't have mattered if he had missed it. He would have taken the next one. He was in no great hurry, which was one of the reasons he had taken this roundabout route instead of just flying to London. On the contrary; since he didn't yet know what he was going to do he needed quiet time to think, and trains were always useful for that purpose. The other reason for his complex traveling, of course, was ingrained security. Though no one could possibly be looking for him, better safe than sorry.

At Le Havre he boarded the Hovercraft for Brighton, and now stood leaning over the side of the ship as they skimmed the waters of the English Channel, thinking how easy life had become since the European countries had banded together and decided that people should be free to travel between any of their countries without formality or restrictions. It was like the days before the First World War, when no passports were needed. Unfortunately, it was true only for travel within Europe. To go back to America he needed the document he had come here to get.

"I'm afraid we'll have to ask you to come inside, sir."

He turned to look at the hostess, just a bit startled to find her there.

"We're getting reports of choppy water ahead," she explained. "A sudden north wind coming down on us. It's nothing to worry about, but all passengers are requested to stay inside until we reach port in fifteen minutes."

"I thought the whole point of these Hovercraft was that they were steady," he said as she opened the door for him. "Skim over the water, smoothing out the bumps."

"Yes sir, in normal water. But when it gets particularly rough we do tend to ride up and down the troughs and crests, and you could get tossed over if you were on deck."

It was crowded inside, and immediately Naman began to feel uncomfortable. He could hear the whir of the air-conditioner under the babble of conversation, but the air seemed to hang heavy, not moving. It became difficult to breathe. *Oh Christ,* he thought, *not again.*

The floor began to shift under his feet, but that didn't bother him. It wasn't the motion that induced the tightening he began to feel in his chest, the difficulty breathing. *Damn*, he cursed under his breath, feeding his anger to combat the panic. He didn't even notice the motion; it was the tightness of the cabin, the closed doors—the *locked* doors. He saw the steward locking them with his key, and the realization that he *couldn't* get out—even though there was no reason for him to *want* to—was overpowering. The familiar cold sweat squeezed out of his pores on his forehead, his hands began to shake, and he lowered himself into a seat and shut his eyes tightly. If he kept his eyes closed it didn't matter if the doors were closed or not, he told himself; he could pretend he was just sitting here with his eyes closed and any time he wanted to get up and go outside he could, he told himself.

But he *couldn't* go outside, and he couldn't fool himself. He opened his mouth to breathe better, sucking in great dollops of air, but somehow they didn't make it to his lungs. He was sweating profusely now, and his skin was clammy cold. His eyes popped open—

The boat was rocking now, jumping up and down over the choppy whitecaps. Inside the cabin a few people were looking green. As he watched, one woman grabbed the paper bag her companion was holding and bent her head violently over it and threw up in great spasmodic heaves. The odor quickly permeated the room, too powerful for the air-conditioning, and two other people followed suit. He had to get out of here.

He stayed in his seat. He exerted all his willpower to hold back from the edge of panic. He wanted to just get up and stroll casually over to the doors and try them. If he knew he could get out, maybe he wouldn't even want to. . . . No, oh no. If those doors opened he would go outside, he didn't care if he fell overboard, he didn't care if he died, if he could just get out of here—

He shut his eyes tightly and began to recite poetry to himself. The doors were locked, he had seen the steward lock them. His fingers dug into the arm of the chair, the sweat flowed down over his clenched eyes, and he tried desperately to leave this world with poetry. . . .

> Sah ein Knab' ein Röslein stehn,
> Röslein auf der Heidn,
> War so jung und morgenschön,
> Lief er schnell es nah zu sehn,
> Sah's mit vielen Freuden.
> Röslein, Röslein, Röslein rot. . . .

It didn't work, it wasn't working, instead of seeing the free flowing fields of roses he saw only the black walls marked with terrible scratchings and splats of blood as the fingernails gave way to flesh and the flesh tore against the concrete, instead of the singing wind he heard the shouts of *"Schnell! Mach' schnell!"* behind him as the doors clanged shut and he was locked in the cavernous room with a dozen other boys and hundreds of dead bodies—*"Schnell!"* rang in his ears and he shivered and began to clamber with the other boys over the piles of dead bodies, slipping in their excretions, prying open their mouths—

"It's all right, it's going to be all right. Can you hear me?"

He nodded his head, afraid to open his eyes.

"Good. Now just hold on a moment."

He felt a sting in his arm, and then fingers massaging it. "Come on now," the voice said in his ear. "Try to stand up now. You're going to be all right."

He shook his head, he couldn't move.

"You'll feel better if you stand up and walk around. There's lots of room in here. We can walk around and look out the windows. It's not the motion that's bothering you, is it?"

He shook his head.

"I thought not. I just gave you a shot that will make it go away. Trust me."

He opened his eyes, and there was a crowd of people around him. He shut them tightly again, nearly screaming, and heard the man who was holding him say, "Clear back, can't you? He's all right, just leave us alone." And then, a moment later, "They're gone now. It's all right, there's plenty of room."

He opened his eyes again, cautiously, just a peep, and saw that a space had cleared around them. He sat up, and the man helped him to his feet and they began to walk around the cabin.

"If I could just go outside for a second," he asked.

"Much too dangerous in these seas," the man said. "Never mind, it'll be all right in a minute or two."

Naman nodded. "Feeling better already. It's fading."

"Good."

"Thank you."

By the time the boat docked and they opened the doors he was all right. "What did you give me?" he asked the man.

"Just a shot of sedative. Basically a liquid form of Valium, get it into your bloodstream immediately. Does this happen often?"

Naman shook his head. "Once in a while," he admitted.

"You should take Valium before you travel. Get your doctor to give you a prescription."

Naman shook his head again. "I don't like drugs," he said. "I don't like this feeling." He smiled, because he had to admit the feeling was rather wonderful. No problems, no anxiety, the illusion of a wonderful world. "I don't like not being in control."

"Well, don't worry. This will wear off in an hour or two. Better not drive a car for a while. Other than that, you're as good as new."

Better, Naman thought as they parted. *Much better than new. But it's not me.*

In the train from Dover, still under the influence of the tranquilizer, he looked out the window and saw it all again. But dimly and altered, as through a darkened, cracked mirror: Auschwitz, Lise the Germans' whore, the blond lieutenant, his fall from grace, the ovens, the final week in hell . . .

It wasn't real. None of it affected him. He sat in the train and looked out the window. Out there, beyond the window, there were the passing fields of unsurpassed green and the sheep who looked back at him, while in the window's reflection he saw all the old familiar horrors. But he found they had lost their power to terrorize him. Maybe he would get a doctor's prescription after all, and live on Valium the rest of his life.

By the time the train pulled into Victoria Station an hour later the euphoria had worn off and he was his old self again. The claustrophobia had been terrible and he was grateful the doctor had taken care of him this time, but he was glad to be rid of the artificial euphoria. He preferred the claustrophobia— No, he had to be honest, there was nothing in this world more terrible. But it was part of him and he would deal with it himself, not with the aid of drugs. It had been his own fault, anyway. He knew better than to get himself into those situations. But the ads for the Hovercraft said it was so smooth; he had never anticipated being locked in the cabin.

At any rate, he was all right now. He got off the train and checked the schedule for his connection, looking up at the great billboard in the cavernous hall. He had well over an hour. He walked out into the crowded courtyard, carrying his small valise. He stepped carefully through the maze of taxis and buses until he was clear of the overhanging roof, and looked up into the sky. It was cold, and he pulled his coat tighter around him, buttoning the top collar. The weather was crisp and clear. There were black clouds scuttling across the skies, blown by the stiff north wind that had chopped up the waters of the Channel, but they were being blown so swiftly they didn't look as if they'd have time to drop rain or snow on the people below. And he had always loved London. He decided to take a walk.

He ambled through St. James's Park, as happy as he had been in years. Happy to be free of the boat trip: Escaping from the grip of a claustrophobic attack was like the feeling when a migraine finally faded away. The peace was wonderful. Happy to be out now in the open air, strolling through this most lovely of parks, watching the ducks in the pond and the children feeding them, feeling the biting wind but warm enough against it. Happy to be back in England, even if only for a short visit. A wonderful country. People in America, his adopted land, were always saying things like "Only in America . . ." whenever someone succeeded, when a peanut farmer or an actor became President. But England had already elected a Jew and a woman as prime ministers, and he didn't think he'd live to see the day when either of those happened in America.

A lovely country it was. And then slowly, as he made his way through the park, he began to remember why he was here. He checked his watch. He had time for some quick food.

He came out of the park by Admiralty House and found the Silver Lion on Whitehall. He had a shepherd's pie and a Scotch egg and a pint of best bitter, and asked the barmaid for four bottles of Newcastle Brown to go. But they hadn't an off-licence, and so she directed him to a grocery store around the corner. By the time he had collected the bottles it was time to hurry back through the park to Victoria, to catch his train. As he left St. James's and walked through the narrow, twisting streets toward Victoria he began to regret the clear weather. On these streets of London a thick fog should always hang, he thought. It should always be night, with shadowy figures moving dimly through the fog, appearing and disappearing like apparitions.

And in the hollow cavern of Victoria there should be great clouds of steam pulsing out of the locomotive engines. But as he walked down the platform toward his train there was nothing but the invisible energy of electricity filling the air. Ah well, at least the air in here was damp and chill.

He bought a *Guardian* and sat reading it until thirty minutes past the announced departure time, and then finally the train lurched once or twice and moved out of the station.

He was the only one to leave the train at Ravenscrag. He walked down the wooden path of the unattended station, closing the gate behind him, and headed down the hill toward the village. He passed the pub and found the photographer's cottage still there. A bell rang as he opened the door, and a voice called out from the room behind the counter, "Be with you in a moment."

Naman wandered about the shop, touching things, looking at the pictures of English scenes—the mountains of the Lake District a few miles away, the Cornish coast, the River Avon—and marveling at how some things never changed and how lovely that was, and then François Gilbert came out from the back room, shuffling a bit but still unstooped and with the same fine head of flowing white hair. He blinked once or twice at Naman and then cried joyfully, "Walter! They said you're dead!"

"Well, yes," Naman said when he finally disentangled himself from Gilbert's joyful hugs. "As a matter of fact, I am."

"Ah," Gilbert said, understanding. "And so you come to see me."

Walter shrugged. "If a man is dead, he must be someone else, *nicht wahr?*"

Gilbert wagged his finger in his face. "Take care. You know I hate that language. Just last week a Hun tourist came in here and I didn't answer the bell quickly enough. He called out *'Achtung!'* " He shook his head sadly. "It took three days to clean all the pieces of blood and skin off the walls. We still haven't found all the camera parts."

François Gilbert was a terrible liar, but a wonderful man. He had come to England with De Gaulle in 1940, one of the few Frenchmen to escape at Dunkirk. When he spoke French to the British crew of the trawler that had rescued him, he was nearly thrown back into the sea like an undersized flounder. In those days they looked on the French as traitors whose cowardice had let the Nazis encircle the British line and cause the Dunkirk debacle.

That voyage across the Channel had filled him with hatred for the British, but in the months following he had learned to love them, as that first surge of anti-French hysteria died down and they showed their normal selves. He worked for De Gaulle in the documents section of the Free French Army, rising to command its British section by D-day, turning out identity cards and passports for the Special Operations agents who parachuted behind the lines. Not a single life was ever lost due to inspection of those documents. De Gaulle personally forbade François to join the invading forces, but somehow he evaded the command. He had to walk on French soil again, with Free French soldiers; and so he had, but when the *boches* counterattacked at Bastogne his battalion was cut off from the rest and he was captured. The German interrogator who vetted the prisoners was good at his job and spotted something in Gilbert's manner or in his eyes. He was taken off for interviews by the Gestapo. The interviews lasted two weeks, at the end of which he was broken in body but not in spirit. He had revealed nothing of his work in secret documents, and finally they gave up on him. He spent the rest of the war in one of the stalags, and when it was over he returned to England instead of staying in his beloved France. He had found a woman in England, a WREN who worked with him before he was captured.

He married her and returned to live with her in her native village, Ravenscrag, where he set up three shops. One was a normal photographer's shop, taking pictures of weddings and newborn children and grand parties up on the hill. Another did secret work for the authorities who were now fighting the cold war, and another did even more secret work for those who were *not* the authorities and who were fighting a series of their own little wars.

François had closed down the latter two shops five years ago, living semiretired, taking pictures of the small village, but he kept all his equipment in fine order and still did the occasional job of work for a few old friends.

Naman said, "I have a lovely Canadian passport."

François took it in his hands, turned it over a few times, opened it, and read the information. "Age is just about right," he said. "You'll have to scrunch down a bit, hunch your shoulders, for the height. Shouldn't be any problem." He glanced up at Naman, measuring him briefly. "You haven't put on an ounce in twenty years, have you? The man weighs about thirty pounds more than you."

"The picture was taken almost three years ago. I've lost weight since then."

"Remarkable loss. How'd you do it?"

"Smoking. Two packs a day, and the weight just drops off."

François agreed. "Of course. Because of the cancer." He laughed. "I suppose they'll buy that. Well, let's see what we can do."

They went into the back room and Walter sat on the stool in front of the camera while François took several rolls of cotton out of a drawer and stuffed them in his mouth, high and low along the gum line, then stepped back to inspect the effect. "Not bad. With the proper shadowing we'll get away with it."

He adjusted the light to emphasize the swollen nature of Naman's face, and took the photos. Walter took the cotton out of his mouth and asked how Joan was.

"Dead," François said. "Last year."

"I'm sorry. I didn't know."

François gave one of those Gallic shoulder gestures he had never lost. "Her heart was bad. She just couldn't stop smoking," he said.

"Oh God. And I make stupid jokes about it."

François smiled softly. "When I first saw her, in 1943, I said I'd give my right arm for thirty minutes in bed with her. Once I'd had that, I said I'd kill for a whole night. And when we had that, I told God I'd never again for the rest of my life ask for anything else if he'd just give me one entire weekend with her."

He took the plates out of the ancient camera. "He gave me forty-nine years. One can't complain, after that."

Walter had learned, when people talked to him of personal relationships in general and sexual ones in particular, to nod understandingly while understanding nothing. He could remember the one day in Frau Berthold's attic when he had felt his only surge of sexual excitement. He could remember that day, but could no longer understand the feeling he had had then. He had never experienced it again; since Auschwitz there was nothing inside him that could respond. Something was missing, something that other people had. It used to bother him tremendously, but over the years he had learned to live with the empty hole inside him; he felt only a slight prick of envy when people spoke this way. He focused on the envy; it comforted him. It was the only thing that attached him to the rest of humanity.

He brought out the four bottles of Newcastle Brown, and they drank the beer and talked about old times while François developed the picture, aged it, and carefully attached it to the Canadian passport.

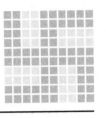

8

1

FRAU HELMUT SCHLANGER closed the door quietly behind her and put the suitcase down gently, but immediately a voice came ringing down from upstairs: *"Bist du es, Hilde?"*

She called out that it was, took off her overcoat and hat and went up the staircase, finding Helmut reading in bed. "I thought you'd be asleep," she admonished.

"I can't sleep without you. Have a good visit? Family all well?"

"You know Father." She smiled, unbuttoning her jacket. "If he were well, he'd be sick about it. Everyone else is fine. And how are you?"

Schlanger nodded. He put down the magazine he had been reading and took off his glasses. He dropped the magazine to the floor beside the bed and put his glasses on the night table while his wife undressed. He lay there propped up in bed while she showered and brushed her teeth. When she came back into the bedroom she picked up the trousers he had left hanging over the back of the chair and hung them up, then straightened out his shoes. "I hope you dressed properly while I was gone," she said.

"The deed is done," he said.

"Oh my God!" she gasped. "He's dead?"

"Quiet!" He shushed her with a raised hand and glanced around nervously. He had already had Vorshage's men check the place thoroughly to be sure there were no bugs, but he couldn't help looking around fearfully, half expecting police or storm troopers to come charging out of the closets and arrest him. He forced himself to speak calmly: "We must be careful what we say and where we say it. For the rest of our lives." He lifted a warning finger for emphasis.

She hated it when he did that. She had a terrible compulsion to pick up a carving knife and cut off that finger. But all she said was "Tell me."

He patted the bed beside her and she sat down. "Everything is in motion. The man is hired and paid for."

"You got the money—"

"From Hauptmann." He smiled in triumph. "He doesn't know what it's for. I simply told him it was for necessary and urgent use, of a secret nature."

"He trusted you," she said admiringly.

"It's more than trust. It's a pact. He thinks that accepting his money puts me in his pocket."

"Well, it does, doesn't it?"

"It puts *him* in *my* pocket. When Waldner is dead"—he couldn't help glancing around to be sure they were alone—"and I become chancellor, it will be an interim appointment only. Everyone will begin maneuvering. But who will Hauptmann want in office? Some *verknabe* who owes him nothing? Or me, in whom he has already invested?" He couldn't help laughing. "He'll never know what the money bought, but he'll know he gave it to me and that I'll be grateful for it. And so he'll support me. There'll be more money coming, and all his influence, his connections . . ."

"You're really going to be chancellor, then?"

"Oh yes. Yes, my darling, I am."

She slid into bed and pulled the quilt up around them both. He laid his head on her bosom and she spread her arms around him. "Helmut," she asked after a moment, "he really is a Nazi, isn't he? There isn't any doubt?"

"No doubt at all. Vorshage has shown me documents he dug up, taken me to cell meetings, laid out a list of things Waldner's done to protect his damned storm-trooper thugs. Yes, he's a Nazi, all right. He has to be removed. For Germany's sake."

She nodded. "Thank God for Vorshage," she said. "Or you'd never have known." She bent down and kissed him. "And thank God for you. Not many men in Germany would be brave enough to do this." He snuggled against her breasts, and she reached up and turned off the light.

2

CARLOS GRASS never panicked. He could make a mistake, he could be tricked by a master like Naman, but this meant only that he had more work to do; it was not a cause for panic.

By the time he had been sitting in the cab outside the Bonn airport for half an hour, he began to wonder. And by the time an hour had gone by he was sure that something was wrong. Still, he didn't panic. Either Naman's chartered plane had crashed or the man had tricked him. Either way there was nothing to gain by rushing around like a chicken without a head. If Naman had tricked him, he had done it well enough that he was now gone. It was simply a question of getting down to work, slowly and carefully.

He walked back into the operations terminal and asked if the pilot who had brought him in was still here. The clerk told him that the plane hadn't gone back to Berlin yet and the pilot could probably be found either wandering around the hangar or in the snack shop.

He found him at the counter, drinking coffee and reading the *Zeitung*. He told him that he had been expecting to meet a friend here who was also flying in by charter airplane, but the man hadn't shown up. How could he find out what happened to him? The pilot finished his coffee and took Grass back into the operations terminal, directing him through a small door and up a steep flight of steps to the flight service office.

Grass told the man in charge there that he was worried about his friend who had chartered an airplane from Berliner Flugzeug Mondrach several hours ago to fly here. He should have arrived by now. The man asked if he knew the aircraft identification, and Grass said no but he knew the exact time of takeoff.

"I'll see what I can do," the man said. "It should take just a few moments. If you would wait over there, please?"

Grass took a seat and leafed through copies of *The Aeroplane* and *Der Spiegel*, and then the man beckoned him back to his desk.

"Nothing to worry about," he said. "There wasn't any accident. Your friend simply seems to have changed his mind. He left Berlin on aircraft two-seven-alpha, and shortly after taking off the pilot filed a change of flight plan by radio. They flew to Munich and landed there safely forty-five minutes ago."

"The son of a bitch," Grass said, then laughed. "And here I am dropping everything to drive out here to meet him, and he doesn't even tell me he's changed his mind."

The man shrugged. "People are like that, aren't they? A young man, I bet."

Grass nodded. "My nephew."

"It's the television," the man said. "All the things they see on television, they never learn to think of anybody else. Turn it on when they want, play it as loud as they like, watch what they want." He nodded. "I blame the television."

Grass blamed Naman's naturally suspicious mind. He didn't think Naman could have any inkling that he was being followed, not this early in the game; he was just careful by nature, the old bastard. Well, it was good to learn these things early on in the game. Grass vowed he wouldn't be so easy to shake off next time. He thought of flying to Munich after Naman, but discarded that idea right away. If Naman was careful enough to have evaded him like this, he certainly wouldn't leave any traceable trail at the airport there. With a false identity he could have flown out of Munich to anywhere in the world, or he could just have taken a tram into the center of town. Either way his trail would be impossible to pick up.

The old bastard. Grass sat down and thought about things. He would have the passenger lists from Los Angeles to Berlin checked for the day Naman had flown in. He would also have all of today's passenger lists out of Munich checked—he glanced at his watch: all lists for planes leaving after one P.M.—to see if the same name showed up on both lists. If it did, he would not only know where Naman had flown to today, but also what identity he was using.

But that was too much to hope for. Any man careful enough to avoid him the way Naman had today would not be careless enough to use the same identity coming and going. If Naman left Germany by train or bus he wouldn't even have to give a name when he bought the ticket. No, Grass thought; he'd have to have it checked out but he had no hope of success there. Walter Naman could be anybody right now, traveling to anywhere in the world.

He was discouraged, but only for a moment. Naman was good, but Carlos Grass was better. Wherever Naman was, whoever he was, Carlos Grass would find him.

3

"FREUD SAID there is no such thing as a coincidence," Melnik said as he came into the room.

Horner looked up from his paperwork. "Five thousand years of civilization you guys got, and you don't know enough to say hello?"

"Einstein, on the other hand," Melnik said, sitting down and smiling, "did not believe in probabilistic determination. But recent experiments in quantum mechanics have shown him to be wrong. Do you think Freud could have been wrong too? Hello," he added.

Horner was feigning annoyance at the interruption, but actually he was glad of any excuse to put down the paperwork. "Depends on the coincidence," he said. "Like, if you happened to be in some hotel room with your floozy and suddenly there's a banging on the door and you open it and there's your wife standing there, I'd say that's not likely to be a coincidence. Freud was right."

Melnik shook his head. "I don't have a wife. Nor, at the moment, a floozy."

"You're not fooling around with Miss Wintre?"

"No. Certainly not."

"Shame. I would, if I were a few years younger."

Melnik shook his head. "Nothing there," he said. "Business relationship. And not such a good one, at that."

"You two don't get along?"

"It's not that. She's a beautiful woman, charming, intelligent. You'd have to be a cretin not to get along with her."

"But?"

"She lies to me. She's supposed to be my liaison with the FBI, but in fact she told them not to pay any attention to me. That's why I didn't mind when she said she had to get back to Washington this morning. We can get more done without her."

Horner considered this. "She wouldn't have said that to the feds on her own," he said.

"No," Melnik agreed. "She does what she's told to do. But for whatever reason, I've got a problem with her."

"So what's the coincidence?" Horner asked, going back to their first topic.

"Charley Lingano is in Philadelphia."

"I don't know . . ."

But Melnik was not to be put down. "We're looking for three people who could be anywhere in the world," he said. "And one of them turns out to be within a hundred miles of the scene of the crime. It's just like your example of the hotel room and the wife; I think Freud was right."

"He was wrong in almost everything else," Horner pointed out.

"Details. He was wrong in details. But with the concepts he had great insight."

"Did he really say that? About no coincidences?"

Melnik shrugged. "I don't know. I think I read that somewhere. Maybe it was Kafka."

"Yeah. Well, if Kafka is your choice of a philosophic guide to reality, I think we're all in trouble." Horner paused, thinking about that. "I don't know," he said again, rubbing his back. "It's getting pretty complicated for a simple assassination plot."

"That's the story with all such plots. The problem is the same one Shakespeare talked about in *Macbeth:* 'If the assassination could trammel up the consequence, and catch, with his surcease, success . . .' The problem is not the assassination, but the consequences. You've got to trammel them up. That's what complicates things."

"Yeah. I guess. How did you find out Lingano is in Philadelphia?"

"Ve haff vays of finding zings out," Melnik said in a stage Teutonic accent.

Horner nodded in admiration. "I've never worked with any of you guys before," he said.

"Who are *us guys*?"

"Super-duper crime stoppers. Mossad, CIA, Secret Service. Closest I've ever come is the FBI a couple of times. I really envy you guys."

"What for?"

"Are you kidding? Resources, money, contacts. Like with Lingano. You want to find these three guys who limp and maybe killed Kremble so you sit down and call Israel, and next day you've got an answer. I can just imagine the computers whirling, agents flying around the world first-class on jets. . . . If I want to make a call to New Jersey, for God's sake, you wouldn't believe the paperwork I have to go through. 'Is this call really necessary? Couldn't you write? Semaphore? Send smoke signals?' "

"It's a luxury," Melnik admitted, "being able to spend money, having resources. It's a luxury I could do without. Mossad gets a lot of Israeli money that should be spent on other things: education, improvements in the life of the people, medical care. But we spend it on Mossad and the air force because we're surrounded by enemies. Our existence depends on these 'luxuries.' "

"You think we don't got enemies? It's just we *pretend* we don't. You think I'm not fighting a war here in this city every goddamn day?"

"I didn't mean to—"

"Look, this last war over there, when Iraq was firing Scud missiles at you guys and everyone in America was saying they wouldn't go overseas for love or money. *Especially* they wouldn't go to Israel. Well, there were more people killed on the streets here in New York, murdered by their fellow citizens, than were killed in all of Israel by all those Scud attacks. And it's not just New York. The same thing's happening in Chicago, Detroit, Washington, L.A., every city in the country. But we don't want to admit it. So we don't spend any money on it, and so it just gets worse and worse. If I had in one *year* what we spent fighting Iraq in just one *day,* maybe I could make a dent in the problem." He paused and leaned back. "I don't know. Maybe I couldn't."

They thought about that for a while. With the new job that was due to come through any day now, Horner told himself, there ought to be enough money to do things right. He guessed he'd probably have to fight for the money. That was probably what the job was going to be about, fighting for money. He wondered if he could do that.

Melnik got up and took a cup of coffee from the pot Horner kept going on the sideboard. "Either way," he said, "I guess it is a coincidence."

"What?"

"Lingano. If he didn't have anything to do with Kremble, it's a coincidence he's right here in Philadelphia. But even if he did, it's a coincidence: The reason we picked up on him so fast is a Mossad hit squad's been after him for months because of an airline bombing. They're just about ready to move in, so when the request for information came they replied right away."

"What do you mean, hit squad?"

Melnik smiled sadly and sipped his coffee. "The funny thing about America," he said, "is you meet naïveté in the funniest places. A New York cop you'd think would know everything." He sighed. "You envy *us?* You've got the biggest luxury of all: You can arrest people, have a trial, turn over the punishment to others, and forget about it. If we arrest someone for bombing an airliner we get riots in the West Bank, bombings in Jerusalem; families on isolated farms get their throats cut and the children are hung out on telephone poles. We don't have the luxury of arresting and trying our murderers; we just eliminate them."

Horner didn't want to hear any more. He put his papers back into his in tray and reached for the telephone. "Maybe we better go talk to Lingano before your guys get itchy fingers. I'll call the Philadelphia cops and get us squared away—"

Melnik reached out and put his hand over Horner's on the telephone. "No," he said. "Better not say anything to anyone. Just let me go with my friends."

"Philly won't like us moving in there without clearing it."

"We're not moving in. *I'm* moving in, and they won't not like it because they won't know anything about it. You don't know anything about it, either. I never told you."

Horner sat back in his chair. "Explain," he said, although he understood, and Melnik knew he understood.

"Two reasons," Melnik said. "Number one is that even if he doesn't have anything to do with Kremble that doesn't negate his role in the airliner bombing. We want him for that. But if he's found dead after the Philadelphia police know we're interested in him . . ." He shrugged. "It could complicate international relations, right?"

"Number two?"

"Number two, we'll find out the truth quickly."

"And we cops won't?"

Melnik raised his shoulders. "You have the luxury of civilized laws. We have the necessity of protecting our people. Luxuries are pretty, but they're not as efficient as necessities."

Horner arched his back, trying to stretch it out. He looked up at Melnik, really seeing him for the first time. "You're going to kill this guy," he said. "And before you do that, you're going to make him talk."

Melnik shrugged again. "It's what I do," he said. "For a living."

4

WHEN FRANÇOIS GILBERT finished the passport they left his workshop and walked up the hill to the pub. It was night by then, cold and dark along the unlit road, and they trudged along with their hands in their pockets, seeing their white breath only by the occasional lights of a car swooshing by in the darkness. But when they opened the door to the pub all the cold and dark and quiet were pushed aside, and they stepped into a crowded smoky room, warm with a burning fire and alive with talk.

They ordered two more Newcastle Browns, took them to a corner near the fire, and settled down to warm their toes and their stomachs. They talked about the state of the world and of old friends, and watched the flickering flames, and dozed off with the glasses in their hands.

Naman found himself thinking about Gilbert's wife and the lifetime they had had together. The warmth of the fire and the beer, and perhaps the lingering effect of the afternoon's Valium, brought words up from somewhere inside him. He choked them off before they came out of his mouth, but then he looked over and saw that Gilbert was asleep. He reached over and took the glass from his fingers, putting it on the small table in front of them. And he began to talk quietly to the sleeping man.

"I decided to rescue Lise," he said, staring into the flames, receding into the past. "We were children, in a concentration camp from which no one had ever escaped, but to see her like that was intolerable and so I decided we must run away. I had no idea how, but as soon as I made that decision I felt better."

He nodded to himself. He glanced over at François Gilbert, who had asked God for one weekend with a woman and had been given a lifetime, and who was now asleep dreaming of her. *I too,* he thought. *I too . . .*

"You must understand," he told the sleeping man, "that I didn't even know where she was. The girls—the whores—had no assigned rooms. Each day they were thrown into a room as one might throw in a mop or pail, and when their time was up they were taken back to their barracks—into which I could never get.

"So it was not possible for me to plan an escape with her. I would have to be ready to run the next time chance threw us together. It was an altogether impossible idea.

"So what happened? It was a short time later—weeks, possibly, though I have no firm idea of the passage of time during those years—that I did find her again. I was making the rounds with my little supply of soap and towels, and I entered one of those rooms and saw her huddled on the floor in a corner. She had been beaten rather badly—which of course was nothing unusual for those girls. Between the continual rape and the beatings, they never lived very long. I knew that, of course; it was one of the reasons I had decided we must escape.

"At any rate, I came into the room and hurried over to her without noticing that there was someone else still in the room. I began to wipe away the blood when he shouted at me. It was the blond lieutenant who had 'hired' me. He was lying naked and angry on the cot, and began to berate me for attending to the whore, when he recognized me and smiled. Lise told me later he had been unable to—it seems ludicrous to say 'make love': He had been unable to fuck her.

"Now he called me over to his cot and began to rumple his hand through my hair as he had the day he found me with the commandant's boots. He was mumbling, ranting and rambling, about the *'verdammte jüdische Hure'* and all her deficiencies, and he took my hand and placed it on his chest and began to rub himself with it. He pushed it down to the scene of his disgrace, and immediately he began to revive. You understand that in the past few months I had seen every sort of sexual activity, but at the same time I had seen nothing; I had existed as a fish in a fishbowl exists, swimming around in little circles with the whole room open to view, but seeing and understanding and thinking about nothing except the water in my own small bowl. Only now, for the first time, did I *see* a man's sexual arousal."

He looked around the room. It was crowded, but in the corner they were alone. No one was listening except François, and he was asleep. Walter got up and walked over to the bar, asked for two more bottles of Newcastle Brown, and brought them back. He put one on the table in front of François, and held the other in his hands.

"And now," he said, "the blond lieutenant puts his hand on my head and pushes it down to his penis. I am revolted, but I dare not resist. This has nothing to do with sex; it is as if he told me to lick his dirty toes or smear his excrement on my face—which, incidentally, was not unheard-of in that place. I felt no shame; all such feelings had long ago disappeared. My natural revulsion forced me to pull back, but the hands on my head tightened and forced me down. If I had resisted further, he would certainly have shot me. And so I opened my mouth and allowed him to move my head back and forth on him, gagging a bit more from the essence than the existence, as Sartre would put it.

"The door opens. I hear it but cannot see who it is. The lieutenant at this moment is obviously incapable of either hearing or seeing anything, for he continues to use me—until suddenly there is a horrified shout. My head is thrown back, I stumble and fall against the far wall. An officer is standing in the doorway, obviously an officer far superior to my lieutenant. He begins to shout and curse, and I find that I am a 'dirty Jewish degenerate' and a 'disgusting piece of filth trying to corrupt an officer of the Third Reich.' I am hit repeatedly by both the officer and my lieutenant, and I am condemned on the spot to death. A guard is called and I am dragged away. As my head bangs on the door jamb, just before I am yanked out into the corridor, I see Lise still sitting on the floor in the corner where she was when I entered, the blood still drying on her face."

A sudden spurt of sparks flew out of the fire, and Walter jerked back in reaction. His bottle of beer was empty, and so he switched it with Gilbert's.

"My life at this point was not in my own hands," he continued, "but was totally dependent on outside occurrences. I was taken to the death barracks and given a number. The disposal process at this time, near the end of the war, was no longer being run with typical German efficiency, in an orderly manner. I was told that there were no beds available at the moment, but that one would undoubtedly open up with the next removal. From other inmates I found that I had a life expectancy here of probably six days: They were running that far behind.

"But everything changed suddenly the very next day with the sighting through binoculars, by a group of prison guards on one of the towers, of a Russian soldier. They fired at him and he disappeared back into the woods which fringed the compound, but where one Russian walked could others be far behind?

"The immediate result was evidently to inspire the commandant to rethink his chances of disposing of us all before the whole Red Army appeared at his gates. Perhaps it would be better to pretend that we were all good friends. Suddenly the ovens were turned off, the gas showers ceased, and everything was in turmoil.

"I walked outside the death barracks and found no guards. I left the compound and walked through the camp without being stopped. Near the brothel I encountered a sergeant I knew from my duties there who asked me where I was going. He seemed more frightened than frightening, and I told him I was looking for Lise. It was all very confused. The soldiers were running this way and that; no one seemed to be in charge anymore. The sergeant took me into the girls' compound and stayed with me while I found her. I remember he seemed to be talking to me all the time, but I can't remember anything he said. I told him I wanted to leave with Lise, and he walked me to the front gate and told the sentries to open the barrier. I don't know if I realized then that he was now more afraid of the Russians than of the commandant, and that he was asking me to tell them that he had helped us. I do remember that he kept repeating his name. I don't think I answered him. I took Lise by the hand and we walked through the gates. I looked up at the sun, which was beginning to set. The Russians would be coming from the east. I had heard in the camp stories from eastern Jews of how the Cossacks were worse than the Germans. The Americans, I thought, would be coming from the west, and so I turned Lise toward the setting sun and we began to walk down the road toward America.''

François stirred and opened his eyes. "So you see how it was," Naman said to him. François drew the back of his hand over his mouth, wiping away the spittle that had gathered there while he slept, and nodded.

"Time, gentlemen," the publican called, and they pulled themselves to their feet and went out into the dark night.

"America," Naman said wonderingly. "What did I know? We walked out the gate and turned right, toward America."

5

"So good of you to meet with me, Mr. Secretary."

"Not at all, not at all," William Hagan said. "We're all part of the same team, aren't we? If I can be of any help, it will be my pleasure."

Randolph Burroughs smiled thankfully. He had been a bit nervous about meeting the deputy assistant secretary of defense for politico-military affairs. The man had a reputation as a mean son of a bitch. But it was immediately clear that such a reputation had been bred by the jealousy of others rather than by the man himself. The really big ones, Burroughs thought, are always the most humble.

Never again, Hagan was thinking. *Never again will I hire a woman assistant. They are untrustworthy and incapable of rational thought.* He had been irritated when he came back from lunch yesterday and found a message from Miss Wintre saying that she had gone to New York with that Israeli. He thought he had made it perfectly clear to her that her task involving the "Jewish plot" was simply to keep it out of his hair; it was not important enough to interfere with her other duties, certainly not important enough to take her away from her desk for days at a time. Particularly not without his specific permission. (*Yes,* he admitted, *I told her to get back to New York and see what the Yid was up to, but I didn't tell her to* stay *there.*)

When she had finally thought to call him this morning and bring him up to date he had tersely told her to get her little ass on the first plane back to Washington. He had taken pains *not* to take pains to be polite. If the Israeli wanted to stay in New York and pal around with the police there, that was no skin off his nose. But he wanted her back at her post immediately.

Presumably she was on her way back now, but she was not here yet and so he was sitting at this dreary table in a second-rate Washington restaurant with this dreary little man, a minor functionary of that most overrated of all agencies, the CIA. It was Miss Wintre who should have been here; his time was too valuable.

He glanced at the menu and thought, not for the first time, that he really should have put off this request for a meeting until Wintre had returned. But, he had to admit, the man had intrigued him with his guarded reference over the telephone to an urgent problem in the European Community. "Can you recommend anything?" Hagan asked, although judging by the man's tie his taste was not to be trusted. "I don't believe I've eaten here before." *Nor shall again,* he added silently.

"The brook trout is excellent. If you don't mind the bones."

"Rainbow?"

"I beg your pardon?"

"Rainbow trout?"

"I don't know," Burroughs said, abashed. "It just says brook trout."

"Yes. Then it's not likely to be rainbow, is it?"

"Would the gentlemen care for a drink before lunch?" a suddenly materialized waiter asked.

Burroughs's face lit up, and Hagan paused just long enough to let him get out the beginning syllables of the word "martini" when he broke in over him, "No, we're working men with a big afternoon ahead of us— Oh, I'm sorry, Burroughs. Were you about to have a drink? Go right ahead, don't let me stop you."

"N-n-o," Burroughs stuttered. "I just thought perhaps you might like— No. No, of course not. Shall we order?"

"I'll have the swordfish if it's fresh," Hagan said.

"Yes sir."

"Not fresh frozen?"

"No sir. Flown in daily."

Hagan nodded and Burroughs ordered the same. Hagan smiled. The swordfish was the most expensive dish on the menu, and would probably put this young lout over his expense allowance for a CIA lunch. "I think I'll have a shrimp cocktail first," he said to the waiter. "And perhaps a cold beer with it. Will you join me, Burroughs?"

"Ah, yes. Of course. That sounds very good. Two shrimp cocktails," he told the waiter, "—and two Buds," he added before Hagan could ask for something imported.

As soon as the waiter left with their order, Hagan took a sip of ice water and said, "And now to business. What's this all about?"

Burroughs pulled his chair closer to the table and leaned over it. "We've been getting rather interesting reports from our man in Berlin, and as I was doing a group correlation on the computer yesterday afternoon I came upon your recent interest in the Israeli reports—"

"Damn. Excuse me," Hagan interrupted suddenly. "My beeper's gone off."

Burroughs looked confused. "I—I didn't hear anything."

Hagan patted his breast pocket. "It's a silent, vibrational beeper." He smiled paternally. "It wouldn't do for everyone at the National Security Council to have beeping beepers; the conference would turn into a cacophony." He half stood, looking for the waiter. "Where is the damn man?"

"I don't think they'll have telephones to bring to the table, sir."

"Really?" Hagan expressed astonishment. "But surely they must have a telephone somewhere in the establishment."

"Oh yes sir, I'm sure they have a coin phone. Possibly by the rest rooms?"

Hagan grimaced and said, "I wasn't prepared for such a contingency, I'm afraid. Would you have a quarter?"

Burroughs handed it to him, but by then the waiter appeared and when the situation was explained he immediately brought over a cordless phone. Hagan sat down, pocketing the quarter, and dialed his office.

"Good afternoon, this is the office of the deputy assistant—"

"Hello, Edna, it's me. What's up?"

Edna Pherson wasn't flustered or even terribly surprised by this greeting. Hagan had done it before, whenever he wanted to impress someone or get out of a meeting. "The circumstances are altered whenever the Italian pilot peregrinates," she said, just in case anyone was listening in.

"I see," Hagan said seriously, frowning. "All right, have the papers ready for me, I'll be right there." He hung up and turned to Burroughs. "The White House," he said. "I hate to leave before the swordfish, but . . ." He shrugged helplessly.

"Your shrimp, sir," the waiter said, putting the chilled dishes on the table. Hagan took one, dipped it in the sauce, popped it into his mouth, and stood up. "Call my office and set up another appointment," he told Burroughs, turned to leave, but then stopped, swallowing and sucking his lips. "Excellent shrimp," he said. He took another one, and walked out of the restaurant still chewing.

. . .

He was furious with himself. He never should have agreed to meet with a man like Burroughs, a minor player in the game, a paper pusher. What had he been thinking? What had he to gain from such a meeting? It had been a moment of weakness: There had been nothing on his agenda for the afternoon, and he had given in to the temptation to strut a bit in front of a little man who would be awestruck at having lunch with him. Yes, the man had mentioned a "European problem" he wanted to discuss with him. . . . Hagan snorted. What could he have expected the man to say that might have interested him? No, it was vanity, personal vanity, that had induced him to accept the invitation instead of sending the proper person to respond to such an invitation: his assistant.

Miss Lisle Wintre. Immediately Hagan's anger transferred to her. If she had been in her office this morning as she should have been, Burroughs's call would have been transferred to her automatically and this near embarrassment would have been avoided. He calmed himself as he taxied back to his office by repeating those words: *near* embarrassment. A near thing, yes, but his quick thinking had pulled him out of it.

"Rather interesting reports from our man in Berlin," Burroughs had said. "Came upon your recent interest in the Israeli reports," he had said. Damn. He had nearly been forced to comment. To reveal his hand. Only his quick thinking had saved him.

He leaned back in the taxi and closed his eyes. So long as he maintained total deniability of any involvement in the purported German assassination, he could come out on top no matter how the cookie crumbled. If the plot came to nothing, he could take credit for knowing it was merely a figment of the Israeli imagination. Or, if the assassination took place, he could claim that Wintre had been acting on her own, while at the same time he moved in quickly with a prepared course of action. But it was all-important that he himself never talk to anyone about it, that he maintain total deniability.

By the time he reached his office he had drawn a cloak of calm about his shoulders, and was seething only inwardly. His quick thinking had saved a situation brought on by Wintre's unforgivable absence from duty. "Ah, there you are, Wintre," he said as he entered the office. "Good to see you again. Good trip to New York? When did you get back? Hungry?"

"Yes, sir. I mean no sir. I'm not hungry. The trip was fine; I got back just a few minutes ago. Sorry I'm late, the early-morning flight was canceled. Engine trouble or something. I can report on New York immediately if you like—"

"No time for that right now," he said pleasantly. "I'm sure you must be hungry. Go immediately to the Seagate Restaurant on Eye Street, there's a small gentleman named Burroughs there eating two plates of swordfish." He laughed at her surprised expression. "I had to walk out of a meeting with him. Something urgent came up on the beeper. He wants to talk about the German thing. CIA." He glanced at his watch. "If you get there quickly enough there might be some swordfish left. I'm told it's quite fresh."

6

DAVID MELNIK took a morning train into Philadelphia, though his appointment wasn't until that evening. He had visited the place once before, but hadn't had time to see it properly; he was interested in the city where this republic had been founded. He had never, in fact, been to downtown Philadelphia, and his impression as he left the Thirtieth Street Station was rather depressing. The walk down Market Street could have been a walk through any modern, dirty, falling-to-pieces city anywhere in the world; the beggars, the color of their skin disguised by layers of filth, could have been in Babylon or Bombay, Baghdad or Boston—though not in Berlin or Beijing.

He thought the central square had a nice European touch, and Horner had told him about a small take-out place nearby that sold the best subs on the Eastern Seaboard. "Which means the best subs anywhere in the world. Of course," he added warningly, "they're not kosher."

"What is, these days?" Melnik had answered. As he turned the corner into Twelfth Street he thought that the subs' not being kosher would have prevented his father from trying them. But his father was dead, his ashes blown out of the tank in which he had been cremated while still alive twenty years ago. Those ashes were drifting now over the desert sands, and the fact that the best sub on the Eastern Seaboard wasn't kosher wasn't relevant any longer.

Though it was not yet noon, a line was already forming at the take-out place, and he had to wait ten minutes before it was his turn. And certainly those subs weren't kosher, he thought, as he watched a wide assortment of meats and cheeses being thrown in. On the other hand, all those spices and oils and peppers must certainly have purified it. And at any rate, he thought, as he wandered down the street chewing his first bite, it really was the best sub in the entire world. It smelled like it too, judging from the envious stares of the people he passed.

He found his way down to the waterfront, which had been rebuilt to resemble the original city, and spent the afternoon wandering through the shops and museums there. He had dinner at Bookbinder's and by the time it was over he thought Philadelphia might be the nicest city he had ever seen in the United States. But now evening was approaching, and what he had to look forward to wasn't very nice at all.

"I don't want to take him off the street," Zerolnik said, "because someone might notice and though they're not likely to interfere, we don't want them calling the police and sending out word that a citizen's been kidnapped. We don't want any fuss."

Melnik agreed.

"I also don't want to take him in his own room," Zerolnik went on, "because he may be prepared for such an eventuality, and you never know what little reservoirs of surprises he might have stashed around the place."

Again Melnik agreed. This man knew his job. As well he ought. Zerolnik was the leader of the hit team sent out by Israel to eliminate terrorists. They had been after Lingano for seven months, and were ready to strike. Melnik knew they couldn't be happy to see him; they wouldn't look on any interruption happily. But Zerolnik was a pro, and was willing to cooperate—so long as it didn't mean Lingano would be set free.

"What do you suggest?" Melnik asked.

"His people have a safe house. We'll spook him into going there. On roller skates," he added.

Melnik wasn't sure what the joke was. "Roller skates?" he asked.

Zerolnik smiled. "I love it," he said. "I'm recommending Tel Aviv supply us all with them."

It had been a good game, the Flyers winning with a flurry of goals in the final two minutes, and Charley Lingano returned home on a high. He bounced up the stairs, his limp forgotten, his legs whole and strong again, flailing an imaginary opponent with an imaginary hockey stick, giving him a wicked chop across the face. He skated by him up past the second floor and around the turn in the stairs toward the third, where the instinct he relied on brought him up short and back into this world with a skidding halt, his left leg collapsing slightly under the weight.

He had wired an electric switch into the door so that when the door was opened the light in the apartment came on, just like a refrigerator. The only difference was that this light stayed on, even though the door was closed again, until it was deliberately shut off. Someone entering the apartment surreptitiously, to ambush him, would see only that the light was on when he opened the door, would suppose Lingano had left it on, and would therefore leave it that way.

Lingano was always careful to turn out the light before he left the apartment. Now, as he came up the stairs to the third floor and his head reached floor level he saw, unmistakably, light shining out from under the door. He stopped dead. He tried to think back to the last few seconds: As he came skating up the stairs swatting opponents out of his way, had he made any noise? Would they have heard him from inside the apartment?

He thought not. He hoped not. Quietly he backed down the stairs again until he reached the second floor. Then he turned and hopped quickly down the rest of the stairs and out the front door. He got back into his car and drove away, and saw in his rearview mirror a pair of headlights as they came on. They belonged to a car parked across the street from his apartment house. He watched in the mirror as the car pulled out into the street and began to follow him.

Sons of bitches, he thought. He didn't know who they were but he was willing to bet it was the Jews. They never let you alone, those bastards. He couldn't wait for the day when they were all dead. Yet he smiled as he drove down the street. They thought they were so fucking smart. They were in for a surprise.

He drove slowly, not making any attempt to shake them off. He could just imagine the conversation on the airways right now. "He's heading north on Broad Street, nice and easy. Doesn't seem to know he has a problem. . . ."

They probably thought he had simply forgotten something, and that was why he hadn't entered the apartment. His next stop would reinforce that belief, and by the time they woke up it would be too late.

He turned right on Cheltenham and drove two more blocks, pulling up in front of a twenty-four-hour 7-Eleven. He left the engine running and walked casually inside, noticing that the tailing car had pulled to the curb a block behind him and was waiting there. He almost laughed out loud. They'd be waiting a goddamn long time.

He walked into the store, went straight up to the counter, and took a card out of his wallet and shoved it in front of the face of the Puerto Rican on duty, who was leaning over the counter reading the *National Enquirer*. The kid pushed the card away and stood up and asked him what he wanted. Again he pushed the card in the kid's face, and again the kid backed away and asked what the hell he wanted.

"What do you mean, what do I want? Read the fucking card," he explained.

"I ain't reading no card, what you think I am? You want something, you go pick it up and bring it over here. What you think I am, man? You never been in a store before?"

"You goddamn dumb Spick!" he shouted. "I want the fucking key!"

"What key, man? You crazy? We don't sell keys here. You want a quart of fucking orange juice? You want milk, ice cream? A newspaper? Candy? You want keys, you go someplace else. Leave me alone, huh?"

Lingano would have pulled out his knife and slit the dumb Spick's face open, but he wasn't sure that would do any good. If the key wasn't in the cash register he wouldn't know where to look—

And then the manager came in from the back room. "You got a problem here?" he asked.

"You're goddamn right!" Lingano cursed, and showed him the card. "You read English?"

"Oh yeah," he said, looking up at Lingano with interest as he read the card. "You want the key?"

"Yes, I want the goddamn fucking key. Why don't you teach this dumb Spick here what's he supposed to goddamn do when someone comes in? What are you getting paid for, huh?"

"He's new, he's new. Relax. No problem."

"What do you mean, no problem? What if I come in here and you're out taking a leak or something and this dumbo doesn't know what I'm talking about? What then?"

But the man only smiled and opened the cash register, and Lingano calmed himself down. What was the point? The man took the key out of the cash register and handed it to him, and opened the door to the back room. He reached behind the door and took out a heavy plastic sack, which he handed Lingano, then closed the door behind him.

Lingano sat down on a wooden chair and took a pair of roller skates out of the sack. They were the old-fashioned kind that fasten on to one's shoes. He slipped them on and tightened them, then put out the light and coasted over to the back door. He opened it and stepped out into the alley, moving cautiously at first on the roller skates but then faster and faster as he found his balance. He came to the corner, turned right, and whistled off down the street faster than anyone on foot could possibly have followed him, cutting through narrow alleys so that no one in a car could, either.

He didn't have to worry, though, he thought, stopping to look behind him. Those guys in the car were still sitting there on Cheltenham Avenue, waiting for him to come out of the 7-Eleven.

He hurried on and within five minutes was at the subway station. He dumped the roller skates in a trash can, went in the entrance, and caught the first train south. He took it down to the Spring Garden station, got out, and hurried up Vine Street.

No one paid any attention to him; no one was following. He had evaded them.

He reached the apartment house at 1815 Vine, inserted the key in the front door, and entered. He took the elevator to the fifth floor and limped down the hall, breathing easily once again. From here he could call his friends and get money, a passport and clothes, and be out of the country before the Yids knew they had missed him. He inserted the key into the door of apartment 515, clicked it open, and walked in. He turned on the light, and Zerolnik said, "Good evening, Johnny. It's nice to see you," as the door was pushed shut behind him.

"I've got good news and bad news," Melnik said. Zerolnik had kindly allowed him to take charge of the interrogation. "First of all, we're Israelis."

"Yeah. Like I didn't think you were the Catholic Legion of Decency. So what's the bad news?"

Melnik smiled. "That was the bad news, for you. The good news is that you're not necessarily a dead man. If you're lucky you may know something that we're interested in."

"Yeah, well, the Flyers won tonight so I guess this is my lucky day so far. Go ahead and try me."

"First let me explain the situation," Melnik said. "We know you were in Greece and planted the bomb on El Al flight twenty-one last Novem—"

"I never been in Greece. You want to go back to my apartment? You guys've already been there anyhow. Check the entries in my passport. I never been there, I don't know nothing about that."

Melnik let him finish, then went on. "You don't quite get the picture yet. I'll go slowly, since you're obviously not too bright. I was telling you what we *do* know. The way you might save your life is by telling us something we *don't* know, not by lying to us about the things we do know. Now that's reasonable, isn't it? Simple enough to understand? Have you digested that yet? Good. Now let me go on. We know you put the bomb on that airliner and killed a hundred and eight people.

Women, children, whatever. These gentlemen here''—he gestured to the group that surrounded them, half hidden behind the circle of light from the single lit lamp—''have been tracking you since then and now they want to kill you. I agree with them. You are scum, and everyone in the world would be better off if you were dead. However, it is just possible that you know something I am interested in finding out about. And if you do I am willing to bargain your life for the information.''

''Sure. If I know something, you're willing to let me go and kill more of your people, sure you are.''

''Not quite. You'll be on sort of probation. We'll send you to some-place pleasingly remote, and you'll constantly check in so we can be sure you haven't left. But you'll be alive.''

''Yeah. Well you better get out the electric wires, but let me tell you you're going to burn an awful lot of electricity before you get me to tell you fuckers anything.''

Melnik shook his head. ''For someone who's been in the business as long as you have, you're extraordinarily stupid. We're not going to torture you; we're going to kill you. Let's not waste time playing games. You do what you do because they pay you, and I suppose because you enjoy it. But you have no great moral commitment. If we were to pay you to kill Arabs you'd be happy to do it, so don't waste my time. Zerolnik here wants to dispatch you and get away before anyone else comes wandering by.''

At this, Zerolnik pulled the gun out of his pocket and fitted the silencer to it.

''You probably don't know anything but I thought it was worth my time to take a trip here and find out. If you have anything to tell me about the Kremble murder say it now. Otherwise I'm leaving and you're dying.''

Lingano gave a little laugh. ''The Kremble thing? Well, what the hell. Okay, like you say, I don't owe those little brown-skinned fuckers anything. What do you want to know about it?''

Melnik shook his head. ''No questions. Too easy to lie about specific questions. Just tell me what you know.''

Lingano licked his lips nervously. That crazy fucker with the gun was leaning forward, smiling. He *wanted* to kill him. Lingano wondered who the hell Kremble was and what he might be able to say about it. ''Look, it's a complicated business,'' he said. ''You tell me what you want to know and I'll—''

''Forget it,'' Melnik said, standing up. ''Save your breath for your prayers. It's obvious you don't know anything.''

"Hey, wait a minute! Don't go and leave me with these— Look, maybe I don't know anything, but I can find things out! If my Arabs were involved I can find out—they trust me."

"No," Melnik said, "they don't trust you. Nobody trusts you." He turned to Zerolnik and said, "He's yours."

Lingano started up from his seat, saying "Wait a minute—"

Zerolnik reached into the pocket of his jacket and took out his wallet. Without putting down his gun he extricated a picture and held it out to Lingano, who after a moment's hesitation took it. "What's this?" he asked.

"Look at it," Zerolnik said.

"Yeah, I looked. So what?"

"*Look at it.*"

Lingano looked at it. It was a picture of a young woman and two children.

"My wife," Zerolnik said. "My kids." He took back the photo and carefully replaced it in his wallet. "They were on El Al flight twenty-one." He raised his gun and in the same motion pulled the trigger; Lingano's head splattered against the wall. His body fell backward against the chair, and in a moment the only things moving in the room were his blood and the little shards of skull sliding stickily down the wall.

In the silence Melnik said, "I'm sorry about your family."

"Not to worry," Zerolnik said. "They live in a kibbutz below the Heights." He put the picture away. "But somebody's wife and kids were on flight twenty-one. Lots of wives, lots of kids. I wanted the bastard to think about that with his last thought."

Melnik nodded and looked at Lingano's body. He had been disappointed even before seeing the man. He had heard him limping down the hall toward the apartment, and thought that such a pronounced limp was not what Miss Angstrom had described. And then when the man came into the room and they told him to take a seat in the corner, Melnik had seen the limp with his own eyes. It was not what she had called "scarcely noticeable; someone not trained to see these things might not notice it." No, Lingano had not been their man. "Are you going to leave him here?" he asked.

"Why not?" Zerolnik answered. "It's their apartment. Let them clean up the mess."

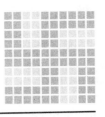

9

1

BEFORE RETURNING to Germany Naman stopped in at the British Museum. Though he had visited here before fairly frequently, losing himself for hours in the Antiquities Hall, he had never had occasion to use the Reading Room. He now followed the signs and came down the narrow hall behind a man who approached the double doors, flashed a card to the guard on duty, and went in. Naman walked up to the guard and said, "I'd like to use the Reading Room." Through the glass panel in the doors he could see the domed room made familiar in dozens of movies; he could almost imagine he could see Karl Marx hunched over a table at the end of one row.

"You'll need a visitor's card, then, won't you?" the guard replied, pointing back down the hall to an office.

Naman went in, explained that he was a visitor from Canada and wanted to use the Reading Room for a few days. The woman gave him a form to fill out. He listed his Canadian name and hotel. The last item on the form was for a reference from his minister. He wrote down "The Reverend François Gilbert, Ravenscrag," and handed it back to the woman. She glanced at it and asked if he had brought the letter of reference with him. He said no. She said, "That's all right, we'll write and ask the Reverend Gilbert to send us a letter. We should have the card ready for you by next week."

Naman had no doubt that Gilbert would be able to put together an official-looking piece of stationery, but he didn't want to waste several days waiting. "I'm in rather a hurry," he suggested.

"You could give the Reverend a phone call and ask him to send the letter right along," she suggested.

"But I'm only here for a few days."

"Well then," she said, beginning to lose patience, "you should have written us before you came, shouldn't you?"

He tried again. "I'm a professor at McGill University in Montreal. I have to do some research while I'm here and I won't have time to wait for the Reverend's letter. I'm sorry I didn't understand your rules before I came, but after all how could I? Couldn't you give me a temporary permit?"

"Oh yes, if you're a professor we can do that. May I see identification, please?"

He handed her his passport.

"No, I mean something identifying you as a professor at McGill."

He smiled apologetically. "I'm afraid I didn't think to bring along my identification card. I thought my passport would be sufficient ID for anything I wanted to do here."

"But it doesn't say you're a professor at McGill, does it? We're always happy to accommodate visiting scholars, but we must know who they are, mustn't we? Otherwise anyone at all could walk in here, couldn't they?"

"What would be the harm if they did?"

"Oh, we couldn't possibly have that," she explained, and that was the end of that. Naman had to smile despite himself. Britain is a land of nearly total freedom, he thought, but they do have this thing about doing things their own way. Anybody in the world is free to come in and use the British Museum Reading Room, but you have to do it their way. The word "stubborn" takes on new meanings in England.

He wandered back into the Antiquities Hall for an hour, then decided he'd try the *Times*. He relaxed on the bus, got off at the corner, and walked back to the building and straight into the lobby. He told the guard at the reception desk that he wanted to look at old copies of the paper, and was directed to the fourth floor. He told the lady behind the desk what he wanted, and she smiled brightly and handed him the microfilm for 1988. "You know how to use the machines, do you?" She gestured to a bank of them lining one wall.

"Yes, thank you," he said, and that was that.

He fed the microfilm into the reader, and started in on January 1.

Since he didn't know what he was looking for, he realized the search might take quite a while. But here was where it all began.

2

BY THE TIME Wintre had arrived at the Seagate Restaurant, Burroughs had left, and so she called him and suggested that she meet him at his office the following day. She found him in a small room on the third floor in the east wing at Langley. She was beginning to get a feel at work for the outward embellishments of power, despite her feeling that such knowledge was degrading, and she realized that this office meant that Burroughs was not exactly a mover and shaker. She was determined not to become the kind of Washington insider who was influenced by such knowledge; knowledge could be power, but it could also be a trap. She had an idea that many people sank into the quagmire of impotence simply from knowing too much about who was important and, more particularly, who was not. So she pushed these thoughts out of her mind as she shook hands with Burroughs, shuddered under the impact of the awful tie he was wearing, and sat down.

Burroughs, for his part, was happy about meeting with this Miss Wintre. He realized he could never have fobbed off the deputy assistant secretary with a cup of coffee, and would have been forced either to pay for today's lunch himself or to attempt to explain to the officious Miss Rogers in accounting why two lunches were necessary for one meeting with the same man. So he had been pleased with Wintre's suggestion that they meet in his office. And when she walked in and he realized that instead of feeding the obnoxious Mr. Hagan he was going to be chatting with a lovely woman, his spirits absolutely soared.

They exchanged pleasantries and he expressed gratitude at her willingness to come all the way out to Langley. She told him she was still learning her way around Washington and was glad of the opportunity to pay a visit and to get to know the place. "It's exciting just being in a building where more is known about the rest of the world than most people know about their husbands and wives," she said.

Yes, that was exactly how Burroughs felt. Even after five years with the Company it still gave him a charge every morning to walk into this building. "That's actually a very good analogy you used," he said, "because sometimes we get the same kind of unpleasant surprises that people can get from their husbands and wives. Matter of fact, that's what I wanted to talk to you about. Our job is principally to avoid those kinds of surprises.''

Wintre was too polite to suggest that the Company hadn't been too successful with that of late. From the Shah of Iran through the Lockerbie disaster to the resilience of Saddam Hussein, there seemed to have been one surprise after another in store for the United States and its intelligence services.

''We understand that Mr. Hagan has some information on the Nazi resurgency in Germany,'' Burroughs said. ''We wondered if you'd be good enough to share his insights with us.''

''I'm afraid there's been a misunderstanding,'' Wintre replied, wondering what was going on. ''Mr. Hagan gave me to understand that you called our office with information that you wanted to share with us. Isn't that the way it usually works?'' She smiled sweetly. ''The intelligence agencies tell the Department of Defense what's going on in other countries, not the other way around. Isn't that what you exist for, after all?''

He returned her smile, more warmly than she had expected. He liked this woman; she was cute as a button, but a tough little cookie. *Wow*, he thought. *Talk about mixing your metaphors.* ''That's the usual course of events,'' he admitted. ''But we're all on the same team, aren't we? Ordinarily the fullback blocks for the quarterback, but if there's a fumble and the fullback picks up the ball—well, the quarterback's got to throw his body into the breach and do what he can, doesn't he?''

''Did you fumble the ball?'' Wintre asked innocently.

Burroughs laughed. She was a tough cookie, but she had a sense of humor. He reminded himself that humor or not, a woman who had managed to get the job of personal assistant to Hagan was probably one of those damn feminists, not only tough as nails but also edgy as a razor. ''I'll show you mine if you'll show me yours,'' he said heartily, man to man. She cringed, and he cursed himself for acting like a jerk whenever he met a pretty woman. ''There is a Nazi resurgency in Germany,'' he plowed on. ''We have full dossiers documenting the fact. These are available for your perusal. But we are receiving conflicting information on the role of the chancellor in all of this. There are indications that Waldner is being supported by the Nazis and in return is giving them protection beyond the bounds of the law: leaking secrets of upcoming police raids, letting files vanish, that sort of thing. On the other hand there are also indications of an opposite nature—signs that he doesn't even know what's going on.''

"And your analysis of the situation is?"

Burroughs spread his hands wide and smiled apologetically. "Premature. Any judgment at this time would be premature. We're still in the information-gathering stage."

"Then why am I here?"

"We have indications of a plot against Waldner's life. The information we have is sketchy, fragmentary, untrustworthy, but it keeps popping up. We're interested because any instability on the part of our allies is naturally of interest to us, but even more so in this case since Waldner is planning a trip to the United States next month and we wouldn't want to be embarrassed by an assassination in our own country. As the fella says, you gotta be clean at home."

She looked at him wonderingly. " 'As the fella says'?" she repeated.

"Just an expression from back home."

"Oh my God," she said softly. "And where is home?"

"Missouri."

Not St. Louis, she decided. "Rolla?"

"No, just a small town. You wouldn't have heard of it. Micanopy."

"I don't believe it. I was born in Carbondale, just down the road."

His face lit up and they smiled at each other for a moment. Then she said, "We left there when I was eight years old." For the first time since joining Hagan's staff she felt worldly, sophisticated, superior. No wonder he was stuck here in a tiny basement office. "If you're running for election," she said gently, offering him some free advice, "that kind of down-home stuff might go. But in any of the civil services, particularly in the CIA, you want to project an air of quiet sophisticated efficiency, not good-old-boy redneck wisdom."

"It's just the way I was brought up," he said with a soft smile.

"Yes, well, you've *been* brought up, haven't you? Now it's time to bring yourself up into the world of Washington. Our backgrounds may be a hindrance, but we're not condemned to live there the rest of our lives, are we?"

He smiled again. "I reckon not." And when she smiled he added, "I surely thank you," laying it on with a trowel. "And any other hints, little lady, I'd surely be thankful for."

She closed her eyes. "Don't ever, *ever,* call any woman you're working with 'little lady.' Does your wife actually like that kind of talk?"

"Not married," he said.

"Well, that explains it."

"What?"

"The tie."

He glanced down at it, shamefaced. "No," he said, "it doesn't."

He was quiet, and she said, "Okay, tell me."

"I'm kind of ashamed; it's childish."

She smiled, suddenly understanding. "You *know* your tie's atrocious, don't you?"

He nodded.

"It's your rebellion, isn't it?" she asked. "Your attempt to buck the anonymity demanded by the Company."

"You make it sound like a philosophy," he said. "It's really just obstinacy."

She nodded. "I've always admired obstinacy," she said.

He lowered his gaze, then forced himself to look up again, right at her, and said, softly, "Maybe you could help me brush up on my manners and ties and things."

"No." She thought a moment, and said it again more firmly. "No. I'm sorry, that's not my thing."

He nodded, chastened, and she went on briskly, "I still don't understand why you're talking to me about the Germans at this time, if you don't have enough information to suggest action."

"Information is the name of the game," he said with forced vivacity, and then leaned forward over his desk. "And some of our information is very disturbing. A funny thing, for example, happened in L.A. A guy got killed. A car bomb went off, is what happened. Dead as a doornail, burnt to a crisp. Maybe not so unusual these days, but the guy's name was Walter Naman. Mean anything to you?"

It struck no chord in her memory. "Is he a German?" she asked. "Connected with the Nazi movement?"

"No and yes," Burroughs said. "Naman's an American citizen, but he was born in Germany. Grew up in one of the concentration camps. Jewish. He came to America after the Second World War and went to school here. Ended up working for us. He was a good man, I'm told, one of the best, but he had this thing about the Nazis. That's all he really wanted to do, round up all the old Nazis and prosecute. Or just kill them, if you can believe all the stories they tell. He's actually been running a consulting business out in L.A., advising big business how to avoid getting their people kidnapped or knocked off in Latin America, that sort of thing, but what he's really been doing is going after the old Nazis.

"Now, we don't have any information that he was ever involved with the neo-Nazi movement in Germany. All our information is that he was after the old guys, the real Nazis from the Second World War. But what makes me wonder is that car bomb going off in L.A. and killing him."

"You think this may be related to the supposed German assassination?"

"Well, who knows? Maybe he was on to something, found out something about what was happening, or maybe even they just thought that he might because—no matter about all the publicity about Wiesenthal—he's really the number one Nazi-hunter in the world. The most effective, you know what I mean? So maybe he knew something, or maybe they just wanted him out of the way in case."

"Maybe," Wintre agreed. "And maybe he'd made other enemies."

"Oh sure, that's possible. A man in his business is going to make enemies, no doubt about it. Maybe he foiled one too many kidnapping attempts in Bolivia or Argentina, and somebody decided they didn't need this guy bothering them anymore. Sure, it's possible. On the other hand . . ."

"Any clues to the bombing?"

"*Nada*. Boom, burn, that's the end of it. Any possible evidence goes up in smoke. A professional job for sure, but who the professionals were, the L.A. cops have no idea. So, like I say, maybe it's nothing to do with the Germans, but it makes me wonder. Anyhow, while I was computer-regressing all informational inputs on the situation I came across a statement from our FBI friends that you had reported to them that Israel had reported to you that there was indeed to be an assassination attempt during Waldner's visit here, and furthermore you reported that the Israeli report was not to be taken seriously. If this is true, it's important in fitting together all these conflicting data that are coming out of Germany today. Could you please tell me how you can be so sure that the Israelis are wrong?"

"No," she said without missing a beat, and then said nothing else.

"No?" he asked after a moment. "No, what?"

"No, sir?" she asked, and they stared at each other for a moment until he realized that was a joke. He smiled politely, but then repeated his question. She shook her head. "I'm afraid I can't tell you anything about our sources. I don't have the authority to reveal them." And despite another round of questions and mildly veiled threats, she wouldn't budge another step.

As she left the building she was thinking: Does Hagan really know anything that indicates the German assassination plot is a phony? She hadn't realized that the CIA actually had hard information, and that a man had been killed.

She thought she'd better find out just exactly what it was that Hagan did know.

3

THE VIEW was incredibly bleak, the wind incredibly bitter. It blew with wicked intensity directly from the white-capped North Sea, rose straight up over the sheer cliffs, and spilled over against Carlos Grass's face.

"That's him sitting by the edge," the nurse said. "We put that bench there for them to use in the summertime, but Herr Geiss likes it all year 'round. I think he prefers it in the winter because there's no one else out there to bother him."

"I hope he won't think I'm bothering him," Grass said.

"Oh no." She laughed. "The people who bother him are the other patients who want to talk about themselves. Anyone who comes here to ask him to talk about himself will be more than welcome, I assure you. He's expecting you, Herr Lindemann. He's been looking forward to it since you called."

"Thank you," Grass said, setting off down the path to where the white-haired man sat bundled in blankets. The wind brought water to Grass's eyes and made his nose run, but he didn't mind. He never thought about such things as whether he was comfortable or not. The only thing that bothered him was that he might be wasting his time, and that worry he brushed from his mind. For there was nothing else to be done; to find a man, you had to know the man. To know the man, you had to talk to the people in his life. You had to gather details, you had to be patient. And finally, when you knew the man, you knew what he would be doing, where he would go. Finding a needle in a haystack isn't so terribly hard if you have a metal detector.

This was a funny place for a nursing home, he thought; but then, maybe not. Maybe it was good to get slowly accustomed to the chill of death rather than plunging in without thought, as most of us do. "Herr Geiss," he said softly as he came up, not wanting to surprise the old man and shock him into a sudden heart attack. Not before he talked to him, at any rate.

Herr Geiss paid no attention, and so Grass stepped around the bench to come in front of him and said again, "Herr Geiss?"

The old man's eyes blinked open, and he looked around in astonishment, obviously not knowing where he was. Grass hoped this wouldn't be another wild-goose chase. He had already been to see two other people; one of them had died six months before, and the other proved senile but had at least given him Geiss's name and address.

Geiss blinked twice more. The final blink seemed to do it: His eyes lost the vacant stare and focused on Grass's face. "Herr Lindemann?" he asked.

That was a good sign. Maybe this wouldn't be a wasted visit after all. "Yes," Grass said. "I phoned yesterday and you were good enough to say you'd talk to me."

"Glad to talk to you. Glad to talk to anyone sensible. Don't get much of that around this place. Sit down, sit down, make yourself comfortable." He edged sideways on the bench, and Grass sat down beside him. "You should have brought a blanket," he went on. "It's cold out here, with that wind."

"You seem to be enjoying it," Grass said.

"Enjoying it! Are you out of your mind? It's colder than the depths of hell here."

"I thought hell was supposed to be hot," Grass said mildly.

"Cold," Geiss insisted. "Cold as the depths of hell. It's what we deserve, it's what we all deserve. We'll freeze for eternity."

And Grass thought: Here we go again. Another babbling idiot. But then Geiss calmed down. "That's what you said you wanted to talk about," he said.

"Hell? No, I'm afraid not. You must have misunderstood me."

"The Nazis," Geiss said. "The Third Reich. *Der ganze Führer*. The Leader who led us all into hell."

"Not exactly that either."

The old man turned back from the wild North Sea in surprise. "When Sister Anna told me yesterday that you called, she said you were writing a book about the beginnings of the Nazi movement and wanted to talk to me about what I remembered."

"Well, yes. But I'm a bit more focused than that. I'm trying to follow the career of a friend of yours. Walter Naman."

Geiss stared out over the sea and then suddenly, without warning, broke into violent tears which the wind whipped away from his cheeks and flung off into the air, leaving behind little frozen patches of red skin. "I'll freeze in hell forever for what I did to that boy!" he wailed.

"I understood you were his friend."

"Of course I was his friend! His father's friend, and so his friend.

And what did I do? Murdered his father, murdered his mother, destroyed the boy's soul."

"You were a Nazi?"

Geiss huddled deeper into his blankets and stared out over the sea. "How could one not be a Nazi?" he asked. "I was a lawyer, they were the government. . . ."

"His parents died in the concentration camps. What was your connection with them?"

"Connection? Mine?" He started up suddenly. "I—I had no connection. I didn't even know about them!"

"Then what did you mean, you killed his mother and father?"

"I *should* have known about them. We all should have. We didn't want to know. Those swine couldn't have done all that if we all hadn't, each of us, managed to look the other way. When they took the Namans away, they said they were resettling them in the East. We *wanted* to believe they would be well treated."

"But Walter survived," Grass plodded on after the man's voice had drifted off into silence.

"Survived? Yes, he survived. He came to us in 1945, showed up on the front doorstep like a wet rat, starved and shivering, him and little Lise Berthold. You know about Lise?"

"No," Grass said. "Tell me."

He had expected this trip to be a waste of time, Grass thought as he walked back up the path toward the nursing home. He had come because you never knew what information was going to turn out to be useful. He had hoped at best to learn something about Naman's formative years, about the kind of man he would have had to grow into from such a beginning. As it turned out, Grass had done somewhat better.

Geiss had joined the party in 1934, he said, because it seemed like the only group that could establish order out of the anarchy of the twenties. Later, when he saw how evil the Nazis were, he wanted to quit—but he was being given rapid promotion, as the Nazis established their own people in power, while if he quit they would have destroyed him. So, caught between the carrot and the stick, he stayed and prospered. Grass could understand that.

In the spring of 1945 Walter Naman had appeared suddenly on his doorstep. The front doorbell had rung; he had gone to answer it; and when he opened the door there was Walter, shivering with fever, clothed in rags, crusted with dirt—and he looked *good* compared to the girl he pointed out, who was sitting on the ground beside the front gate; she had been too exhausted to walk those last few steps, or perhaps too frightened to ask for help.

They were only children, filthy, frightened, and exhausted. They had escaped from Auschwitz and walked across Germany, all the way back home. They had come to Walter's father's friend Hans Geiss, and literally collapsed in his arms. He had taken them in, of course, now that the war was nearly over and it was clear that the Nazis had lost.

Geiss's house was still standing in 1945, but few others were. There were no private doctors left, and the hospitals were jammed with soldiers. He fed Walter and Lise, and Walter began to recover. Lise did not. God knew what those monsters had done to her, Geiss said. When he finally managed to talk a doctor into attending her he said her wretched body was racked with syphilis and gonorrhea; it was simply shattered inside. She never even talked; Geiss never heard her speak a word. She just stared at people and shivered all the time. God alone knew how she had managed to walk across Germany with Walter.

Walter recovered, in a manner of speaking, though he would never be normal. At first he was afraid of everything. If someone knocked on the door he thought it was the Gestapo and ran away to hide. He was afraid of the dark, of bright lights, of noises, of silence, of people, of being alone. Slowly he got better; slowly these fears left him. He began to function. But he would never be normal. One fear that never left him, Geiss said, was a terrible fear of being shut up anywhere. Even in a plain room, the doors had to be open. At night they had to leave his bedroom door open. He never got over that, not up to the day he left. "You know why?" Geiss asked.

"It's understandable," Grass said.

"No, you don't understand, not yet. First you have to know what his first job at the camp was. They separated him from his parents, tore him away and threw him in with a bunch of boys. They gave him a bucket and a pair of pliers, and when the gas chamber was finished they sent the boys in and locked the doors behind them. The boys climbed over the dead bodies and pulled the gold teeth out of the mouths of dead bodies that had been their parents, uncles, aunts. . . . And if later, when the bodies were being carted to the ovens, if the guards found any gold still in the dead mouths they showed the boys how to do the job better by tearing out their own little teeth."

"Terrible," Grass sympathized. "Where did he go when he left you?"

He had relatives in the United States. Geiss got in touch with them.

They agreed to take the boy, and Geiss had enough connections to get him the proper papers. Six months after Walter showed up at the door, Geiss put him on the tram for the airport, and he left for America.

And that was that, Grass thought, preparing to leave, but Geiss wasn't through. "Walter didn't want to go," he said. "He didn't want to leave Lise. But his relatives didn't want a dying girl who had been the Germans' whore." He shrugged apologetically. "I told them the truth about her. My wife wanted me to lie so they would take her, and Walter couldn't—or wouldn't—understand how sick she was, but I knew she couldn't have made the journey; she would have died on the way, and I couldn't accept that. Not in here." He gestured to his breast.

Spare me, Grass thought impatiently. He had heard enough about the girl, but he couldn't stop the flow of words.

"The day before Walter left," Geiss went on, "the doctor came again. Lise was getting worse, not better. We fed her, but she stayed skinny and her belly was swollen and getting bigger every day. The doctor told us why: She was pregnant. So of course Walter didn't want to leave. But the visa was explicit and it would have been impossible to get a delay. There were so many people wanting to go to America that if he had turned it down he would have been swamped behind all the others. I told him she would be all right, we would take care of her and then send her and the baby to him, and finally he left."

The old man shook his head sadly. "Of course she died. The baby inside killed her. The last little Nazi. *Ach so,* at least it died with her."

Grass nodded thoughtfully. He was glad now of his patience in listening to the story. You never knew—it might come in handy. "Did you stay in contact with Walter?" he asked.

Geiss shook his head. "We wrote that Lise and the baby were dead, and he wrote back a few times. And that was all."

"You never saw him again?" Grass asked, standing up.

"Not for many years. He wanted to cut his childhood out of his life, to forget it. You can't blame him for that. When he did come back it was only because he was grateful to me. I blame him for that."

"What do you mean?"

"It was about ten years ago. I had pneumonia, and somehow he knew about it. I looked up from my fever and there he was, out of nowhere. He said he wanted to come see me before I died." The old man laughed. "He talks like that, you know. Very straightforward. None of the social graces. He said he was grateful because I saved his life, and he wanted to thank me and tell me what he had done with it."

"How can you blame him for that?"

"I was the one who broke his life. Me and everyone else like me who didn't do anything when that *verstunkene* bastard Hitler was taking power. He should have come to curse me on my deathbed, not to bless me."

"To forgive is divine," Grass said.

"Maybe." He gave a coarse cackle. "I hope so. I can't forgive. It would be a pleasant surprise if God turns out to do so. Well, you know what Heine said."

"Who?"

"Heine, the great poet. On his deathbed they brought him a priest who asked if he repented all his sins. And he said no, he repented nothing in his life. And then he said, 'God will forgive me anyhow; that's his profession.'" He cackled again, then stopped suddenly. "Somehow I don't think so," he said.

"What did he tell you? Naman, when he came back to see you."

"Oh, you must know all that. How he grew up in the United States. Worked with the CIA. That's why you're interested in him, isn't it?"

"Yes, of course. But I'd like to talk to as many individuals who knew him personally as possible. Did he mention any names?"

"People he worked with, you mean?"

"Or friends."

"He had no friends. He grew up without any way to talk to people, to make contact. In his heart he never left Auschwitz. He saw everyone as either guard or prisoner, to be feared or avoided. The only hope of survival was to be alone, ready to move on when the other person died."

"Didn't he mention anyone? He must have had somebody."

Geiss sat there for a while, staring off over the sea until Grass thought he had forgotten the question, and then he began to nod his head. "Yes," he said. "There were two men. No women." He glanced up at Grass. "He never had a woman in his life, did you know that? When little Lise died . . ."

"Tell me about the men."

Geiss scrunched up his eyes, trying to remember. "One was a German. A spy, or something like that, what do you call it? An intelligence agent." He shook his head slowly. "Can't remember his name."

"Müller?" Grass prompted, picking a name at random.

Geiss shook his head.

"Telemach?" And again the old man shook his head. "Vorshage?" Grass asked, and this time Geiss smiled and nodded vehemently. "Yes, that was it!" He was happy to have remembered the name, but Grass was not overjoyed; Vorshage was the one man he already knew about, and the one man he couldn't talk to. "You said there was someone else."

"What?"

"You said there were two men."

Geiss nodded, pursing his lips in thought. "Yes," he said. "An older man. My age. Someone who had worked in the French underground while Walter was in Auschwitz. I suppose that made Walter feel he could trust him."

"Is he still alive?"

Geiss laughed. "Who knows? An old man like me, why would he still be alive?" He stopped laughing and asked bitterly, "Why would he want to be alive?"

"But you don't know?"

He shook his head.

"And his name?"

He was silent. Grass waited. He had no real hope that this old man would remember anything of use; he had come here because he had nowhere else to go, he hadn't been able to find anyone else who had known Naman. And then suddenly the old man said, "Nevermore."

Grass waited, standing there in the North Sea wind while the old man's mind wandered through a maze of memories, trying to sort out the clue that would bring the name to his lips. "Nevermore," he mumbled again, his eyes looking vacantly into the distance. *Einmals war ein Mit'nacht traurig* . . . 'The Raven'!" he broke out. "Ravenscrag! He lives in Ravenscrag. In England," he explained. "Walter's friend."

"You said he was French."

"Yes, an old Frenchman. Escaped to England when the French surrendered, worked for De Gaulle, returned to France when the Allies invaded, was captured by the Gestapo, tortured, but freed when the Americans came. Went back to England to live after the war. A photographer. Yes, Ravenscrag."

"What is his name?" Grass was busy scribbling down the old man's words on a notebook he had pulled hurriedly out of his pocket.

Geiss shook his head. He couldn't remember the man's name. But the name of the town had stuck in his memory. "Ravenscrag," he kept repeating. "That's where he lives in England. Isn't that a funny name?"

He was looking up at Grass, proud of himself for the strength of his memory, and he smiled happily. For the last time in his life. Grass smiled too, and reached out and patted him on the cheek, then slid his hand down to the old man's throat and found his carotid artery. It took amazingly little pressure, and only a few seconds, to cut off the blood supply to the brain. The old man's hands were tangled in the blanket; they struggled to get out, but fell lifeless before they could. He was so feeble that Grass didn't have to squeeze very hard at all, and when he finished he saw that there was no obvious bruising on the neck. In a place like this, with a man so old, no one would suspect anything. And if by chance anyone else came to talk to him, they would never know that someone had been here to ask him about Walter Naman. Grass adjusted the blanket around him and walked back up the path to the nursing home.

He hadn't expected this visit to be terribly productive, he thought, glancing down at his notebook as he walked. But at least he had obtained another contact. He wished the old man had remembered the name, but Ravenscrag certainly wasn't one of England's larger cities; how many photography shops could there be there? He put the notebook back in his pocket as he approached the main building. He told Sister Anna that they had had a nice chat about Herr Geiss's role in the government of the thirties, and that now he was dozing in the cold sun. Sister Anna said she'd give him another hour, and then bring him in for tea. Grass thanked her for her kindness and drove back into town.

4

BASICALLY THERE WERE three ways to kill a man like Waldner, who was surrounded by security agents whose only mission in life was to detect and thwart an assassination attempt. One way was with a bomb. But Naman couldn't use a letter bomb, because Waldner didn't open his own mail. A car bomb conceivably might work, but gaining access to the chancellor's car would be extremely difficult, if not impossible. There was the further—and to Naman's mind, overwhelming—objection that a car bomb must necessarily kill more than the one person targeted.

The second method was with a gun: A long-range sniper, properly positioned and with the requisite skill, could do the job, as was demonstrated by the Kennedy killing. But again there were objections. He himself, Naman thought, no longer had the eyesight or the steady hand needed to pull off such a job; that meant bringing in someone else, and once you brought in a second man the secret was being shared and likely to be leaked. Furthermore, the target could never be expected to be alone in any situation where the killer might catch sight of him, and it took a great deal of patience to wait, holding a long-range rifle, while other people continually drifted into and out of the gunsight between you and your target. The temptation to let loose a fusillade of shots, knocking the other people out of the way and creating a clear line of fire, was almost overwhelming. Even in the classic Kennedy killing, an unintended victim was hit. Still, this might have to be the method of choice, unless the third method could be worked out.

The third method was simply something else—anything else—neither gun nor bomb. It was an instrument tuned to one particular frequency, chosen to resonate to the frequency given off by the target. It was a method, any method, chosen because it fit the personality or physical characteristics or mode of operation or psychological weakness of that particular target and of no one else. But in order to choose such a method one had to know the target intimately; one had to find a parameter that identified and exposed the target and no one else.

And the problem, Naman was finding as he went through *The Times* dating from the year Waldner had taken office, was that the man seemed to be a chameleon. He took on the colors of his background; he did not stand out in any way.

Or, at least, not in any way brought to the notice of *The Times*. It would have been lovely if Waldner's hobby was skydiving, or if he liked to camp out in the wilderness by himself, or if he frequented brothels or any other place where he would be trying to divest himself of his security guards. But nothing in *The Times* suggested anything of the sort.

Walter stepped outside the building and breathed in the cold air to clear his head. These results were discouraging, but hardly unexpected. It would have been wonderful if something had jumped off the page and shouted "This is the way!" But as he wandered through the foliage of Gottfried Waldner's life, none of the bushes had burst into illuminating flame and spoken to him. It would have been wonderful if something of the sort had happened, and it would be wonderful if this evening the sky should suddenly blaze with light and a harmonious voice announce that there would be peace on earth from now on; it would be wonderful, but Walter wasn't counting on it.

Nor had he counted on coming up with the answer on his first day of research. Still, it *would* have been nice. . . . He glanced at his watch. It was just after three o'clock, which meant that he had missed all chance of a pub lunch. It was so silly; he knew they would have had food left over from lunch, food that they would put out again in a few hours for evening snacks, but if he went in and asked for something to eat he would be greeted with the simple reply that it wasn't eating hours, and no appeal to reason would have the force to break through that simple wall.

He paused outside a Wimpy's, hating to go in but finding no alternative. With the pubs not serving food and the fish-and-chips shops all gone from central London, the only alternatives were a full meal at a restaurant or some fast food at a Wimpy's. His palate hated the fast food, but his intestinal system couldn't take a full meal in the middle of the day without putting him to sleep for the rest of the afternoon.

And so he reluctantly pushed open the door—and suddenly stopped. A small sign on the door warned those seeking admittance that a microwave oven was in operation behind the counter. With a sudden dazzling clarity he saw again *The Times* of a January 13 several years old, a full-page profile in depth of Gottfried Waldner, at the time a growing influence in West Germany's Christian Democrat Party. He scrolled mentally down to the next to last paragraph in the middle column, and there it was: the clue that jumped off the page at him, the burning bush.

"Watch it, mate!"

"What? Oh, sorry." He stepped back out of the entrance as a young, cloth-capped man led his three children out. Naman turned around, all thoughts of a Wimpyburger forgotten, and hurried to find a phone. He had to call Gilbert immediately and get him to write or phone the British Museum. He had to get access to the Reading Room as quickly as possible. He had a lot of technical research to do.

Part
Three

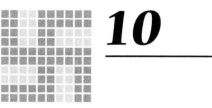

10

1

"I've got good news for you," Assistant Commissioner Ronald Waxman said. Horner smiled and sat down. He didn't expect that his new office would be anything like as plush as this one, but it would be a big step up from the space he shared back at the precinct.

"That new job we've been talking about for you," Waxman said. "Well, you can forget about it."

Horner didn't believe he had heard right. "What?" he asked. And it was only then that he noticed the look of embarrassment on Waxman's face.

"Yeah," he said. "Like, I had to pull some strings, you know, but what the hell. You've worked long enough and hard enough, and that back of yours wouldn't be getting any better sitting hunched over a desk all day. And all night too; you know what those jobs are like. So anyhow, I managed to convince the powers that be that if anybody deserved a rest, you do. You can take early retirement starting July first. Beginning of the fiscal year."

Horner just stared at him until Waxman lowered his eyes. Then Horner said, "Okay, boss. The press conference is over. There's nobody in here but you and me. What gives?" He asked the question that had to be asked, but already he didn't give a damn. He knew what the answer would be. He didn't know what form it would take, what words would be used, but he knew from what Waxman had just said that the decision was already made.

"Shit, Jolly, I'm sorry," Waxman said, his gruff good humor collapsing like a spent condom. That was one of his favorite similes.

The apology helped a little. At least it was better than the phony winning-the-lottery-congratulations crap he had started out with.

"You know I wanted you for this position," he said.

"Who gets it instead?"

"Nobody gets it! It's gone. Wiped out." Waxman threw up his hands in exasperation. "What am I gonna tell you? You know the situation as well as I do. This goddamn city doesn't have a pot to piss in, let alone they should have a pot they can take money out of for new jobs."

"It's a job that needs to be done, for chrissake."

"Sure, sell me on the idea. Go ahead, argue with me. You think I don't know? You think I didn't go down on the mat with them on this? There's just no fucking money."

"Okay." Horner nodded. He had been working for the city long enough so that Waxman's last line had become a refrain more familiar to him than "Stardust." "But what's this crap about taking early retirement?"

"I got you a disability pension, too, for your back. You'll make out fine."

"What the *fuck* are you *talking* about?" Horner shouted.

"Christ, take it easy. I did the best for you I could. It's not just new positions," Waxman said. "We've got to *cut* positions. Each of us— uniforms, detective, maintenance, even administrative. We've got a quota to meet. Now I can either kick a couple of new detectives back to the street, which means uniforms kicks two rookies out on their ears with no pension, no money, no nothing, after they've just finished their training, or I can find someone like you who makes enough money to cover two rookie salaries and lay you off with a full pension plus disability which will bring you damn near as much as you're getting now, for the rest of your life, for doing nothing. I don't want to be the mugger, Jolly, I want to be the good guy. So you tell me, which would be the fair way to go?"

"You think I'm not as effective as two rookies?" Horner asked quietly. "The department's going to be better off this way?"

"Shit no, you know I don't think that. The department's not gonna be better off, not today, not tomorrow, not this year or next year. But the world doesn't come to an end next year, you know? We gotta look to the future. If we start cutting all the kids, pretty soon the word gets around and then we don't get any more kids looking to join, you know what I mean? Not good kids, anyway, not the kind we need. I gotta protect the kids, kid.''

Horner looked away. For some reason he felt ashamed. "There's nothing wrong with my back," he muttered. "Just a little twinge once in a while."

"Don't go around telling anyone that outside this office, okay?"

They were quiet for a moment, and then Horner broke out: "If you're going to pay me retirement and pension, it's almost as much as I'm making now. So how are you saving the department any money by getting rid of me?"

Waxman just looked at him and shook his head, and Horner answered himself: "Yeah, yeah, I know. Retirement and disability monies come out of a different pot, right? They don't come out of your salary sheet. So it doesn't really save the city a penny, but it makes the books balance, right? Hizzoner announces he's slashing police costs, only he's not saving the citizens a goddamn penny, is he?"

"What am I gonna tell you, Jolly? You know the game as well as I do."

"Yeah. Yeah, I do," Horner said, and they both digested that for a moment. Had the breaks been just a little different, Horner could have looked forward to sitting in Waxman's chair a few years from now. Instead he'd be rotting his ass away on a rocking chair in Florida.

"You stay on the payroll till June first," Waxman said, "but I'm not gonna expect you to break your butt. I'll leave it up to you what you want to work on."

"Right," Horner said, and heaved himself up out of the chair. At the door he stopped to turn around. "Any chance of this, you know, changing?"

"Any chance? Sure. The comptroller finds ten million bucks he didn't know he had somewhere in the books. Donald Trump dies and leaves his money to the police department. Hizzoner decides to put barbed wire around Harlem, the South Bronx, and Red Hook, and legalizes prostitution, drugs, and gambling. Any or all of the above, and we'll be able to afford you again. And, oh yeah," Waxman said as Horner turned again to leave, "if Christ Almighty fucking Jesus comes back walking across the East River and declares the Kingdom of Heaven on Earth this fiscal year, I guess maybe things will be okay. Short of that, I wouldn't count on anything changing."

"The scum's so thick on the East River *I* could walk across it," Horner said. "But I guess that wouldn't count for much."

Waxman shook his head. "No, not much," he said.

2

"IT'S A QUESTION of sensitivity," Reynolds was saying. William Hagan nodded encouragingly. "It's not really a big thing," Reynolds went on modestly, "but in its own little way it's a new concept. A breakthrough, really, for the next generation of fighter planes. It would be a shame not to develop it." He paused. "It would be a crime."

Hagan made the proper noises, and Reynolds went on. "What we have is a 512-channel laser photometer which is going to change the nature of the whole ball game. The reason you can't see our Stealth fighters on radar is not because of any magic—no one's repealed Maxwell's laws of electromagnetic transmittal and reflectance—it's just that little by little we've developed techniques to cut down on radio reflectivity." He paused for a second. "They call it reflectivity, but really it's a question of absorptivity and re-emission." He waved his hand negligently.

"These details don't matter. The concept is the important thing," Hagan prompted him.

"Exactly. So if you put the wings and tail on at the proper angle you cut down resonance, and the effect is that the radar signal is diminished. You make things out of carbon base instead of iron-based alloys, and this diminishes both absorption and re-emission, and again you're cutting down the radar signal. You start putting all these things together and little by little you get a plane that's more and more invisible to radar, and finally you get something you can put into production as a Stealth fighter or bomber. But there's no big breakthrough anywhere along the line. You haven't made it invisible, like with the Invisible Man, you ever see that picture? Claude Rains?"

"A classic," Hagan agreed.

"Well, it's nothing like that. You've simply cut down the intensity of the radar signal the plane will send out when a beam hits it. The radar signal's still there, but it's lost most of its intensity. So all you have to do to render the target visible again is make a receiver that's more sensitive, that will pick up these lower intensities. That's what we've done."

"You haven't actually done it yet," Hagan pointed out.

"That's what we're developing, then. The idea is simple, like all good ideas. A laser beam instead of a radio beam. Radio beams spread out and cover a wide angle, which is good. But this causes them to diminish in intensity, which is bad. A laser beam has zero diminution over distance, which is fantastic, but it doesn't spread out, which is bad: It's like a gun, you only hit what you're aiming at, and the whole idea of radar is to search a wide area. So what we're doing is to combine the two. We have 512 different laser beams, in effect, which means we can search in 512 different directions, which means we can cover the whole damn sky and still maintain the sensitivity of each individual beam. With the new flat diamond chips we're developing, which are a thousand percent more efficient than silica chips, we can miniaturize the whole thing to fit into the nose of the new Advanced Tactical Fighter. This means no matter what kind of a Stealth fighter the other side develops, our boys will see it and shoot it down. I'm talking about a device that will give our country technical superiority and security in the air through the twenty-first century. And we're only talking a few billion dollars here. You don't get bargains like that every day."

Reynolds smiled expansively with this irrefutable close to his argument, and Hagan nodded and said, "Of course you still have the Fessenden problem."

"Beg your pardon?"

"Reginald Fessenden, the man who invented radio."

"I thought that was Marconi."

Hagan shook his head. Reynolds was CEO of one of the country's biggest defense corporations but he didn't know diddly-squat about the technical side of things, no matter how he went on about 512-channel analyzers and flat diamond chips. He could have been selling shoes or brassieres. Hagan liked to impress these people with his own technical knowledge; he took the time to learn what he was talking about. "Fessenden invented the heterodyne receiver," he said, "which made wireless transmission of the human voice possible. Marconi was a talker and a businessman; Fessenden was a scientist."

Reynolds wiggled his fingers in dismissal. He hired scientists when times were good and fired them when times were bad, like janitors. He was not impressed by them.

"Fessenden's heterodyne receiver," Hagan went on, "proved the answer to radio transmission. But not until someone asked the right question. At the time he invented it all transmissions were being made with spark-gap techniques, and the heterodyne had no advantage over the coherer receiver for picking up such signals. It was only when

General Electric came up with a continuous-wave transmitter that the heterodyne came into its own. It took twenty years after Fessenden got the patent before anyone would put up the funds to build the thing."

Reynolds glanced at his watch. "So?"

"So that's what I call the Fessenden problem. An invention that addresses a tough problem isn't going to be built until someone asks the right question. And right now people are asking the wrong question."

"What's the right question?"

"The *wrong* question is, Why do we need a defense against Stealth fighters when we're the only ones in the world making them? You don't seriously propose that Iran, Iraq, or Syria is going to come up with Stealth technology? China isn't interested, and the U.S.S.R. doesn't even exist anymore. What you've got is a defense against a threat that doesn't exist."

"We're talking about the future," Reynolds said.

Hagan agreed. "What we need is for someone to start asking, What are those guys up to now?"

"Who are 'those guys'?"

"*That* is the right question," Hagan said. "And the answer is that we've got to identify a potential enemy capable of producing the threat before we can sell the countermeasure." He offered Reynolds a cigar.

Reynolds lit up and puffed out a cloud of smoke. "Who do you see on the horizon?" he asked.

"Nobody. That's the problem."

"And what's your solution?"

"We've got to look *over* the horizon." Hagan paused. "What would you say to a resurgent Nazi Germany?"

Reynolds thought about that, then smiled. "You're a good man, Hagan," he said. *The man is an asshole,* he thought, *but he knows his way around.*

"And the higher I go, the better I'll be. For my friends."

Reynolds nodded. "Gratitude is the name of the game," he said. "You scratch mine, I'll scratch yours. And I've got lots of scratch."

"So our friend in the CIA thinks this fellow Naman was killed as a prelude to a real assassination attempt?" Hagan asked. "Is that it?"

Wintre said, "It's a possibility. But not if you have definite knowledge that the assassination plot is phony."

"Definite knowledge?" Hagan repeated the term. He seemed amused by it, he swirled his lips around it. "Def-i-nite knowl-edge. When I was a boy I had definite knowledge that God had parted the Red Sea for the

Israelis. The Bible told me so. What could be more definite than God's word?" He laughed and shook his head. "When you grow up and learn that not even God's word is 'definite knowledge,' what is? No, I don't have 'definite knowledge' that the assassination is a paranoid fantasy. So I want you to stay with Melnik and learn whatever he learns, and tell me about it so we can decide how best to cope. But I want you to keep in mind that there are ten million different plots floating around Washington on any given day and if we were to take official action on all of them the government would be paralyzed." He paused. "I can't give you details," he added slowly, as if reluctantly deciding to let her in on official secrets, "and I don't pretend to call it definite knowledge, but reliable sources tell me that the Israelis are pumping up this story for their own purposes. I would be very much surprised—*very much*—if these sources were wrong. So don't get taken in by this man Melnik. Your presumptive mode must be that it's all nonsense. Don't let him bother people without clearing it with me first."

"I'm to block his efforts?"

"You're to act as a buffer between him and our people. If he wants something done, you let me know, and together we'll decide."

"He's not to know this, of course."

"Of course. Nor is there any need to tell him about the Naman death; I'm sure it has nothing to do with anything." Hagan smiled warmly, chillingly. "You understand your position. You're his liaison, his help-mate, his wife. In the Washington sense"—he smiled again—"not the biblical." He paused, dropping the smile. "And like any wife, you'll lie to him when you think it necessary." He waved his fingers in dismissal, unconsciously imitating Reynolds.

If Hagan was telling her that her job was to spy on and, not to mince words, *sabotage* Melnik's investigation, Wintre decided, she would find out why; she would find out what Hagan knew. It seemed to her a long time since she had come to work for Hagan, and in those two and a half weeks she had not wasted her time. He had made it clear at the outset that he expected her to find her sea legs on her own, and she had set about to do it. She had begun by cultivating and making friends with Hagan's secretary, and from there had gone on to do the same with all the contacts she had been able to pry out of her. She discovered who Hagan's men were in the FBI and at the CIA, at the various defense departments, in the White House, and among the press. She now set about calling or visiting each of them in turn, and found out nothing. Or rather, she found that they knew nothing.

She was convinced finally that no one had told Hagan there was nothing in the Israeli story; none of them knew anything about any supposed assassination. There was always the possibility that Hagan had a super-secret source, but Miss Pherson had been with him since before he became deputy assistant secretary of state, and Wintre didn't believe he had any sources Miss Pherson didn't know about. Miss Pherson would at least have known there was someone she didn't know about, because Hagan would be incapable of not letting slip little bragging hints about his new contact.

What was his game? she wondered.

3

"I'M NOT ASKING for tea and sympathy," Melnik said. "I don't want you to hold my hand."

"I know," Horner said. "You think I don't know? You think I haven't been there? It's a bitch." He took a bottle and a couple of glasses out of his desk drawer and poured them each a shot.

Melnik shook his head. "It's too early in the morning."

"Sure it is," Horner agreed, handing him the glass. "*L'chayim,*" he said, and Melnik laughed bitterly. "I mean it," Horner insisted. "To life." He raised his glass; Melnik nodded reluctantly and they both drank.

"You squash an insect," Horner said, "a mosquito, and you think good, another pest gone, the world's a little bit safer for the rest of us. You don't look at the crushed mosquito, and if you do all you see is a tangle of little black threads. But you kill a man like Lingano and you see blood and guts splattered all over the wall, dripping on your shoes."

Melnik finished his drink, and looked at his hands holding it. "Here's the smell of the blood still," he said. "Will these hands ne'er be clean?"

"Exactly," Horner said. "That damned spot will never come out. Look, the man is scum. You tell yourself that by killing him you've saved the lives of dozens, maybe hundreds of people the bastard would have murdered if he'd had another ten years of life. You tell yourself that, but your eyes tell you there's blood on your hands. And you can't help thinking, Once upon a time that scumbag was two years old, learning to talk, cute as a button, the hope of the world's future. And you killed him."

"Thanks a lot," Melnik said. "You're really making me feel great."

"It's the only thing I can do for you, buddy: remind you that you're not the only one, that others have been there too, and we know what it's about. That's why cops never stay married long. 'Cause their wives haven't been there, they don't know what it's about, they can't understand." Horner paused, beginning to think his own thoughts. "That, and the fact that we lie and cheat on our wives."

Melnik glanced up, aware that the conversation had suddenly changed. He wanted it to change, he didn't want to think about Lingano anymore, but Horner just stared into his glass a few minutes and then finished off the whiskey, looked up, and smiled. "What the fuck," he said. "That's the official motto of the New York Police Department, did you know that? They're gonna start printing it on our badges. What the fuck . . ."

There was a knock on the door. Horner called out, "Come on in," and Lisle Wintre came into the room.

They nodded their greetings. She looked at the two of them and said, "Early in the morning for boozing it up, isn't it?" Then, quickly, she apologized. "None of my business," she said. "Sorry."

"You're right, though, about one thing," Horner said. "It's early in the morning. What are you doing here in New York? You must have caught the early flight from DC. Anything up?"

"That's what I came to ask you," she said. "Anything happening?"

The two men looked at each other. "You want the good news or the bad news?" Horner asked.

"I could use some good news."

"Yeah, couldn't we all. Doesn't matter, it's both the same. We found—" He stopped and nodded at Melnik. "His boys found one of our limping killers."

"Good," she said.

"Bad," Horner said. "He turns out not to be *our* limping killer."

"How do you know?"

Horner glanced again at Melnik, and Wintre turned to him. "Take my word," he said. "He's not the one we want."

"No, thank you," she said.

"What?"

"I *don't* take your word. Tell me how you know."

"I talked to him," Melnik said.

Wintre waited, but he didn't say anything else. "That's it?" she asked. "You talked to him?"

Melnik nodded.

"Oh. Right. I understand. You asked him if he killed our man, and he told you no he didn't. Is that it?"

"More or less."

Again she waited, and again he said nothing. "You tortured him, didn't you?" she asked quietly.

"No," he said. "If he had been our man it would have been hard to get information out of him, and so we would have had to try very hard. But he wasn't. We didn't torture him. We killed him."

There was a short pause. "If he wasn't our man—"

"We killed him because of other things he did. Can we drop it now, please? Can we forget about it? Can we put it behind us, as your presidents are fond of saying, and get on with our lives?"

"No! How do you *know*—"

"Look!" Melnik stopped and took a deep breath. "We wanted him for other crimes. We caught him and told him about those crimes. He knows the penalty. We told him if he was the one who killed Kremble and would tell us about it, we'd spare his life. He tried to lie, to pretend, but he couldn't say anything about it because he didn't know who Kremble was or what happened to him."

Again a pause. "So you killed him. Just like that."

"Just like that, lady. That's the way the game is played."

She nodded her head. "I see. No laws, no rules to the game, just do what you want, kill anyone who gets in your way—"

"What do you want? You think this is a tea party? You think we're playing games?"

"It was *your* metaphor."

"Okay! You want to learn the rules of the game? Okay. There are two rules. The first rule is that you play for keeps. And the second rule is that there aren't any other rules."

"He's right," Horner said, breaking into the conversation. "Have a drink and forget it. The question is, where do we go from here?"

She stood there looking from one to the other, furious with their hypocrisy, with their blatant irresponsibility. Did talking about it as if it was a game diminish the reality for them? Didn't they realize they were talking about killing people? She was furious with Horner, more so with Melnik—and even more, she realized, with herself. She had come here this morning contrite and ashamed about her role in lying to him on Hagan's orders. But instead of apologizing she just started jumping all over him—

She took a deep breath. "Let's just go over the whole thing," she said after a moment. "Let's see where we stand. Why are we even involved in all this?" She turned to Horner. "Your man Kremble was carrying a briefcase containing a lot of money, possibly a weapon, and with a bomb rigged to go off if anyone tried to force the lock. He might have been carrying an assassination weapon and payoff money, or he might not. It might have been any kind of illegal funds. The weapon—if it was a weapon—could have been for his own use."

Horner nodded. "And then he was killed by our limping assassin," he added. "So clearly there's more than this one individual involved. There's a conspiracy of some sort."

"But what do we have to link it to the Israeli story of an attempt on the German chancellor's life?"

Horner shrugged.

"Right," she said. "Now, about the assassination plot: Do we really have any hard information on it?"

"Our operative in Germany reported quite definitely," Melnik said.

"And then he disappeared. So there's no confirmation."

"We tend to look upon his disappearance as confirmation."

She shook her head. "If he was discovered spying for Israel—"

"Our two nations are not at war," Melnik reminded her. "When spies are discovered in such a situation, as happens not infrequently, formal complaints are lodged and the spies are either arrested or deported. They are not summarily executed without trial and their deaths disguised as accidents."

"Perhaps it *was* an accident."

"Possible," Melnik admitted. "In the same sense that it is possible next February's average New York temperature will hit ninety degrees. You can't be sure that it won't. But I wouldn't bet money on it. I certainly wouldn't bet my life on it. And we *are* betting somebody's life, you know."

"My boss thinks you're crazy," she said.

"I know."

"You do?"

"We are actually rather an efficient intelligence service. I know that there's a plot against the German chancellor's life, and I know your boss wants to hamper cooperation between me and the American intelligence agencies. I know that you, following his orders, have told the FBI that there is nothing in my paranoiac ravings for them to worry about. What I do not know is who is plotting against the German chancellor or how they intend to strike, or why your Mr. Hagan has taken his attitude."

"I'm not sure why either," Wintre said, abashed. She hadn't known he knew about Hagan. She took a seat. She wasn't sure exactly what she was going to say next until she heard herself saying it. "Walter Naman is dead." And with that statement it was as if a balloon had been punctured; she felt the pressure suddenly leave her chest and vanish. She had made a decision without even realizing it, but now she knew what she had done, and she was glad. Scared, but glad. To hell with Hagan and his unreasonable strictures; she was working with these two guys now.

Horner reacted with no reaction at all; he obviously didn't recognize the name. She glanced over at Melnik. His eyes had gone hooded, like a cobra's. "What happened?" he asked.

"A car bomb in Los Angeles, a week ago."

"Tell me everything you know."

"I already have."

"Who is Walter Naman and why should we care?" Horner asked.

"German Jew, in Hitler's time," Melnik said. "Lived through the concentration camps and came to America. Worked undercover for the CIA, one of their best field operatives. Retired a few years ago to spend his time hunting Nazis. Something of a legend; everyone in the business knows of him."

"Like . . . what's his name?"

"Wiesenthal. Yes, except Naman usually doesn't bother to bring them back for trial." He turned to Wintre. "Identification is certain? He'd be a tough man to kill."

"Seems to be, although the body was burnt to a crisp. The car was in the parking lot of the building where he has his office. His secretary left him working late, and about an hour or so later the car blew up. He hasn't been seen since."

Horner picked up the phone and told the station operator to put him through to the L.A. police. "Long distance to L.A.," he said to Melnik and Wintre as he waited, and laughed. "Peters in accounting is going to split a gut."

"You can put the call on my phone card," Melnik said.

"Nah. By the time the paperwork comes in I'll be long gone from here. I'll be sitting in Florida thinking about it and laughing."

Melnik started to ask what he meant, but Horner waved him down. "Tell you about it sometime," he said, and into the telephone: "This is Detective Paul Horner of the New York Police Department. Like to get some information from you about a car bomb incident, February—?" He raised his eyebrows at Wintre, who lifted one finger. "February first, in L.A. Victim name of Walter Naman. Right, I'll be here." He gave his number, then put the receiver down and looked up at the others. "They'll call back. It's gonna take some time. You got anything you want to do?"

"Come on," Wintre said, getting up. "I'll treat you to a great Jewish brunch."

Melnik smiled. "I live in Israel, remember?"

She said, "This is New York, and I've been to Israel. Believe me, they don't know from a great Jewish brunch over there. Come on, we've got something to celebrate."

"What's that?"

"Our new cooperation," she said. "Our team."

Melnik nodded. "I'll drink to that," he said.

4

THE ENTIRE VILLAGE of Ravenscrag consisted of nothing more than a single curved street one block long with four houses on one side and on the other a pub, a greengrocer/butcher, and the photography shop. Grass had walked the half mile from the railroad station and now stood at the end of the street looking at the village and wondering how a community of four families could provide economic support for a photography shop.

Of course there were other villages nearby, which explained the pub and the butcher's, and perhaps one could build enough of a reputation as a photographer to bring in business from the outlying districts, but if you were searching England for a location to set up a new business you couldn't possibly pick a worse spot than this small village. And yet Ravenscrag was where the old Frenchman had chosen to set up shop.

Grass permitted himself a small smile. If one were looking to set up a business someplace where one wouldn't be overly inconvenienced by the presence of customers demanding attention, this village would be an ideal spot. For example, suppose one were setting up business not to specialize in family portraits or pictures of children or weddings, but instead to process documents for the secret services or for the band of fringe and even illegal mercenary troops that flourished in Europe after the Second World War: This would be the spot to choose.

And if a man like Naman wanted to put together a false passport or two, this might indeed be the place to which he might come.

For the first time since embarking on the flight to England, Grass felt a surge of excitement. He had tried to call from Germany to find out if the man Geiss told him about was still alive and living in Ravenscrag, but the long-distance operators had proved less than helpful. He had managed to get through to the Direct Enquiries operator of the trunk line servicing Ravenscrag, after a succession of London operators with Jamaican accents had insisted there was no such place anywhere in the British Isles, but after winning the battle he had lost the war: "What name are you looking for in Ravenscrag?" the operator had asked.

"I don't know the name. A photography shop."

"Our listings are only by name."

"There can't be that many photography shops there. It's a small place, isn't it?"

"Our listings are by name only. I have no way of looking up simply a photography shop. If you don't know the name, I'm afraid I can't help you." She maintained a cheerful politeness that was as unbreakable as it was unhelpful and Grass finally hung up, left with a choice. He could either forget the Frenchman in Ravenscrag or he could fly to England and see for himself.

It was really no choice, since he had nowhere else to go, nothing else to do. Now, standing here on the village street, he thought there must really be a God in heaven who looked after poor fools such as himself, and he crossed the street and entered the photography shop.

A bell tinkled as he entered, but no one responded. He stood waiting a few moments while his eyes became accustomed to the gloom inside; then he looked around. The place appeared to be a standard if under-nourished photographer's supply shop. He walked behind the counter and pushed open the door to the rear room.

Ah, this was more like it, he thought. Plenty of equipment here to enable one to take passport photos, make copies of documents . . . and there in the corner was even a small printing press. To create documents? He stood quietly looking around, thinking there was too much equipment here for a simple country photographer, but quite the proper amount for a man dealing in illegal documents.

He heard footsteps coming haltingly down the stairs, so he went back into the main part of the shop. A moment later an old man emerged from the stairwell and hobbled in. "Sorry to keep you waiting," he said, with the hint of a long-forgotten French accent. "Heard the bell, but I was lying down, and it takes a while for me to get up these days. What can I do for you?"

Grass smiled at the sight and sound of him. It looked as if Geiss had steered him right. *"Vous parlez français?"* he asked.

Gilbert had thought, when he came into the room and saw that his customer wasn't one of the locals, that this must be a lost tourist off the A65, come in either to ask directions or to buy a roll of 35mm Kodak. Now he peered at the man more closely, but it was no one he had ever seen before. "Do I know you?" he asked politely.

"No. We've never met. I'm a friend of a friend. Walter Naman."

"Ah," Gilbert said, and then was silent, waiting.

In that long moment Grass knew there was no point in going on like this any further. Gilbert's entire history was evoked by that one monosyllable and by the inscrutable patient wait that followed. He would offer no information, he would say nothing, Grass knew. Still, there was not much to lose by giving it one more try.

"He's dead, you know," Grass said.

Gilbert lifted his eyebrows in surprise. "One doesn't hear much news in this far corner of the world," he said. "I'm sorry to hear that. My sympathies."

"He was your friend, too, I believe?"

Gilbert shrugged.

"I'm trying to write a short article about him," Grass said. "Sort of a memorial. *The New York Times Magazine* has expressed an interest. I thought perhaps you might be willing to tell me what you know about him? Especially if you've seen him recently."

"No, it's been years. I never knew him well. I don't think there's anything I can tell you."

"No, I didn't think so. Still, one must try, mustn't one?" He reached into his jacket pocket and pulled out a gun.

Gilbert blinked at it twice, then raised his hands and took a step backward. "All the money I have is in the cash register."

"I wouldn't take your money," Grass said comfortingly. "I just want to talk." He backed up to the front door, not taking his eyes off the old man. Gilbert had worked for the Resistance, after all, and was at that age where he might want to be a hero one more time. Grass backed up to the door and flipped the sign in the window from OPEN to CLOSED. He pulled down the shades and they were alone, isolated from the village.

"What do you want to talk about?" Gilbert asked.

Grass looked at him unhappily. If he, Grass, had had the luck that secret agents always seem to have in the movies, this obstinate old man in front of him would be a young and lovely woman. Grass enjoyed extracting secrets from women, but hardly ever had the opportunity. With an old man like this, the process gave him no thrill of pleasure, no rush of hormones into the blood. Still, what had to be done had to be done.

"Take off your clothes," he said.

5

"There doesn't seem to be any doubt that it was Naman," Horner said. "But that's about all the L.A. department is sure of. It was a clean, professional hit. Nobody saw anything, nobody noticed anything unusual until the bomb went off. Then blooey, and there was nothing left."

"Positive make on the body?" Melnik asked.

Horner shook his head. "Not enough left to play with. But Naman's secretary says she left him working late at the office. An hour later someone opened his car door and the bomb blew up. Naman hasn't been seen or heard of since. *Sum ergo sum.*"

"Have they checked out the body's teeth with Naman's dentist?"

"No could do. For one thing there's no record of his ever having visited a dentist in the L.A. area. For another, there wasn't enough left of his teeth to help. We're not talking just fire here, we're talking blast furnace. Even the gold fillings were melted."

"Bingo," Melnik said softly.

"So this may be part of your plot," Horner continued, "but I don't see how it's going to help—" He stopped. Melnik was grinning. "What did you say?" he asked.

"He said, 'Bingo,'" Wintre provided.

"Go directly to go," Melnik amplified. "Do not stop in Jail. Collect two hundred dollars and live happily ever after."

"You're trying to tell me something," Horner said. "I'm noted for my intuition, so I can tell that right off. Now I could either requisition a Ouija board and we can wait till dark and then sit down in a circle with our hands on it and see if it spells out your message, or you could save us all a lot of time and spit it out right now."

"The dead man isn't Naman," Melnik said, and then he paused.

"Okay," Horner said. "I can see you're a real hotshot superspy type, and you can tell more about what happened at a murder from three thousand miles away than those poor suckers at L.A. can do right at the scene. I don't doubt that for a minute. But us poor New York cops are no smarter than the L.A. dicks, so you're gonna have to explain to me exactly how you come to your conclusions."

"Well, I'm making an assumption, of course."

"Of course."

"I'm assuming that when you said, 'even the gold fillings were melted,' you weren't just making a point about the heat. There really were traces of melted gold in the corpse's mouth?"

"What was left you couldn't properly call a mouth," Horner said, "but there was certainly melted gold in what used to be the oral cavity."

Melnik grinned broadly. "Then it wasn't Naman. He went through Auschwitz. He had nightmares the rest of his life about what they made him do there. They sent him into the gas chambers and made him pull out the gold teeth from the dead bodies there. Can you imagine what that was like? A ten-year-old kid being thrown into a warehouse, crawling over dead bodies, opening their mouths, and pulling out teeth with gold fillings?" Melnik shook his head. "There is no way that Naman would ever have let anyone put a gold filling into his mouth. Whoever died in that car-bomb explosion, it wasn't Walter Naman."

6

THEY WERE in the darkroom, the only light provided by a deep red bulb in the ceiling. Grass had taken Gilbert in there because it was located in the bowels of the building, the room farthest from the outside; his screams would go unheard, especially muffled, as they would be, by the cotton rag stuffed into his mouth.

Gilbert lay naked on the developing table, tied down securely. The table was wet, and so was he; although it didn't really matter, Grass had found that psychologically this was helpful. People associated being wet with conducting electricity. In fact the current would flow through the interior of Gilbert's body, and whether or not the skin was wet would make no difference at all.

Grass had cut the cord from a table fan and splayed the interior wires to a length of several inches. He had found a candle in the old man's kitchen and cut off an inch of it. The ends of one wire he wrapped around that chunk of candle, and then he inserted the candle like a suppository into Gilbert's anus, pushing it up past the sphincter, where it lodged securely in place. The ground wire he attached to the metal leg of the table, and the third wire he wrapped around the old man's testicles. He plugged the cord into a rheostat that had been used as a light-dimming switch. He smiled at the old man and twisted the dial slightly.

Gilbert's body stiffened and arched, lifting for a moment off the table. A scream from deep in his throat reached the air only as a rumbling moan through his cotton-stuffed mouth. Sweat broke out on his face and under his armpits, as if a faucet had been turned on.

Grass turned off the current and pulled the rag out of Gilbert's mouth. "When did you last see Walter Naman?" he asked.

The old man only stared at him.

Grass was not happy. There was no pleading, no begging, not even any unnecessary talking; Gilbert didn't try to invent a year when he had last seen Naman; he didn't pretend that he couldn't remember. The old man knew that none of this would matter to Grass. The question was whether he had seen Naman within the last few days or not, and he wasn't going to answer that. Which meant that he had seen him, that he had information Grass wanted, and that it was going to be difficult to extract it. It was going to take longer and be messier than he had anticipated. The old man seemed to be made of nothing but leather and bones as he lay tied to the developing table, and although Grass knew that inside that body was a network of nerves that would cause excruciating pain, he also knew that a man's stubbornness can be an awful nuisance. He stuffed the rag back in.

One way to break the stubbornness was to confuse the will. Grass had done this before, and it always worked like magic. He searched around the room and soon found a bottle of distilled alcohol. He dribbled it, drop by drop, around Gilbert's left breast, until an area from the nipple to the collarbone was soaked. He took a box of matches out of his pocket. He paused.

"Different compounds burn at different temperatures," he said. "Gasoline would burn too hot; it would kill you too quickly. Alcohol burns at just the right temperature, hot enough to incinerate your skin without killing you right away. I'm going to burn your skin off, one patch at a time."

He lit the match, held it for a moment in front of Gilbert's wide eyes, then touched it to the pool of alcohol on his left breast. It flared up immediately, and within seconds the stench of burning flesh filled the room. Gilbert strained against the cords, twisting and writhing, choking on his own saliva as he silently screamed.

It took nearly a minute before the fire burned itself out, leaving a mess of charred tissue where Gilbert's left breast had been. It was more fun with a woman, Grass thought, but really just as effective with a man. And now came the beauty part. He placed the rheostat next to Gilbert's right hand, and loosed the cords enough so he would be able to reach it. "We're going to try a little experiment," he said. "We're going to play a little game."

He picked up the bottle of alcohol and began to dribble the liquid onto Gilbert's forehead. He moved the bottle around so that the drops fell on his cheeks and across his nose. He pulled the rag out of Gilbert's mouth and asked, "Do you want to talk? Last chance before we play the game?"

Gilbert didn't answer, only closed his eyes. Grass stuffed the rag back into his mouth and soaked it with alcohol. The fumes made the old man start choking. Grass pulled back Gilbert's eyelids and dribbled the alcohol into the eyes, so that he now lay choking and blinking with pain.

Grass lit another match and held it over Gilbert's face. "Which would you prefer?" he asked. "The fire or the electric shock? Or would you prefer to tell me what I want to know?" Gilbert didn't answer, and Grass went on. "There are two ways to prevent me dropping this match onto your face. One is to tell me about Naman. If you don't want to do that, you can still stop me by turning on the electricity yourself and sending the current through your body. Isn't that interesting? No? Well, I'll be generous. After your face starts burning you can still stop it, perhaps before the fire reaches your eyes. You won't be able to talk, of course, but if you give yourself the electric shock I'll blow out the flames. Of course then we'll start all over again, and again and again until you talk. And the really exquisite part is this: You don't know how much of a jolt will make me stop. A little bit of a tingle, like I gave you before? No, that won't do it. But it's close. Just a bit more might work. Are you ready to begin?"

He lowered the burning match toward the old man's face. Gilbert tried to pull away, but his motion was limited to a few inches and the burning match in Grass's fingers followed inexorably, coming closer and closer.

The psychology was simple. Make the victim torture himself and his will breaks down in confusion. Reality vanishes, and with it all loyalties and inhibitions are forgotten. There remains no reason not to say whatever will stop the pain.

The flame came close enough to Gilbert's face for the old man to feel the heat. Another fraction of an inch and the alcohol would ignite.

Gilbert's hand jerked spasmodically toward the rheostat, took hold of it, and in one sudden motion spun it all the way on, catching Grass by surprise. The surge of electricity, the full 220 volts, rushed through his body, lifting it off the table, jerking it spasmodically.

Grass dropped the burning match and yanked the rheostat out of the old man's hands, spinning it around back to zero, but it was too late. François Gilbert had been tortured fifty years before by the Gestapo. That was a long time ago, but some lessons one does not forget. It was better to be dead than to go through that again.

"*Scheisse!*" Grass cursed, staring with hatred at the dead body arching on the table, its muscles still contracted. He had underestimated the old man, God damn him.

He kicked the leg of the developing table in helpless frustration.

Grass walked around the shop, and the more he saw the angrier he got. The equipment here was clearly not what could be needed for a village photographer's shop. Gilbert had certainly been in the business of providing documents under the table, and Naman would certainly have come to his old friend for help in obtaining new passports and identification.

He opened drawers, taking everything out one item at a time, inspecting it, dropping it on the floor. There was nothing, no clue anywhere. It was possible, he thought, that Naman hadn't yet come here. Grass could, perhaps, sit here and wait for him, like a spider in her web. But Gilbert's refusal to talk had convinced Grass that he had indeed seen Naman within the past few days.

And how long would it be before someone missed Gilbert? Was he a recluse whose disappearance from village life no one would notice for weeks? Or did he go to the pub every evening? Would his friends come knocking on the door in an hour to pick him up?

Damn the old man's guts, he thought angrily, and continued ransacking the place.

The first thing he had checked was the big trash can near the rear door. He had nearly finished the entire shop when he noticed the small wastebasket under the desk. He went through this as carefully as he had everything else, but even then he almost missed it.

It seemed to be the draft of a short letter, written on letterhead that proclaimed "The Vicarage, Ravenscrag, Lancashire," addressed to the British Museum, providing a reference for a Professor Fred Nagle of McGill University in Montreal, Canada, who evidently wanted to use the Reading Room for scholarly research.

Grass would have dropped it with the other rejected items on the floor, if at the last second he had not noticed the signature. The letter was signed by the Reverend François Gilbert. The Reverend . . .

Grass looked back to the scorched dead body, and began to laugh. He examined the letter closely; it was very good, the letterhead was perfect.

And why would the old man print a phony letterhead and write a personal reference to the British Museum? Only to support someone who had no identification. It could have been someone other than Naman, some other man on the dark side of the law, but the coincidence in timing was too tight. He might be wrong, but he felt it now in his guts: Walter Naman was Fred Nagle of Montreal, Canada, and with a little luck might still be doing his research in the Reading Room of the British Museum.

11

1

"CAN I HELP YOU?"

"Oh yes, I certainly hope so," Grass said. "I'm very worried about my boss. I— I'd better explain."

"Yes, please do," the woman said. She was politely concerned, exuding an air of efficiency and competence.

Grass liked the British; they were so polite. He smiled ingratiatingly and said, "We were supposed to meet last week at the Cambridge University library, but he never showed up. I even called the university booking office at home, and they said he left on time. So I just don't know what's happened to him. And then I thought, before I talk to the police I ought to check here because we were supposed to spend our second week doing research here and I thought maybe he got mixed up and came here first?" He tried a small laugh. "Maybe he's even worried about *me* not showing up? I wonder if you could possibly check and let me know if he's been here."

"Well, we'll certainly see what we can do. Now, what is his name?"

"Fred Nagle. Professor Nagle, McGill University, Montreal."

"I seem to recall him," she said, opening a large book and turning the pages. "Yes, here it is. He was issued a Reading Room card on February twelfth."

"But did he actually pick up the card? Has he really been here?"

"Oh yes. He made an application back on February eighth, and the card was issued to him personally on the twelfth."

"Well, thank God for that," Grass said. "He does get things confused. Or maybe I shouldn't say that, maybe it's me who got it backwards. Is he here now, do you know?"

"We don't keep records of their comings and goings. Once one is issued a card, one simply shows it at the door and the guard passes one in without making a record."

"Could I just take a peek and see if he's there now?"

"Yes, of course. But if you're going to be working here you'll need your own card."

"Well, if he's finished here he may want to go right on to Cambridge. I'd better check with him first."

The woman accompanied him past the guard through the door to the Reading Room and waited while he walked around.

Naman was not there.

Grass hired a private detective to keep an eye on the museum, telling the man that he was Professor Nagle's brother-in-law and that the professor's wife, his sister, was trying to pick up the professor's trail, for the usual reasons. He left a full description, which he was sure would not be necessary; the detective would simply bribe the Reading Room guards to let him know if anyone used Professor Nagle's pass. But because several days had elapsed since Naman had first used the Reading Room, Grass was more concerned with the possibility that he might have finished his work there and moved on.

He had been unwilling to let Hauptmann know that he had already lost contact with Naman, but there was no harm if word got back to him that Grass was searching for a Professor Nagle of Montreal. He placed an international call to the contact Hauptmann had given him in Germany and asked that surveillance be placed on the use of that name for travel to and from England during the period from February 12 till the present time, and continuing until Nagle was located.

In twenty-four hours he heard nothing from the private detective at the Reading Room, but received word from Germany that a Fred Nagle of Canadian citizenship had flown yesterday from London's Heathrow to Munich.

Damn, Grass thought, just missed him.

The telephone voice continued, saying that at the airport in Munich Nagle had booked a seat on Delta nonstop to Los Angeles tomorrow.

Of course, Grass thought. He wouldn't be carrying the money with him, going through customs from Germany to France to England and back again. Since he had flown from Berlin to Munich, it stood to reason he had left the money there. He had gone back to collect it and now he was going to Los Angeles, probably to reestablish contact with his people there.

Grass called a private detective agency in Los Angeles. Using the name Ralph Berner, he arranged to have immediate surveillance set up both at Naman's home and at his business, World Security Consultants. But Grass was a cautious man who dealt not in probabilities but in certainties. He himself would be at the airport when Naman arrived. He stopped in at a travel agency and bought a ticket for that night's flight from London to Los Angeles.

2

THINGS WERE GOING WELL, Naman told himself; things were going beautifully. Right on schedule. He knew basically how he was going to do it, and had learned from his researches in the British Museum Reading Room not only the rough outlines of how the apparatus might be built but also the name of a small American company that should be able to do it. He didn't yet know the precise details but that was because he didn't know *where* the incident would take place. That was the next step.

He didn't anticipate any problems. He wasn't worried about finding the exact procedure; he was confident that that would be evident when he found the proper location. From Vorshage, he knew the chancellor's schedule in the United States and so the next step was to investigate the locus of his engagements, and all else would follow.

The apparatus would be rather expensive and so he had to bring the money into the United States with him. That would present a minor problem, but it wasn't what was worrying him now. In fact, Naman told himself, he had nothing to worry about now. Even if the concept of Vorshage's plot against Waldner had leaked—and he had to be prepared for that, since there wasn't an undercover organization in the world impervious to penetration—still, nobody but Vorshage himself knew that he, Naman, was alive; he trusted Vorshage not to divulge that information.

And even if someone should find out he was alive, nobody knew that he was using a passport in the name of Fred Nagle, nor where he was, nor what his plans were.

Nevertheless, one should still be prudent. That was why he had taken the precaution of rerouting his flight out of Berlin in midair, and of traveling to Britain by rail and boat. He hadn't had to give a name when buying those tickets, and the passport-control people kept no record of whom they let in or out.

But he was not going back on that Hovercraft again. He tried to tell himself that the weather conditions had been unusual, but it was no use; nothing in the world could have induced him to set foot on that boat. Which meant that he had to fly back to Munich to pick up the money he had left in the locker there, and that meant he had to give a name to the airline. And though they didn't ask for identification, the name on his ticket had to match that on his passport when he passed through passport control.

He told himself he had no reason to fear using the name of Fred Nagle, and he agreed with himself. One couldn't afford to get too paranoid in this game. But also, he reminded himself, one must equally well refrain from not being paranoid enough: Precautions might be unnecessary, but they were never wasted.

And so as soon as he landed at the airport in Munich, he had booked a flight as Fred Nagle in two days' time to Los Angeles. He then left the terminal, took the tram into town, and recovered the money from the athletic-club locker. In the locker room he tore up the Los Angeles ticket and flushed it down the toilet. He took a train to Frankfurt, booked a room under a false name in the Nordling Hotel, had dinner in the dining room, took a walk around the block, and retired for the night.

In the morning he went to the airport and waited until thirty minutes before the Lufthansa flight left for New York. Then he bought a ticket and boarded just before they shut the doors. Minutes later he was climbing past ten thousand feet on his way to cruising altitude, on his way to New York, with six hours to work out the solution to his next problem.

3

THE STEWARDESS bent over the arm of the seat and spoke softly into the passenger's ear. It was unusual but not unknown for first-class passengers on the transatlantic flight to be important enough to have messages delivered to them by the plane's radio. She smiled softly and gave it her best husky low-throated voice: Anyone important enough to rate this service was rich enough for her to be interested in. "Sorry to bother you," she said, and the man looked up at her. "Your office would like you to call in. There's a telephone upstairs in the club room. Shall I show you the way?"

Grass shook his head and pushed up out of his seat so quickly that she nearly tripped backing out of his way. He ignored her and climbed the curving short flight of stairs to the jumbo's lounge, where he put his card into the telephone and dialed the number. He couldn't imagine what could be serious enough for Hauptmann's office to contact him like this. "Hello," he said when the call went through. "This is me."

"Yes, Henvig here." That was the man Grass had put to work tracing "Fred Nagle's" movements. "I'm afraid I have bad news for you."

"Get on with it."

"The professor boarded a flight from Frankfurt to New York six hours ago."

"What?"

Henvig repeated his statement. "He bought the ticket at the last moment. The flight took off before we became aware of his change in plans. It will be landing any moment now."

There was a pause, a long pause.

"Is there anything I can do?" Henvig asked.

Grass stood there looking at his watch. *Too late,* he was thinking, *too damned late again.* There was no one he could get to the airport in time. And he himself was stuck thirty-seven thousand feet in the air over the North Atlantic, stuck on this damned airplane until it landed in Los Angeles, a continent away from New York.

"Is there anything I can do?" Henvig repeated, breaking Grass's reverie.

"No," he said, and hung up.

The stewardess watched him come back into the first-class section and sit down. From the expression on his face she guessed he was not in the mood to consider feminine companionship once they landed. And no one else on the flight seemed interesting at all.

Oh well, she thought. Mother said there'd be days like this.

4

THE LONG LINE of people filed slowly off the airplane in Los Angeles, tired and stiff from their long flight. As soon as he could Grass stepped past them and stalked angrily through the airport toward the first bank of telephones. He dialed the number of the Jay Preston Detective Agency.

Mr. Preston wasn't in, but he identified himself as Ralph Berner to Preston's secretary and told her to cancel the surveillance he had ordered at World Security Consultants and at Naman's home.

"Is this temporary or permanent?" Miss Fellowes asked.

"Permanent. Cancel it," Grass said, and was about to hang up when she went on to say that their operative was not within telephone contact at the moment and they would probably have to charge Mr. Berner for the remainder of the day's expenses before they could cancel the surveillance. "Fine," Grass said. "Just cancel it as soon as you can."

"If anything comes up in today's surveillance will you want to be notified?"

"Just cancel it!" he said irritably, and slammed down the phone. He turned and moved off down the hall toward the lobby, to buy space on the next flight to New York. As he hurried along, his limp accentuated by stiffness, he passed two men and a woman emerging from a New York–to–Los Angeles flight.

David Melnik noticed the man hurrying past, noticed the limp, and thought what a fine world it would be if the good Lord only saw fit to deliver up the people you were looking for as easily as that. As long as he was dreaming, he thought, it would be nice if the Lord would also send him a woman to love—not just to sleep with, he pointed out to God, but to love and live with forever. He glanced sideways at the one striding alongside him toward the baggage claim area. Beautiful she certainly was, but not, he thought, the marrying-and-settling-down type. Too smart, too ambitious, too tough. He was glad they seemed to have settled their differences and could begin to work together, but there was nothing else there. A shame, really; he bet she'd be good in bed—

"Penny for your thoughts," Lisle Wintre said.

He was embarrassed, and shook his head.

"I knew it," she said. "Lascivious thoughts."

"Not at all," he protested. "Why do you say that?"

"You had a lascivious grin on your face if ever I saw one. Was it that blonde we just passed?"

"You do me wrong. As a matter of fact I was looking at that man who was limping—"

"What man?"

Melnik turned around, but the man was gone. He shrugged. "I was just thinking how lovely it would be if we just bumped into our man without effort."

"Right," Horner joined in. "And if all women in the world were Marilyn Monroe."

"Yes," Melnik agreed. "That too."

There was no one there and the door was locked when they got to the office of World Security Consultants, Inc., but a few moments later they heard heels clacking on the stairs and a short, chubby woman burst into view. "Sorry I'm late," she said, breathing hard from the exertion and opening her handbag as she hurried down the hall. "I hope you haven't been waiting long, but I couldn't get my car to start and then the cab got lost—"

"We just got here ourselves," Melnik assured her.

Norma Middler introduced herself and managed to get her keys out and open the door. "You flew in from New York?" she asked, and when they nodded she said, "I still miss the city. I came out here with Mr. Naman when he started this business." She sighed. "Christmas shopping. Isn't that silly? But that's what I miss, the Christmas shopping. It isn't the same here." They followed her in and waited while she scurried around turning on the air-conditioning and the lights. "Paul Horner," Horner said when she turned back to them. He held out his wallet with his NYPD identification. She leaned forward and read it carefully, then nodded. "You're the one they said to expect. The Los Angeles police."

"Yes, ma'am. They called you?"

She nodded. "They said you're investigating a murder in New York that might be connected to Mr. Naman's death."

"As a matter of fact," Melnik said, stepping forward, "we're not sure that Mr. Naman is dead."

She turned to him. "David Melnik," he said, holding forth his open wallet. "Mossad. Israeli intelligence."

"Of course he isn't dead." She looked him over critically. "I thought you'd never show up," she said. "What took you so long?"

Since it *had* taken them so long, she insisted that they take a few moments longer and sit down and relax while she made coffee. "It's a habit I picked up from my father," she explained as she set mugs out on the small table in the inner office. "He says he can't think without a cup of coffee in his hand."

"How do you know he's not dead?" Melnik asked, but she just shook her head and went on finishing the coffee setups. When the coffee had finally perked and settled down, and she had filled the mugs to the brim with a thick dark brew and sat down herself, Melnik asked her again.

"How do you know Mr. Naman's not dead? And if he isn't, who was the man who was blown up in his car?"

"Jean-Paul Mendoza, I should think." And she told them of Vorshage's visit. "That's why I didn't think he was dead. Anyone can be taken by surprise, but Mr. Naman knew about his danger. He was expecting it. He might have been cut down by a sniper, but he certainly knew about the bomb in his car."

"How do you know that?" Melnik asked.

"After Mr. Vorshage's warning, he set up a series of surveillance devices. One was a camcorder taking a continuous tape record of his car in the parking lot. He would have seen anyone tampering with it."

"People get careless," Melnik suggested. "Perhaps he didn't check the tape before he got in the car that day. Maybe he was in a hurry: Someone called with an urgent message and he ran out—"

"No," she interrupted. "The first thing I did when I heard about the bombing was to check the tape. It's missing." She looked around at them triumphantly, but Melnik only shrugged.

"Like I said, people get careless," he said. "He forgot to put the tape in that day. How long had it been since Vorshage visited? A week? Ten days? After days and days with nothing happening, he simply forgot to put a tape in the camcorder that morning."

She shook her head defiantly. "That was my job. I put the tape in every morning. And I put it in that morning."

"You can't be sure," Melnik suggested.

She set her lips primly. "I knew Mr. Naman's life might depend on that tape. Perhaps you can't be sure because you don't know me. But I am perfectly sure."

Wintre leaned forward and put down her cup of coffee. She wanted to nail this down. She told Miss Middler of Melnik's theory about the gold teeth in the mouth of the bombing victim.

Miss Middler smiled. "That was clever of you," she said. "Nobody told me about the dead man having gold in his teeth."

"Naman didn't have gold teeth, did he?"

"No, of course not," she said. "And then there was the telegram."

"What telegram?"

"I guess you don't know about that, either," she said, and told them about the telegram asking her to get a tape of Waldner speaking English and to send a copy to Audio Technology Associates for digital analysis, to be held under the name of Henry Larkinson. "I didn't know if it was really from him. It was signed 'Walter,' so I did it, but it was strange."

"Contacting you by telegram?"

She nodded. "Why wouldn't he call me? But I didn't know, maybe he had his reasons, so I did it."

Melnik immediately nodded to Horner, who picked up the phone, dialed New York information, and was soon connected with Audio Technology Associates. He identified himself and said, "I believe you're holding a package for a Henry Larkinson?"

He waited while the man on the other end checked his records, then thanked him and hung up. "It's there," he said.

"Get someone on it," Melnik ordered.

Horner sighed. "That's exactly what I would do," he said, "if I were a hotshot Israeli agent. But I'm nothing but a New York cop. You think we got rooms full of eager young detectives sitting around with nothing to do, just waiting for my phone call? You think they're gonna jump up and organize a three-man, twenty-four-hour surveillance operation for maybe a couple of weeks, waiting for somebody to pick up this tape? You think maybe there's a single cop anywhere in New York with time on his hands and nothing to do but help you out?"

"Sorry," Melnik said. "What do you suggest?"

Horner sighed again. "I'll see what I can do."

Miss Middler interrupted, a puzzled expression on her face. "Excuse me, but . . ." She stopped, confused, looking from one of them to another. She had been thinking over everything they had said before, and now she asked, "Is that how you knew Mr. Naman is still alive? The business about the gold in his teeth?"

"It's what made us suspect," Wintre said. "We're glad you've confirmed it."

"But if you don't know all about it, what are you doing here? I thought—"

"What did you think?" Horner asked.

"Well, him being Mossad and all . . ." She nodded at Melnik. "I mean, I expected you'd be bringing me the message."

"What message?"

"To tell me where he is, what he's doing. What he wants me to do."

"You don't know where he is?"

"No. Don't you? When you said you were Mossad, I thought you'd be working with him. I thought you were going to tell me what was happening. But you don't know anything about it, do you?"

"Well," Melnik had to admit, "we don't seem to know very much."

5

WILLIAM CONRAD had taken a walk around the block. Strictly speaking, he wasn't supposed to let the offices of Worldwide Security out of his sight, but there were limits to how long a man could sit in a car or hang out on the sidewalk without attracting attention. There were no bars or coffeehouses within line of sight of the office windows and so he felt it was mandatory to move around every once in a while—besides, there was the simple relief of doing so. There can be nothing on earth more boring than continual surveillance of an empty office.

When he came back around the corner from his jaunt around the block, however, he saw that the lights in the office had been turned on.

He crossed the street and entered the building. He ran up the stairs to the third floor and then quietly walked down the hall past the door with the Worldwide Security sign. The upper half was frosted glass, and he could see that the lights inside were still on. He stood waiting at the end of the hall, by the elevator.

Luckily it was not a busy building and no one came by for nearly twenty minutes. Then the door to Worldwide Security opened. Two men and two women came out and stood there for a moment while one of the women turned off the lights and locked the door. As they turned to come down the hall toward the elevator Conrad pushed the button and sneezed loudly, whipping out a handkerchief and bending over to smother the sneeze. They glanced up at the sudden noise, which hid the click of the minicamera concealed in his hand. By the time they reached him he was wiping his nose daintily and smiling apologetically, and then the elevator came and they all got on and rode down to the ground floor.

He crossed the street and got into his gray Plymouth. He watched as the group got into two taxis, one of the women taking one and the three others taking the second. He had been told to follow whoever showed up at the office, but he couldn't follow two groups. Since the single woman's taxi headed off in the direction his car was pointing, he went after her while the cab carrying the other three took off in the opposite direction.

"So we know that Naman's not dead," Wintre said. "And we know his apparent death was triggered by a visit from Vorshage."

"We don't know enough to make any decisions," Horner argued. "But at least we know enough to take some action on."

"Try to find Naman?" Wintre asked.

"Why not? At least it's a name, and something to do. What do you think, Melnik?"

Melnik had been looking out the window. Now he leaned forward and tapped the taxi driver on the shoulder. "Make a U-turn," he said. "And follow that car."

He turned back to an astonished Horner and Wintre. "I've always wanted to say that." He smiled.

6

WALTER NAMAN'S one extravagance in life was a first-class seat whenever he flew, and actually it was a necessity rather than a luxury: He could never face the ordeal of being long entrapped in the clawing cluster of the crowded tourist cabin. In first class he had room for his feet, room to move his arms and squirm around, aisles wide enough to walk around in, room enough to keep his claustrophobia at bay. During the flight from Frankfurt to New York he got into casual conversation with his seatmate, an older man who introduced himself as Harry Carstairs and who was returning from his first vacation in years, traveling alone because his wife had died. By the time the plane made its North American landfall, over Nova Scotia, Naman had worked out how he would bring the money in.

They were seated in the last row of the unfilled first-class section; the seats across the aisle were empty. When Carstairs excused himself to go to the lavatory, Naman took down both their carry-on bags from the overhead rack. Unnoticed by the passengers in the forward seats, he quickly picked the simple lock on Carstairs's bag and moved the money from his own bag to it, removing enough clothing and books to balance the weight. When Carstairs returned Naman steered the conversation until he learned the man's address in Greenwich Village, and then remarked that he also lived in lower Manhattan, was being met by a limo, and would be glad to give Carstairs a ride home. As the jumbo jet landed in New York they agreed that if they were separated in customs they would meet directly outside.

As they entered the cavernous customs area Naman managed to lag behind, enabling several pushing passengers to come between him and Carstairs. The older man waved back to him as he passed through passport control first and disappeared into the interior. When Naman came through he saw Carstairs wheeling his luggage along, but made no effort to join him. Instead he took his own two small cases toward the other end of the room. He saw Carstairs looking around for him, but he remained unseen; finally Carstairs decided to go through and wait for him outside as they had arranged.

Naman watched as Carstairs passed easily through the "nothing to declare" line without being stopped, and so all was well. He now started to go through himself, but as he did an inspector came up to him and asked to see his luggage. Naman smiled and patiently opened his bags; it meant only a moment's delay, and proved that his caution had been justified. He waited while the inspector checked his passport and luggage, and a few minutes later he walked through the gates into the crowded concourse.

Carstairs had already passed through and, not seeing Naman in the concourse, headed outside to wait. Just before he reached the door he was stopped by a white-gowned nurse asking for donations for one of the standard sucker "charities." Angrily he said no, and when she began her spiel he spun away from her. The suitcase he was carrying swung wide and hit her, knocking her down. She screamed and people turned to watch. Afraid of being arrested and sued, Carstairs dashed outside and took the first cab he could find. He gave the driver his Greenwich Village address and breathed a sigh of relief as the cab pulled away before any pursuit came after him.

By the time Naman got through customs and went outside, Carstairs was gone. He didn't understand that; he thought he had taken the measure of the man, thought Carstairs would certainly have waited and met him as agreed. He went back inside and looked around carefully, but Carstairs was nowhere to be seen. Well, at least he had the man's address; he took a cab and headed for the Village. With luck he would get there before Carstairs opened his luggage, and from there he would play it by ear.

Carstairs's cab pulled up to the Village brownstone, but instead of getting out he began to cry. The cabdriver buried his head in his hands—why did these things always happen to him?—while his passenger said, "I must be losing my mind." This address, it seemed, was where he and his wife first lived in New York fifty years ago. He lived in Darien now. The cabdriver asked if he should drive him to Darien, but the passenger said no, he couldn't afford that, please take him to Grand Central.

When they arrived Carstairs was so upset that he left without his hand luggage, taking only the large suitcase the cabbie had put in the trunk of the cab. The next passenger called the cabbie's attention to the carry-on left on the rear seat, but since it was locked there was no way the cabbie could find the man who left it. He put it on the floor of the front seat and took it home with him that night. He hoped the man might call and offer a reward, or if he didn't call within a few days that there might be something useful in it.

When Naman arrived at the Greenwich Village address he found not only that Carstairs was not there, but that no one had ever heard of him. He tried to insist—he was sure he had the right address—but the young woman didn't want to hear about it. Nobody named Carstairs lived there, nobody by that description had ever lived there since she had moved in three years ago.

Finally she shut the door firmly in Naman's face, and he stood there on the steps. Had he been snookered? He didn't know, but the money was certainly gone.

Carstairs never bothered to call the taxi company about his bag, since it had held nothing but some old clothes and books, and he wasn't even sure where he had lost it. The cabbie, after waiting a few days, forced it open and found the money. He hid it in the basement prepared to swear he knew nothing about it if the passenger called the taxi office. A month later, when no one had called, he quit his job and moved to California, where he lost it all on the horses.

7

WILLIAM CONRAD followed Naman's secretary to her home and then called the office to report his triumph. "I'm glad you called in," Miss Fellowes said. "The client has canceled. The case is closed. You can come home now."

"Come home? You mean you don't care about these people?"

"I've always said you were one of our brightest boys," Miss Fellowes said. "You don't miss a thing, do you? That's right, the client has canceled."

"But I've even got pictures of all the people who came to the office."

"Well, hoorah for you," she replied unperturbed. "The client doesn't care, he isn't interested, the case is closed. Come back in for reassignment."

"But what shall I do with the film?"

"Well, that depends," she said studiously. "Are you using the Olympus mini with thirty-five millimeter or the Canon with microfilm?"

"The Canon, but—"

"That's all right, then," she interrupted brightly. "Take the film out of the camera and rewind it as tightly as you can. It'll make a very neat, small roll. Then you take the roll between your thumb and your forefinger and stick it right up your—"

Conrad hung up.

12

1

NAMAN WAS IRRITATED by the loss of the money. He could do nothing without it. What he had planned to do next was to fly directly from JFK to Washington, which was the city Waldner would visit first, and search around for a good assassination site. But without money or a credit card he couldn't buy the airline ticket. He couldn't even get a hotel room in New York, because without a credit card he would have to pay each night's bill in advance, and he barely had enough money in his wallet for a decent lunch.

He did have that much, however, and so he went to eat at Crêpes Suzette, a Forty-sixth Street French restaurant he remembered as the sort of place local residents frequented. He arrived toward the end of the lunch hour, nearly two o'clock, but the place was still crowded. He was given a table for one against the wall, and ordered an excellent cream of broccoli soup followed by rack of lamb. When he finished he called for the bill and then sat at the table sipping strong black coffee.

While eating he had been paying attention to as much conversation from the surrounding tables as he could hear, and he had picked out three likely possibilities. Finally one of them lurched to his feet, clearly on his way to the men's room. Naman got up at the same time and they reached the entrance to the stairs together. Naman stepped back and allowed the other man to go first. In single file they clumped down the narrow stairs into the basement cooking area and turned left toward the tiny men's room. They urinated nearly in unison in the cramped quarters, and as they turned from the twin urinals Naman clumsily bumped into the man. He excused himself, the other man backed off with a nod, and Naman rinsed his hands and left the room.

He went back to the dining room, picked up his check from the table, and carried it to the register at the bar near the front door. He took an American Express card out of the wallet he had lifted from the gentleman in the men's room, and paid the bill. As Naman was signing the bill he saw the wallet's owner reaching into his pocket for the wallet to pay his own bill. Naman retrieved his luggage from the cloakroom, leaving a dollar tip, and left the restaurant while the other man was still looking under the table and his companion was suggesting he might have dropped it in the men's room.

Naman caught a cab on Forty-sixth Street and took it straight to the Pierre Hotel, stopping on the way to dash into a theatrical costumer's and pick up a few items. He used the American Express card to check in at the hotel, then went up to his luxurious room. As soon as he was alone he showered and then sat down before the dressing mirror and opened the plastic bag he had brought from the costumer's. He dyed his hair black and carefully applied thick black eyebrows and a wide mustache. They weren't much, but they changed his appearance completely. Not even his mother would recognize him. Especially not his mother, for she had died in Auschwitz when he was still a child.

As his hair dried Naman prowled around the hotel room, inspecting it closely. Waldner would be staying at this hotel while he was in New York, after Washington, and therefore it too was a possibility for the assassination site. But first, Naman thought, he'd better finish off the business of the credit card.

He looked for Carleton Genever, the name on the card, in the several telephone books the hotel provided, and found an address in Forest Hills. He called the main Post Office number and asked for the station closest to that address, and instructions on how to get there from Manhattan. He left the hotel, took the E train and the Q-33 bus, and found the post office forty-five minutes later. He asked for a change of address card and filled it in, changing Carelton Genever's address, for three days, from 111-25 Seventy-ninth Street to the Pierre Hotel. He spent the remainder of the day and evening wandering through the hotel, investigating it thoroughly. He didn't know what he was looking for, but he knew he'd recognize it when he saw it.

He found nothing. The next morning he called American Express and said he had lost his card and was checking to see if his secretary had properly reported the loss. The woman asked him if he knew the number; he read it off to her. She said that yes, it had been reported stolen yesterday and a new card had already been mailed out. He should have it within twenty-four hours. Naman thanked her. He went down to the lobby, asked for the manager, and told him that the American Express card he had checked in with had been stolen last evening; he would be receiving another one today or tomorrow. The manager asked him to please revalidate his reservation with the new card when it arrived, and that was that.

Again he spent the day prowling around the hotel, and again came up with nothing. He thought he had better pick up some money before going on to Washington. His new American Express card came on the following morning and would be safe to use for another day or two, while the real owner was waiting for it to arrive, but not beyond that.

He hated to make contact with Vorshage's men, but decided it could no longer be avoided. He checked out of the Pierre Hotel, getting a three-hundred-dollar cash advance on the card to tide him over, and took a cab to Penn Station, where he caught the next train to Philadelphia. He nearly threw the card away as he used the men's room in the train station, but instead he put it back into his wallet. It might be necessary in an emergency.

2

LOS ANGELES INTERNATIONAL was one of the first airports in the world to be equipped with the new neutron-activation luggage-surveying equipment, computer-driven to scan for high nitrogen-to-oxygen ratios. All luggage to be deposited in an airplane's cargo compartment passes first under neutron scrutiny, and if a high ratio is discovered sirens sound and men come running, for such a signal is a virtual fingerprint of plastic explosives such as the type that destroyed Pan Am flight 103 over Lockerbie, Scotland, several years ago.

But Grass was not worried. The small package of amorphous plastic, wrapped in clear plastic and resting among his underclothes, was the newest type of explosive. Its nitrogen-to-oxygen ratio, unlike that of early versions, was well within the range of ordinary materials. Once again the forces of antiterrorism had concocted a multimillion-dollar solution to a problem that had advanced beyond their comprehension.

No sirens went off, no men came running, and the Los Angeles–to–New York flight departed on time. The plastic did not explode, of course; it wouldn't do that until Grass had set it to go off at the right place and the right time.

Nevertheless, it was not a pleasant flight. Throughout it Grass glowered and cursed under his breath, and he arrived in New York accompanied by an almost paranoid conviction that he was in the wrong place. Waldner's itinerary called for him to fly to Washington first, spending two days and nights, meeting with federal officials and the President, and giving three public speeches, after which he would fly to New York for a couple of days to address the United Nations, then to Florida for a gathering of the governors of the fifty states, and then on to California.

Washington was therefore the most likely hit site. That Naman had flown to New York meant nothing: There simply were no direct Munich–Washington flights. He had probably stepped off the plane in New York and gone straight to Penn Station and taken the Metroliner to Washington.

But Grass knew that as soon as he flew to Washington he'd be assailed by doubts suggesting that the hit was to be made in New York, and that Naman was even now making his preparations there.

Patience, he counseled himself. Patience and thoroughness. As long as he was here he'd see what he could see. He took a cab to the Pierre Hotel and registered as Ralph Berner. As he signed the register he asked if his friend Fred Nagle had arrived. The reception clerk checked, and told him that they had no reservation in that name. Grass went to his room and kicked the furniture. Naman could be anywhere in the United States by now, he thought. Well, not quite. He'd have to go to one of the places Waldner would be visiting; preparations for the kill would have to be made.

Grass left the room and checked the hotel dining room and lobby, then went and stood in the small plaza across the street. If Naman was in New York, he'd be staying at the Pierre. He would have to enter and leave the hotel, and so Grass thought he could wait for him here in the plaza. But within ten minutes Grass was telling himself that there was really no necessity for Naman to stay at this hotel: If he was going to hit Waldner in New York it would probably be during his talk at the United Nations.

Damn, damn, damn, Grass thought. *The son of a bitch could be anywhere.*

Impatiently he left the plaza and took a cab to the United Nations. He spent the next three hours there, taking the tour, wandering through the public halls, walking around the neighborhood. He was looking not only for Naman but for whatever Naman might be looking for: a place for the hit, an opportunity, something, anything . . .

He found nothing. Since he didn't know what Naman's plan was he didn't know what to look for or even in which city to look; he had no way of even guessing at what preparations Naman might have to make. He had no hope of catching up to Naman, he thought. His only chance was if Naman were to contact one of Vorshage's men.

But there was no reason for Naman to do that since he already had all the money he needed. Damn, Grass thought. Well, meanwhile he could take care of some business. He had things to do. He walked down the street to the subway and took the E train out to Jamaica. He took a taxi to the offices of Audio Technology Associates, and walked in. It was a small office with a counter at one end. A buzzer went off as he entered, and in a moment a young man appeared and asked if he could help him.

"Henry Larkinson," Grass announced. "You're holding a package for me."

The young man behind the counter checked his records, went into the back room, and came back with a small package, which he put on the counter. Grass paid for it in cash. As the young man wrote the receipt, Grass took the gun out of his pocket and screwed in the silencer. The young man finished writing the receipt and looked up to hand it to him, and Grass lifted the gun to the man's face and pulled the trigger.

The young man's body bounced backward with the force of the bullet that shattered his head; he hit the wall and fell to the floor, leaving streaks of gray matter and red blood on the wall. Grass waited a moment to see if anyone else in the building came running out, but no one did. There had hardly been a sound worth mentioning.

He turned and walked out.

He went back to the Pierre, took the elevator straight up to his room, and called the Sheraton Park in Washington. He asked to speak to Fred Nagle. The receptionist replied that no one by that name was registered or expected. Grass called the Breakers in Palm Beach, the Hyatt in Los Angeles, all the hotels where Waldner was scheduled to stay during his trip, but found Nagle registered at none of them.

Grass's resources were extensive, but at the moment useless. He could place surveillance at each of the hotels, and even along the routes Waldner would take for his public appearances, but he had no one who knew Naman personally. He could distribute pictures, but even the slightest makeup could change a man's appearance from his pictures. And clearly Naman was, if not suspicious about being followed, at least extremely cautious.

He wondered if perhaps he shouldn't have canceled the surveillance on Naman's office; maybe Naman would go back there for some reason. No, at this point he would never go anywhere he might be recognized. But perhaps he might yet need one of Vorshage's contacts. . . .

Not likely, but Grass recognized that one who is drowning must grasp at whatever straws come to hand. He picked up the telephone and put through calls to detective agencies in Philadelphia and Chicago, identifying himself as Ralph Berner, asking them to place surveillance on the Vorshage contacts. They wouldn't recognize Naman, but he left instructions to follow anyone who showed up, with particular attention to be paid to an elderly man, about five foot eight, with gray hair that might be dyed dark, weighing one hundred fifty pounds that might be augmented by padding.

The third and last contact was in Los Angeles; Grass called the Jay Preston Agency again. He was put through to Preston and gave him the same order. He nearly hung up then, but before he could Preston said, "There's something else. I was hoping you'd call. We had some results on the earlier investigation you ordered, but I had no way to contact you to let you know."

"Results? What do you mean?"

"Yesterday, just after you called to cancel, several people visited the office. We have a clear photograph. Would you like me to send it to you?"

"Describe the people."

"Yes sir. If you'll hold on for just a moment I'll see if I can locate the film right away." He put down the phone, checked with Miss Fellowes and found that Conrad was in his office, and walked down the hall. "About that photograph from the Worldwide Securities case," he said without preamble as he entered. "Could you get it for me?"

Conrad had been a million miles away. Well, four thousand five hundred, to be exact: sunbathing naked on the beach at Pago Pago with Madonna and Marilyn Monroe. But he was quick on the uptake. In the flicker of an instant he saw his chance for revenge. The photo had suddenly become important. "Miss Fellowes told me to destroy it," he said.

"What?" Why did these things happen to him? Preston wondered. Why couldn't he ever hire competent help?

"Yes, sir," Conrad went on. "Matter of fact, what she told me to do was to take the film and shove it up my—"

"You didn't do it?" Preston pleaded.

"No, sir, of course not!"

"I mean you didn't destroy it?"

"As a matter of fact, I didn't," Conrad said in his best James Bond voice. "I thought it might be important, and so I took the responsibility of saving it despite her orders."

Preston began to breathe again. He didn't know how he could have explained to his client that the evidence had been destroyed after telling him a moment ago that they had it in their possession.

In point of fact, Conrad had planned to clean out his office today and intended to dispose of the film. He would already have done so had he not been seduced by the glinting sunlight outside his windows, reminding him of what life could be like on Pago Pago with Madonna and Marilyn. Had he been the well-organized, industrious boy his mother had always intended him to be, the evidence would even now be burning in the building's incinerator. Instead, Conrad reached forward on his desk and picked up the photograph. Preston took it, returned to his office, and described it for Grass. "There's a middle-aged dark-skinned woman and a young good-looking Anglo woman. There are two men. One is tall and slim, middle to late thirties, aquiline features. The other is a black man, even taller and very heavy, a real giant, probably in his late fifties."

Neither of them was Naman, Grass thought.

"The group split up after leaving the office," Preston continued, "and our operative chose to follow the older woman. He followed her to her home, and from our contacts with the telephone company and later conversations with her neighbors he ascertained that her name is Norma Middler and that she served as secretary to Worldwide Consultants."

"He didn't follow the others?"

"He couldn't follow both groups, I'm afraid."

"Fax me the picture," Grass said, giving him his hotel address in New York. "Start the surveillance again, and if anyone comes follow the visitors, not the secretary."

Well, he thought, that was unexpected. He wondered who the people were and what their visit meant. Two things at least were clear: Someone else was looking for Walter Naman, and grasping for straws should never be neglected.

3

By the time Melnik had finished explaining to Horner and Wintre that they were following the gray Plymouth because the man in it had snapped their picture when they came out of Worldwide Security, several corners had been turned and it was clear that the Plymouth was following Norma Middler's cab. Melnik told the driver to stop the chase and take them instead to police headquarters. "It's 3 HET 275," he said to Horner, who nodded. At the last traffic light they had pulled up close behind the Plymouth, and he too had noted the license number.

At police headquarters they climbed out of the cab. As they walked up the steps Horner said, "I been thinking. You know, that wasn't a very smart thing we did, on the phone with Audio. What if they're a cover, a front? What if they're in on it?"

"Damn," Melnik said. Maybe Mazor was right, maybe he was getting too old. Or maybe he was just stupid. If Horner was right they had just tipped off the other side that they were on the trail. "I'll check them out with Tel Aviv right away," he said. "See if we know anything about them."

"I know somebody in the CIA," Wintre put in. "I'll call him and see if he's ever heard of them."

"Right," Horner said. "Meanwhile I'll find out what we know about 3 HET 275."

When they came back together again several hours later Horner greeted them with a gruff smile. "I've made some progress," he said. "Have you?"

"Audio seems clear," Melnik said, and Wintre nodded. "Neither Mossad nor CIA have anything on them. So that's okay. What did you find out?"

"The man in the gray Plymouth is William Conrad. Motor Vehicles gave us his Social Security number, and the IRS—with some prodding from my friends here—gave us his place of business: the Jay Preston Detective Agency. The people here tell me it's totally legit, which is bad news because it means he won't name any of his clients, and we don't have any lever to prod him with."

Melnik nodded. "You done good," he said. "From here on in it looks like a job for Super Mossad. I'll go in tonight and see what I can find."

"Well, yes," Horner admitted, sucking his teeth. "You could do that."

Melnik looked at him with curiosity. "Or . . . ?"

"Well, I checked some records, and they didn't pan out, and then I checked some things that *did* pan out."

"And?"

"Well, like I said, you *could* break the law and smash a window in the Preston Agency offices tonight and sneak in and look over his books, and maybe you'd find something, and maybe you'd get caught, because after all it *is* a detective agency and these people can reasonably be expected to be sort of security-minded. . . ."

"Or?"

"Or you could go talk to the man. I checked the charitable foundations in Los Angeles, and it turns out that Mr. Jay Preston is an extremely heavy hitter with the Hadassah Mount Sinai Hospital in Tel Aviv, and with the United Jewish Relief Fund."

Melnik smiled. Horner spread his hands. "The man's a Zionist," he said. "And I bet he's never in his whole life met a real, honest-to-God secret Israeli Mossad agent."

It was the following afternoon before Melnik caught up with Jay Preston, but when he did he found that Horner had been right: Preston was thrilled when he introduced himself and produced his Mossad identification. Melnik told him that Walter Naman had been on the trail of a high-level Nazi—

"I had heard stories," Preston said eagerly.

—and that he, Melnik, was interested in whoever was interested in Naman's death, in whoever was keeping surveillance on whoever happened to visit Naman's office.

Preston was silent.

Melnik said, "We know that you're keeping a watch on Worldwide Security."

Preston shook his head. "I couldn't possibly give you the name of my client."

"I understand," Melnik said. "You have principles in your profession, and you don't want to compromise them."

Preston nodded. He bit his lip.

"You have principles in your life, too," Melnik went on, hitting hard. "We're talking about a resurgent Nazi plot here. We're not talking about something that happened fifty years ago. We're talking about something that's happening right now. Somebody killed Naman because he was on to them, and they're keeping a lookout to find whoever he was working with. The problem is, he wasn't working with anyone;

he was a loner. And we don't know very much about what's happening, and we've come up against a stone wall. We've got no more leads, we have nowhere to go. Unless you give us something."

He waited. Preston didn't say a word. Melnik noticed that he had begun to sweat. "He canceled the surveillance at Worldwide," he said reluctantly. "He told us to keep an eye on another place now." He gave Melnik the address. "We're supposed to follow anyone who shows up. He's specially interested in the same person he was looking for at Worldwide: an elderly man, five eight, a hundred and fifty pounds."

Naman, Melnik thought. Somebody else knew Naman was alive, and was looking for him. "It's important that we know who ordered this surveillance," Melnik said. "Without that we're just spinning our wheels while the plot unfolds."

A long moment went by. "I don't think I can help you," Preston said finally. "We don't have an address for him. He calls in for our reports—" Preston stopped. He gave a little grin, almost to himself. "The son of a bitch goofed," he said, remembering. "He had us fax him the picture Conrad took of you."

"Where to?"

Preston glanced in his desk diary. "Mr. Ralph Berner, at the Pierre Hotel in New York. It might not be his real name, and I don't know how long he's going to be there. You'd better hurry."

4

HORNER TELEPHONED to New York and got hold of his partner, Jeff Blank. He told him to get a handle on a Mr. Ralph Berner at the Pierre.

"Is this a warrant-type thing?" Blank asked.

"No, we've got no probable cause, and Waxman won't authorize it, you understand? This is just a personal favor I'm asking, an informal, friendly look-see."

"Gotcha," Blank said, and hung up.

"I think maybe the best thing now is we call Audio and ask them for some cooperation," Horner suggested. Melnik agreed and Horner put the call through. He reached the manager, and his face fell. He talked for several more minutes, then hung up. "Too late," he said. "Someone picked up the package yesterday afternoon."

So they had made a mistake at Audio after all, Melnik thought, only not the one they had feared. If they had tried to arrange cooperation immediately, they might have caught their man. "Can they identify him? Someone must have seen him. If it was just yesterday they'll remember what he looked like and—''

Horner shook his head. ''The guy who picked up the tape dusted the clerk. Shot him in the face. No motive, nothing stolen, and the clerk wouldn't have had any reason to resist turning over the package. Shot at close range in the face. Other people in the building heard nothing, so it was a silencer. They found a receipt made out to Henry Larkinson. No one but the dead clerk had seen him, so there was no description. Could have been Naman,'' Horner concluded.

Melnik shook his head. ''Not his style. Mr. Naman doesn't walk around killing people.''

''The man with the limp does,'' Lisle suggested.

Melnik nodded. ''I wonder,'' he wondered, ''if Mr. Ralph Berner limps?''

5

DETECTIVE JEFF BLANK got to the hotel within fifteen minutes, with his jacket held casually in one hand over his shoulder, Kennedy-style, tieless, his white short-sleeved shirt undone at the collar and with the sleeves rolled up a half inch. The dark-gray pants of his business suit and his black working shoes would have given him away, but he walked quickly through the lobby and up to the telephone receptionist before she glanced up; by the time she did so, all she could see of him was the top half. He flashed her a quick glimpse of his best Robert Redford smile, then turned away and glanced just a bit furtively around the room. When he turned back the smile was just a haunting image and his eyes showed a casual concern. ''Hi,'' he said.

''Can I help you?'' she asked.

''I sure hope so. I've got a delivery to make to Mr. Ralph Berner, but I've forgotten his room number.''

''Just a moment.'' She glanced down at her records and then looked up again. ''I'll ring him and see if he's in.''

''No,'' Blank whispered violently, leaning across the partition. He pulled back and glanced over his shoulder again to make sure no one was listening. He leaned forward again, with just a touch of the old Redford magic. He enjoyed doing this. The trick was not to do it so that you came across as charming, but rather so that you seemed sincere, as if you were unaware of the charm—which would then take care of itself. ''I've got a *delivery* to make,'' he whispered. He pulled out of his pocket a small plastic envelope full of white talcum powder and flashed it quickly at her. He slipped it back into his pocket. "I'm supposed to remember things like people's room numbers. He'll get hysterical if you call him for me. He'll think everyone on the hotel staff knows he's getting the stuff, you know what I mean? Something like this could be worth my job, and it's a real good-paying job."

"I'm not supposed to give out anyone's room number without permission," she said.

"Well, I know that. But I bet there are also a few things your mother told you you weren't supposed to do, with or without permission, which maybe you do once in a while, am I right? I'm sorry, I shouldn't have said that," he apologized, backing down immediately and flashing her that boyish grin again. "It's just that, like, you know."

"Well," she said.

He should have been an actor, he thought, leaning forward again on the partition and giving her the full benefit of his smile. If he was going to linger on the edge of poverty with a cop's salary, he might as well plunge right into it with an actor's salary; at least then he'd be getting applause for a performance like this.

"Sixteen-eleven," she whispered. "But don't tell anyone I told you."

He went to the house phone and dialed 1611. There was no answer. He walked to the cashier's desk in the front lobby and said, "Sixteen-eleven, checking out."

"Yes sir," the young man said, and a moment later presented Blank with the computerized bill. Blank glanced at it and said, "There must be some mistake. I didn't make any long-distance phone calls."

"Let me check that," the young man said. He came back a few moments later and said, "They're clearly recorded on your phone, Mr. Berner."

"Could I see the numbers, please?" he asked. The clerk showed him the computerized list. "Let me just check these out," he said, pulling a small notebook from his pocket. As he looked from the list to his notebook, flipping pages as if searching for his records, he memorized each of the four numbers. Then he looked back up at the clerk and said, rather embarrassed, "These are all phone numbers of my wife's relatives. I guess I'm going to have to pay the bill. I just wish she'd tell me when she does this."

"Yes sir," the clerk said, smiling in return.

Blank looked back down at the bill. "There's another mistake. You've got a date missing, the fourteenth."

"No, sir. Today is the sixteenth, and you're leaving today so there's no charge."

Blank looked up at him in astonishment. "Isn't today Wednesday? The seventeenth?"

"No sir, it's Tuesday."

"Oh, I'm so stupid. Excuse me, will you? I thought it was Wednesday. I'm not checking out after all. I'll be here another night." He grinned self-consciously, turned, and walked out. As soon as he got outside he wrote the phone numbers down in his notebook, before he forgot them, then came back in and went straight to the gift shop, killing time until the clerk he had talked to left for a coffee break.

There wasn't much more he could do. He was always happy to spend an idle hour helping out a partner, but he really couldn't stay much longer. No way he could hang around and wait for Berner to show up; Horner might be on semi-vacation, but Blank had his own work to do. When the clerk left the front desk he slipped on his jacket and took the tie out of his pocket and tied it around his neck. He went back to the desk, showed his badge, and asked to speak to the manager. He was taken down the hall and around the corner to an open frosted-glass door beside which stood a handsome man ten year's Blank's senior, Paul Newman to his Robert Redford.

"I'm Mr. Cartwright," the man said. "Please come in." He ushered Blank into his office and asked what he could do for him.

"We're interested in the man occupying room 1611. He's registered under the name of Ralph Berner."

Cartwright lifted his eyebrows. "May I inquire how you know his room number?"

Blank smiled engagingly. "That's not really relevant, is it? In fact, the fact that he's staying in your hotel at all is not relevant."

"I'm glad to hear that."

Blank nodded. "With your cooperation there won't have to be any mention at all of the hotel when he's picked up. He simply happens to be in New York."

"What can I do to help you?"

"Well, the situation is this. We want him, and we can do it either of two ways. I've got a warrant now for his arrest, but it doesn't specify where he is. I can go back and get a new warrant made out including the fact that he's in room 1611, and I can come back here with a dozen uniforms and block off all the entrances and go up and kick the door down. That's one way."

Without missing a beat Cartwright said, "You mentioned there were two ways."

Blank nodded. "I can wait until he leaves the hotel and pick him up on the street. Less fuss, less bother for everyone."

Cartwright agreed. "That would certainly be preferable from our point of view."

"Only problem is, I don't know what he looks like."

"I'm astounded. You seem to know so much about him."

"Except what he looks like. So how am I going to pick him up on the street?"

"I see your problem," Cartwright said.

"So I really ought to just go in and take him from the room. But I know you wouldn't like that, and we like to cooperate with our citizens."

"I appreciate that."

"So if you'll just let me know when he checks out, we can follow him outside and pick him up."

Cartwright thought that over. "Could I see your identification?" he asked. Blank handed it over to him. Cartwright read it carefully, then handed it back. "How do I notify you?" he asked.

"What I want you to do is tell all your desk clerks to be on the lookout for this guy. When he shows up at the desk to check out, you take his picture—"

"How can we do that?"

"I thought we weren't playing games with each other," Blank reprimanded him. "You know and I know, and you sure as hell oughta know that I know, that you've got an automated camera set up in the registration area to take pictures any time you want. Like when people cash checks, or when someone passes a note over the counter asking for all the money or he'll kill everyone in the lobby. So you tell your people to just reach out with their little toe and click the camera when he shows up. Then you call this number"—he leaned forward and scribbled a number on Cartwright's notepad—"and that will get through to me. I'll hop on my horse and be here as quick as I can. You hold the guy up, without making it obvious."

"I don't see how we can procrastinate if he wants to check out."

"Mr. Cartwright," Blank said sadly, shaking his head. "The computer goes down, right? You can't get his itemized bill ready. I dunno, every time I check out of a hotel it seems to take an hour or two. Look, I don't want to ask too much of you, for my sake as well as yours. I don't want him suspicious that you might be stalling or he'll take off running. So just do the best you can. If you can't hold him, you can't. But make damn sure you get his picture. Or, like I say, if you'd rather—?''

Cartwright stood up and extended his hand. "We're always happy to cooperate with the police. And I appreciate your taking the trouble to spare the hotel any unnecessary fuss."

"My pleasure," Blank said, shaking his hand. "Maybe someday you can do me a favor." He left Cartwright's office feeling satisfied with himself. He didn't think he had much chance to keep tabs on Berner when he checked out, but at the very least he had the list of phone numbers Berner had called and a good chance of getting his picture. Horner ought to be happy. And it never hurt to have the manager of a fancy hotel in your debt.

He walked through the lobby to the bank of pay telephones and called Horner, collect.

6

EVERY MORNING Klaus Vorshage felt like Snow White's wicked step-mother. He would go to his office, and the first thing he did there was ask the magic mirror: "Mirror, mirror on the wall, / Who's the fairest of them all?" And every day the mirror reported that he was, and he would turn from it and get on with his life.

Those were not quite the words he used, of course, and he didn't exactly use a mirror. It was actually a computer screen, and instead of talking to it he would tap into the central computer and access a program he had written himself. He wouldn't speak to the mirror, but he would type in the opening command. The video screen would then print out the response: "*Nichts.*" He would sign out of the program and begin the day's work.

Today, however, when he keyed in there was a slight pause, and then a quite different message came on the screen, the equivalent of "Hair so black, skin so white, / The fairest in the land is now Snow White." What it actually said was

London Times. February 18. Page 63. Francois Gilbert, a French-born English citizen, was found tortured and murdered in his photography shop in the village of Ravenscrag, Lancs. Neighbors had reported to the village constabulary that Gilbert, 75 years old, had not been seen for several days. Upon entering his shop, police found him strapped naked to a table with electrical wires attached to his genitals and anus. They theorize that a break-in occurred, and when no money was found the victim was tortured to reveal its whereabouts, although they do not discount the possibility that it was a crime of sexual deviation.

Gilbert came to England with Free French forces in 1940, and fought under De Gaulle for the remainder of the war. He opened his photography shop in 1945 and married an Englishwoman. . . .

"Merde," Vorshage muttered. He had programmed the computer to track all stories in major newspapers around the world relating to anyone whose name was linked to Naman in the Bundesnachrichtendienst files. He hadn't really expected anything to show up. Of course it was possible that the *Times* was right, that the murder was a simple break-in or a "crime of sexual deviation." It was also possible that someone was looking for Naman and had tortured Gilbert in order to discover his whereabouts. But why Gilbert?

Vorshage leaned back in his chair and let his memory drift. A photography shop . . . Yes, of course. Gilbert was not only Naman's old friend, he was in the business of providing documents to those who needed them. Naman might very well have gone to him for a new passport. But who would know about Gilbert and his relationship to Naman? People Naman had worked with: the Israelis, probably; the CIA, possibly. People with whom, perhaps, Naman had had a beer or two, and let down his guard and talked about the old days. There would not be many such people.

He read the article again. This did not seem like the work of those people. But you never knew, these days. Well, nothing to be done now except warn Naman. He erased the message from the computer, picked up his telephone, and dictated a short message to be placed in the London and New York *Times*.

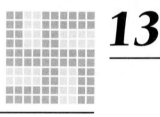

13

1

WILLIAM HAGAN was not happy. Things had been going badly for the past few months, and had been crashing disastrously over the past week or so. During the preceding few years he had managed to establish himself in the eyes of the high-tech defense industry as the man who got things done: the man who took the credit for all the multibillion-dollar contracts for smart bombs, intelligent missiles, laser-guided juggernauts with onboard computers that not only mimicked but transcended human intelligence in terms of split-second decision-making capabilities. This reputation had enabled Hagan to extract promises and credits for future financial support when he made his move toward a more important national office. And this coming year he was poised to make that move, and right now the bottom was dropping out of the weapons market.

In truth he had been no more than a skilled surfer these past few years. He had ridden the crest of the wave with such dexterity that people watching thought he controlled it. But he had no more power over the waves than any other surfer, and when the waves stopped coming he could no more raise his hands and cause them to rise and flow than old King Canute had been able to make them desist.

It was a desperate time for him; he needed another wave, he told himself, as he sat in his living room sipping his third whiskey of the evening, watching his wife watch television.

She wasn't watching a damn thing, he thought; she was seeing something the FCC would never allow broadcast. She was seeing naked bodies writhing in passion, exploding, sucking, absorbing. . . . Looking into her languorous face, he could nearly see those images himself, and his groin began to pulse. If he were a violent man, he thought, he could take great pleasure from picking her up by her throat and throttling her while her toes kicked and dangled inches above the ground—

"Penny for your thoughts," she said, and he realized with a start that she was looking at him instead of the television set.

He shook his head. "Nothing you'd be interested in," he said. "Business."

"You looked so intense, and you were staring at me."

He forced a smile. "Didn't know what I was looking at. Afraid I was a million miles away." *In a different universe,* he thought. *We don't inhabit the same universe, you and I.* . . . He wondered what would happen if he simply spoke up and told her what he was thinking. No—he shook his head sadly as she turned back to the television and her own thoughts—if two people can't communicate the least they can do is shut up. Tom Lehrer, he remembered; he couldn't remember from what song.

What really rankled, he thought, was that she was a stupid damn woman who hadn't the faintest idea what his world was about. If he tried to tell her about his career problems she wouldn't even know what he was talking about. She had no idea how to manipulate politicians or the system, how to squeeze a rich living out of a democracy, how to make a place for oneself in society. Without him she would be nothing and nobody, flotsam in the sewer-stream of life. And yet she was making a fool out of him, and he was helpless to stop her. He could manipulate and control people because he understood them and the world in which they operated. He knew what they wanted and how to get it for them. But of all the people in the world, the one he understood least was his own wife. The world she dwelt in was as alien to him as if she were an exotic species of bug: He saw her flitting from flower to flower, but he hadn't the faintest idea why.

The doorbell rang. Hagan glanced at his wife. Had she forgotten he was going to be home this evening? Had she gotten mixed up in her dates, and was he now going to see her lover face to face for the first time? The thought excited him, and he got a positive thrill when she turned from the television and looked at him with sudden realization in her eyes. "Oh dear," she said. "I forgot."

He got unsteadily to his feet.

"That'll be your Miss Wintre," she continued, and he nearly fell back into his chair. But all he said was "What?"

"I'm sorry, love, I forgot to tell you. Your office called today while you were on your way home, to say that Miss Wintre was returning from Los Angeles and wanted to see you. Your secretary said she told her to come here this evening, and asked me if I thought that was all right. I said yes. It probably could wait till tomorrow, but I know how you like to stay on top of things."

Everything she said to him these days seemed to be loaded with a hidden sexual connotation, as if she were either teasing him or making fun of him. He wished he knew which.

She got to her feet. "I know you'll want to be alone, and this will probably take hours, so I'll run out to a movie."

"No. It'll just take a minute or two."

"Oh." She appeared so contrite. "I just naturally assumed you'd be busy all evening. I mean, if it was so important that she had to come here instead of waiting till tomorrow. So I went ahead and made a movie date." She glanced at her watch. "I really ought to be going. Unless you want me to cancel?"

"No," he said. "You go ahead. It'll probably take longer than I think."

"That's what I thought," she said. "I'll go get ready, then."

He watched her run upstairs, then went to the front door. It was indeed Miss Wintre, and he took her into his den.

"Something is going on," she said without preamble.

He gestured her to a seat, took his own behind his desk, folded his hands, and nodded encouragingly.

"Walter Naman's secretary is convinced he didn't die in the car bomb. A man named Vorshage, an old buddy of his who coincidentally now runs the German secret service, warned him several weeks ago of a threat to his life."

Hagan lifted his eyebrows and leaned back in his seat, and she told him everything she, Melnik, and Horner had discovered in Los Angeles. Midway through her recitation he heard his wife's footsteps coming down the stairs and going through the front hall, and the door opened and closed. Miss Wintre, of course, paid no attention. "There is definitely something going on," she concluded. "Melnik's story of a wholesale Nazi uprising may have sounded farfetched at first, but it's beginning to look a lot less silly now."

Hagan nodded. So often when he was ostensibly listening to people talking earnestly about the major concerns of their life he was actually thinking of other things far more important to him. But now, with his wife on her way to her lover's bed, this conversation *was* the really important happening in his life. Maybe there was a God in heaven after all, he thought. But he had to tread carefully. He mustn't end up taking any blame for letting it happen, nor must he allow it to be prevented from happening. "You and the Israeli make a good team," he said. "Are you still working with the New York policeman?"

"Yes. He was the one responsible for getting the Los Angeles Police Department to cooperate."

"Good. Although I don't imagine there's anything more he can help us with. You may as well let him return to New York and his other duties. Nor is there much for this fellow Melnik to do just at the moment. I'll arrange for FBI surveillance of the three posts you found out about, and you tell Melnik to lie low for a while. Meanwhile, I'd like you to go to Germany and see what you can find out."

She nodded eagerly.

"Play it rather cool," he said. "I don't want you to make any official contacts. If what Melnik says is really happening, this movement may pervade the entire German government. Until we know how far they've infiltrated the political apparatus we won't know whom we can trust. Talk to people at the lowest possible levels, without giving anything away, and see if you can get a feel for the situation. I'll be looking into it from the highest levels over here, and when you get back in a week or ten days we'll put our heads together and see where we stand. Maybe at that point we'll be ready to take some action."

And that was his Rubicon, he thought as he stood at the door watching her drive away. Strange how the river of decision in one's life is suddenly just there with no warning. One always imagines that one will see it in the distance, faintly at first, growing with each advancing step until finally one stands on the shore of the raging waters while the thunder roars and the earth shakes, and it is then that one makes the decision that will change everything one way or the other. But in real life you walk through a fog, where events have no chance to cast a shadow into the future, and suddenly the water is lapping at your feet and a decision must be made. And you make it, and what happens next is in the lap of the gods . . .

No, he thought as he closed the door thoughtfully. What happened next was in his own hands. He held the cards, and he would play them and win the game. If the event actually happened, if the German chancellor was done in and the specter of a Nazi beast rose from his grave, there would be questions asked of him. But only if anyone knew that Miss Wintre had come here tonight.

He counted off on his fingers. His secretary knew that Wintre was coming; Melnik and that policeman would know; but none of them could prove that she had actually arrived. Yes, she was supposed to have seen him tonight, but she had never shown up. No one could say differently except his wife, and he could trust her.

He smiled at that, but it was true. In a matter like this, he could trust her.

Wintre would tell Melnik about their conversation, but Hagan was confident he could have him shut up. And if not, he could still deny that Wintre had ever come here, had ever told him what they had discovered in Los Angeles. The policeman could do no more than corroborate Melnik's version; there might remain the question of why Wintre had lied to them, had not come to him as she should have, but there would be no proof against him.

If he were lucky, of course. A man had to have some luck, or all the plans in the world were of no use. Napoleon might have all the generals in France plan every aspect of his campaign, but if winter came early and the roads turned to mud and the snows came pouring out of heaven all those plans were useless. If winter had been late he would have conquered the world; but winter had come early, and his empire had crashed.

As for himself—he smiled—if he was lucky Wintre would never come back alive.

He couldn't actually see to that, of course. He couldn't have had her killed even if he had the means; he wasn't that sort of man. But she was naïve enough, and tough enough, to do as he suggested: He had seen her eyes light up with the challenge as he asked her to investigate the German roots of the conspiracy. And so if she was wrong, if there really was nothing in this supposed plan to kill the chancellor, she would find nothing in Germany and would return empty-handed and nothing would ever come of it. So no harm done.

But if she was right she would almost certainly blunder into someone's path. She could hardly help coming to the notice of the participants, who would have no hesitation in putting her out of the way. And then there would be no one, after the assassination, to ask why in fact

Hagan had never notified the FBI, had never asked for surveillance on the three posts Wintre and Melnik had uncovered, had done nothing to stop the plot.

What plot? He knew nothing about it, nothing beyond a vague warning from an obscure Israeli agent. What could he have been expected to do about that?

Wintre was furious at Hagan as she left the deputy assistant secretary's house and got into her car, furious that he should take her for such a naïve fool. Did he really believe she was stupid enough to think she could go into a strange country and ferret out these things? Melnik was right, she thought. Hagan was trying to slow down their investigation without actually derailing it or ordering it to cease. He must know that if she did as he said she'd be simply spinning her wheels in Germany while the investigation was put on hold. She didn't know anyone in Germany; she couldn't even speak the language properly. She couldn't possibly walk into a strange country and learn secrets of a most sensitive nature. She felt a hot flame of anger as she realized what he must think of her.

And then she flushed as she thought back to how naïve she actually had been when she began to work for Hagan a few short weeks ago. *Yes,* she thought, *he does believe that of me.* And she realized that she was furious not so much at Hagan as at herself, for ever having been such a fool.

She was also rather angry with Melnik for having been right, and then again she realized it was herself she was angry with in this case too, for having been so stupid as not to see from the very beginning that he might be right. She had believed the sophisticated sophistry of Hagan, and now was being forced to eat, if not her words, at least her thoughts—which tasted no less bitter for never having been uttered aloud.

When Blank reported to Horner and Melnik the list of phone numbers Berner had called they immediately recognized one of them: the Jay Preston Detective Agency in Los Angeles. The other two numbers were in Philadelphia and Chicago.

"Contact houses," Melnik said immediately, and Horner nodded agreement. "In three cities, and this guy doesn't know which one Naman will go to. Five'll get you twenty those other two phone numbers are private-detective agencies like Preston's."

"No bet," Melnik agreed. "But what are the odds they're Zionists like Preston?"

When Lisle Wintre reported back to them that Hagan had said he would set up surveillance at the places they had discovered from the Ralph Berner phone list Blank had provided, Melnik was happy. "Good," he said.

She shook her head. "I don't believe him." She told him what Hagan had told her to do in Germany, and Melnik smiled bitterly. "Of course," he said. "Lisle Wintre, girl spy, will walk into Germany and discover all the secrets we've been unable to find in two months."

"Exactly," she said. "He just wants to get me out of the way. I don't know what his game is. I thought at first he was right and you were being silly with your story about a plot to kill Waldner, and then I thought he was still right not to believe it even though it looked as though something might be happening because there wasn't any real proof, but now it's clear that something is happening and he still doesn't take it seriously. And worse, he pretends that he does."

Horner agreed. "That's much worse," he said. "He's got some kind of hidden agenda."

"Do you think he's in on the plot?" Wintre asked, then shook her head. "No, no. It's so easy to get paranoid in this game. That would be too much."

Melnik agreed. "It's not impossible, but it would be stretching the lines of communication so far that I'm sure we would have picked up a hint by now. But who knows what weird political motive he's got up his sleeve? At any rate, we certainly can't trust him to do as he says." He turned to Horner. "Can you get us any help from the New York police in setting up a surveillance?"

Horner shook his head. "The reason I'm with you on this is that I'm on unofficial leave from the department prior to retiring for good. They don't care what I do. But there's no way they're going to give me any help that costs money for a problem that's not New York's. I can get a buddy like Blank to help us out for an hour or two without going through channels, but I can't do more than that."

"We'll have to do it ourselves, then," Melnik said. "I'll take Philadelphia, you take Chicago, and we'll have to trust Preston for Los Angeles."

"You don't want me to go there?" Wintre asked.

"No," Melnik said. "You're not trained for surveillance work, and it's tougher than it looks in the movies. You'd stick out like a sore thumb to any experienced operator, and we have to assume whoever we're looking for is no amateur. You'd not only lose him, you'd alert him that we're after him."

"So what should I do, take up knitting?"

Melnik smiled. "You go to Germany, like Hagan wants. Just don't do anything stupid like wandering around asking loaded questions. I can't believe he really wants any harm to come to you, but that's a good way to get yourself killed. Go visit the Wall and a few museums, take in the Berlin Philharmonic, see an opera or two, and come home. Tell him that you couldn't find out anything and let's see what his reaction is."

"And meanwhile you two guys have all the fun."

"It's a cruel world," Melnik agreed. "Unjust, no doubt about it."

2

WALTER NAMAN sat munching a bagel in the deli on Broad Street in Philadelphia. This time of day, mid-morning, it was uncrowded and he had a table by the plate-glass window. He had spent the morning looking for the perfect location, and this was it. The window was tinted against the sun, and with the sun at its morning angle no one from the outside could see in. He had called the contact house twenty minutes ago, and had been answered with a simple "Hello."

"This is Monroe," he had said. "Whom am I speaking to?"

There was a short pause, and then the man answered correctly, "Taylor. What's up?"

"Thought I'd take a walk on the cliffs today."

"Not for me, thanks. It looks like rain."

"Maybe you're right. Let's go to a movie."

So everything was okay. "I need the money," Naman said. "Do you have it in the house?"

"It's in a safety deposit box," the man answered. "I can get it for you right away."

"No, not quite yet." Though the man had said there were no problems, Naman was afraid there might be things he wasn't aware of. "Take a walk up to Broad Street," he told him. "Turn south and stop at the first phone booth." He hung up.

Naman glanced at his watch. He had walked by the house himself first thing this morning, and had seen nothing out of the ordinary. It was a typical Philadelphia row house on a typical street. That was the problem. There were at least thirty houses facing it from the other side of the street, most of them broken up into flats, which made sixty or so possible places from which someone could be watching. In addition the street was lined with parked cars, including several closed vans.

It might all be perfectly ordinary; on the other hand, it might not. Naman looked at his watch again. He had timed the walk from the house, and within a few minutes of his estimate he saw a man come down Broad Street and stop at the phone booth across the street. Naman got up and went to the phone hanging on the wall, dropped in a quarter, and rang the number. Looking through the window he saw the man pick up the phone as soon as it rang.

They went through the same litany as before, and then the man asked, "Is anything wrong?"

"There doesn't appear to be, but it pays to be careful. Continue on, please, and you'll find another phone in about three blocks. Stop there again; if you don't hear from me, go home and wait."

He hung up and went back to his table. The waitress came by and asked if he wanted more coffee. He nodded and she filled the cup as he looked out the window at the man disappearing from sight. Thirty seconds later another man came, walking in the same direction. He stopped at the phone booth, looked it over quickly, and then continued on in no apparent hurry.

Damn, Naman thought, even as he felt a slight surge of gratification that his efforts at caution had not been in vain. You could never trust anyone, he thought. There was always some kind of screw-up. He had been afraid that Vorshage's men would be watched, and now he knew that indeed they were.

"Something wrong with the coffee?" the waitress asked from behind the counter.

Naman turned around. "No. No, the coffee's fine. Thank you."

"Sometimes this damn pot makes it too strong."

"There's no such thing as too-strong coffee. That's an oxymoron."

"What?"

Naman smiled, left his money on the table, and left the deli.

_____

3

GRASS RETURNED to his hotel room late that night after another fruitless day snooping around the Pierre Hotel and the United Nations building, trying to pick up a hint of Naman's whereabouts. Well, no, the day hadn't been entirely fruitless. He had dealt with another bit of necessary business in the morning, arranging the next step in his plan. He had taken the digitized analysis of the Waldner tape to a converted second-floor warehouse off Houston Street in lower Manhattan. The sign on the door read HardSoft; inside there were soft lights, muted music, and a fat man with a beard. Grass explained that he worked for a man who hated bothering with keys.

"A fucking nuisance," the man agreed. "But what are you gonna do?"

"He has an idea," Grass explained. He produced the package and laid it down on the desk. "We've made a digitized analysis of his voice. We'd like you to come up with a software program that recognizes the individual patterns and won't confuse it with any others. The program should provide a signal when the voice is recognized, triggering a solenoid valve to close, thus opening the lock on the door to which it will be attached. Can you do that?"

The man smiled and nodded. "Cute," he said. "So all you have to do is walk up to the door and say 'Open Sesame,' or whatever, instead of fumbling around with a hundred different keys."

"That's it. And put it all on a microchip."

"Well, it's gonna be more than just a chip, you know? You got a little circuitry here."

"How big? Physical dimensions?"

The man held up his thumb and forefinger, making a small circle, and Grass nodded his satisfaction.

After leaving HardSoft he frittered away another day at United Nations Plaza, searching for Naman. His satisfaction at arranging for the Waldner voice-to-solenoid apparatus slowly gave way to anxiety. His fingers began to twitch in frustration. He would never find Naman like this. Hauptmann would have his head. His reputation was gone, vanished in the slipstream of the plane out of Berlin on which Naman had evaded him. He would end his life mugging old ladies for pennies.

He started to laugh. Yes, it was so easy to fall into depression. And so ludicrous. Nothing in life counted if you were not lucky: not skill, hard work, nothing. Edison or one of those old farts used to tell people that genius was one percent inspiration and ninety-nine percent perspiration. He never bothered to mention that there was one ingredient missing; that you had to have point one percent luck, and without it the other ninety-nine point nine percent wasn't worth a damn.

And Grass was lucky. He always had been lucky and always would be. He sat down on the bed, kicked off his shoes, fluffed up the pillows, leaned back, and stretched out his feet. Very consciously, he forced himself to relax. He concentrated on his toes first, willing them to unstiffen, and then worked his way gradually up his legs and torso. It worked okay until he got to his neck. The muscles at the back of his neck just wouldn't unclamp. He heard the sound of laughter, of people laughing at him. He heard them telling each other about the old Jew who had given him the slip. His fingers began to quiver as he thought of how he'd like to put them around the old bastard's neck and twist it as he had the neck of the old man in the nursing home on the shore of the Baltic Sea—

He took a deep breath and closed his eyes. He would wait, that was all. He would sit here like a spider in a web and wait. Nobody could pull off a job like this totally without help, and as soon as Naman tried to contact Vorshage's plants he would be notified. And yet a nagging voice whispered, *If Naman* could *do it on his own* . . . Well, there was nothing he could do about that now. He had laid his snares and now there was nothing to do but wait for Naman to walk into one of them. Sometimes a man had no cards to play but his patience. And his luck.

He lay there with his eyes closed, concentrating on breathing slowly and deeply, slipping into depression.

He was sound asleep, still dressed, early the next morning when the phone rang.

4

STANISLAW PRZYBYLOWICZ had lived in the same house since he fled Poland in 1939. The neighborhood had been all white when he moved in during the war years; working-class, yes, but at least white. The neighbors hadn't been particularly friendly; actually, they hadn't liked the idea of a Polack moving in. Many of them were Jewish in those days, so who were they to be snotty? A lot of them were even from Poland, but they didn't consider themselves Polacks, or even Poles. It hadn't been easy to make friends.

Now he thought of those years as the good old days. Today he was a minority in the neighborhood not because he was Polish, but because he was white. The neighborhood was split fairly evenly between black, Arab, Asian, and white, which left everyone in the minority. Some people liked that. Przybylowicz didn't. It wasn't like the old days. The Jews might have been stuck-up, but at least they kept the streets clean.

And they didn't come breaking into your house at night. Not that anybody would dare come breaking into the Przybylowicz house. He kept a shotgun beside his bed, and he had a huge black Doberman who slept at his feet. The Doberman was named Stalin, so that Przybylowicz could get additional pleasure from hitting him.

Stalin wasn't as mean as the small woman who slept by Przybylowicz's side, but he was a lot noisier. The neighbors could hear the dog barking two or three times every night, when Mrs. Przybylowicz got up to go to the bathroom. Everybody knew about the dog and the shotgun. They knew that anybody sneaking into the Przybylowicz house would evoke a cacophony of frantic barking, and they knew that old man Przybylowicz—though not as mean as his wife—was plenty mean enough to enjoy pulling the trigger of his double-pump 004. He made no secret of it. He lived for the day when one of these smart-ass nigger or wog kids would be stupid enough to come sneaking into his house in the dead of night.

Mr. and Mrs. Przybylowicz lived in the end house on a block of typical Philadelphia row homes, each house sharing a wall with the house next door. Their back door had three locks on it, but the upper half of the door consisted of four panes of glass set in a wood frame. At two o'clock in the morning Walter Naman approached the door silently, and from his pocket took a roll of heavy cellophane tape. Carefully he taped the pane of glass next to the lock, then smacked it hard and sharply with his elbow. The glass cracked softly, the tape holding the pieces in place. He pulled them one by one out of the frame and laid them down on the floor. He worked slowly and cautiously. A man had to be patient. Then he reached in through the opening and quietly slid back the bolts of two of the locks.

The third one was a dead-bolt mechanism, key-operated from both inside and outside. The key was not in the lock. He felt around with his fingers on top of the doorframe, or beside it for a hook on which the key could have been left. There was nothing there.

He went back down the steps to the alley and tried the cellar door. It had only the original lock. Again he taped the window, broke it, and reached inside. He slid back the lock bolt and the door opened easily. *Idiots,* he thought gratefully. Although it didn't much matter. If he hadn't been able to get into this house, the one next in line would have done as well. Of course, it was best to make his entrance into the house farthest from his target, and thus farthest from any possible surveillance.

He crept quietly up the steps from the cellar to the first floor, lighting his way by flashlight.

.   .   .

In Przybylowicz's bedroom Stalin's ears lifted straight up. His eyes blinked open. He lay quietly, breathing heavily, his mouth open, listening.

Naman went quietly through the kitchen and dining room, finding the stairs that led up to the second floor. As he made his way up them, stepping gingerly on each stair—next to the wall instead of in the center, to minimize the possibility of creaking—suddenly there was an explosion of loud barking above him.

Przybylowicz was out of bed before he woke up. He came to consciousness nearly falling down beside his bed, holding on to it for balance, all his nerves shattered by the barking, which went on and on, climbing in intensity and fury.

"Goddamn dog!" he shouted, as he did every night.

He took two steps to the foot of the bed and slapped the dog, hitting its head with an open but hard palm. Stalin growled angrily; the barking subsided. He hid his head on the floor between his paws.

"Every goddamn time you get up to piss," Przybylowicz mumbled to his wife as he lumbered back into bed, "that goddamn dog thinks it's a burglar." He fell into bed and was asleep again in a minute.

Mrs. Przybylowicz opened her eyes for a second, wondered what was going on, and immediately fell asleep again.

Naman waited, straddling the fourth and fifth steps, not moving until the house was quiet again. He wondered if perhaps he should back out and find a house without a dog. But he had come this far, and dogs were vastly overrated as defense mechanisms. He had a way with them, dogs and children. He thought he'd give it a try. Once more he began to move up toward the second floor.

Stalin growled, but he growled softly. He didn't want to be hit again, but he knew that something unusual was going on. He got up and padded out into the hallway to see for himself.

Naman reached the top step and shone the light from his flashlight along the hall. His blood froze for a second when the light suddenly reflected in the mean eyes of the giant dog. For a moment the two of them stood there quietly, looking at each other.

Stalin wanted to bark, but didn't dare. Instead he growled quietly and came slowly forward, baring his fangs. Naman reached out and touched him on the top of the head, ready to pull back and slam the dog over the head with the flashlight if he snapped at his fingers.

Stalin didn't snap. He wasn't sure what was going on. Naman rubbed him between and around the ears.

This was better than being cuffed on the head, Stalin thought. He had hardly ever had his ears rubbed softly. He liked it. He lowered his head and enjoyed it.

Naman spent a good five minutes with him, crooning into his ear, rubbing and scratching. Then he rose to his feet and continued softly down the hall, Stalin following behind.

He searched the upper floor of the house, hoping he wouldn't have to climb out the window and up the side. In the bathroom a short metal chain hung down from the ceiling. Naman smiled and thanked his stars. Then he closed the bathroom door and pulled the chain quietly, opening the skylight. He closed the toilet seat and stood on it. Reaching up, he caught the edge of the skylight, reached out with one foot to the top of the medicine cabinet, and managed to pull himself up. The next moment he was through the skylight and out onto the flat roof of the house. He wasn't as young as he used to be, he thought as he stooped there, waiting for his heart to pump back to normal, but he wasn't an old man yet either.

He crossed the roof house by house, stooping to stay below the raised gutters at the edge of the roofs, staying out of sight of anyone watching, until he reached the contact house, then entered it through an identical skylight and crept through the rooms until he found a sleeping man. He slapped his hand suddenly and tightly across the man's mouth, simultaneously waking him and keeping him quiet. "I'm Monroe," he said. "Who am I speaking to?"

He waited a moment for the man to come fully awake and absorb what was happening, then took his hand from his mouth. "I'm Taylor," the man said. "What's up?"

"Thought I'd take a walk on the cliffs today."

"Not for me, thanks. It looks like rain."

"Maybe you're right. Let's go to a movie."

The man sat up in bed. "What's wrong?" he asked.

"You were followed this morning."

"That's impossible. Who could—"

"Who knows? I don't have time to find out. Give me the key to the deposit box."

The man reached into the drawer of his night table and handed it over.

"It's in your name?" Naman asked. "Write it for me, as you sign it at the bank." He held the flashlight on a piece of paper while the man wrote. Naman studied it briefly, then put it into his pocket. "Go back to sleep," he said.

"What about the man following me?"

Naman smiled. "Let him follow. It'll keep him out of trouble."

Mrs. Przybylowicz woke up, hacked a couple of times, wiped her nose with the back of her hand, sat up in bed, and pulled her legs over the side. Unsteadily she stood up and walked around the bed.

Stalin growled. She slapped him hard over the head, and he whimpered as she left the room, walking unsteadily down the hall toward the bathroom.

Naman went back up through the skylight, back across the rooftops, and down again through the skylight into the bathroom of the house he had entered. On his way up he had left the skylight open, and had crawled through it without making a sound. This time too he was as silent as a ghost, but as his feet dangled down feeling for the toilet seat, they encountered the head and shoulders of Mrs. Przybylowicz, sitting on the toilet.

She screamed in terror as the feet swung down in the darkness and clambered over her, imagining her worst fears of the night to have come true—rats, thousands of rats, emerging from the subterranean depths and swarming all over her. She bolted from the bathroom as Naman dropped to the floor on hands and knees. He pulled himself to his feet, and was blinded as the light came on. There in the bathroom doorway stood Mr. Przybylowicz, his shotgun held with shaking hands but pointed straight at Naman's gut.

As Naman raised his hands in surrender, Stalin sidled in past Mr. Przybylowicz and rubbed against his legs, recognizing his new friend and wondering why he wasn't getting his ears rubbed.

5

MR. HAROLD AITKEN, of the Philadelphia private investigation firm Bradley Phillips, had taken the trouble to talk to the policemen on the beat that included the house they were staking out, asking them to be on the lookout for anything unusual. Mr. Aitken was a favored person with the Philadelphia police, being known as one who asked easy favors and paid promptly for them. And so Patrolman Mike Larson woke Mr. Aitken with an early-morning call to tell him that there had been a break-in just down the block from the house they were interested in, and that the man had been caught. It was Mr. Aitken's call, in turn, that woke Carlos Grass from his slumber in the Pierre Hotel.

"Do you have a description?" Grass asked, instantly awake.

"A pretty old guy, the officer said—"

"Where is he now?"

"South Street station. He's been remanded overnight for a hearing first thing in the morning."

Grass glanced at his wristwatch. It was nearly six. "Can you get the hearing postponed? Keep him there till I get there?"

"I can try. I know a few people."

"If I don't get there in time, stay with him. I'm on my way."

"Yes sir, you can trust—" Mr. Aitken stopped talking when he heard the dial tone. He hung up and hurried down to the South Street station.

Jeff Blank was in the interview room at the precinct station just north of Times Square, discussing modern life with a street punk who might or might not have robbed and raped an elderly lady in her flat off Twelfth Avenue. Blank didn't much care whether the kid had done it or not. If he hadn't, he had certainly done other things in the same vein, and Blank didn't much care what they got him on. The case would never go to trial anyway, whatever charge they made would be bargained down, but at least the kid would get off the streets for a few months.

And so Blank's heart wasn't really in it and he was only mildly annoyed when his beeper went off. He left the kid with his partner and went off to answer the phone.

"Sergeant Blank, this is Mr. Cartwright at the Pierre. You asked me to call you about—"

"Yes, I remember. Is he checking out?"

"Even as we speak. The clerk has told him he's having a small problem with the computer."

"Do you have his picture?"

"Yes, we snapped that right off."

"He didn't see you do it?"

"If he did, he didn't mention it."

"Oh, he would have mentioned it, all right. I'm on my way."

It would have taken too long to get a station car checked out, even if Blank had had an official story to tell. He ran outside without bothering to go back upstairs and grab his overcoat, and stepped out the doors into a sudden, swirling blizzard. *Wouldn't you know it,* he thought. He looked up and down the street; he'd never get a cab in this weather. He started running, and in the third block he saw a cab pulling over in front of a restaurant. By the time he reached it the passenger had gotten out and was paying through the window while three different people were arguing over who had rights to it. He stepped up to them and flashed his badge. "Sorry to pull rank, folks, but this is an emergency."

Blank still got a thrill out of the way people backed off when you said something like that. Well, not a thrill, exactly; he was too jaded for that, but it was kind of nice. He settled back in the seat and wiped the snow from his head and shoulders as the cab took off for the hotel. He thought that with any luck Mr. Ralph Berner would also have had trouble getting a cab and might be waiting there for him.

No, he thought. It might be hard to get a cab elsewhere in the city but when it snows or rains cabbies head for places like the Pierre, where they'll pick up a quick series of fares who can't walk in this weather the two blocks to F.A.O. or Cartier's and who, being out-of-towners, are embarrassed at leaving less than a five-dollar tip no matter how short the ride.

He reached the hotel in less than five minutes. As he ran up the steps he found Cartwright standing there waiting for him.

"I'm sorry, he's gone. We couldn't hold him."

"Christ!" Blank exclaimed. "How come when I try to check out of a hotel it takes all day, and when you're *supposed* to slow a man down he's away and gone in less than five minutes?"

"My man told him the computer was down and it would take a few moments to get his bill ready, but he said he had a plane to catch and couldn't wait, to just put the charge on his card and send him the bill." Cartwright gave the merest hint of a shrug. "There was really nothing I could do."

Blank paused. "You don't think he saw you take the picture?"

"There wasn't anything to see. The camera doesn't move or make an audible click, and the clerk activated it with his foot from behind the counter."

"Yeah, but did he give it away? Did he look nervous or suspicious?"

"This is the Pierre," Mr. Cartwright said. "Our staff are never nervous, and they never *look* suspicious."

"Then why did he run off without waiting for his bill?" Blank worried.

"He was rushing before he even reached the counter; he was practically running through the lobby."

2 5 0

"Yeah?" Blank thought about that. "Maybe he really was late to catch a plane."

"At any event he didn't catch it."

"Why not?"

"Because he didn't go to the airport."

"How do you know that?"

"When I saw what was happening I followed him through the lobby and outside—apologizing for the delay, you understand. He was shocked when he stepped outside and saw that it was snowing. I apologized all the way to the curb, where he jumped into a cab, seemed to hesitate for a moment, and then told the driver to take him to Penn Station."

Blank looked at the man admiringly. "Okay," he said. "I'll take a look at that videotape now. And then I'd like to use your phone for a moment."

Cartwright fetched the tape and set it up on the VCR in his office. They watched the five-second video. Blank nodded. The guy didn't have any particular distinguishing features; he didn't have two heads, or green hair on either of them. There wasn't much of a description he could give that would enable anyone to pick his quarry out of a crowd. He asked Cartwright to run the tape through again for him. And then again. He searched closely, looking for identifying characteristics, trying to estimate Berner's height and weight. Then he picked up the telephone, took a piece of paper out of his pocket, and dialed the number written on it.

"I'm calling Philadelphia," he said to Cartwright. "It'll just be a minute or two. I'll pay you."

"That's all right—"

"Hello, who's this? Melnik? Right. This is Blank, Horner's partner in— Right. Your man just left the hotel here to take the train to Philly. How do I know? He left here in a rush, saying he had to catch a plane. But when he saw the blizzard we got here he changed his mind to the train. So number one, he's in a hurry and was afraid the plane might be delayed or even canceled because of this weather. And number two, no matter how long the plane might be delayed, if he's in a hurry he's not taking a train to Chicago or L.A. It's got to be Philly. Well, 'gotta be'? Who knows? But that's how I figure it. So look, he left here maybe ten minutes ago and he's in a hurry, so he'll be on the next train. He's a big man, a good six foot, weighing I'd say about one-ninety. Trim and tough. Brown hair, cut medium short. Heavy features, thick nose, but nothing really distinguishing. Wearing a gray parka— Hold on a minute."

Cartwright was gesturing at him as he talked. "What is it?" Blank asked.

"As he was rushing through the lobby I noticed he was limping. Not very much, and perhaps just because he was hurrying—"

"Man here says your guy limps slightly. Yeah, that's interesting? Well, we aim to please. Go get him, kid."

6

Thirtieth Street Station, the main Amtrak stop in Philadelphia, is a mausoleum, a monument to what the railroads once were. To a generation for whom space is money it must seem wickedly extravagant: a huge, high-ceilinged, nearly empty room, populated only intermittently when the occasional train pulls in and disgorges its load of passengers.

Melnik stood in a corner by the soft-drink dispenser, behind the newsstand, from where he could see the passengers coming up the steps from the tracks below. The announcement board clacked its messages like a slot machine, and finally came up with the winner: The New York train had arrived. It was another minute or two before the first passengers came clambering up the stairs, led by Ralph Berner.

He was easy enough to spot. He fit the description Blank had given, he was the man most in a hurry, and as he crossed the wide floor Melnik could see the unmistakable though slight sign of a limp. He pulled the Pentax Microzoom from his pocket and clicked off a half-dozen snapshots as Berner hurried through the station without looking around. Then Melnik followed him out the door.

He had to expect that Berner was a trained operative and would be able to lose a tail whenever he chose. The important thing was to avoid alerting him, to keep from being noticed. Melnik had to be prepared to lose him rather than be seen. The important thing at this stage was to identify him, and the photographs would probably do that.

Still, it didn't hurt to try. He took the third cab in line after Berner's and easily managed to stay behind him as they entered the curving ramp leading down from the station into the city. There was plenty of midday traffic, which made conditions just about perfect for a tail. Melnik kept the cab driver a dozen cars behind their quarry as they snaked their way through the city. When Berner's cab pulled up in front of the South Street Courthouse Melnik told his driver to keep going and turn at the next corner. He jumped out, leaving the door open, and ran back to the edge of the building, peering around to see if Berner had stopped only as a ploy and was about to drive off again. But he saw him standing outside the cab paying off the driver, and so he ran back to his own and did the same. He came back to South Street in time to see Berner disappear up the steps and into the courthouse.

This was a bit tricky now, Melnik thought. He would have liked to know what Berner was doing here, but the only way to find out was to go into the courthouse and look for him room-to-room. He had been lucky in following him so far, but there was no way he could search the courthouse without standing out to any man with a suspicious mind looking for possible followers. All in all he thought it better to wait here until Berner came out, and then see what developed.

He had just about decided to do this when the door of the courthouse opened and Walter Naman walked out.

14

1

"Does it occur to you," Lisle Wintre had asked, "that Hagan may want me to go to Germany just to get rid of me? To send me on a wild-goose chase?"

Melnik looked at Horner with that conspiratorial expression men use when they're dealing with girls—not women, but girls. "Of course," he said. "That's the whole point. Let's be honest with each other. We've had agents trying to penetrate this plot for months. Trained agents, the best in the world, and we haven't learned very much, have we? We know it's guarded at a very high level, at least as high as Vorshage and probably higher. Do you really think I expect you to wander over there and ferret out the secrets in a few days?"

"Then why am I going?"

"Hagan wants you to go."

"Yes, but if he's—"

"If he wants you to go and you refuse, he'll know you're suspicious of him. He'll worry about what we're up to and he'll start to nose around, and we don't need him interfering with us. Look," he explained, "what's needed now is plain old-fashioned detective work. We've got to find Naman and whoever is after him, and learn whatever it is they know. At that point we may need United States cooperation, but for right now all we need is to be left alone. That's your job."

"But if I'm over in Germany—"

"Exactly. You're in Germany and so Hagan is satisfied that you're chasing wild geese because there aren't any ducks around. *Verstanden?*"

"So in essence I'm to do nothing?"

Melnik shook his head and smiled. "Not in essence, darling. In actuality. In total and absolute actuality."

Right. Sure. Give the little girl a lollipop and send her on her way. *Well, not* this *little girl,* Wintre thought. Back in her office, she picked up the phone and called Randolph Burroughs, the man in the CIA who had questioned her about the Nazi plot. "This is Lisle Wintre," she said, "in Secretary Hagan's office. We met a few days ago."

"Well, sure," he said immediately. "Have you got something for me?"

"Not exactly," she admitted. "I called to ask a favor."

"If I can, it's yours."

She told him that Hagan was sending her to Germany to see Vorshage, and she needed some background on the man. He called her back within two hours. "We have nothing deleterious on him. He's loyal to Germany rather than to us, but I suppose you really can't fault him for that, can you? He's been very steadfast. Until *Anschluss* his chief enemy was the East Germans, but since they got together he hasn't shown any grudge. They're all good Germans now. Staunch anticommunist—"

"Would that perhaps make him a Nazi?" she asked.

Burroughs laughed. "You mean like in the good old days? When the only people fighting the Nazis were the Commies? No, not a chance. His parents were old-time landowners, Junkers. Classy people. They died at Buchenwald. I'm afraid if you're looking for Nazis, you've got the wrong man."

No, she thought, I've got exactly the right man. Stooge around on a wild-goose chase while Horner and Melnik did the men's work, would she? *Well, we'll soon see.* "Thanks," she said, hung up the phone, and grabbed a cab to the airport.

"Lisle!" a voice screamed as she moved through the International Departures Lounge. "Lisle Wintre!"

She turned and saw a woman waving at her, moving toward her through the throngs. For just a moment she couldn't place her, and then the woman came up and threw her arms around her and it was Mugsy Farrow. They hugged and agreed how remarkable it was to meet like this after all these years, and Mugsy dragged Wintre over to have a celebratory drink. "If you've got time," Mugsy said. "I've got just half an hour before my plane leaves."

"Same for me," Wintre said. "Where are you going?"

"You'll never believe it when I tell you."

"Well, where?"

"I'm not going to tell you. Guess."

Oh God. Mugsy hadn't grown an inch since college. They had been the best of friends, they looked so much alike that people thought they were sisters, but she could drive a person crazy. "North, south, east, or west?"

"East. All the way across the Atlantic."

"Paris."

"No." Triumphantly. "And not London or Rome."

"Where then?"

"Where else is there?"

"Mugsy, we've only got half an hour—"

"All right then, I told you you'd never guess. Berlin! Imagine that! I've been bitching and moaning for five years for us to take a real vacation and I guess finally Jerry couldn't take it any longer and told me I could go anywhere I'd like if I'd only go by myself and shut up, and so I just said the most ridiculous thing I could think of. Berlin! He didn't know what to say. It's in Prussia, you know. What used to be Prussia. So he had to say okay, and here I am actually going and to tell you the truth I'm scared to death, although I'd never admit that to Jerry. Where are you going?"

Lisle didn't know whether to laugh or cry.

They ended up sharing a suite at the Adlon. When Mugsy suggested it, Wintre protested that her salary didn't quite run to such extravagances, but Mugsy had shouted her down. "Jerry will pay for it, he doesn't know what to do with his money and he can't expect me to stay in Berlin all by myself. He's just lucky that you're an old girlfriend instead of a new boyfriend, not that he'd mind, probably. Sometimes I wonder if he would. Oh, but it'll be such fun! We'll be able to talk all night long!"

Which was precisely why Wintre didn't want to share a room with Mugsy, but she couldn't quite bring herself to say so.

2

THE BUILDING was just as she had imagined it might be: large, block-faced, and austere. Vorshage himself was not at all what she had imagined. The CIA men she had met were either furtive, officious, or pompous—except for Burroughs, who somehow didn't quite count—while the FBI were so cold and official-looking. Vorshage was a pussycat.

He reminded Wintre of her father. He was much older, but then it had been a long time since her father had been murdered. Vorshage looked like what he might have one day grown into. She was glad she had ignored Hagan's expectations and Melnik's advice; she was glad she had come straight to him. She was not fool enough to believe that since Vorshage looked honest, he was. Or that it was not possible that he himself was involved in the plot. But she *was* fool enough to think that she would be able to tell something from his reactions if she sat down in front of him and with no warning blurted out the story. "We think there's a plot against your chancellor's life," she said.

Vorshage lifted his eyebrows. "I would be deeply in your debt if you would tell me about it," he said.

And so she did.

"I will be honest with you," he said when she finished. "I appreciate your coming here to tell me, I appreciate your concern, but I'm not sure there is anything to your story."

"Number one," she insisted, counting off on her fingers, "Walter Naman is supposed to be dead but he's alive. Number two—"

"Don't get angry, please. You didn't let me finish. I'm also not sure that there is *not* something to your story."

She waited, but he only sat there looking at her, drumming lightly with one finger against his desk. "What do you have in mind to do about it?" she asked.

"More to the point, what do *you* have in mind to do? The attempt, if there is to be one, will be made in the United States, *nicht wahr?*"

"We are taking all precautions," she lied, not wanting to go into details about Hagan's reaction. "It would help if we knew more about it from this end, who is after Waldner and why. Our indications are that it is connected with your Nazi uprising."

Vorshage looked pained. "We are all deeply ashamed about that. It seems filth can never be completely swept away. But I don't quite believe they are yet well enough organized to be dangerous. Perhaps it's one of them—yes, that might be possible—perhaps it's one of them acting on his own. A lunatic like your Lee Harvey Oswald—"

"There is more than one person setting this up; there is an organization—"

"Ah, but many of your people think the same about the Oswald affair. It's so hard to know for sure. I tell you what. How long can you stay with us? A few days?"

She nodded.

"Good. You understand that I have operatives keeping an eye on our Nazi friends, as a continuing matter. I will press them to find out if there is anything cooking there. We cannot expect answers immediately, but we should get indications, hints, if anything as big as this is being planned. Give me two days? Come back then. And let me have your address in Berlin."

"I'm staying at the Hotel Adlon, suite 615."

"Good. An excellent hotel. Let us meet again here on, say, Wednesday. If anything comes in sooner than that I'll ring you."

Forty-five minutes later a fat man named Helmut Begemann entered the lobby of the Hotel Adlon and asked for the key to 615. Guests at the Adlon are given a card that they are supposed to show when requesting their key, but no one except tourists ever does that, and even the tourists begin to ignore the rule when they realize the clerks never bother to look at the card. Begemann was given the key without any problem. He took the elevator to the sixth floor and walked down the hall. He inserted the key and turned it, pushed open the door and entered.

"Who is it?" a female voice asked.

"*Entschuldigung,*" he said. "They gave me the key to this room."

"Well, I'm sorry, but this is my room," the woman said, coming toward him.

He hesitated, a look of confusion on his face, until she stopped a few steps away. She had been writing at the table and still held the pen in her hand. She waited, but he stood there. "Would you please leave?" she asked, and he put the key in his pocket, took out an old-fashioned razor, flipped it open with one hand, stepped forward as she froze to the spot, and with one quick movement slashed open her throat.

He caught her as her head fell backward, no longer supported by the neck, and her body slumped forward. He dragged her to the bed and dropped her on it. He lifted her skirt and pulled down her panties. He dropped his own pants and found that he didn't have to masturbate himself, he was already hard.

Her head hung back over the edge of the bed, dangling downward, and he put a pillow over the still spurting neck. And then he made love to her.

When he finished he hung a "Do Not Disturb" sign on the door and left. He checked himself in the elevator's mirror and found blood on his clothing, but nothing that would be noticed on his way home. He would burn the clothes, of course. As soon as he got home he picked up the telephone. "Job executed," he said.

"No problems?" Vorshage asked. "You waited for her in her room?"

"She was already there. There was no fuss, no bother. I'm afraid I left a small mess, though."

"It will be taken care of. Thank you." Vorshage hung up, congratulating himself for having acted so quickly. She must have gone straight back to her room after their visit, but she wouldn't have had time to report home on their conversation, and he could decide later what they had said. Perhaps on her first visit she had merely introduced herself and asked for a further appointment to discuss her reasons for visiting Germany. For a moment he wondered if instead he should have simply stalled her, put her off . . . But no. He couldn't have stalled her forever, and once she realized what he was doing she would begin to wonder why. It was best this way. Regrettable, but best.

3

AFTER HER CONVERSATION with Vorshage, Lisle Wintre had not gone straight back to the hotel. She had walked the Kurfürstendamm, looking in the shop windows, strolling through the small parks, killing time. She hadn't wanted to go back to the Adlon because Mugsy would be there. As soon as they had arrived in Berlin it had become obvious why Mugsy had been so insistent on their sharing digs, and the reason was even worse than her stated one of staying up all night talking over old times: Mugsy was scared to death.

This was the first time in her life she had ever gone anywhere, done anything, by herself. Her frustration at her husband's boredom with her had driven her to scream Berlin in his face, but now that she was here she was afraid to go out on the streets by herself. She was afraid she'd get lost, be waylaid, get hit by a taxi, fall off the face of the earth. Lisle knew that whenever she returned she'd find Mugsy sitting there, writing postcards to her friends, waiting to suggest they do something together.

She wandered through the zoo, hugging her coat about her in the frigid wind, telling herself she had to stay here in Berlin a few more days and she couldn't spend all her time hiding from Mugsy. And yet she simply couldn't bring herself to return and face the bright face and chirping questions. She felt for Jerry, she really did.

She looked at her watch. It had been barely an hour since she left Vorshage. Her toes were beginning to freeze; they felt as if they might just crumble and fall off. She couldn't wander around the city day after day. She would have to face her fate, she would have to return to the hotel.

Her worst fears were confirmed: There was a "Do Not Disturb" sign hanging on the door; Mugsy was in. But as soon as Wintre entered the suite she saw that something was wrong. The desk drawer was upside down on the floor; some clothes were scattered about. "Mugsy?" she called.

Her mind told her that someone had been here, and might still be here. She should run out and get help. But while she was thinking that, while the message was making its way slowly to her feet, those feet kept walking into the room and toward the bedroom door. Wintre opened it and saw Mugsy lying half naked on the bed, her red-and-white blouse pulled up around her neck—

No. It was a white blouse. The red was—

"Mugsy!" she whispered, and took another step forward, stepped around the bed, and saw Mugsy's head dangling over the edge of the bed, held to her body by a thin strand of wet scarlet neck.

It was like being hit by a bolt of electricity. One moment she was in the bedroom staring at the dead body, the next moment she was out in the hall, leaning against the wall, quivering, shaking, unable to remember how she had got there. She hung on to the wall, fighting down the nausea, sucking in deep breaths. Finally she pushed away from the wall and took a few seconds to make sure her legs were strong enough to hold her, and then she started to run.

No.

She stopped.

What had happened? She had to stop and think. What had happened? Had Mugsy picked up some rough trade on the street and brought him back to the room? Impossible.

She didn't want to think. The dead body was horrible enough; what she was thinking was worse. Had Mugsy opened the door and found a mad rapist standing there? Had the man wandered into the Adlon and picked the sixth floor for some astrological reason?

Nonsense.

Had a hotel burglar come knocking on the door and, when no one answered, picked the lock and entered, found Mugsy there, and killed her to keep her quiet? No; the "Do Not Disturb" sign would have alerted him that someone was inside. And if someone had come in, well, Mugsy would have been waiting for Wintre to return; she would have jumped up at the first sound of a knock on the door or a key in the lock, would have started talking even before the door opened.

Then what?

She knew, she knew what must have happened, the only way it could have happened. She hadn't told Vorshage there was another woman in the room; there had been no occasion to. She had simply told him that she knew of a plot against the chancellor and she had come to Berlin to investigate it and that she was staying in suite 615 of the Hotel Adlon.

Again her legs were cold, numb, without feeling. But this time the cold was inside her. What was she to do? If she ran down to the front desk and reported what had happened, the police would come, but Vorshage *was* the police.

A man came walking down the hall. A fat man, shuffling heavily toward her. She was terrified; she would have run from him, but her legs wouldn't move, she was paralyzed as he came closer. He came straight toward her, passed, then stopped. She could hear his steps stop. She was afraid to turn around.

"Entschuldigen Sie?" his voice asked.

She couldn't answer.

"Gnädige Frau?" he asked again. "Excuse, please? Something is wrong? Perhaps could I be of help?"

"No," she said, turning to him, forcing a smile. "No, thank you. I just forgot something." And she opened the door to her suite and went back in.

Not back into the bedroom; she couldn't do that. But she managed to cross the room and pick up the telephone. She asked to be connected to United Airlines. She asked the man who answered if she could get a ticket to Washington, D.C., today. Yes, he said, there were seats available. Was this to be round-trip?

"I already have a ticket. This is a return. I want to change it to today's flight."

He explained there might be a penalty charge if the ticket she had bought was nonrefundable—

"I don't care," she said. "I just want to leave today."

"You'll have to be at Tegel Airport within two hours—"

"Yes, I can leave right away."

"Very good, madam. Your name, please?"

He waited.

"Madam, the name, please?"

She had no idea what connections Vorshage might have with the airlines. Would he hear that she was buying a ticket half an hour after she had been killed?

"Madam, I must have the name please, for the ticket?"

She panicked. She couldn't think of Mugsy's married name, she couldn't think—and then it came to her. "Walker," she said. "Carolyn Walker."

And now came the hard part, she thought as she hung up; now came the impossible part. She had to go back into the bedroom. She had to go back into the bedroom and find Mugsy's handbag and get her airline ticket and passport.

She stood up and found herself walking across the softly carpeted room. She walked right up to the bedroom door, and then she opened it, and then she stepped in.

And vomited right on the rug.

4

FIFTEEN MINUTES LATER two men dressed in overalls and caps stepped out of the service elevator on the sixth floor. Trundling a cart with cleaning equipment on it ahead of them, they walked down the hall to 615, where one of them knelt in front of the door and began to fiddle with the lock. It was a good lock, and it took him nearly five minutes to open it. Then they went in, surveyed the damage briefly, and got to work.

They laid Mugsy's body on the floor, pulled the blood-soaked sheets off the bed, and wrapped her in the sheets. They cleaned up the vomit on the floor with bath towels and threw those in with the body. They stuffed Mugsy and the towels and the dripping red pillows into a large green plastic garbage bag they had brought along. The mattress was also soaked in blood and they couldn't carry it away with them, so they washed it as best they could and turned it over. It would have to do for the time being. In a few days, when the room had been used by a couple of other people so nobody would think of the missing Miss Wintre, a lit cigarette would be left in the bed. The room would burn, and all trace of the killing would be gone.

For now, they opened two bottles of red wine they had brought along for the purpose, and poured them over the blood and vomit stains on the carpet. They left the bottles in the room, one on the night table, the other lying casually on the floor. They took out a bottle and sprayed deodorant around the suite, masking the malodor.

They opened the closets and drawers, packed all the clothes in the suitcases they found, and left the luggage sitting in the middle of the room. They slung the garbage bag onto their cleaning cart, arranged it tidily among the other debris there, and left. The door was of the type that could not be left unlocked; they taped the latch so it couldn't click shut and made sure the "Do Not Disturb" sign was in place. They took the service elevator down to the cellar, loaded the cart with the garbage bag into their van, and left.

Ten minutes later a young woman came up the elevator, walked down the hall, and entered suite 615. She picked up the phone and called the Hotel Paischer in Nuremberg, making a reservation for Lisle Wintre. Then she called the front desk. "This is suite 615. I'm checking out. Can you send up a boy to help with my bags, please?" When the boy came she indicated the two suitcases and he carried them down to the lobby. The bill was waiting for her at the front desk. "If you will just sign the American Express slip?" the clerk said, pushing it toward her. If she had looked at it she would have seen the name Carolyn Walker and would have realized that something was wrong, but she merely shook her head and took cash out of her handbag. The clerk tore up the charge slip and she paid without looking at the bill. She left as forwarding address the hotel in Nuremberg, and the bellboy carried her bags outside and put her in a taxi.

15

1

NAMAN WALKED DOWN the steps of the courthouse in Philadelphia, glancing at his watch. It was nearly two o'clock; the banks would still be open. He nodded in satisfaction. The hearing, luckily, had turned out to be not much more than an irritation. When he had left his hotel the previous night he had taken along the passport identifying him as Mr. Fred Nagle of Toronto, Canada, and his wallet containing nearly two hundred dollars in cash. You never knew when documents, identification, and money might come in handy. The police had confiscated all this, of course, together with the safety deposit key he had collected in the contact house.

When his case was called the arresting officer told the judge what Mr. Nagle had had in his pockets, and that the police computer had found nothing against him in its files. The judge nodded and turned to the miscreant. What was it all about, then? Nagle hung his head shamefacedly and begun to mumble about having met a woman last night, they had gone out drinking, and somehow she had left him, he didn't remember too much, he must have been awfully drunk. So he had flagged down a cab and given the driver the address he thought he remembered from earlier in the evening's conversation. But when the cab dropped him off he had found the door locked and the house dark. And when he turned back to the cab, he found it had already gone.

He walked around the back of the house and— He guessed he must have been drunker than he thought, because it never occurred to him that he might have the wrong house, or even that the woman might not want to see him. He didn't really remember breaking in through the cellar door, but he guessed he must have, if the officer said so. He was just so terribly ashamed.

Naman didn't know if the judge believed any of this story, but after the courtroom full of scum the judge had already seen that morning— most of whom had been given suspended sentences because the jails in Philadelphia were already full, and long past full—in Nagle the judge saw a solid citizen with no previous record of trouble. And was he going back to Canada?

"Oh yes sir, absolutely, this afternoon. As soon as I finish my business here," he said before he could stop himself. That was a mistake; never volunteer information. If the judge should now ask him what his business was he'd have to think up something, and his story might be checked, and—

The judge wasn't about to ask him anything of the sort. "Thirty days, drunk and disorderly. Sentence suspended." The gavel rapped; Naman felt a hand on his arm; he turned, and was pointed to the door leading out of the courtroom. He found his way to the corridor and two minutes later he was walking down the front steps and a young man came up to him and said, "Mr. Naman, I presume?"

Naman smiled blankly and continued down the steps, but the man came after him. "David Melnik," he introduced himself. "Mossad."

"I'm afraid you have the wrong—"

Melnik shook his head. "It's no good, Mr. Naman. Your hair has been dyed black and the mustache is awfully good, but you're well known to us, you know. And since we're on the same side, why don't we have a little chat?"

2

CARLOS GRASS had run into the courthouse and looked around. There were signs directing people to the Pennsylvania Bureau of Motor Vehicles (Registration), Bureau of Motor Vehicles (Licenses), Bureau of Motor Vehicles (Violations); the Philadelphia Department of Public Safety (Traffic violations), Department of Public Safety (Summonses), Department of Public Safety (Miscellaneous); Civil Court, Criminal

Court, Appeals Court, Marriage Licenses and Ceremonies, the Cafeteria, and the Institute for the Blind.

He found a uniformed guard standing by the metal detector with his hands clasped behind his back and his eyes gazing around the ceiling, and asked him where a man arrested for burglary might be arraigned. He was directed to the fourth floor, and it was while Grass was riding up in the world's slowest elevator that Naman had come down in its twin on the other side of the corridor.

He found the proper courtroom, but Naman was not there. A small black man was being asked if he wished to plead guilty to beating up on his wife. The man replied, "She be bitchin' around." The judge explained that before that might be considered as a defense the accused would have to decide if he was pleading guilty or not guilty. "Bitchin' around," the man replied. "Your Honor," he added, and smiled.

Grass asked a guard if all the people being arraigned were in the courtroom. No, he was told, they were brought in when their case came up.

"I'm looking for my father. Our name is Nagle but he might have given a different name." Grass started to give a reason for this, but the guard wasn't interested. "What's he up for?" he asked.

"He evidently broke into someone's home last night. He's not well, you see."

"What's he look like?"

"What can I say? An old man, about five foot eight—"

"You from Canada?"

"Yes. Well, not originally, but he lives there now—"

"Yeah, that's the guy. I think the name was Nagle, something like that. He was just released, suspended sentence."

"Where would he be now?"

The guard shrugged. "Gone. Back to Canada, I guess."

Damn. Too late. Why couldn't trains be made to run on time? Grass ran down the stairs and searched through the main lobby, but Naman was not there. He went outside and stood at the top of the steps, looking around at the people going in and out, wondering where to go next, when a small man came walking up the steps, hesitated, and then approached him.

"Mr. Berner?" he asked. "I'm Harold Aitken."

3

"SO HOW ARE THINGS on the other side?" the young man asked, and Naman wasn't sure what he meant. They were sitting in the delicatessen across the street from the courthouse, and the waiter had just brought them coffee. "What other side?" Naman asked.

"Isn't that the American expression? 'To pass over to the other side'?" Melnik smiled pleasantly, and then said more seriously, "You died two weeks ago, you know."

"Oh that." Naman dismissed it as an event of no consequence, and sipped his coffee. "You wanted to chat," he said. "So chat."

"I wanted *us* to chat. But I'll begin." Melnik paused, stirring his coffee, gazing out the window. "There is a plot against the life of the chancellor of Germany. It seems to be linked to the Nazi uprisings there which have been increasing since unification. We think perhaps the attempt on your life is linked to that, and are wondering why you are working on your own in this respect. In the past you have not hidden your activities from us."

Naman waited, smiling as if he were the Sphinx and knew everything there was to be known. He was waiting to hear what else this young Mossad man would say, but soon it was apparent that there would be no more. Did they know nothing after all, or was the young man playing his cards close? At any rate he sat there quietly and patiently now, saying no more, waiting for Naman to speak. And so Naman did. "I'm not exactly hiding my activities," he said. "I'm working with Moshe Sharon of your Shabak." He knew that Mossad and Shabak—the Israeli counterintelligence service—had a relationship more antagonistic even than that of the CIA and FBI, often not speaking to each other about matters which should involve them both, each going off on its own to the detriment of both. "I really can't tell you anything without his permission. But if you can contact him and straighten things out, perhaps we could work together on this little matter."

Melnik nodded. He should have known there'd be an administrative foul-up. He leaned back in his chair, and saw Berner come out of the courthouse across the street. "That's the man who was trying to find you," he said.

Naman looked across the street and studied the man. "You haven't been following me, then?"

Melnik shook his head. "I've been following him."

"Who is he?"

"No idea. Name of Berner. Probably false."

As they watched they saw the other man come up to Berner. The two men talked briefly, then started down the steps and across the street toward the deli.

Naman rose. "I will go now. I'm staying at the Downtown Ramada, room three-twenty-one. I'll be there till Wednesday." He walked quickly through the swinging doors into the kitchen, and out through the rear.

Melnik sat hunched over his coffee as Berner and presumably the detective who had summoned him came in. The two men glanced around the room, and then sat down. Melnik sat there unconcerned, amused, as the two of them grew more restless, as they began to wonder if perhaps Naman was not in the men's room. Finally the smaller man, the detective, got up and headed for the men's room. He was back in a moment and said something to Berner, who then left the restaurant.

Too late, Melnik thought. Naman would be well on his way by now. Unfortunately, the small man then sat down and studied the menu. He had obviously seen him, Melnik, take Naman into this restaurant and was planning on following him while Berner tried to find Naman. Which meant that Melnik could not follow Berner, he'd have to let him go. Well, he supposed that didn't matter. The important person was obviously Naman. He'd have to get on the telephone to Mazor and find out what the hell Shabak was doing involved in this, and then get back to Naman at the Ramada.

He stood up, paid his bill, and left. He stood on the corner while several taxis passed. When the light turned to red, one taxi was stopped at the corner. Melnik got in and told the driver to take a right-hand turn. As they disappeared around the corner he saw the detective, who had followed him out of the deli, looking around desperately for another cab. *Too bad, old son,* Melnik thought. "Left at the next corner," he told the driver, looking behind them. After they had passed several more traffic lights with no visible pursuit he relaxed and glanced at his watch. It would be late at night in Israel, he thought. His call would wake Mazor. Good, he thought. Why hadn't the son of a bitch known about Shabak's involvement?

4

GRASS STEPPED OUTSIDE the restaurant and looked up and down the street. Useless. Naman was gone.

Luckily, Grass knew where he was going. What he didn't know was whether he would be in time or not. He looked up and down the street, but there were no cabs in sight. He began to walk quickly to the corner, but before he got there the lights changed and an empty taxi came around and stopped at his signal. He got in and called out, "Philadelphia Savings Fund Society, quickly."

"What branch?" the driver asked.

Verdammt! Aitken had told him that when Naman's case was called the arresting officer had testified that he had had in his possession when arrested in the house on North Ninth Street a passport in the name of Fred Nagle, a couple of hundred dollars in cash, and a safety deposit key for the PSFS. What else could he have picked up in the safe house but the key?

But what branch? If there were many branches it could be any one of them— No. "Is there one near North Ninth Street?" he asked.

"What hundred?"

"I don't understand."

"What hundred? What's the address?"

Oh, the house address. Naman had broken into—what was the number? "Yes, forty-nine fifty-three North Ninth."

"Yeah, that's pretty far from here. You want I should take you?"

"Please."

It took half an hour, but finally the cab pulled up in front of the bank on North Broad Street. "This'll be the closest to that address, buddy," the driver said, and Grass paid him and hopped out. He limped quickly up to the front door, pulled on it, and was stopped. The door was locked. He yanked on it twice before he read the sign.

"This office will be closed on February 17, Presidents' Day."

Grass read it twice, and then he began to laugh. Suddenly he had lots of time.

5

MELNIK TOOK A ROOM at the Ramada and put the call through to Israel, enjoying Mazor's irritation at being awakened. He did not, however, enjoy his own irritation five hours later when Mazor's return call returned the favor. Nor did he enjoy Mazor's message.

He got dressed and hurried down the hall to the elevator. He took it to the third floor, nearly ran to number 321, and banged on the door. He banged again and again, until the door was opened and a sleepy face peered out from behind the night chain. The face was not Naman's. "What the fuck do you want?"

"Sorry, wrong room," Melnik said, and walked more slowly back to the elevator as the man cursed after him. He took the elevator down to the lobby and approached the front desk, even though he knew it was no use. Mazor had told him the simple result of his inquiry. There was no Moshe Sharon working for Shabak, nor was anyone there working on the German problem. "Help you?" the man at the desk asked.

"My friend Mr. Naman told me he's staying here in room 321 but I just went up there and it's the wrong room."

"Just a moment, let me check." The clerk studied his computer screen for a moment and said, "That's right, it's the wrong room. A Mr. and Mrs. Golden are in there." He looked up. "I hope you didn't wake them."

"I'm afraid I did."

The clerk shook his head. "You should have checked with me first. What was the name? Naman?" He shook his head again. "I'm sorry, you must have the wrong hotel. There's no Naman staying here. You want me to check the other Ramadas in town?"

"Please," Melnik said, but he knew it would be no use. He had been snookered.

Well, it wasn't the first time and probably wouldn't be the last. The thing was, he thought, that usually when someone fooled him he at least knew why. This time he didn't even know that.

What was Naman up to?

6

THE NEXT DAY was the most remarkable day in Walter Naman's life, a day he would remember if he lived to be a hundred—which was an event rendered extremely unlikely precisely by the events of that day.

It began at ten o'clock in the morning. He had risen much earlier, breakfasted, walked about, bought a small valise, made a reservation on Delta to Palm Beach, and then killed time until the bank opened. He was waiting by the door when it did, and he went in and straight to the safety deposit vault. He signed in and passed over the key, and the box was brought to him in a small enclave.

So far so good. The money was there, and he put it in his valise and left. He signed out and walked across the bank's lobby toward the front door. As he pulled the heavy door, a man stepped out from the side of the bank and came up to him as if to help him open it. He recognized the face immediately: It was the man the Israeli had said was following him.

And he recognized the gun the man held in his hand, sliding it out of his pocket so Naman could see it before he hid it again. It was a Glock 25, and he could feel its tip pressing against his side as the man held the door wide and gestured for him to emerge.

"You know the story of the peasant and the mule? No? Well, it seems that a peasant sold a mule," Grass said as they strolled away down Broad Street, "promising the buyer that it was a good and obedient mule, which would follow all orders if spoken to gently. And it seems that two or three days later the buyer brought the mule back to the peasant and complained that no matter what he told the mule to do, the mule simply ignored him. 'Did you speak to him kindly?' the peasant asked, and the new owner assured him that he had. 'Watch,' he said, and he turned to the mule and said, 'Giddyap,' but the mule never moved. He begged, he pleaded, he scolded and shouted, but the mule ignored him and stood there chewing placidly. Whereupon the peasant picked up a large two-by-four and hit the mule smack across the forehead. 'Giddyap,' he said gently, and the mule started to move. 'See,' the peasant said to the buyer. 'Speak gently. But first you have to get his attention.' "

He drew the gun partially out of his pocket so Naman could see it, and he pointed it at his own side and squeezed the trigger twice. It clicked on empty cylinders. "The gun was merely to get your attention," he said. "So you wouldn't run away from me before I had a chance to explain."

"Why would I run from you? I don't even know you."

"Ah, but you've been running from me since Berlin. You hired a plane to fly to Bonn, and so I did the same. But when I got to Bonn you were in Munich. I nearly caught up to you in the village of Ravenscrag, but again you ran from me. You flew to New York while I foolishly followed your trail to California."

"Why have you been chasing me?"

"Not chasing, following. In order to be at your side if you should need me."

"And why should I need you?"

"Perhaps you won't. But it's not an easy thing to do, to kill a chancellor."

They walked on in silence for a while. Finally Naman asked, "Who sent you?"

"Vorshage, naturally."

"He knows I don't want help."

"Because you trust no one. He thought you might trust me."

"Why should I do that?"

"What man doesn't trust his own son?" He smiled broadly and yet shyly. "I've wanted to say this for so long: Father." He said the word simply, and waited.

16

1

LISLE WINTRE caught a glimpse of herself in the mirror as she walked into the ladies' room of Berlin's Tegel Airport, and was shocked. That woman in the mirror was obviously terrified. She was almost visibly shaking.

Wintre locked herself in the stall, sat down, and composed herself. When she came out ten minutes later and washed her hands she was gratified to see that the woman in the mirror looked no different from those on either side of her. Inside she was still just as frightened, but on the outside nothing was wrong.

She walked back out into the international departures lounge and when her flight was announced she crossed to the waiting passport inspectors and handed over Mugsy's ticket and passport, looked the man right in the eye, and smiled.

He looked at her and came halfway out of his somnolent reverie. This woman smiled too brightly; she was frightened of him. He glanced at the documents, which seemed all right. If she was carrying drugs—or, more likely, a diamond ring she didn't want to pay U.S. import duties on—it was none of his concern; let the Americans worry about it when she entered Washington. He handed the ticket and passport back to her, motioned her through, and drifted back into his somnolent state. And so before Vorshage knew she was alive, she was climbing to thirty-five thousand feet and heading back to the United States of America.

Safely on her way now, she began to relax and think about what had happened. She tried to make a detached, logical assessment of the possibility that Mugsy had not been killed as a result of mistaken identity, that the murder had been one of the random, senseless acts of violence that permeate cities everywhere. She tried very hard, but she couldn't quite convince herself.

When the flight landed at Dulles International she was no longer frightened. If passport control should notice the difference between her face and that on the passport, it no longer mattered. She was safe in America now, beyond Vorshage's power; the police here were *good* police.

But since she was no longer frightened she gave off no air of irregularity and passed right through the checkpoint. She wasn't sure what to do now. She had to report what had happened, but to whom? She walked to the first bank of telephones and called Paul Horner in New York, but he was still out of town and unreachable. She called Melnik's hotel room in Washington, but there was no answer.

She wasn't sure what to do. She had left Germany and entered the United States illegally, using a dead woman's passport and identity. Hagan certainly had the clout to straighten these things out, but she was afraid of his reaction. He would certainly keep her out of jail, if for no other reason than that it would be a black mark against him if she were arrested, but going by his previous views of the assassination plot he wouldn't believe the killing had anything to do with her visit to Vorshage a half hour earlier. She could hear him now: "Not even the Germans are that efficient!" And then the bright, cold smile. He would think she had panicked and run away like a hysterical woman. Girl.

No, she couldn't go to him, but she also couldn't ignore what had happened. For one thing, Mugsy's family had to be told. She wasn't sure what to do, where to go. And then she remembered Randolph Burroughs of the CIA. She wasn't confident that he had the know-how or authority to do anything, but at least he would believe her.

"That's unbelievable," Randolph Burroughs said.

Wintre sighed. "That's exactly the way it happened," she said.

"Oh, I believe that. What I find incomprehensible is that you walked into Vorshage's office like a nun sashaying into a whorehouse, all innocence, bright-eyed and bushy-tailed. Didn't your mother teach you *any*thing?"

"You said he wasn't a Nazi."

"I didn't say he wasn't *some*thing. I *did* say, if you recall, that this thing might go all the way up the line. Which means, little lady, that no one over there is to be trusted."

"Don't—"

"I know. Don't call you 'little lady.' I'm sorry, but when I think you damn near got yourself killed—"

"No. I wasn't going to say that." She felt tired, so tired. "I just wanted to ask you not to yell at me."

He looked at her a long time, then smiled quietly. "I wasn't yelling at you. I guess I was yelling at me. I shouldn't have let you go—" He stopped himself. "I reckon there wasn't no way I could stop you, was there?"

"I reckon not," she agreed, and he laughed.

"I'll take care of the details," he told her. "You go home and get some sleep." He looked at his watch. "There was a 'Do Not Disturb' sign on the door, right? They probably haven't discovered the body yet. That makes it easier."

"Can you really take care of it?"

He nodded. "You'll have to give a formal statement, but that can wait." He paused. "You no longer pose a threat to anyone. Once you got back here safely and talked to us, there'd be no point going after you again. But you never can tell what kind of nuts you're dealing with. It's not necessary, but what I'm thinking is I'd feel safer if you didn't go home."

"Where else can I go?"

He took out his keys and threw them across the desk to her. "Stay at my place. —Just till I get everything cleared up," he added hastily. "A day or two, max."

2

"I FEEL LIKE a total idiot, losing Naman like that," Melnik said.

"Forget it," Horner told him. "The question is, what do we do now? Go after the other contact houses? Pick up the people and grill them?"

Melnik shook his head wearily. "Not enough time, not enough manpower, and not much chance of success. What we'll find is someone in each house with a locked suitcase or a safe-deposit-box key, with instructions from the person who hired him—who will be someone he doesn't know—to turn the stuff over to someone who gives him the right password. That won't take us anywhere."

"So we go back to surveillance, and hope Naman or Berner turns up again?"

Melnik sighed. "I feel so stupid."

"Not your fault," Horner reassured him. "In fact, I still don't understand it."

"Neither do I. Why would Naman want to ditch us?"

"Maybe something just came up. Maybe he'll be showing up at the Ramada in a day or two."

"No way," Melnik said. "He has no reservation there; he gave me a room number, and that room hasn't been specifically reserved in the next few weeks for anyone under any name. He couldn't possibly be intending to show up and check into a particular room unless he had made arrangements in advance. No, he just wanted to get rid of me."

"Maybe he didn't trust you to be who you said you were. Maybe he wants to check you out before he contacts you."

"He doesn't know how to contact me."

"Through his secretary," Horner suggested. "If he knows we know who he is, then he must know that we know where his office is. He's got to figure we'll be in touch with her."

"I guess that's possible," Melnik admitted. "Not likely, but possible."

"What else have we got?"

Melnik shrugged.

"So give her a call."

"What are the odds?" Melnik asked dispiritedly.

"Maybe one in a thousand."

"Ten thousand."

"Whatever. It's the only game in town. So let's play."

Melnik nodded listlessly, and picked up the phone.

3

He doesn't believe me, Grass thought. *He knows it isn't true.*

Grass knew from what old man Greiss had told him that Naman couldn't believe he was Naman's son, since Naman had never slept with Lise. But the only thing that was important was for Naman to believe that *Grass* believed the story. As he told it he heard how flimsy it sounded; he felt that Naman would never fall for it . . . and yet he saw

-----

something in Naman's eyes that didn't quite disbelieve, some glint that wanted to believe it.

Not a word, Naman thought. *Not one word of this do I believe.* And yet, if it was all a lie, how did this man know such things? Only Vorshage knew; to no one else in all the world had he ever said these things. So he listened as Grass talked of his childhood in Munich, of his mother who had been forced to play the whore in Auschwitz and who had escaped at the last moment with the one man she had ever loved. He told of how they had walked all the way across Germany and found refuge with friends in Munich, and how this man, Grass's father, had left for the United States and a new life.

He told Naman how, after the child's birth, Lise had forbidden their friends to write the truth to America. She was sick, dying, and she didn't want her love burdened with a sickly son. She had begged them to write that the child had died at birth, and soon afterward she herself had died.

He had been brought up as the son of these people, who had soon emigrated to Argentina. His given name, Karl, had been changed to Carlos, and when he came of age and they finally told him the story of his parents he had thanked them for their kindness and left them, returning to his homeland, to Germany. He had changed his name; he wasn't angry at his "parents," he was grateful to them, but they weren't really his mother and father and he didn't want to carry their name. Instead he took the family name of the famous German novelist.

He had wanted to go to America to find his father, Carlos said, and at the same time he didn't. Not yet. He wanted to prove himself first. And so he worked for the German intelligence service, slowly working his way up, and always he heard stories of the great Walter Naman, and never did he tell anyone that the great Walter Naman was his father. And finally, he said, a few weeks ago he had been called into his office by the head of the service, Klaus Vorshage, and told to go to America to help the great Walter Naman in his greatest assignment.

Naman didn't want help, Vorshage had cautioned him, and had been allowed to leave Germany on his own, but on second thought Vorshage thought perhaps Naman would need an assistant. And so Grass had been sent to find him and to look after him and to do whatever Naman would tell him to do.

"And do you know what my assignment is?" Naman asked.

"Of course. To eliminate our Nazi chancellor when he comes to America."

It made sense, Naman had to admit as he listened. The story held together. Lise would not have wanted the boy to know he had been conceived during repeated rapes, nor would his adoptive parents. It made sense that they would have tried to make the story a little easier to bear, that they would have told him he had a real father somewhere in America. And yet it was preposterous! Surely they would have written. If at first they had obeyed Lise and told him the boy had died, surely when Lise died they would have written—

Unless they had wanted to keep the boy. People did that, he knew. People loved, and love distorted their senses. . . .

It was the eyes that made him want to believe. The boy's eyes reminded him of Lise. Was it his imagination, or did he see her in those sharp blue eyes? Those eyes in the attic, staring at him scornfully and yet lovingly as she dropped the red dress from her shoulders—

He shook his head and turned away. Nonsense, the whole story was nonsense. . . . And yet—

Naman was a one-dimensional personality living in a four-dimensional matrix of space and time. The universe existed in the past, in the present, and in the future; but he constrained himself to live only in the present. The past was full of horrors, and it had taught him that the future held unimaginable terrors. All his life he had forgotten the past and had not dared imagine a future; held tightly in the present, he could exist, he could live.

Now the past was thrusting itself in upon him, and he turned from it—and then paused. Was he turning away because he didn't believe the boy, or because he did? Was he being cautious in the face of real dangers, or cowardly before imaginary ones? Was he turning away precisely because he didn't *want* to believe?

"So stay," he muttered, and walked to the window, stood there, looking out. What could it matter? Whether he was truly Lise's son or not, Vorshage had sent him to help; he wanted to help; so let him help. Forget Lise, forget the dead; still, the boy could help.

Forget Lise, forget the past. Only psychotics torment themselves. Life today is good, Naman told himself. He nodded; everything was going well. He knew what he was doing, he knew how to do it, he saw clearly the steps in front of him. And if he failed, well, at least he would still have the million dollars in the Bahamian bank. He would not likely be alive to enjoy it, but she would. This thought came unbidden into his mind, startled him with its ambiguity; for a moment he thought it was Lise who would inherit his newfound wealth, then he shook that nonsense away. It was Norma, Miss Middler, and he smiled at the thought of her receiving the news, of her surprise.

She was the closest thing he had to a friend in his life, though she herself didn't know it. He had hired her as his secretary when he began his consulting business nearly twenty years ago, and she had been with him ever since. He never talked to her about anything but the business, he never saw her outside the office, and yet she had somehow become integrated into his consciousness. She was someone else, some other person, someone he could touch; barely, imperceptibly, yet she was there.

Enough, enough, he told himself without words. Whenever his subconscious began to drift into dangerous territory he brought it up sharply and buried it deep. There was work to be done in this world without drifting somnolently into darker worlds where unknown terrors lurked.

Yes, there was work to be done. He had wanted to carry out this assignment strictly on his own, without contacting anyone in the world, but clearly that was no longer possible. Already at least two people knew about him, so he decided to find out if anyone else knew he was alive. That was why his thoughts had drifted to his secretary, he told himself: He had to bring her into this now. He picked up the phone and called her in Los Angeles. He didn't want to frighten her—after all, she thought he was dead—so he purposely disguised his voice. "Sit down and don't start screaming," he said when she answered the phone. "Do you know who this is?"

"And why shouldn't I?" Miss Middler answered calmly. "Haven't I listened to that voice for twenty years?"

Naman was skeptical: She must be confusing him with someone else. "I want you to listen quietly, and not say anything," he told her in his normal voice. "I am not dead."

"So who thought you were? I hope you haven't started believing your own publicity."

He had to laugh then. "I didn't fool you? Not for a moment?"

"Well, maybe just for one moment."

"Ah. And did you cry for me?"

"Never! Not a tear. I just wondered if you remembered me in your will."

"Diamonds and rubies, Norma. The Naman jewels, all yours. So tell me, did I fool everyone else?"

"Not quite, Mr. Bigshot. Some people have been looking for you, and someone else sent me a telegram using your name."

"Tell me about the telegram," he said, and she did. He didn't know what it could mean, but certainly he was not as alone as he wished to be. "Describe the people looking for me, please."

She did; he didn't know the black man or the woman, but from her description the other man was clearly Melnik. "All right," he said. He told her he would be working with these people, but had lost contact. If Melnik called—

He already had, she said. He had left a phone number in New York to be called if she heard anything at all about Naman.

"Good," he said. "Call him and give him a message. Tell him I'm sorry, and ask him if he can meet me in front of the Delacorte Theater in Central Park at three o'clock on Wednesday."

He discussed the telegram with Grass. "A digitized analysis of Waldner's voice," he said. "It must be for identification, wouldn't you say? Perhaps someone wants to call Waldner's hotel room and be sure that the person answering is indeed him."

"Makes sense," Grass agreed.

"But who? And why? And why try to do it through my office?"

Grass shrugged. "There's too many people interested in Waldner. And in you."

Naman nodded. "This fellow Melnik worries me," he said. "I would like to know what he knows. Even better, I would like to distract him, put him out of the way until it's all over."

"Easily done. I'll put him out of the way forever."

Naman was shocked to hear the suggestion come so easily out of Grass's mouth. "Why would we want to kill him?" he asked.

Grass shrugged again. "Why not? It's the easiest way to put him out of the way."

"Killing someone is so easy for you? Perhaps it's even pleasant?"

Grass smiled.

"That amuses you?" Naman asked. "Killing people is a subject for mirth?"

"You live in a different world," Grass said. "Think of this world. Every day we do things that aren't 'pleasant,' as you put it. We do them because they're necessary, and because they're both necessary and unpleasant we don't spend our lives thinking about them and wishing we didn't have to do them. We blow our noses and we go to the toilet. We ingest the bodies of dead animals, we chew them up and swallow them in order to live. Some people shudder at the thought of killing animals, some people won't step on an ant or a cockroach. Are such people morally superior to you and me?" He smiled again. "You want Melnik out of the way? I'll step on him."

Naman sat quietly, staring at the big man, seeing Lise in his eyes and hearing the voice of the Gestapo in his words. If Grass's story were true, his real father had been one of the concentration-camp officers, perhaps the young blond lieutenant who had nearly killed him with the same zest he would have felt stepping on an ant, on a cockroach.

And yet there must be more of Lise in the boy than merely his eyes. He thought of what Grass's childhood must have been like, growing up in a battered and destroyed country with no one to really love him, with no mother. He thought of his own life in America, free of all responsibility—free of the responsibility of Lise's child, who had grown up to think no more of killing a man than of stepping on an ant. Was it too late? Naman wondered. Or was he being given a second chance?

First things first. "If we work together," he said, "you must follow my orders. Is that understood?"

"*Jawohl, mein Führer,*" Grass answered with a smile.

"You think that condition excessively Teutonic?"

"It's your manner when you say it," Grass said, and Naman saw from his mirth that he was still a child; it wasn't yet too late.

"Fly to New York tomorrow," he told him. He took out his wallet and peeled off several bills. As he did so he noticed Carleton Genever's American Express card still there. Stupid to keep that, he didn't need it any longer. "You wouldn't have a scissors?" he asked, holding the card out.

"What for?"

"I used this a couple of times. It shouldn't be used again."

"Leave it to me," Grass said. He took the card from Naman, held it out in his huge hand, and crumpled it up.

"That's not good enough. Cut it into pieces, and drop the pieces at different places. It mustn't be traced back to us."

Grass nodded. "I'll take care of it." He turned casually and wandered away. As Naman began to count out the money for his trip, Grass took the card out of his shirtsleeve where he had slipped it when pretending to crush it, and put his hand—and the card—in his pocket.

"Meet Melnik and find out what he knows," Naman instructed, handing him the money. "Send him off on a wild-goose chase, get him out of our hair for a while. And forget about killing people."

"Isn't that what this is all about? Have I misunderstood something? Or have you forgotten?"

"Later," Naman told him. "We'll discuss things later. For now, just do as you are told."

Grass jumped to his feet and raised his right hand in the old Nazi salute, clicked his heels, and left the room.

Children. Naman sighed, shaking his head. Always a problem.

<hr />

4

"Unbelievable," Melnik said.

"I know," Wintre agreed, "but it's true, every word of it."

He stared at her, shaking his head. He turned to Horner. "Do you believe this?"

"It's true," Wintre insisted. "He tried to kill me! He *did* kill Mugsy—"

"Do you believe," Melnik asked Horner, "that anyone could be as stupid as this woman? Do you believe that she is *surprised* that Vorshage tried to kill her? Do you believe that she didn't listen to me when I told her this plot went up *very* high in Germany, maybe all the way up to the top? Do you believe *any* of this? Is it possible? Could God make a woman so beautiful and forget to give her even the slightest *hint* of a brain?"

Wintre's ears began to tingle, to burn with shame. She tried to defend herself. "He looked so—"

"Kindly?" Melnik turned back to her. "Like a father? He listened patiently to what you had to say? He appeared to believe you? He took you seriously? Treated you like a grown-up?"

She nodded, ashamed, angry at herself, furious at him.

"Yes, he took you seriously, all right." He started to say more, then stopped. His first impulse when she told him what she had done had been to grab her by the throat and shake her like a dumb rag doll. She could have gotten herself killed. Now suddenly he wanted to put his arms around her and rub her ears. It was the eyes that did it. Not the fact that they were filling with tears in her humiliation, but that she was refusing to let the tears flow: The fierce determination not to be vulnerable made her so terribly vulnerable he wanted only to protect her. Instead, he turned away and changed his tone. "Well, as it turns out," he said, "you did damn well. You found out more than we were able to: You found out that Vorshage is definitely in this plot."

"The question now is, What do we do about it?" Horner said.

"We don't bother with Vorshage," Melnik said. "It's too late to go after the root of the problem. What we have to do is cut off its hands before they aim the gun and pull the trigger. Naman's clearly involved somehow, so the next step is obviously to meet him as he suggests and see what he wants to tell us."

"Have you thought of the possibility," Horner suggested, "that he may be involved in a way rather different from what we've been considering?"

Melnik nodded. "The less you know about something the more possibilities there are. And we know damn-all about what's going on here."

"You took him by surprise in Philly," Horner went on, "and his first instinct was to get away from you. That is not a healthy reaction. Now he wants to get in touch again. Why? Because he's checked you out and now knows he can trust you? Or is it just to find out what you know? Maybe even to set you up?"

"Naman?"

"Right, Naman. What are you saying, a nice Jewish boy has to be on the side of the angels?"

"Actually," Melnik said, "what I had in mind was for you to keep an eye on me."

"Not so easy unless I actually come along. He'd be tough to tail without getting spotted."

"Right. But I don't want you to come along and perhaps spook him. To tell the truth, I'm not at all happy with Naman. You never know what's going on in anyone's head, and Naman's head has been twisted and shaken a lot. He's killed a few Nazis in his time rather than bring them back for trial, and when a man does that he begins to think—well, I don't know." The problem was, Melnik was thinking, he *did* know; he knew all too well.

"You're not thinking he's the one who's after Waldner?"

"I'm not thinking anything. I'm saying we don't know. And since we don't know, I'd feel better if you were hanging around." He took out of his pocket two small buttons with Velcro-like patches for backs. "These are microtransmitters," he said. "I'll keep one on me so you can keep track of us, and try to slip the other into the lining of his coat so if he ditches me, which is a clear possibility, you can follow him." He showed Horner the receiver, which looked like a small Walkman radio except for the indicator dial, which pointed like a compass to the transmitter. "It's got a range of about a mile, two at most," he said, "so don't get too far away. But it'll enable you to keep track of us without being obvious. Unless, of course, something goes wrong."

"What could go wrong?"

"In a city like this, almost anything could interfere. Listen to it," Melnik said, putting the earphone from the receiver into Horner's ear. A steady clicking sound ensued. "That tells you you're listening to it. It operates on a single frequency not in commercial use. But sometimes almost anything else can put out a signal at that frequency. A kid's toy radio, a kitchen utensil, a microwave or electric mixer, even a toaster. If the interfering signal is stronger, the receiver will home in to it. So listen to the clicking, that tells you you're hearing me. An interference will be more of a buzz, or something. I don't know, you might even hear music."

"That would be nice," Horner said.

Melnik nodded, not listening, and turned toward Wintre. She had regained her composure, at least on the outside. She sat there quietly.

"Music would be nice," Horner said again.

They didn't hear him. They were looking at each other. It was embarrassing. Horner cleared his throat. "Well, I got things to do," he said.

They didn't answer. He left the room.

5

GRASS TOOK A CAB from Penn Station to the software company on Houston Street. The same fat man with the beard was sitting at the same desk when he entered. "It's all ready," the man said. He went into the back room and came back with a small package. Grass opened it, looked it over, nodded and handed him Naman's stolen AmEx card. "I noticed the guy has an accent," the man said. "He'll be speaking in English, won't he? Because the program focuses on English-language sounds, not German."

Grass nodded, and the man took the AmEx card and entered the numbers in his computer. He frowned at the answer he got, looked at the card again, and entered the numbers again. Then he looked up at Grass, irritated. "What you got here," he said, "is a card that's been reported missing. Well, stolen is what it's been reported. You want to give me some cash, or what?"

"Or what," Grass said. He lifted his gun and shot the man in the face. The gun made only a little poof of a noise, but the clatter when the man fell was considerable. Still, no one seemed to have heard; no one came running. Grass leaned over the desk and saw the fat man lying on the floor in a widening circle of dark red blood, his hand still clutching the AmEx card.

Grass picked up the package and walked out.

"Two feet by a foot and a half by seven feet," Grass said.

"Coffin-sized," the man said. "Just about, anyway. No problem. When do you want it?"

"Tomorrow."

"No way, José. A week from Tuesday."

"How much?"

"It's gotta run five hundred. Custom job, you know what I mean?"

"Fifteen hundred," Grass said. "Tomorrow."

6

OH DEAR, Lisle Wintre thought. Things were getting confusing. Mr. Burroughs had been so nice when she came to him, had even taken her into his flat and given her a place to stay— God, she thought, she had to call him, he'd be worried because she hadn't come home last night.

What was she doing, she wondered? He was so nice, and David Melnik had been horrid. Angry, even mean. He was a hard man. She turned her head and looked at him, and he opened his eyes. "Penny for your thoughts," he said.

She'd have paid a good penny herself to hear her thoughts articulated so that she could understand them. She didn't know what she was thinking, she didn't know what was happening. "Well," she said, "at least when I tell Mr. Hagan what happened he'll have to believe that you're right about the conspiracy."

Melnik rolled over in the bed and took her in his arms. He held her a while. This was a mistake, he thought. He shouldn't have done this. He hadn't needed another quick roll in the hay, really he hadn't. What he needed was to find a real woman and settle down and have children and grow up with them, and this woman was just a child herself. What had happened last night? he wondered, and then he remembered, and smiled. When she told him she had nearly been killed he had wanted to kill her himself. And then the reaction had set in. . . .

After a while he said, "No. No, I don't think so."

"Hagan won't believe you?"

"We won't even tell him."

"But why not? How can he doubt what's going on after this?"

"Tell me your story," Melnik said, "imagining that I am Mr. Hagan who does not believe that there is any conspiracy to kill the German chancellor."

"Well, what's there to tell? I went there to see Vorshage to tell him what we know about the conspiracy, and half an hour later he tried to kill me."

Melnik chuckled and patted her head paternally. "Dear child," he said, imitating Hagan's tight-lipped and supercilious New England accent so perfectly that she began to laugh, "of course you're upset. I don't blame you. I understand. But let's look at this just a bit more clearly before we dissolve in hysterics. If you had been mugged in downtown Washington on your way to the airport, would you have claimed that the Washington police are part of this conspiracy? If you were attacked in New York would you blame it on the Eastern liberal establishment?"

"This wasn't a mugging, this was murder!"

"Perhaps. But it wasn't *you*, dear child, who was killed. It was a friend of yours who knew nothing at all about the supposed conspiracy."

"But the killer mistook her for me!"

"Ah, you know all about the killer then?"

"No, of course not—"

"You know what was in his mind? You understand him so perfectly that you know—"

"Don't be silly!"

"Silly?" Melnik asked in tones of great hauteur. *"Moi?"*

And they both dissolved in giggles at the thought of Hagan's reaction to being called silly by one of his staff.

"But seriously," Melnik then went on, "what would he say? That it's possible, barely possible, that your interpretation of the killer's motive is correct. Possible, but hardly probable." He slipped back into Hagan's voice. "Highly unlikely, I should say. Shouldn't you? Berlin is a big city after all, and as in every big city in this wicked world, crime is rampant there. Particularly now, with over three million ex–East German unemployed and unemployable. No, I would imagine that your friend is much more likely to have been an unfortunate victim of hotel robbery gone awry."

"Okay, maybe he'll think that," she said, pulling away from him, a bit upset, sitting up in bed. "But maybe he won't. Maybe I can convince him."

"Yes, maybe," Melnik agreed. "On the other hand, imagine that perhaps I am not Mr. Hagan who doesn't believe in the conspiracy, but Mr. Hagan who is *part* of the conspiracy."

She looked at him wide-eyed.

"In that case," he went on calmly, "what is my reaction when you tell me your little story?" He smiled coldly. Suddenly his hands shot out and his fingers snapped closed around her throat. He held her without squeezing, but tightly, in a grip of loose-fitting steel. "Your lovely neck would be like American corn flakes," he said. *"Snap, crackle, pop."*

She was silent for a moment. Then she said, "Rice Krispies."

"What?"

"Never mind. You can't really believe that Hagan is involved in this?"

Melnik shrugged. "Go know," he said. "At the moment I don't believe anything because I don't know anything. But I certainly believe it's possible. Think over his behavior and then tell me you're sure it isn't. Sure enough to risk that lovely little corn-flaked neck?"

She thought about it. "Rice-Krispied," she insisted, but she insisted on nothing else.

7

NAMAN VISITED several stores, returned to his hotel room, stripped and stood in front of the bathroom mirror, and got to work. The Israeli, Melnik, had seen him in his black hair and mustache. He would be circulating photos of him with and without those modifications. And so Naman stepped into the shower and washed his hair thoroughly. Then he lathered it with shaving lotion and proceeded to shave it off.

He dried himself and examined the result in the mirror. He went over his head again with the razor, smoothing away the last vestiges of hair. He removed the mustache and clipped the eyebrows down to a narrow line and bleached them white. He opened another bottle and splashed a little of the dark oily substance into his palm, smeared it around with both hands, and then spread it on his head. It was bottled suntan, and as he worked it into his skin it darkened from a gleaming white into a dull brown, and finally into a rich darkness suggestive not only of a lifetime in the sun but of generations before him who had lived there.

He spread the suntan over his face, working it carefully into the creases, the eyelids and the ears. He took it down over his neck and below the collarbone. He spread it on his arms up nearly to the shoulders, and on his feet from the toes to the calf.

When it had dried he put on a slight white beard, nothing ostentatious, rather dignified in fact, running casually along his chin line into an understated Vandyke. Then he dressed, slipping into the pair of Western-style boots and the conservative gray suit he had bought. The boots concealed platform soles and hidden heels, which added a full three inches to his height. He examined himself carefully in the full-length bathroom mirror. He thrust out his lower lip and contracted his mouth and forehead into a slight scowl, the kind he could maintain all day long without thinking about it. He smiled, maintaining the scowl as he did; yes, it was a permanent part of his face, part of his appearance. He nodded. Melnik might recognize him; someone familiar with him who was looking for him might penetrate the disguise; but no one else would. Hotel clerks and taxi drivers, airline attendants and policemen, shown his picture and given his physical measurements, asked if they had seen him, would certainly shake their heads with regret.

He straightened his tie and left the hotel room.

He flew to Palm Beach, where Waldner was scheduled to address a national convention of U.S. governors. He checked into the Breakers, where the meeting was to be held, and wandered around. He found nothing. He began to get nervous; there wasn't much time left to make preparations, and he still hadn't found the proper place to do it.

He hadn't yet checked out Washington or Los Angeles, but they didn't hold much hope. He wanted to stay away from Washington because security was naturally tighter there, and he knew Los Angeles well enough to know he wouldn't find anything new by visiting there. He hadn't found anything in New York, and now Palm Beach seemed lackluster. Naman was not a happy man.

He returned to his room with a headache. He opened the medicine cabinet and, reaching for his aspirin bottle, caught his finger on something. There was a small but sharp pain and he yanked his hand away and sucked on the finger, tasting blood.

It was a nasty little cut, and he felt around in the cabinet to find the cause. It was a small but sharp projection in the rear lower corner, a thin slab of metal that didn't quite fit in place. Peering closely at it, he realized that it was actually a latch that hadn't closed properly and had been painted over as it lay. He pressed on it, but the paint held it fast. He pushed harder, and suddenly it popped open and the entire rear wall of the medicine cabinet swung away, opening silently into a dark cavern beyond.

He leaned into it and found a pair of ropes dangling there. He pulled down on one, and as he did the other began to move up, and he realized what he had here. It was a dumbwaiter, used in the old days of glory to bring food up from the kitchen to the individual rooms, now long disused and probably forgotten by everyone.

And Naman knew, finally, what he was going to do.

He went down to the front desk and told them that he had just checked in this morning.

"Yes, sir. Is everything satisfactory?"

"Well, yes and no. The hotel is lovely, and I'd like to spend a few weeks here. But I find the room rather small."

The clerk lifted his eyebrow. The Breakers had been built early in the century, and its rooms were immensely large compared to those of newer hotels.

"A friend of mine recommended a particular suite," Naman went on. "I wonder if it's available? Number 3148."

"That's the Henry Flagler Suite, number 3148/52. It's a full three rooms. Let me just check, but this is high season so I don't know." He hit some buttons in the computer. "How long would you be wanting it?"

"Oh, I don't know. Say three weeks? Four if it's available."

"It's occupied at the moment, but will be coming free this weekend, if you could wait?"

"I suppose I could manage where I am till then."

"We do have other suites which are nearly identical—"

"No, if I'm going to stay I'd prefer to take one that was recommended."

"Let me just check further. I'm afraid we have someone booked in for next week, but let me see if I could switch them around. They didn't request that room in particular, so . . ." He pushed a button, then a couple more, and then another half dozen before he looked up smiling. "If we can wait till this weekend, there won't be any problem. Shall I book you in for four weeks, did you say? Suite 3148/52."

"That will be nice," Naman said. "It's a pleasure to get such attentive service."

"Our pleasure," the clerk said.

And mine, Naman thought.

Chancellor Waldner was due to arrive in ten days' time. He would stay in the Presidential Suite. Number 2148/52.

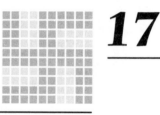

17

1

CHILI WAS NOT a big man, nor a vicious-looking man. He was a kid, really. He was six feet tall when he stood straight, but he never stood straight. Hunched over as he was now, skinny and shaking in the cold, the bottoms of his jeans not quite reaching to the top of his sneakers with the bare skin of his ankles showing between, he was a child of the twentieth century, God save us all.

He half stood, half leaned against the side of the building with the poster in the window: JUST SAY NO TO DRUGS. He had learned to read well enough to make out the words if he took the trouble, but he never bothered to. He had never understood the *concept* of reading; he had never learned that there was anything of interest to be learned from reading. A shame. He would have gotten a laugh if he had turned and read the poster. "Just say no to drugs"? What for?

It was cold on the street, and he was getting tired of standing there with his hand out, cupped and jingling the few coins he had. A couple of quarters had been dropped in the last hour, hardly enough to make a difference. He looked at them disgustedly, then threw them scattering and clinking over the sidewalk. People glanced at him and walked away, moving their eyes quickly, afraid of making contact. He wasn't a big man, not a vicious man, he didn't frighten them; but he made them uncomfortable. They didn't like to acknowledge that such as he inhabited the same world as they, that he was joining them for a stroll up Fifth Avenue on this lovely winter's morning.

He walked up Fifth past the sixties and turned into the park.

Many years ago new cars used to come with full-sized spare tires, and with four-pronged tire irons to loosen the hub nuts and jack up the support. Now we have small tires, more efficient jacks, and a tire iron consisting of a single length of solid metal with a hub joint on one end and a sharp point on the other. This was a great help to Chili.

He couldn't possibly have walked around with the old-fashioned four-square tire iron under his arm, but the new one could be taped to his forearm and caused hardly a bulge under the sleeve of his loose-fitting sweatshirt. The sweatshirt itself was insufficient covering for this February weather, but it was all he had. It let the wind in and the heat of his body out, and as Chili climbed the hillocks of the park he was cold. He knew he needed to get warm, but his thoughts did not turn to a dwelling or a coat. He knew what he needed for warmth: a hit of coke.

And for that he needed money, more money than the few quarters he had collected on Fifth Avenue and which he had scornfully thrown into the street. He saw an elderly, well-dressed woman approaching. She wore a fur hat and a long fur coat, and her handbag looked heavy. He stepped into a cluster of bushes as she approached, hunched over with his back to her, and rolled up the sleeve of his sweatshirt. He began to pull the tape loose, half freeing the tire iron, but his fingers were cold and they fumbled the job.

The woman passed by and gave him a wide berth. From his half-crouching attitude there she thought he must be urinating. She yearned for the good old days when she took her children ice skating in the park, when you saw policemen instead of vagrants, when the air was clear and clean. She passed Chili by and hurried on, and by the time he had cleared the tape from the tire iron and turned around she was gone.

He pulled the sleeve down over the iron again, but held it clasped in his freezing fingers rather than taping it up again. He wasn't worried about losing the old woman. There would be someone else.

Ray Durbin had wanted a Nintendo set for his birthday, and all he got was this stupid walkie-talkie. He sat around all morning pissed off with his mother, until Charles Wilford showed up. Charles was interested in stuff like that; he thought it was neat.

"Neat? Man, what you saying? What you gonna do with a stupid piece of shit like this? We gonna go in separate rooms and tell secrets with this, like a couple girls, huh?"

"I ain't talkin' stupid shit like that, man. I be talking money here, real big money. You hear what I'm saying?"

"Shit, man, you ain't saying' nothin'."

"Don't shit me, man. We can be top doggies in this town."

"What you mean?"

"Man, you *are* a dumb shit. If we be on the street doggin' an' the man come by, what we do? If we be anyone else we go runnin', right? An' they see us runnin' an' they come runnin' and there we be, right? But with this fancy piece of shit we just call up right there, you hear me, man? You be on the street and I be next block over and you see the man, you just saunter away nice and easy and turn your back and put in a fuckin' phone call is all. And I run up and tell the folks, and we be the best fuckin' doggies on this street, man! We pick up some big change soon as people hear 'bout us!"

"You think?"

"Why not?"

"Let's try it out, man! Let's us see if it be workin'."

And so they took off down the street, one on one side, one on the other, talking and jiving back and forth, getting real excited about this, you know?

Melnik leaned against the railing alongside the Delacorte Theatre, waiting for Naman to show up. He felt the cold only as something extrinsic to him. Years of training, years of experience in uncomfortable climes and ugly places, had inured him to the external world. What really made him uncomfortable today was the thought that Waldner's visit was fast approaching and he still didn't know what was happening.

Melnik had been surprised and disappointed when Naman ditched him. Naman's reputation put him squarely on Mossad's side, and even though he worked independently he had not been known to spurn the Israelis when they came into contact. He had been surprised again to get the telephone call from Naman's secretary, apologizing and offering to meet him here. What had happened to change Naman's mind?

Perhaps the man was simply being wary. Perhaps he had left Philadelphia only to check up through his own contacts on Melnik's credentials. That might make sense. He wondered what Naman knew about the project. It couldn't be too much or he would have contacted the authorities. If he knew enough about the plot to name names and locations he would have come forward already. Still, it was clear that he was involved somehow, he must know something.

Though Melnik mused through his thoughts like this, he never relaxed his vigilance, and so he saw the man he knew as Berner as soon as he made his appearance. Melnik continued standing where he was, leaning against the railing, as Berner came straight across the snow-speckled grass toward him.

"Herr Naman offers his apologies for the mixup at the Ramada in Philadelphia," Berner said to him without preamble, "and wonders if you would be so good as to accompany me to his presence."

Well, it was always something unexpected, wasn't that the way of the world? Melnik had thought that this man was pursuing Naman; it now appeared that he had been seeking to join up with him. For the mention of the Ramada was as good as a password; no one but Naman would have known about it.

He nodded and joined the man known as Berner, and they walked quickly across the park toward the west.

Horner sat on a park bench, the single earphone in his right ear looking like a hearing aid but giving forth a steady clicking sound which indicated that the transmitter was active. In his hand he held the Walkman look-alike, and was gratified when the needle started to flicker and then to move determinedly to the right.

Which meant that the transmitter was in motion, moving off in that direction. Horner got up and slowly began to meander around until the needle swung dead center. Then he wandered off in that direction, careful not to walk too fast, not to catch up to them, careful to keep the needle centered, to follow in the right direction.

Careful. Not careful enough. Forgetting, in his careful attention to work, the first rule of survival in New York City: Always be aware of your surroundings.

Concentrating on the needle quivering in the palm of his hand, he walked along the park path.

Chili saw the big black man with the hearing aid coming toward him. He didn't like big men, especially big black men, but the hearing aid and the slow walk combined with the man's downturned eyes to convey an appearance of age and carelessness. He wasn't as well dressed as the woman in the fur coat, but with men you couldn't tell nowadays. And Chili wasn't a greedy man, he wasn't looking to get rich, he only wanted a hit of coke to get warm again.

He passed by the big man, turned, and slid the tire iron down out of his sleeve and into his hand. He lifted it and hit the man across the back of his head. The man went down without a sound and Chili dragged him off the path into the bushes. He paused there a second, listening for the sound of running footsteps or screaming voices. There was nothing. He found the man's wallet and quickly took out the money without even looking, without even noticing the gold badge, peering all the while through the bushes for any sign of alarm. He dropped the wallet on the ground; credit cards were too hard to turn into cash, impossible for him to use. He knew he didn't look like an American Express holder, and each time he had tried to use a stolen card he had had to run away while the store owner called the cops.

Not worth the trouble. All he needed was some cash. Once he was away from the bushes there'd be nothing to connect him with the dead body inside. Cash is nonincriminatory; you can't prove where it came from.

He pushed the bills into his jeans pocket and stepped out onto the path. No one saw him; he was safe already. As he started to walk away he saw the Walkman lying at his feet. Radios were good, he thought, you could always get a few bucks for a radio. If it hadn't broken when it fell.

He bent down to pick it up, and saw the needle dial. It wasn't a radio, it was something else. It might be valuable. But he didn't know what it was. The hell with it. He had money in his pocket now, and he was beginning to feel warm already. He hurried away, out of the park, toward the nice warm hit.

"Where you be, Raymond?"

"Just comin' roun' Thirty-eighth 'n' Twelf'. You readin' me loud an' clear? Over an' roger."

"I hear you, I hear you good, man. This is fuckin' great, you know?"

"Now let's rendezvous, man."

"Say what?"

"Meet me, man! You goin' to Tenth and Fortieth, you hear me?"

"Roger, man! Hee-hee!" He slapped his side in happy exuberance. They bein' kings of all fuckin' creation!

Grass led Melnik out of the park and across Seventy-second Street, past Amsterdam and past Broadway. They turned and headed south. As he stepped off the sidewalk Melnik stumbled and nearly fell forward into the street, into the path of a speeding car, but Grass caught him by the arm. Melnik swiveled around and grabbed hold of Grass to stop his fall, then pulled himself upright. "Thanks," he said. He laughed. "A man like me, to almost get killed crossing the street in New York, it's kind of funny."

Grass didn't laugh, nor did he reply. He was not interested in polite small talk. Melnik let the matter drop. He had done what he wanted: In grabbing hold of Grass he had slipped one of the microtransmitters under the back of his parka collar.

"Herr Naman would be interested to know how you learned of his involvement in this little affair," Grass said as they continued on down the block.

"What exactly is his involvement?"

"If you don't already know, why are you so interested in him?"

"My father always used to answer one question with another. I found it very irritating."

"Perhaps you would prefer to talk to Herr Naman directly. We will soon be there."

They kept walking, however, block after block, down through the sixties and the fifties and the forties. As they passed a subway entrance Grass started down it, but Melnik stopped. Grass looked up at him and he shook his head. "I can't use the subway," he said. "Claustrophobia." He was afraid the radio signal would get too weak down there, or that a train might take them out of range before Horner could follow.

Grass laughed. He seemed to think that very funny. "All right," he said, and instead they took a bus. Grass sat looking back down the street. Taking the bus would frustrate any follower on foot, and he kept a watch to be sure no cab or car stayed with them. In the upper thirties they got off and struck out further west, past Ninth Avenue, past Tenth. Suddenly, as they were passing a boarded-up, deserted old brownstone relic, Grass put his hand on Melnik's shoulder and turned him. "In here," he said. They went down the outside steps and he pushed open the door. He led Melnik through a long passageway and then gestured him in front of him. "Up the stairs," he said. They climbed up silently and then Melnik felt Grass's arm again on his shoulder. "Down this hall," Grass said, and as Melnik turned he felt a sudden stab of pain in his neck.

He twisted away and kicked around at Grass with a roundhouse motion, but Grass stepped back and Melnik fell down. He tried to get up but couldn't. He felt the poison racing down through his neck, he felt the floor coming up, he felt nothing.

• • •

Horner felt a god-awful ache in his head.

"You're lucky to be alive enough to complain," the doctor said. "Anyone with a normal head would be past these earthly troubles. You have any Irish in your blood?"

"A paternal grandfather, they tell me, gone these many years."

"Well, he must have left a thick Irish head somewhere in your genes. Get some sleep, you'll feel worse in the morning, but you'll live."

"I've got to get home," Horner said, and tried to sit up.

The doctor pushed him back down onto the bed. "Tomorrow, maybe," he said. "We'll do some more tests and see."

"I've got work to do."

"Not today, you haven't. You've got a concussion, and you've got to rest. Now just relax and sleep a bit—"

"I don't have insurance to pay for this," Horner lied. "So unless you're going to pick up the bill—?"

Twenty minutes later he was out on the street, on his way back to Central Park. He went straight to the Delacorte with his Walkman in his hand, but the earphone made no sound and the needle gave no flicker. He walked up and down, around and around the theatre, spiraling farther and farther out, but couldn't pick up any signal. Melnik had said it had a range of a couple of miles at best.

His head ached, he felt dizzy and nauseated, but still he walked and walked until he came to the edge of the park. He stared out then over the city spreading out miles in every direction. Miles.

He leaned on the stone fence. He felt weak, and dizzy, and nauseated, and angry. But mostly he felt scared.

Melnik awoke in utter darkness. He lay still and waited for his senses to return. His hearing seemed normal—he could hear the sound of a distant buzzing—but his vision didn't return. No matter how he squinted or looked out of the corner of his eyes, he saw nothing but blackness. He reached up with his hands—

They banged against a wooden roof a few inches above his face. He reached out to the side, and came up against the same wood a few inches beyond his body.

He began to feel suffocated. He found it hard to breathe. He tried to feel the outlines of his jail with his hands and feet, but everywhere he moved he found only inches to spare. And then his hands hit against a small box on his stomach. He felt around it and realized it was a small tape recorder. His fingers found the play button and he pushed it.

"Good evening," Berner's voice said, strangely loud and resonant in the close confines. "In case you are wondering, you have been buried alive. You are in a coffin, and are buried seven feet under the basement of the abandoned house I took you into. The buzzing sound you may have noticed is a battery-operated air pump. They tell me it will last ten days. I tend to believe them, but after all it is not my life that rests on it. You will also find a container of fresh water, which you may sip through the attached tube. It is a full liter. There are, I am afraid, no refills.

"I want to know why you are interested in Walter Naman. I want to know how you discovered he was not dead, and why you care. I want to know what you think you know about the assassination of the German chancellor.

"I will come back to ask you these questions. I will come back in six days. Six days. So you have sufficient time to think about whether you want to answer these questions or not.

"I will ask them once. If you give me answers that I believe, I will ask you for a phone number. Whatever number you give me I will call, and tell them where you are. Of course, I will not do that for another three days, to make sure I am long gone and untraceable. If you do not answer my questions properly, I will simply walk away. There will be no second chance. Give it some thought. Give it some serious thought. Good-bye for now."

The silence closed in as the tape stopped playing. The silence closed in, and the darkness. . . .

Melnik splayed out his fingers and gently traced the outline of the box as far as he could. He couldn't sit up or bend over; he could barely lift his hands over his face. He kicked out with his feet. He banged on the coffin. He cried out.

He stopped. There was no sound answering him except the steady hum of the battery sucking in air from the ground seven feet above him.

He kept very still. He knew that if he started to scream he would never stop.

2

THAT MORNING Walter Naman left the Breakers Hotel and drove from Palm Beach westward across the state to the town of Sarasota, where in 1927 John Ringling had settled down, building a palatial home and bringing his Ringling Brothers and Barnum & Bailey Circus for winter quarters. Ringling's arrival marked the true birth of the town, as performers came from all over the world to join the circus, and tourists came to see the midgets and acrobats and animals in their winter hibernation. The town, sitting on the Gulf Coast and boasting some of the finest beaches in the state, became the center of the circus business in America. And that, rather than the fine beaches, was why Walter Naman drove there.

Sarasota has a variety of shops and facilities that cater to the circus trade. Naman looked through the local yellow pages and marked several of these. He visited a couple of them before he found what he wanted. He told the manager he ran a small children's carnival outside Houston—a few ponies and a carousel and a few rides—and he was building a house of horrors. He had a funny mirror, he said, and he would like to set up a system with a battery of flashing lights that would go off when someone peered into the mirror. He didn't know if it could be done, but—

"Easy," the man said, "but expensive."

Well, Naman said, he had the money.

"Not worth it, though," the man said. "Easier to sit someone by it, behind a door, and run it manually."

But they'd cotton on to that, Naman said. These Texas kids were smart. Damn smart. No, he'd thought of that, but he wanted it fully automatic, so they would think it was ghosts.

"Well," the man said, "an infrared sensor could do it. Catch the heat of the human body and trigger a solenoid relay to set off the bulbs."

Naman clapped his hands ecstatically. Yes, that was it. What a great idea!

"Not worth it, though. Too expensive."

Damn the expense! He wanted it. . . . How much?

"Couple of thousand, easy," the man warned. "Have to check into it. Maybe more."

Oh, that much?

The man nodded. "Not worth it," he said.

Well . . . Well, what the hell, Naman thought aloud. His wife would kill him but he had his heart set on it. How long would it take to put it together?

"Oh, no time at all, if you really want it. A couple of weeks? And two thousand bucks," the supplier repeated. "Maybe more—have to check the price list on a bunch of stuff."

"How about five thousand dollars? And one week?"

"Done," the man said.

And though Naman had been lying about it all, he had been quite serious when he clapped his hands for joy. He did indeed have his heart set on it.

3

"I DON'T SEEM to be able to locate Miss Wintre," Miss Pherson said.
Hagan glanced up from his papers.
"She's checked out of the Hotel Adlon in Berlin."
"Forwarding address?"
"A Hotel Paischer in Nuremberg. I called there, and they did have a reservation in her name, but she never arrived. I suppose she changed her mind, but now we don't know where she is."
Hagan considered that a moment, then smiled. It was probably not that she had changed her mind, but that she was purposely not leaving a trail, acting like a real spy. He wondered for a moment if anything had come up in Berlin to make her think there might really be something to the plot, then dismissed the thought. Whatever happened, he would be all right. He turned back to his work.

4

"WHAT THE FUCK, MAN?"
"Say what?"
"Shit, man, you hear me?"
"What you sayin'?"
Raymond and Charles were having problems. Their equipment had been working beautifully all over the neighborhood until they had straddled this abandoned building on Tenth. They had begun to notice a clicking in their earphones, which got louder and louder as they came closer together, closing in on the building, until now they could barely hear each other's voices over the noise. They came together outside the building and discussed the situation as clearly as they could.
"Shit, the fuckin' set be broken already, man!" Raymond said, already seceding from Charles's dreams of financial glory.
"Ain't broken, man, they made in *Japan*! Fuckin' Japs build these things, they be lastin' forever."
"Yeah, so what you sayin', man? You sayin' you don't hear nothin' but noise, man? 'Cause if you sayin' that, you don't know fuck nothin'!"

"There be somethin' wrong," Charles had to admit.

"Huh!" Raymond turned and held his walkie-talkie high, reared back, and prepared to throw it through the window of the old building. Charles watched him, and then at the last moment grabbed his arm. "Wait, man. It ain't the set."

"What ain't what set?"

"The noise, man!"

"Shit, you don't know nothin'. It sure as hell be in *my* set."

"No, man, what I mean, it somethin' *else*."

"What else?"

"You 'member *Rambo*?"

"What Rambo?"

"*Rambo,* man! Shit, the movie!"

"What Rambo movie you talkin' 'bout?"

"Shit, man, I don't 'member which movie. One of them. He lost in the jungle and he listenin' on his walkie-talkie and he be hearin' this *noise*? It be interference!"

Raymond laughed. "Right, man! We be in the fuckin' jungle and the Vietnamese be sendin' out signals! Whoo-ee!"

"You really an asshole, Raymond, you know that? What I sayin', somebody be sendin' out some interference. It ain't no Vietnamese."

"Who be it?"

"I don't know who the fuck!" He paused, and then he smiled. "Let's find out."

It started to snow. Light, powdery flurries, no nuisance in themselves but a reminder of the wind as they flitted and flirted around Horner's eyes and nose. His fingers and ears were the coldest, but it wasn't the cold that bothered him. It was the sheer futility. He had no doubt that he had been mugged by an accomplice of Berner's, and the fact that Berner had had no way of knowing who or where he might be only frightened him the more. He was sure that Melnik had been taken, might be dead already. . . .

Melnik would have been happier dead. He lay without moving, trying not to count off the seconds. He was finding it hard to breathe, and that made him start listening to the whirr of the air pump. Was it weakening? Would it give out? He told himself it would be better if it did: In a closed container, one didn't suffocate gasping for air, but instead by breathing carbon dioxide instead of oxygen. It was a pleasant death, a falling asleep, no more. But just the thought made it harder to breathe.

He began to gasp, to try to suck in great lungfuls of air though he knew this was a mistake, he might hyperventilate, he might panic— He was more afraid of panic than of anything else. Once he began to panic in this tightly closed space he would go mad—

"It be in here, Raymond. It be right in here."

The two boys stopped and looked around. They had climbed to the third floor of the building, kicking rats out of their way, stepping through piles of refuse, kicking up sawdust and spider webs and motes and mites, and the clicking had got louder and louder until finally they had to turn off their sets.

"I ain't seein' nothin," Raymond said, turning around slowly in the dark. A few shafts of light slid in through cracks in the shutters; otherwise the building was dark.

"Listen. You hear that?"

When they had turned off their sets the sudden silence had overwhelmed them; now, getting used to the quiet, Charles was beginning to think he was hearing something else.

"What? I don't hear—"

"Listen! Down that way."

Now Raymond heard it too, a soft whirring, a buzzing. He reached into his pocket, took out a jackknife, opened it. "We gonna go see?" he asked.

Without a word Charles led him on, down the corridor, around the bend, listening every few steps for the sound and hearing it grow, around the bend and in through a far door.

"Shit. What that be?"

It was hard to see in the darkness. In the middle of the room stood a large mound, covered with a heavy blanket. Beside it, on the floor, there was something making the whirring, buzzing sound. Whatever it was, it wasn't what anyone would expect to find in an abandoned house. It was obviously something, though, and the two boys crept forward to investigate, asking themselves "What the fuck?" and "What the shit?" as they circled cautiously around it.

Melnik had fought down the panic and now lay holding it tight to his chest, not letting it free. In the dark solitude of his grave, seven feet buried in the earth, isolated from all mankind as no man had ever been, he heard a voice. It nearly broke him. He knew no voice could be here deep under the ground, he knew it meant he was losing his grip, his tightly grasped grip on his sanity.

For the next moment there was nothing but silence, and he held tightly to that silence, to the certainty that he was alone but he was alive and sane. And then he heard the voice clearly now through the silence, above and beyond the silence of the whirring of the pump: "Shit, man. What the fuck we doin' here?"

And he knew he *wasn't* buried deep within the earth. That was a real voice, he couldn't have imagined that, he couldn't have made it up out of the spirits of his broken mind, never in a thousand years! There was someone standing right outside this box!

"Help!" He screamed, and with that first sound of hope it all broke within him and he began to scream and yell and pound on the side of the box—

"Shit!" Raymond yelped.

"*Fuckin'* shit!" Charles echoed, and the two of them fell against each other and bounced off the walls and fought like whirling dervishes in their flight to reach the door, to get out of that room, to fall, jump, run down the stairs and through the dusty hallway to the broken window through which they had entered, to climb through and fling themselves once more safe outside, in the clouded sunshine, in the snowflakes gently falling, in the comforting familiar clatter of the gentle street.

And once more it was quiet. And once more Melnik gasped for breath and heard nothing more than the dead air rattling in his lungs and the whirring of the air pump, and nothing else. Was he going crazy after all? Was he after all buried beneath the earth, alone and lost? He couldn't bear it, not now.

He felt a salt liquid running into his mouth, and he realized he was crying.

5

HORNER HELD a mug of coffee close to his lips without drinking from it. He held it in both hands, his fingers wrapped around it, letting the warmth seep through while the steam rose into his nostrils. He stared into the black liquid, swirled it a bit, watched the waves rise and die out.

"No luck, huh?" Blank asked, coming into the room.

Horner shook his head. No luck at all.

"Well, you never know," Blank suggested.

Horner nodded. That was true. You never knew. Melnik might be sipping a cup of coffee himself at this very moment in time, sitting in a hotel room or restaurant anywhere in Manhattan, talking to Naman and finding out everything he wanted to know.

It might be happening that way, Horner thought, but somehow he doubted it. Somehow he had this vision of Melnik lying bleeding in an alley, falling from a cliff, drowning in the river; all one vision, really, melding and roiling from one chiaroscuro to another.

He blinked and shook it away. All he could do now was wait. He knew how to do that. He had been a cop all his life.

He sipped the coffee and swiveled around, coming back to life, returning to the precinct station. "What's the fuss?" he asked Blank.

"What?" Blank raised his head from the paperwork he had been filling out and listened. "Oh, that." He laughed, gesturing at the sound of the ruckus out in the hall. "Couple of nigger kids got spooked by a ghost. Beggin' your pardon, I'm sure."

Horner waved it away. He knew what the word meant to a cop: It referred to a social class more than to a skin color. He nodded, returned to his visions, but then the sound of the kids' voices brought him back. And he thought about it. "No," he said. "Couldn't be."

"I'm tellin' you," Blank insisted.

Horner shook his head. "You and me, we got nightmares from watching *The Mummy's Curse* or *Frankenstein*. These kids grew up watching *Halloween*. They suck in horror with their mother's milk. You try to scare them with a ghost movie, they'd laugh at you."

"Yeah? Well you go listen to these two, they're scared shitless. Fuckin' around some empty house and a ghost starts screamin'." He began to laugh. "Can't get them to go home, they're too excited. Go ahead, let 'em tell you the story. Maybe if they tell it a few more times they'll sober up and get out of here."

"Well, maybe I will."

"Sure, go ahead. Take your mind off your troubles."

"Get me some uniforms with guns!" Horner shouted when he burst back into the room.

"What's up?" Blank asked.

"I'll explain on the way. Move your ass, boy!" He was already on the phone, arranging for a car. As they ran down the stairs and into the car he explained. "Kids rumbling through this old building," he said, " 'cause they're getting interference on their walkie-talkie! Melnik *said* the receiver might pick up interference."

"Yeah, but—"

"So the transmitter might *put out* interference, that's what I'm thinking! And these kids go into this room and somebody starts moaning and screaming for help!"

"You think maybe Melnik's tied up in there?"

"Do I know? Let's go find out."

He spread the uniforms out when they reached the place. Standard raid-and-search procedure. They didn't know what they'd find inside. Unlikely to be anyone there armed and dangerous, the kids had said the place was empty, but you never knew. They spread out and entered quietly, guns drawn, and advanced through the building step by step, floor by floor.

On the third floor they entered one room to find a dark blanket heaped over a large bundle, and beside it on the floor a fan whirling. They pulled off the blanket and found a coffinlike wooden box. "What the fuck?" Blank asked, and immediately was answered by the boys' ghost: Screams and shouts came muffled out of the box, and it began to rock as if it were being pounded from inside by a madman. . . .

18

1

NAMAN RETURNED the following day from Sarasota to New York. He took a hotel room in Yorkville and contacted Grass by telephone with instructions, then sat by the window looking out.

Half an hour later he saw Grass come walking up the street past the hotel. He proceeded up to the corner and flagged down a taxi, which then made a U-turn and disappeared.

As Naman watched, the street continued with its business; no one out there panicked, no one jumped into a cab, no cars went screaming into a U-turn to follow the cab.

In a couple of minutes Grass was back. The cab pulled up and he got out, strolled to the end of the block, then suddenly darted down the subway steps.

No one dashed after him.

One minute later he emerged again from the subway, crossed the street to the coin telephone, and began to dial.

The phone rang in Naman's room. He took one last look from the window, then answered it. "No one followed you," he said.

"I could have told you that," Grass answered, but without rancor. He understood the necessity of caution. "I'll be right up."

.   .   .

Grass broke out laughing as soon as Naman opened the door; it was the first time he had seen him since Naman had disguised himself. "Very good," he laughed. "Excellent! An old man disguising himself as an old man."

Naman was amused by his amusement, but deadly serious. "If I could have made myself a young man, I would have." Then he thought about that. "No," he said musingly. "No, I don't think so. Youth is an overrated commodity." Then, briskly, "At any rate, I want you to disguise yourself also. As we get closer to our target we must expect to run into more surveillance." He looked Grass over. "You will not be easy. The best way is to emphasize your characteristics rather than to try to hide them, but with you that will be difficult. To make you any bigger would be to make you too noticeable."

"I am not an amateur. I will take care of it."

Naman nodded. "So what did our friend tell you?" he asked.

"Nothing yet. He has to get his instructions. I don't think he was expecting to be quizzed, but rather to quiz. He has to get authority to tell us anything, but I am confident the permission will be granted."

"Why should you think that?"

"Your reputation," Grass said seriously. "I'm sure they will want to cooperate with you."

"You're very complimentary. Well, it would be nice to know what the Mossad people know, or think they know. But what is more important is to throw them off the track. Distract them."

"Leave it to me. I guarantee this man Melnik will not interfere."

Naman looked at him carefully. "There is no reason to kill him if we can simply distract him."

Grass spread his hands wide in complete innocence. "I promise, *Väterchen*. I won't touch him, not one finger."

2

"I CAN'T DO IT," Melnik said.

Horner looked at him, nodded.

They were sitting in Horner's apartment, or rather Horner was sitting while Melnik walked around. Since they had come here he hadn't been able to sit still for long. He had spent the night in the hospital, where they had sedated him and monitored his metabolism. They had wanted to keep him longer, but Melnik had insisted on checking out. They had come back to Horner's apartment to discuss their next move.

"I know you're right," Melnik said now. "But I can't do it."

Lisle Wintre came in from the kitchen with a tray of coffee, in time to hear his words. "Of course you can't. I *told* you not to ask him," she said accusingly to Horner. Horner had suggested it to her while Melnik was still asleep in the hospital bed, and she had thought the idea monstrous.

Horner shrugged. "It's his decision. He deserved the chance to make it himself."

"Paul's right," Melnik said. "If he hadn't thought of it, I would have. But I just can't do it."

"Of course you can't. No one could."

"And yet . . ." He looked at Horner, who nodded and said, "He'll be back. If he had just wanted to kill Melnik, he could have."

"He's a sadist," Wintre said. "He wanted to torture him."

"He's a sadist, all right," Horner agreed, "but he also wants information. He'll be back to get it, and that's when we can get him. Once old David here is totally recovered, he could do it. But we don't know how long that will take. And the problem is, we don't know how much time we have. He'll be back, but we don't know when. My guess is he said six days just for the torture value. No one could stay sane in that coffin for six days. He could come back any time at all."

"You can't possibly expect David to climb back into that coffin and wait for him—"

"We'll be right there, we'll be in radio contact, we can talk to him continually. Any time he wants to come out, all he has to do is say the word."

"No!" she said. "I won't allow it!"

That brought them up short. Melnik even had to smile. "Don't worry, Mama," he said. "I'll be a good boy." He turned to Horner. "Berner will be back," he agreed, "and it would be great if we could spook him into revealing something about his plans—"

"So far he's been in the driver's seat and we've just been running around after him," Horner agreed.

"If we would rattle him, throw him out of synch, he might give something away, maybe even lead us to Naman." And then Melnik shook his head. "But I just can't do it. Maybe in a month, maybe in six years, maybe never. And certainly not today or tomorrow. There's no point talking about it." He paused. "So what do we do?"

"I'll get in," Horner said.

Melnik didn't think so. "Never work," he said.

"Why not? The jerk isn't going to open the coffin—remember, he's trying to convince you you're six feet underground. He's going to be talking through that airhole, with the pump whirring; he won't know I'm not you."

"I hate to mention this," Melnik countered, "but you have a New York accent that is championship-class. You may sound like a normal human being to yourself and your mother, but to anyone from beyond the boundaries of the East River and the Hudson you come across like a visitor from another planet. He will know it isn't me."

"And he's crazy," Wintre put in. "To do what he did to David takes a very sick mind. Even if he doesn't know it's someone else, he might not like your answers. He could pull out a gun and blast you right through the coffin without any warning."

That was an image that did not greatly appeal to Horner, and he shut up.

"I have an idea," Wintre said finally. "It's probably stupid."

"Stupid ideas are better than null ideas. So tell us."

"Well, it probably wouldn't work—"

"Lisle," Melnik said. "Darling. Just tell us."

"Well, a telephone. You could be somewhere else in the building and speak through a telephone into the coffin, and he'd think you were in there."

"No good," Horner said right away. "He'd see the wire leading in. But—"

"Yes," Melnik agreed, anticipating him. "A radio. He'd be hearing me through the airhole and so the voice would be naturally distorted anyhow. A sophisticated set could provide enough fidelity to fool him."

"And if it doesn't, we have nothing to lose. It's not like you or Paul being in there at his mercy if he realizes he's being tricked."

"I like it," Melnik said.

"Problem," Horner had to put in. "Where do we get this marvelous piece of sophisticated machinery?"

"The New York police must have such things available—"

"The NYPD has trouble keeping billy clubs within its budget. Maybe somewhere in the aristocracy there's stuff like that, but the paperwork to free it will take a week. You need someone with access to it, with clout, and all you got is me. How about the Mossad? You guys probably got radios that fit under your fingernail and sound like the Chicago Symphony."

Melnik shook his head. "The Tel Aviv Symphony," he corrected. "The sound of the Chicago brass section is difficult to capture. Yes, we have such things, but in Israel, not here. It would take too long to get it."

There was thoughtful silence for a moment, and then Wintre said, "Maybe Randy can help."

"Who's Randy?"

"My man in the CIA. I think he kind of likes me. They've probably got stacks of radios in every janitor's bin at Langley. Shall I give him a call?"

"Take care of it," Melnik agreed. "In the meantime"—he turned to Horner—"could you help me find a local magician's shop? I'd like to fix up a little surprise for our friend."

3

"Let's go," Naman said. Grass put on his parka and they left the hotel together, flagged down a cab, and took it to LaGuardia. Two hours later they landed at Logan. Naman rented a car and they drove out the turnpike to Route 128. They turned north and passed Walden Pond and Brandeis University, then turned off into an industrial electronics park. Naman pulled the car up in front of a small firm and entered, leaving Grass in the car.

The shop was tiny and cluttered. Inside, it looked like a small appliance-repair shop in the plains of Texas. The floor was covered with parts of things that might have been vacuum cleaners, ovens, or VCRs taken apart. If one was looking for a place to undertake and deliver on time a piece of sophisticated electronics, the ambience here did not inspire confidence. But the shop's reputation was sound, not only for on-time delivery of equipment that worked, but for a less-than-compliant attitude toward official restrictions.

No bell had tinkled when Naman entered, but he had noticed the electric eye as he crossed the threshold and so he waited patiently. Eventually a man who looked like the janitor entered from the rear. He was short but heavily laden with fat and muscle, bald but white-bearded; a heavy paunch hung forward through his basketball shirt, which proudly proclaimed the Boston Celtics and was dirty enough to be worn by a Lakers fan. "How do," he said. "Bill Hirsh. How can I do you?"

Naman introduced himself as Harvey Kirsten, a procurement officer for Tennessee Valley Geo, a consulting geology business. "We're beginning field exploration studies involving a new method of finding oil.

Our client came up with this idea and is hiring us to check it out for him. What we're doing is, we're putting together a special kind of RV. You know, recreational vehicle?''

Hirsh nodded, his elbows on the counter. ''Hell, you couldn't get me in one of them for no amount of money. I want to go anywhere, I fly.''

''Well, for what we're doing we have to be right down on the ground. In fact what we're going to be doing is taking geological samples and analyzing them right there in the field. Now, this involves melting the rocks to extract entrapped gases, and for this we need an RF induction heater that will fit inside a space two feet by two feet.''

''How much power you talking here?''

''Twenty thousand watts.''

''Impossible. Im-fucking-possible. That's some group of what-do-you-call-'em, geologists, you got there. They don't know their ass from an oil well in the ground.'' He laughed appreciatively, then turned serious again. ''An RF heater generates microwaves, that's what melts the rock. It's like a microwave oven, you know what I mean? And you know how a microwave oven has to be properly closed or it leaks radiation? You remember how everyone worries about that? Well a twenty-thousand-watt RF leaks radiation like a sucker. Detrimental to your health, like they say on the cigarettes, you know what I mean? So you got to shield those suckers and what that means is you can't make 'em small. A twenty-thousand-watter got to be, oh, six or eight feet on a cubic side, easy.''

Naman smiled. ''Forget the shielding,'' he said.

''Can't do that. Too dangerous.''

''Not really. We've worked out a system to operate it by remote control. All we need is the RF generator itself. But it must be small and lightweight.''

''Hell, I can make it, but you're gonna need a special license to operate it.''

''Understood. You make it, we'll get the license.''

''I can't deliver it to you without a copy of the license,'' Hirsh warned.

''Not to worry. But time is a problem. How soon can you deliver?''

''Hell, it's practically off the shelf. Just a standard unit, and I take out the shielding. That's all you're asking for.''

''How soon?''

''I'll have it before you have the license.''

''How soon?''

''Three days.''

"How much?"

"Twenty thousand."

"Thirty thousand, one day, and you don't worry about seeing the license."

"Done," Hirsh agreed without quibbling.

Naman left a cash deposit, returned to the car, and they drove back to Logan Airport.

4

THEY COULDN'T KNOW whether or not Grass had noticed the microtransmitter Melnik had attached to his parka, or indeed if when he came he would be wearing the same parka, but they had to assume he hadn't and he would. They didn't have the manpower necessary to follow him if they had to keep him in sight, especially if he was suspicious—and in all likelihood the result of his interview with the man in the coffin would result in more than suspicion. What Melnik was hoping was that the circumstances of that interview would spook him enough to make him forget his normal caution.

By the time the winter sun was beginning to leave the New York canyons they had their radio system set up in the coffin, together with the little surprise Melnik had fashioned after his visit to the local magician's shop. Melnik was installed in a commercial office across the street, with an unmarked police car parked outside, and Horner was in a similar pad on the other side of the building. Wintre was staying with Melnik. "Hagan doesn't even know I'm back from Germany," she said. "No reason for me to return to Washington."

"This could take a long time," Horner warned. "Maybe up to six days."

"We'll manage," she said.

Horner looked at her. She looked away. He looked at Melnik. He looked away.

"Right," Horner said, and left the room.

Everything was in place. Now, like spiders, they waited.

5

MELNIK WOKE UP screaming; he was having a nightmare. Wintre comforted him, brought him a cup of coffee, and they sat on the bed talking.

"Would you like to know what really makes me angry?" he asked. "When I was walking along the street with that man he started into the subway entrance, and I said no, I couldn't go in there with him. I didn't want to take the subway because I was afraid Horner would lose the trail in there but of course I couldn't say that, so I said I had claustrophobia. And he laughed at that. The son of a bitch, he believed me, and he laughed. He knew what he was going to do to me, and he thought it was funny that I had claustrophobia."

"But you didn't, did you?"

"No, I just said it to keep out of the subway. But if I was lying when I said it then, I wouldn't be lying now." Melnik paused, thinking about it. "I'm really going to get that son of a bitch," he said.

The next day Naman told Grass to contact Melnik again and find out what he knew, while he himself flew back to Boston to pick up the microwave generator. Grass said it was too early, he wanted to give Melnik more time, but Naman insisted.

It was a fine day, cold but clear, the kind of winter day New York used to have in abundance before its streets were clogged with cars and trucks belching black smoke into the restricted canyons. Today the wind came out of the north, and it smelled as if it came straight from the North Pole, blowing the smoke and pollution away as it swept through the city, leaving everyone's cheeks red and shining, and if it also left their noses running no one seemed to mind.

By the time Grass reached the empty building he was in a fine mood, but no less careful for that. It was unlikely that anyone had found Melnik, but it was not impossible. He walked past the building, looking for telltale signs, and circled the block before he made up his mind to enter. In fact, he gave much consideration to not entering, to going back and telling Naman that Melnik had refused to say anything, refused to cooperate. He would simply leave Melnik in the coffin to die, and Naman would never know. The idea appealed to Grass. He didn't really expect to get much information out of Melnik. Whatever Mossad knew, with Melnik out of the way and Naman and himself free and clear, what could Mossad do to hinder them?

But on his circuit around the block Grass saw no evidence of a setup, and he was confident that if there was one he would have picked it up. Waldner was coming in less than a week now, and so the Mossad and CIA and whoever Melnik might have contacted would want to use Grass to find Naman rather than to take him captive and try to make him talk; they would have to expect that by the time they broke him it would be too late. And if they were going to follow him they would have to have a reasonably large number of men in place. They wouldn't know which exit he would use to leave the building, so they would have to have groups all around it. He didn't believe they would be able to do that without his making them—there would be garbagemen stalling around unpicked-up cans, or telephone linemen hanging on the poles, or a bunch of derelicts sitting and drinking beer on a doorstep—and he didn't see anything like that anywhere around the building.

So he thought it over, and decided he might as well go in.

By the time he decided, it no longer mattered. Wintre and Melnik had been, respectively, reading a book and napping when the clicking began. Sporadic at first, it quickly settled down to a steady beat.

With the first clicks, both of them had jumped up and stood over the receiver, waiting for the dial to stop wavering and settle down. It had begun to slew wildly from side to side at the first receptions, which were beyond its effective range, but as the source came slowly toward them the needle steadied. Wintre picked up her radio and called Horner.

"Yes, I've got it too," he said, and gave her his directional reading. Melnik had already drawn a straight line on the city map he had spread out on the table, running it from his own position out in the direction of their signal. Now from Horner's position on the other side of the building he drew a converging line. "He's on Tenth, between Thirty-fourth and Thirty-fifth," he reported.

As they watched the needle move, Horner traced Grass's route toward them. He was coming slowly, obviously on foot. Wintre looked up worriedly when he passed by the building, but Melnik shook his head. *Not to worry.* A few moments later he nodded in satisfaction as Grass's route took him in the beginnings of a circle around the building. They watched in silence as he came back to one of the entrances and went inside.

They told Horner what was happening, and then turned off their communicating radios. Melnik smiled as he turned on the other radio, the one connected to the set inside the coffin.

Grass took no chances. He had seen no evidence of a trap, but he advanced cautiously through the building with gun drawn. He didn't go straight to the room where the coffin lay but instead poked his head into each of the other rooms, climbing slowly to the third floor. Finally he entered the room, and lowered his guard. He walked up to the black-draped coffin and pulled the covers back from the airhole. "Hello, Melnik," he called. "Are you comfortable down there?"

No answer.

"Melnik? Cat got your tongue?"

"Let me out," Melnik whispered hoarsely. "For God's sake get me out of here. Please!"

His voice was rasping, metallic, but Grass noticed nothing over the sound of the whirring air pump. "All in good time," he said. "And of course only if you're a very good boy. Are you?"

"What?"

"A good boy?"

"Please get me out of here!"

Grass smiled. "Are you a good boy?" he repeated.

"Yes," Melnik whispered, defeated, compliant. "I'll be a good boy."

Grass laughed. "Is it possible that the great Mossad has come a bridge too far? How did you get on to my trail?" he asked, turning serious.

"The detective agency."

"They were watching for Naman. How did you know he was involved?"

"The police found out he didn't die in the car bomb. And since he used the incident to disappear—"

"And you already knew of the assassination attempt, of course. Yes, that seems reasonable." Grass was satisfied. They didn't know anything that could be dangerous. He turned to go, then hesitated. As far as he knew, this fellow Melnik was the only one who knew his face. There might be others, but perhaps not. If that was the case, he shouldn't leave Melnik alive. There was little likelihood that the coffin would be found before he suffocated, especially if Grass turned off the air pump, but the wooden coffin wasn't airtight, and reluctantly Grass decided it would be amateurish to take chances. Reluctantly, because he liked the idea of leaving Melnik in there to go crazy and die hammering on the walls, scratching until his fingers were shredded, screaming and crying. . . .

Grass played with the vision, enjoying it. Still, one mustn't be sentimental. He took out his gun and screwed the silencer into the barrel. "Tell me," he said, "would you rather I killed you now or left you to die slowly?"

"You said you would get me out of here! You promised—"

That was funny. It salved Grass's regret at giving him such an easy end. And then he thought: It needn't be easy after all. One bullet in the stomach wouldn't kill Melnik right away. The pain would be terrible, and to bleed to death, caught in the coffin, unable to move—yes, that was the answer. Grass raised the gun, aimed it at where he calculated Melnik's midgut should be, and pulled the trigger. The gun puffed lightly, quietly, and a surprisingly large hole appeared in the coffin.

"You said you would call a phone number for me," Melnik said. "You promised—"

Grass stared at the coffin, unable to believe his ears. The man went on talking as if nothing had happened. Could Grass have missed? Could Melnik have scrunched himself up into a ball in there? He fired again, and again and again, splattering the coffin from one end to the other, but the voice kept on, begging for his life, oblivious to the bullets.

"What the hell is going on?" Grass shouted, losing control, and Melnik's voice suddenly changed.

"Uh-oh," he said. "Have you figured something out?"

Grass picked up the hammer he had used to nail the coffin shut and began to pry open the lid.

"I *thought* I heard wood splintering," Melnik went on. "I hope you're not trying to open my coffin. Vampires don't like to be disturbed, you know."

Grass yanked out several nails, then inserted the tip of the hammer claw and pried the lid up. It came slowly at first; then the wood cracked and it hung loose for a moment, held in place only by its own weight. Grass shoved it hard; it fell aside—

—and with a loud pop a horrible jack-in-the-box erupted out of the coffin.

Grass screamed and fell back, dropped his gun, tripped, and fell to the floor. He lay there for a moment, catching his breath, while Melnik laughed hysterically. "My God, I'd love to see your face right now," he shouted.

Grass picked up the gun and looked into the coffin. He saw the radio there, still laughing at him. He shot it, and all was silence.

6

Some people are just not born lucky. Mike MacDonald was one of them, and so he should have known better. And yet today he was going to do something he never in his life thought he would dare.

He should have known better.

He was pudgy, had always been, but he thought he was looking better now. He sucked in his stomach as he looked in the mirror after showering. Yes, he definitely looked okay today. Some men get better as they get older; not women, poor things. He shaved and smacked his face with after-shave, and he hummed as he got dressed.

He was brought up short, and confirmed in his feelings, by his wife over breakfast. "What's with you?" she asked.

"Huh?" he countered.

"What did my mother used to say?" She tried to remember, and then got it. "You look like the cat that swallowed the canary."

"Your mother never said that to me."

"Not to you, she used to say that when we were kids."

He chewed his toast. "What did it mean?"

"I don't know. Like you were all dressed up and ready to kill."

He shook his head. "Wearing one of my usual suits, nothing special." He kept his voice casual; she couldn't know he was wearing his new underpants.

"I don't know," she said. "I don't think it used to be actually the clothes we were wearing, it was the expression on our faces."

He laughed uncomfortably. "Same old face," he said.

"I guess," she said.

He learned his lesson from that. He kept his expression noncommittal, and when he went to work nobody said anything about his looking unusual, swallowing canaries, or being about to spread his arms and fly out the window—although he felt as if he could, as if he could do anything today. He forced himself to walk and talk and act perfectly ordinary, except for one thing: He couldn't help but look at his watch every few minutes throughout the day.

And finally it was five o'clock. He waited at his desk, his head bowed over a pile of papers, until everyone had left. He should have had his first clue then: Usually the office was empty within thirty seconds of the clock ticking off the hour, but tonight two of the women stood around their desks talking and gabbing while he wondered if they didn't have a home to go to.

It was many long minutes, but eventually they left. He glanced around the office, and relaxed for the first time since breakfast; his face uncreased from its normal frown of concentration and realigned itself into a series of lines that his wife would have recognized instantly. If she had taken one glance at him now, she would have started rummaging among the waste baskets for the bones of the poor canary.

He picked up the phone and dialed. When it was answered he asked for the front desk, and when the deskman finally picked up he confirmed that his room was ready. He wanted to ask if they had any rooms with mirrored ceilings, but didn't know quite how to phrase that. Well, maybe next time.

He smiled openly. He had no doubt there would be a next time. Many next times. He had known Catherine for years, but it was only at last Saturday's party that he had really talked to her, and as they began to draw each other out they found they each had the same frustrated hopes for what grown-up life could be like. Each was tired and bored—not unhappy in marriage, he had stressed that. Oh no, she had agreed, she would never want to make Francis unhappy, which was why she had never . . . you know.

Oh yes, he had said. He knew. He felt exactly the same way himself. He would die rather than cause Gladys a moment's grief. And yet . . .

Yes, she agreed.

It wasn't fair.

No, no it wasn't.

If only—

Yes. . . . She lifted her eyes to his, dropped them shyly, and then in that one shining moment she had raised them again and stared deep into his soul, and he had found the courage that had founded empires, that could press a wreath of stars on the brow of a lover. "I've always liked you," he said.

She lowered her eyes again, but this time slowly, with an invitation for him to follow them right inside to her soul.

Mike hung up the phone and stood up, hurrying now. He put on his hat and coat, turned out the office lights, and nearly ran down the hall. The damned elevator just wouldn't come. He jabbed the button again and again, and finally turned to the emergency door and ran down the steps.

He was sweating when he opened the front door and stuck his face into the cold wind. He felt the sweat cold under his armpits and hoped his deodorant could handle it. Though he was cold he kept his coat open, wondering if the cold wind would freeze the sweat there permanently or evaporate it. He could always suggest a shower first, he thought. He flushed warmly. He could suggest they shower together.

His feet flew over the pavement; he snaked his way through the crowds like Red Grange. He could have bounced lightly and flown over the crowds, except that he remembered he mustn't attract attention.

•   •   •

Horner contacted the two groups of uniformed policemen in their cars. He warned them again that they must follow his instructions to the letter. If they happened to come within Grass's sight they would surely spook him; they were there for the final confrontation only. Horner would direct them along Grass's path but parallel to it, flanking him one on each side, always several blocks away.

Horner, in turn, would be fed information by Melnik. As Grass moved through the city Horner and Melnik would remain on opposite sides of him, and Horner would radio Grass's direction according to the needle on his receiver. Melnik would plot that as a straight line on the map he was carrying and would add another line from his own location in the direction his indicator read; where the lines crossed, Grass would be. Following out of sight they could stay in their unmarked cars and go as slow or as fast as Grass; whether he walked or ran or grabbed a cab or bus they would keep him in "sight." The only problem was the subway, and if he made a move to enter one they would crash after him and arrest him on the spot.

They hoped he wouldn't. They wanted to follow him back to Naman. With any luck, they would. All they had to do now was wait for him to make his move.

Grass crept quietly to the window and considered his situation. He couldn't spot anyone outside, but he hadn't spotted them on the way in either and certainly they were there. He could wait inside for them to grow impatient and come in to get him; he had a good defensive position here and he'd make them pay. But there was no escape for him that way.

He thought of the roof, then rejected the idea: They'd be expecting him to try that route and probably had men posted up there. He stood by the window, and wondered why they hadn't blocked off the street after he entered the building. He saw people walking along the sidewalk, including children. These were obviously not undercover police. If he came out shooting they would get him, but there would be a slaughter of innocents, and they wouldn't want that . . .

He realized what they were up to, and was ashamed it had taken him so long to figure out. They weren't going to try to stop him, they wanted to panic him into running, and they would come running after him. They wanted Naman, and they didn't know where he was.

Fair enough, Grass thought. If he couldn't shake a tail, no matter how many of them there were, it was time to retire and go home to open a tobacco shop and bore his friends with tales of his youth. Not that he had any friends, but never mind, it was the thought that counted.

Grass crept quietly down the stairs. He didn't expect anyone to have followed him into the house, but you never knew. He thought he'd start right off by seeing how well prepared they were, and so instead of leaving by the entrance he found his way around the side and broke a window on the ground floor. Quickly he climbed through and began walking away.

Down the block two men who had been lounging on the steps of an old brownstone, drinking beer from cans wrapped in paper bags, lumbered to their feet as Grass came by. He nearly laughed out loud, they were so obvious. He walked on, and when he got to the corner he glanced quickly back and saw them ambling casually after him.

Did they really think they could follow him as easily as that? He didn't know whether to be amused or insulted.

Mike MacDonald got to the restaurant first. He knew, when making the date, that one is supposed to meet at a bar, but all the bars he knew in Manhattan were either gay or touristy or incredibly expensive. It wasn't that he begrudged the money for the latter, but he knew he wouldn't show up to best advantage there; he realized he didn't fit in. So—rather brilliantly, he thought—he had suggested a small French restaurant on West Forty-sixth Street. Neither expensive nor posh, quiet and intimate, it was the place he always went to with Gladys on their anniversary— He hadn't remembered that, he thought as he walked down the stone steps and opened the door. Somehow that wasn't right. But no time to change plans, he had to plunge ahead.

He went in and knew it was going to be all right. The place hadn't changed at all, it never did. It was early—they had just opened—and the restaurant was empty, which he thought made it more romantic. He was glad Catherine hadn't shown up yet. He spoke to the little old lady who ran the establishment and confessed all: He was having a special evening and he knew nothing about wine. He wanted something good, really good, but not pretentious. She suggested a Château Beau-Site, a Sainte-Estèphe, for eighteen dollars, if they were having red meat.

Yes, he agreed.

They had a bottle of 1987, she said. A very good year.

He had read somewhere that red wines were better in odd years, so that sounded perfect. He was glad he had placed himself in her hands. He thought this was going to be his lucky day.

And then he had a suddenly horrible moment. She would remember him. On his next anniversary, when he came here with Gladys, she would say something—or, even worse, she would wink.

He couldn't worry about that now. He would find somewhere else to take Gladys, make up some story or other, find some place recommended by Gael Greene. He wiped his brow and straightened his tie. He glanced at his watch. Catherine would be here any moment. He asked the old woman, who also tended the bar, for a Manhattan, and casually slid one leg over the bar stool and waited.

The two men followed Grass, or Berner as they knew him, for nearly ten minutes before they lost him. He had obviously been looking for a tail as soon as he left the building, and had taken several evasive maneuvers which they had countered without, as they thought, giving themselves away. They had been told he would be difficult to tail and that they should allow themselves to be seen, if need be, rather than lose him, but he didn't seem to be too tough. Standard double-backs and in-and-outs, nothing too sophisticated, and they were just beginning to think they had his measure and would be able not only to stick with him but to do so without being seen, when he disappeared.

He turned the corner into Times Square, and when they followed a moment later he was gone.

They didn't panic. They took the measure of the square as soon as they entered, estimating how far he could possibly have gone in the short time he had been out of sight. He could have made it to the next corner, but not to the one after that, so they dashed down to Forty-sixth Street and looked up and down it. Not there. So he was somewhere between Forty-sixth and Forty-seventh. Patiently they checked out each of the stores, one waiting outside with an eye on both entrances when there was more than one, the other going in and looking through thoroughly.

They didn't panic until they had been through the whole block. And realized he was gone.

"He's lost them," Horner reported by radio.

"Good. That didn't take long. Any movement on your scope?"

"None."

"Nor on mine. He's holed up somewhere in that block. Tell your men to run around a little and then give up. Be ready to move as soon as he does."

. . .

Grass had turned the corner into Times Square without a definite plan. He had made the two men almost as soon as they began to follow him, and was in no hurry. He would keep walking until something occurred, and as he turned the corner it did. The man who ran the newsstand on Broadway had come out of his wooden shack to set up the new copies of the *Times,* which had just arrived. Grass went up to him and said, "Twenty dollars if you let me hide from my wife for ten minutes."

The man took the money without a word, and Grass slipped around the edge of the shack and into it. He found a small space under the counter and curled up there into a ball.

The newsagent never looked around to see who was following the guy; he was a New Yorker, he didn't care. He went about his business as usual, forgetting the incident within two seconds of stuffing the twenty-dollar bill into his pocket.

Grass stayed there ten minutes, then got up and stepped out again into the street. He headed uptown now. He wasn't sure he had lost the two men yet, but as he walked along, suddenly backtracking and stopping, reversing direction, going into stores by one entrance and out again by another, he finally became convinced that he was free.

As soon as Grass went to ground Horner and Melnik left their hiding places and took up the wait in their unmarked cars. Melnik's radio crackled when Grass started to move again. "Heading north," Horner said.

"Right, got him. Let's go."

Dinner went well. Better than well. Mike had been worried about how to talk to Catherine during a long, leisurely meal, what to talk about. Gladys was always the one who did the social talking when they went out; his role was restricted to an occasional nod and a pucker of interest.

As it turned out, he need not have worried. Catherine was not a talker like Gladys, but somehow there was no need to talk. Nor was the meal a relaxed and leisurely one. Somehow messages were communicated from one set of eyes to the other, from one set of fingers to the other, and out of all these messages an urgency arose almost from the beginning. He had wondered when and how he ought to suggest they go to a hotel after dinner, what excuse he could give. He discovered now that no excuse was necessary, nor had the meal and the wine been necessary. She was as eager for dinner to be over as he was, as eager for the real purpose of the evening to begin.

"Dessert?" he asked.

"I think not. Would you like some?" Her fingers slid the two inches across the small white tablecloth that separated her hand from his, and lightly they touched with a burning intensity.

He tried to say no, choked, finally got the monosyllable out. "Coffee?"

She shook her head.

"Let's go, then, shall we?"

She nodded; he gestured for the bill; she, unable to wait any longer, stood up, and the waiter came hurrying. Mike gave his card and retrieved their coats from the cloakroom. By the time he returned the bill was ready. He signed it without looking, adding a generous tip, wondered for a moment how he would explain that to Gladys when the monthly statement came, and thought he'd worry about that tomorrow. They hurried out into the night.

For a moment, after climbing the steps, they stood uncertainly on the sidewalk. "Where can we go?" she asked, and her meaning was clear, freeing him from his last doubts. "I've reserved us a room at the Skyline Motel on Tenth," he said, and she lowered her eyes and leaned against him. "How clever you are," she murmured into his ear. He put his arm around her and held her for a moment, for the first time, and then a solitary snowflake settled on his nose and he turned and she followed him down Forty-sixth Street.

Grass settled down to a steady walk up Seventh Avenue, passing through the Fifties on his way back to the hotel. He began to breathe normally, and to think again about what had happened. He had been rattled there in the building with the coffin, he had to admit that. The stupid jack-in-the-box had actually scared him! Well, not scared him; *aufschreckend,* startling, that was the word. Silly trick. But they weren't so smart after all, he thought; he had evaded them easily enough.

Perhaps too easily? He stopped for a moment as the thought occurred to him; then he started walking again, more slowly now, thinking about it. Would they have had only two men staking out the building? No, but perhaps two men on each side street, and when he had come out the window the "winos" had been the only ones available to pick up the trail.

Yes. But surely they would have been equipped with radios to call for help, and he had seen no one else. Since he had lost those two he had pulled every trick in the book to expose another tail, and no one had showed. As far as he could tell, he was walking up Seventh Avenue all by himself. But that didn't make sense.

He nodded to himself. They had startled him and hustled him, and he hadn't been thinking clearly. There must be more than just those two incompetents, but then where were they?

Son of a bitch! The memory of Melnik falling into the street flashed before his eyes. He had caught the bastard, who had flung his arms around him and staggered before regaining his balance. Melnik had planted a bug on him! That was why they weren't in sight, they were a block or two away, tailing him at their leisure and laughing at his insouciance—

He flailed away at his pants, his shirt—and then stopped. No panic, now. He resumed his leisurely walk, and as he walked he ran his fingers up and down his pants legs, lifted his shoes and looked at the soles, ran his hands up and around each arm, took off his parka as he walked and looked at the back, at the lining, and under the collar at the rear.

There it was, a small black button hanging on with a Velcro-like material. He had a fierce desire to tear it off and fling it over the rooftops, but anything like that would bring them running, cars would come screeching around the corner, and though they would not have trailed him back to Naman they would have him, and he did not want that.

No, that was not the way. He took the button off and held it carefully in his hand. He put the parka back on without slackening his stride. At Fifty-ninth Street he turned left and headed west. At Ninth Avenue he turned again, to the south.

Mike MacDonald came hurrying up Ninth Avenue, Catherine at his side. Since their one embrace outside the restaurant they had not touched, but the intensity of their passion was growing more and more. The Skyline Motel was on Forty-ninth and Tenth, and on the corner of Forty-eighth he started to cross over, intending to head down to Tenth and finish up on that street, but the light changed right in his face and a charging battery of cars took over the street. Rather than stand on the corner waiting for it to change again, he led her up Ninth Avenue one more block. It was not his lucky day.

Grass passed Fiftieth and decided he had come far enough from the hotel. Now he needed someone continuing on in the wrong direction. As he came to the corner of Forty-ninth he saw a couple cross Ninth Avenue toward him. As they came up onto the curb, looking at each other rather than at their surroundings as smart New Yorkers should, he lurched against the man.

"Sorry," he mumbled, and moved on.

"Check your wallet," he heard the woman say as they walked quickly away.

And then they were gone. He continued on a few blocks, then caught a cab and returned to the hotel.

"He's gone to ground," Melnik called over the radio. "Let's go in and take him."

Horner drove up and pulled into the curb behind him. A few seconds later the two patrol cars came, with the uniformed cops. Horner gave them their instructions while Melnik listened; then they all moved out together.

Two of the cops took up positions by the side entrance. The other two accompanied Horner and Melnik into the Skyline Motel. The desk clerk looked up as they came in, but Horner flashed his ID and told them they didn't need any help. They took the elevator, each of them checking his receiver as they rode up. On the eighth floor each of them said, "This is it."

They got out and followed the quivering needles down one long corridor and around to another. As they passed room 836 both needles swung around.

"Right," Melnik said.

The two uniforms took up their positions, one on either side of the door. Horner raised his foot and kicked, catching the doorknob dead center and splintering the wood. The door bounced open two inches and caught on the chain latch. Horner flung himself against it and the splintered wood gave way. He fell into the room and Melnik leaped over his body, landing with legs spread and his gun held steady in both hands. On the floor Horner lay spread-eagled, with his own gun pointed unwaveringly into the empty room.

For a second they were surprised; then in the silence they heard the shower running. They crept up to the bathroom door, flung it wide open, and sprang inside, guns drawn, pulling the shower curtain back.

It was hard to say who was the most surprised. It was none of their lucky days.

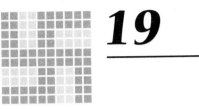

19

1

"THE GOOD NEWS is he tried to kill me," Melnik said.

"The bad news is he failed?" Mazor asked.

"The bad news is he got away."

Mazor sighed. Over the four thousand miles the sigh reverberated through the telephone. "So what's good about the good news?" he asked laconically.

"The good news is that since he tried to kill me, and there were witnesses, Horner can now go after him on an attempted-murder charge and we don't have to worry about getting cooperation from the FBI for the assassination business. We know he's somewhere around here, and Horner's not going to let him get out of the city. They'll clamp a tight watch on airports, planes, trains, and buses, and there are only a few routes by which a car can leave the city. It's really an island, you know."

"I've seen the map."

"Then you know. Anyhow, Horner says he'll get everything covered. They'll close down the entire city. We'll either pick him up or he'll go to ground, and if he goes to ground he can't hit Waldner."

"That still leaves Naman free."

"I can't believe that Naman is trying to make the hit. He must be trying to stop it," Melnik said, but without conviction.

"So why isn't he cooperating?" Mazor probed.

"Do I know?" Melnik had to admit. "Maybe he doesn't trust us. He's probably found out his old buddy Vorshage is in on this, and maybe he's trying to stop it and shield him at the same time. But I think Berner must be the key. If we've got him covered we're probably all right. As long as he's stuck in the city with his head down we're all right."

2

"Close down the city?" Assistant Police Commissioner Ronald Waxman asked incredulously. "Are you out of your mind, Jolly? I mean, who the fuck do you think you are, the police chief of Ruritania, with the king of fucking England coming for a royal visit? I mean, I like to save lives as much as the next guy, so I don't want this guy Waldner to get killed. And particularly I don't want him to get killed in my city, you know what I mean? You hear what I'm telling you? But I also didn't want Carula to get killed."

"Who's Carula?" Horner asked, knowing he shouldn't.

"I'm glad you asked," Waxman said, and shoved a copy of that morning's newspaper across his desk, spinning it around so Horner could read the headlines. "I hate to bother you with this crap," he said. "Seeing as you're so busy with international affairs of state and all. I hate to bother you with little details like this girl Carula. She's just a nine-year-old kid who was raped last night and thrown off a building. A five-story building. So what are you telling me I'm gonna do? Pull out all my cops and close down the gates like a fucking medieval city? And while all my cops are trying to find this guy Grass to save this German guy Waldner's life, how many people are going to get killed on the streets? What are you, nuts or somethin'?"

3

WALTER NAMAN flew back to Sarasota with the induction heater, rented a car, and picked up the infrared detector. He drove to Palm Beach, stopping to buy more supplies at a hardware store on the edge of town, and pulled up in front of the Breakers, where a bellboy carried the two large boxes up to his suite. "Setting up a business here?" he asked as Naman told him to put them down on the desk in the drawing room.

"Presents for the grandchildren," Naman said. "They get heavier every year. I used to be able to carry them myself." He gave the boy a twenty-dollar bill and set to work opening the boxes as soon as he had left.

It took him the rest of the day to get them set up. First he hooked the infrared detector in series to the microwave generator, using a sensitive solenoid valve. Then he shielded the infrared antenna system with Crobar, an infrared reflector, so that the antenna "saw" only the very narrowest of angles; in effect, it could look only straight ahead. By the time he finished it was well past dinnertime, and he was getting hungry. All he had left to do was adjust the sensitivity and then put the whole thing in place. For the latter he would need Grass, and the former would take a long time. Too long to delay dinner.

He showered and dressed and went down to the dining room. It was a beautiful place, reminiscent of the British Museum Reading Room, with a high curved dome ceiling, but featuring an exquisitely dominating chandelier. The service was also exquisite; it was only the food that disappointed. The shrimp cocktail was large and attractive, but the shrimp had been overcooked, which should have given him a clue. He opted for the pompano anyway, and immediately regretted it. Still, first things first, Naman consoled himself as he took the elevator back up to his room. He stripped off his jacket and got back to work.

4

THE MAN SAT DOWN and when Hagan lifted his martini and asked if he wanted one he said no, he wouldn't have a cocktail, he wouldn't be staying for dinner. He was clearly angry, which Hagan had expected—after all, the contract wasn't going through—but he was also out of control, which Hagan had not expected. Hagan had chosen this restaurant because he knew it was going to be a difficult meeting, and he wanted to smooth the way with an expensive wine, a perfect meal, and subservient service. He knew for a fact, thanks to Miss Pherson, that Jimmy Baker had a reservation here this evening, and a casual but warm greeting from him would impress Mr. Reynolds.

But Baker wasn't here yet, and Reynolds wasn't waiting around to be impressed. He didn't see any progress, and he didn't hear anything on TV about any damn German uprising, and his people were giving him hell. "And when I get hell, I give hell! When I put my money on a horse I expect that fucker to *run,* you understand? Or let me tell you, I put my money on another goddamn horse." He picked up his napkin and wiped the saliva off his lips.

The waiter stopped at the table and leaned over them. "Would you care to order a cocktail or wine before dinner?"

Reynolds threw the napkin down on the table and stood up, nearly knocking the waiter down. "My nuts are in the press," he growled, "and that is *not* what I'm paying for. I need action, Hagan, and I want it right away." He took a deep breath, looked around and realized where he was, and with a grimace of distaste he turned and walked out of the restaurant.

The waiter hung back for a few moments, then approached the table again. "Is the other gentleman leaving?" Hagan nodded without looking up, and the waiter continued: "Would you care to order dinner now, sir?"

"No," Hagan said. "I won't be eating. Just bring me the bill for this," he said, picking up the martini and downing it in one gulp.

All the way home he was still thinking about that lousy son of a bitch and the way he had humiliated him at one of Washington's most fashionable restaurants. He hadn't looked around as he left, but he was sure all eyes had been on him. It must have been clear to everyone what was happening. He had been scolded like a child in front of everyone in Washington.

He was still masochistically going over the scene in his mind when he got home and entered the house. It was dark and empty. Charlotte knew he had the dinner appointment and wouldn't expect him before ten or eleven, and she hated dining alone. She'd be out somewhere. God knew where.

From force of habit, without thinking about it, his mind still on his humiliation at the restaurant, he took the tape out of the answering machine and put it in the cassette player. He punched the *play* button and poured himself a stiff scotch.

The tape beeped and then a man's voice said, "Hello? Umm, good afternoon, Mrs. Hagan, it's . . . ah . . . me . . ."

There was a click as the phone was picked up, and then Charlotte's giggle. "Richard, how formal!"

"I didn't know what to say. I mean, this is on the machine, isn't it? Why didn't you pick up if you were home? I almost didn't leave a message."

"I was afraid it would be Melanie, and if she got started I wouldn't be able to get her off and then I'd miss your call. Don't worry about the machine, I'll erase it when we're done. Are you coming over?''

"I don't like it, Charlotte, not in your home."

"He won't be back till late tonight, he's got a dinner meeting with an important backer, he'll be hours sucking up to him."

"It just bothers me. Can't you come here like always?"

And again her giggle. "I can come *anywhere,* with you. All right then, give me half an hour."

"Good. I'll put the fizz on ice."

"And the phallus on fire, please."

"It'll be ready and waiting, I promise you, love. Don't forget to erase this, will you now?''

"Don't *worry* so much. Ciao.'' The line went dead.

And so did he. He stood there with the scotch in his hand, half raised to his lips, listening, waiting for it to go away. But of course it didn't. The tape beeped some more and continued with other long-dead conversations, the cleaners calling to say the things were ready, the butcher calling to say he had some lovely steaks fresh in from Kansas, Charlotte's mother, his father. . . .

He couldn't believe it. He had always *suspected* she was having an affair, but deep in his heart he never believed it. And now . . . In a daze he rewound the tape. He found it hard to breathe; he thought he might be having a stroke. And then he forced it down, forced the rage back into his stomach, forced himself to think. She would be coming home soon, she wouldn't want him to come home and find her gone, and he didn't want to be here when she came. He couldn't look at her, fresh from Richard's bed. Who was Richard? Who was this man she was *sleeping with*?

He'd hit her, he knew he would. He'd kill the bitch!

He had to get out. He went upstairs and packed an overnight case and left a note on the dining room table saying he'd been called out of town for a couple of nights, he'd call when he knew his plans better.

He signed it with love, and left the house.

5

"WE FOUND your man Berner," Mazor said without preamble when Melnik picked up the phone.

"You found him? Great! Where is he?"

"Where is he?" Mazor asked wonderingly. "What do you mean, where is he?"

"You said you found him!"

"I did. We *found* him. In our files."

"Oh," Melnik said without enthusiasm.

"You lost him," Mazor guessed. "You lost Naman and Grass both."

"Who's Grass?"

"Berner. Carlos Grass, we made him from your photos. They were excellent, by the way. Congratulations."

"Yeah. Thanks a lot. Tell me about him."

"German, forty-seven years old, works for the Bundesnachrichten-dienst."

"He works for Vorshage?"

"That's it. And that's why his photo wasn't sent with the first batch you asked for: He's not a free-lance killer."

"If he works for Vorshage, how is he tied up with Naman?"

"Maybe he's not. Maybe he's chasing Naman."

Melnik shook his head, then realized how useless that was. "When I was with Naman he mentioned something to me which Berner—Grass—later knew."

"So maybe he isn't just *after* Naman; maybe he *caught* him. He has a way of finding out things that people don't want to tell him."

"You know more about him?"

"Not sure it's him. But I've had our people looking out for anything that connects with Naman, and something turned up in England. Naman has two friends in an otherwise bitter life. One is Vorshage, the other is a Frenchman he worked with when he was CIA. For some reason they got along together, and have kept in touch."

"And?"

"And the Frenchman was found dead a week ago. In England, a small town where he's lived since the war. The Big War. No one had seen him for a few days, his photo shop hadn't been opened, he was an old man living alone—you know the form."

"Someone called the police, and they brought a locksmith and went into his home? And found . . . ?"

"They found him lying on a table, naked and stinking. He had been electrocuted. There were wires attached to his genitals and up his rectum, hooked to a rheostat for varying the current. Don't know if it was your boy Grass that did it—"

"Oh yes," Melnik interrupted. "It was him all right. That sounds exactly like the son of a bitch."

There was a slight pause. "I would guess," Mazor said, "that you have an interesting story to tell over drinks when you get home. As one raconteur to another, may I point out that the story will prove more entertaining if it has a happy ending? If you find Grass, that is. And Naman too, if he's still alive. On the other hand, if you don't you mustn't despair. You'll probably be able to make rather a decent living as a photographer. Those prints were really quite good."

Mazor hung up the phone.

6

KLAUS VORSHAGE'S secretary rang through to his office. "Just a reminder," she said. "The personals ad you asked me to place in the London and New York *Times* expires today. Do you want me to renew it? We haven't had any response."

Vorshage thought for a moment. It had run for a week; Naman should have seen it by now. "No," he said. "We weren't expecting any response. Cancel it."

7

THE SENSITIVITY FACTOR was as important as anything else in the whole setup, Naman realized, and the only way to get it right was by a series of trial-and-error measurements. Standing in front of the infrared detector, he turned it on; immediately the microwave generator kicked in with a low hum. He backed away, off to one side, out of range of the infrared, and the microwave kept blasting away.

Good. He had set that correctly. He turned off the infrared, stepped to one side, leaned in, and turned it on again; the microwave was silent until he put his hand in front of the infrared, when it immediately started up. So all that was fine.

He turned off the detector, turned it on again while standing to one side, backed away, circled around in front of it, and began slowly to walk toward it. When he reached a distance of ten feet the microwave cut in.

Much too far away. At that distance he was afraid the effect might be a small fizzle, which would warn Waldner that he was having a problem with his pacemaker, and which would abort the whole scheme. It was important that nothing happen until Waldner was right up as close to the microwave unit as he could be.

Security agents would undoubtedly sweep the entire suite before Waldner arrived, looking for bombs, guns, poison, or what have you. They might even come in with radiation detectors, and so it was important that no microwaves be generated until Waldner was alone in the bathroom. Naman had a vision of exactly how it would work. Waldner would come in; the door might be open or closed, he might be talking to somebody in the other room. But sooner or later he would close the door. He would come up to the sink and lean in toward the mirror, inspecting his haggard features after the long travels. He would begin to shave. And as he leaned closer to the mirror the infrared would detect his presence, the solenoid would activate, and the microwave generator would kick in.

He wouldn't hear its hum behind the closed wall at the rear of the medicine cabinet, for even at this time of year the air-conditioning at the Breakers ran full-time. He wouldn't hear it, he wouldn't know what was happening, but it would happen.

The effect might not be immediate. He might feel, at first, only a slight fluttering in his breast as he turned on the taps and began to soap his face, but within a few seconds the pacemaker would flutter and go wild. His heart would begin to fibrillate and he would fall to the floor. He would be out of range of the infrared now, but the microwave would continue to generate its radiation and by the time anyone reached him he would be beyond help.

And no fuss, no recriminations, nobody running around the hotel looking for an assassin. A simple heart attack. Sad, but hardly unexpected for a man his age with a pacemaker. Condolences.

But the solenoid mustn't kick in before Waldner came close enough. It had to be adjusted perfectly. Again and again Naman made the slightest of adjustments, tested it, and adjusted it once again. Finally he had it right. He tested it once, twice, and a third time, and each time the microwave clicked on perfectly at the prescribed distance.

Naman had poured himself a drink and sat down to relax, when the door opened and Carlos Grass walked in. He wore a flaming red wig and thick glasses. That was evidently his idea of a disguise. Naman sighed. It probably didn't matter. "You look good," he said sarcastically.

Grass immediately bristled. He was still upset over what had happened in New York, and didn't need any nagging. "You think it's easy for me to disguise myself? You want me to disappear, right? Become unnoticeable, so no one will remember if they're shown a photo? For you it's easy. All you have to do is change any little thing; who notices an old man like you, anyway? But people *see* me when I walk into a room. There's no way I can stop that. So what do I do? I overpower their senses. They still remember me, but this way they remember the red hair and the—"

"All right, never mind, it doesn't matter. No one's going to see you, anyway. You rented the room?"

"As you said. Number 3142, down the hall."

"Good. And what about Melnik?"

Grass shrugged. "He didn't show."

"That's not possible. If his orders were not to cooperate, not to tell you anything, they would still want him to find me—"

"*Aber natürlich.* He didn't show, but our meeting was staked out." Grass paused, and shook his head admiringly. "They are very good, actually. It took me several hours to lose them."

"Are you sure you did?"

"Absolutely sure. They're still running around New York looking for me."

Naman nodded. If Grass hadn't found out anything, at least he had left the Mossad thinking that New York was the base of operations. "I'll explain everything now," he said.

"It's about goddamn time." Grass sat down and took off his wig and glasses.

Naman told him about the heart-attack machine, and Grass laughed. "That's very good," he said.

"You'll have to help me install it, but that can be done from this room. The only problem is that the power cords have to come out through the medicine cabinet to be plugged in at the bathroom socket, so we have to stay here during Waldner's visit. We unplug them and stuff them down the chute when the maid comes in to clean, then plug them in again when she goes. *Verstanden?*"

"*Jawohl, mein Führer.*"

"That's why we are here; otherwise we'd leave it and go. The problem is, we have to expect security to be looking for us. So we stay right here in this suite. I have enough food in the refrigerator for us to last a week, and we each have our own bedroom. We don't go out, not for any reason. Understood?"

Grass could think of companions with whom it would be more fun to spend a week in isolation, but he shrugged. "The maid will see us if we never go out. We can't hide in the bathroom when she comes."

"That's why you rented the other room. We live in this suite, with a 'Do Not Disturb' sign on the door. When we hear the maid cleaning the other rooms close by we leave and take off the sign. We hurry down the hall to your room and wait there an hour, then return here. Unless we are unlucky enough to bump into someone in the hall, no one sees us."

"Why a week? Waldner comes in two days."

"What would you have us do? Walk out through the lobby when it's full of police investigating the death? No, we stay locked up here until the investigation is over." Naman smiled. "Snug as bugs in rugs. Now let's get to work. You're so proud of being big and strong, let's put it to some use."

Together they rigged up a harness and lifted the infrared detector and microwave-generating apparatus into the dumbwaiter behind the bathroom mirror. Grass lowered it to the floor below, then climbed down the narrow shaft after it. While Naman looked on from above, leaning into the dumbwaiter, Grass anchored the device in place and ran the electrical cord back up the shaft and out into their bathroom. He shaved the ends of the cord to reveal bare wire, and inserted them into the razor outlet next to the bathroom mirror.

"So," Naman said, "our work is done." He nodded in satisfaction, inspecting the setup carefully. "All we have to do now is wait. When it's over we remove the wires from the outlet, drop them down the shaft, and leave the whole setup buried there. No one will find it until they tear the hotel down." He poured them each a drink, stretched his legs, and sighed. It had been a long month since Vorshage had first come to his office in Los Angeles, but now finally it was over. Very nearly over.

8

GRASS LAY IN BED, unable to sleep. He lay there and listened. Not a sound from the other room; Naman was evidently sleeping soundly. Well, why not? His job was done.

So everything was in place. Or so Naman thought. Not quite, Grass told himself as he lay in bed; not quite yet. In two days he would get up early, while Naman was still asleep, and make his own arrangements. It wasn't that Naman's plan was so bad, but Grass was a firm believer in thoroughness and backup contingencies. If Waldner did indeed have a weak heart and the microwave machine worked, well and good. He himself would kill Naman the next day, and when the police found Waldner dead in his suite and Naman dead in the suite directly above, even dumb Americans would think to investigate. They would find the microwave apparatus and realize what had happened, and they would find Naman dead with a typewritten suicide note explaining why he had done it—who could blame him for hating the Germans, with his childhood at Auschwitz?—and that would be the end of the investigation. Hauptmann had hired him for this particular reason: It was very necessary that the investigation stop right where it started. There must be nothing going back to Germany which might unravel and reveal the whole story.

And if Naman's apparatus didn't work, Grass was sure his own would. And nothing would be changed. They would still find Naman dead, and soon enough they would uncover the chain of events linking him to the explosion in the ballroom that would have torn off the chancellor's head: the American Express card, the telegram, the digitizing of the tape.

Yes, in two days everything would be set. But tonight was the problem: Tonight he could not sleep. It was often this way before a big hit. Grass turned over, and over again, but sleep would not come. He still tingled with anger at the jack-in-the-box, at the humiliation of being played with like a child. He still heard Melnik's voice laughing at him. And deep inside still rankled and burned the sweet anticipatory, frustrated pain of lonely anguish as he remembered what he would have done, could have done, to Melnik in the coffin. And his blood burned like acid in his veins.

He stood up suddenly. He swung his arms about. He strode up and down like a restless cat, limping from old jungle wounds, licking his lips in an anxious atavistic search for the taste of blood.

He was hungry. Hungry as a cat is hungry, for something more than food.

He dressed quickly and quietly, not bothering to put on his wig or the glasses, and walked out into the night.

Mimi was bored. It was not one of the good nights. Even the music was boring. Two old fogies in the corner, retirees probably from Century Village who didn't have any right to be here, had complained about the noise and Murphy had turned it down to a point where you could barely feel the walls vibrating. This place was dying, she thought. It was okay on weekends, but she'd have to find somewhere else for the weeknights.

She turned when the door opened, and looked at the newcomer without expectation. He gave off no glow, no vibrations. He wasn't as old as the old farts in the corner, but he was the wrong side of thirty, too old for her. She watched without interest as he limped across the room toward the bar. He saw her watching him, and immediately the limp disappeared. She smiled at that, and turned away toward her drink as he sat down a few stools away from her. It was all so boring.

But when she glanced up he was staring at her, and she saw the delicious hunger in his eyes.

All *right*.

Boring, she thought again. She lay in bed with her eyes closed. Better than nothing, she supposed, but only just. She opened her eyes and turned onto her side, leaning over him, reaching for her cigarettes, and saw that his eyes, too, were open. She had expected him to be asleep after his exertions, paltry as they were. But no, he was awake, and his eyes were burning as brightly as before.

"Not finished, then?" she asked, and slid her hand down his naked body, trailing her nails against his flesh until her fingers came to the limp mass.

Nothing there, though she stroked and probed, nothing there at all. But there was still plenty in his eyes. "I know," she said. "I know what we can do." She reached over him and opened the drawer of her night table and took out a large, erect penis. She giggled. She licked it lightly with her tongue, like a snake with a rat. "You can do me with this," she said. "Would you like to do that?"

She rolled off him, over on her back, and held up the rubber cock. "See this?" she explained, turning the knob at its base as it quivered into life. "It's got batteries. The more you turn this, the more it vibrates. Want to do it to me?"

"You can do it to yourself," he said. "You don't need me."

"Okay, I will. Want to watch?"

He didn't answer, just lay there looking at her as she pushed the covers down and slid the dildo up into her and then slowly turned the knob, just a little at first, and began to quiver.

"I've got a better idea," he said.

She laughed. "I thought it might give you an idea or two. So what did you have in mind?"

He loomed over her, leaning on one elbow. With the other hand he caressed her breast, then reached down and gave the knob another little turn, and felt her pudendum vibrating under his palm and her breath coming fast in her chest. "How would you like me to tie you up?" he asked. "Would you like that?"

She giggled, and quivered, and nodded.

9

"WELL, that's just about settled," Horner said, hanging up the telephone. Although the New York Police Department had officially sent police in all the cities Waldner was about to visit information about Melnik's kidnapping and attempted murder, together with the suggestion that these might be linked to an upcoming assassination attempt on the German chancellor, Horner had followed up with personal phone calls to people he knew in each city.

"Not quite," Melnik said from the couch in the corner, his eyes closed. "There's still Palm Beach."

Horner gave an embarrassed little cough, and tried to smile. "You're a deep one," he said. "Here I am thinking you're dozing in the corner, dreaming dirty dreams, and all the time you're listening to every word I say."

"What's wrong with Palm Beach?" Melnik asked, ignoring Horner's rambling comments.

"Nothing's wrong with Palm Beach. Who said anything's wrong? I just don't know anyone there."

"Yes you do," Melnik said calmly.

Horner waited, but Melnik just lay there, eyes closed, as if he were asleep. But he wasn't sleeping, Horner knew; he was waiting. "Jesus Christ Almighty," Horner said finally. "Don't you ever forget anything? I'd hate to be married to you."

Melnik smiled slightly at that thought. "If I ever propose, turn me down. I promise not to sulk."

"I mentioned once, a million years ago, I've got a friend in Palm Beach." He thought about that. "You know what?" he said. "When we finish with this crap I'm gonna take you to Atlantic City and sit you down with five hundred bucks of my money at a blackjack table, and you're gonna win me a pension and a condo on the water in Maine."

"Why not Florida?"

"Nah, too hot. Too crowded. Too—"

"I wasn't talking about your condo."

"Shit," Horner muttered. He had thought he had successfully changed the topic. "It's just," he said, "you know."

Melnik didn't open his eyes. "Why don't you want to call your friend in Florida?" he asked.

"When I was a young buck," Horner said finally, "full of piss and vinegar, about a hundred years ago, I had this buddy. We had gone through the academy together, Frank Holloway, and then he was my partner, we were in patrol cars then.'' He paused. ''God, it was a hundred and *twenty* years ago, at least. The Two Musketeers, they used to call us, we were inseparable. I was Porthos, the fat one.'' He shook his head. ''I never understood that. I used to stand in front of the mirror naked and look at myself. I wasn't fat.'' He shrugged. ''I am now. Had big bones even then, I guess.'' He drifted off into silence and then suddenly started again. ''So. We used to go everywhere together, ball games, picnics. We were all married, and our wives got along too. One big happy family.''

Melnik closed his eyes again. He didn't want to see the pain in the man's face, but if this had anything to do with their problem today he had to know about it. He sat there quietly waiting but Horner's voice had stopped, and finally Melnik opened his eyes to see the sad giant sitting hunched over, his weight on his elbows on his knees, staring directly at him. He had evidently been waiting for Melnik to open his eyes, to look at him before he spoke again.

''I fucked his wife,'' he said.

''Well,'' Melnik said, ''no one's perfect.''

Horner stared at him hard. ''Sorry,'' Melnik said. ''Didn't mean to make fun of you. It seemed appropriate. The last line of the movie *Some Like It Hot*. One of the two best last lines in all drama. The other one is 'The son of a bitch stole my watch.' ''

Horner turned away; Melnik stood up, walked over to him, and put his hand on his shoulder, kneading it gently. ''It was a long time ago,'' he said quietly. ''Not even Sisyphus suffered forever.''

''I thought he did,'' Horner said. ''I thought that was the whole point.''

''The whole point of the mythology, sure. But nobody believes in that mythology anymore. The suffering stopped when people stopped believing. Maybe it's time for you to stop. Tell me about it.''

Melnik didn't say anything when Horner had finished, and finally Horner said, ''So anyhow, I thought maybe I wouldn't bother this guy I know in Palm Beach. It's, you know, awkward. He'll get the word on the official flyer anyhow.''

''So will all the others.''

''Well, sure. We could have just relied on that, but I figured it's better if we talk to people personally. They get so much official shit all the time, they tend not to pay too much attention, you know what I mean.''

''I know exactly what you mean.''

"But just this one place, I figure we can let it go. Like, there's not much chance the hit'll take place there anyhow."

"Right. There are six cities on Waldner's tour and it could be any one of them. So it's six to one against Palm Beach."

"Right. Pretty good odds."

"If you're betting money."

Horner nodded. Slowly his nod died down. "Not such good odds if you're betting someone's life," he admitted. He sighed. "What the hell." He picked up the telephone.

10

CARLOS GRASS showered until the steam filled the bathroom and fogged the mirrors. He soaped himself slowly and luxuriantly and washed himself off with thick streams of hot water. He stood under the water and felt the heat seeping through his skin, relaxing the muscles underneath. He reached up and took hold of the curtain bar, grasped it in both hands, and bent it in half. The curtain fell to the floor and he stood there in the shower with hot little droplets of water bouncing off his body and spraying out into the foggy bathroom. Finally he turned off the water and stepped out of the shower.

He found a soft, thick towel in the linen closet and dried himself off, luxuriating in the sensual pleasure it afforded. He dropped it daintily in the middle of the bathroom floor and stepped out into the bedroom. The girl still lay on the bed, but he didn't talk to her. He stood in front of her dressing table and looked at himself in the mirror. He picked up her comb and hairbrush and carefully combed and brushed his hair. Then he dressed and went back into the bathroom.

He picked up the towel and carefully wiped off the shower handles and the doorknob. He came back into the bedroom and wiped off all the fixtures he had touched. Taking the towel with him he walked downstairs, opened the front door, wiped off his last prints, dropped the towel on the floor, and left. With the toe of his foot he pulled the door shut after him.

11

"WELL, you win a few, you lose a few," Mazor said when Melnik told him that New York City couldn't be sealed off to find Grass and that they had to assume he could be anywhere by now. "What happens next?"

"It's under control," Melnik told him.

"Thanks, I needed that," Mazor replied. "I haven't had a chance to laugh since Arafat backed Saddam. So?"

"So we don't know where Naman is or where Grass is or what either of them has in his head."

"Oh. For a moment I was worried."

"No point in both of us worrying. What we do have is everything covered, which doesn't reassure me very much."

"By 'everything covered,' you mean . . . ?"

"The routine precautions are in effect. We haven't gotten any further than that officially. Hagan has blocked my efforts at communication. But Horner has contacted people in every city Waldner visits. There are ex–New York cops everywhere these days, what with the city being the traditional major place for a cop and with the city laying people off every year for the past ten years and with the city going to hell anyhow and people wanting to leave. At any rate, he's got friends in every place we're interested in and they're all looking for Grass and Naman. Pictures have been distributed and personal phone calls have been made, and it's probably a better situation than if we had gone the official route."

"But you're not reassured?" Mazor asked.

"Are you? The last time I saw Naman he was wearing black hair, thick eyelashes, and a mustache. No one who didn't know him would have picked him up from a photo. So now I've distributed pictures of him, plus how he looked with the hair and all. But he'll certainly change his disguise. And we can expect Grass to be doing the same. Will they be picked up by cops who've never seen either of them in person? I just don't know. If I knew which city they were planning to hit I'd go there and look around myself. But I don't know which city. I don't know much of anything."

"Well, if that's all that's bothering you—"

"There is one other thing. Naman is good. He's very good, and I don't know what he's thinking. So I'm worried. If Grass is with him, that makes it bad because Grass is a tough son of a bitch. And if Grass has killed him that makes it even worse because that means as good as Naman is, Grass is better. So all in all, I worry. I'd feel better if I had some idea of what was going on."

"If Naman is the problem or if he's trying to solve it on his own, you mean?"

"Right. And whoever is the problem, what are they going to try? A long-range rifle shot, like Kennedy? A car bomb, like the OAS tried with De Gaulle? Poison, like the CIA tried with Castro? A close-up handgun, like Reagan?"

Mazor was silent for a while. "What are you going to do next?" he asked.

"Sit," Melnik told him. "Sit and wait. What else can I do? Pray?"

"I prayed once," Mazor told him. "When my mother got cancer. I was just a little kid. My father put me to bed and told me to go to sleep and not to worry, it would be all right. When he left the room I got out of bed and knelt on the floor and prayed all night."

"What happened?"

"She died."

Melnik was silent. Then he said, "Thanks for sharing that with me. It's a very inspiring story."

You could hear Mazor's shrug over the phone. "You win a few, you lose a few . . ."

They were both quiet, thinking about that. Then Mazor said, "David?"

"What?"

"I'd like you to win this one."

12

WHAT A JERK, Vorshage thought, and rang his secretary. Then his mind wandered off, trying to remember where he had heard that expression. Funny it should pop into his mind like that. It was obviously American; the British would say . . . What exactly would the British say?

"What?" he asked, jarred out of his reverie.

"*Entschuldigen Sie,*" his secretary said. "I thought you rang."

"*Aber natürlich.* What a jerk I am," he said in English.

She spoke English as well as one could wish, but this was a new expression. "*Bitte?*" she asked politely.

"No matter." He had to smile at himself. "That ad I told you to cancel this morning? I've changed my mind. Run it for another week." What had he been thinking? That he could save the department twenty deutsche marks? "One more week," he said.

"*Jawohl, Herr Direktor.*"

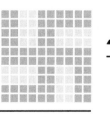

20

1

AT 2:20 P.M. ON WEDNESDAY, an unseasonably warm day after three days of intermittent rain and blowing gusts, Gottfried Waldner's jet landed at Washington National Airport. Horner, Melnik, and Wintre stood watching disconsolately from the private observation balcony, until the welcoming ceremonies were over and the limousine that met Waldner had sped away and the possibility of a fusillade of gunshots had disappeared into the lingering silence with him.

"So far so good," Horner said, and they turned and left.

They took a cab into the city and Melnik stopped the driver at the Mall. They got out and walked down the crushed gravel path, finally sitting on a bench between the Air and Space Museum and the National Gallery. They sat in silence, watching a touch football game on the grassy center strip. The teams consisted of four boys and one girl each, and not much progress was made until one of the girls went out long. Though chased by the other girl she broke free, and the quarterback sent her a high looping pass that came down right into her arms. She turned and gathered it in for a touchdown just as the defending girl ran up to her.

"Touchdown!" she shouted, and the defending girl laughed happily and gave her a high five in congratulation.

"They don't seem to quite understand the concept," Horner observed.

"Nor do we," Melnik agreed. "We don't quite get it. What the hell is happening?"

"It's simple," Horner said. "Vorshage is a secret Nazi sympathizer who's hired Walter Naman, the world's greatest anti-Nazi, to kill the German chancellor so the Nazis can take over the government."

"Or," Wintre said, "Naman is working against his best friend and trying to foil the plot. Either way he's in on it, and either way it doesn't make sense."

"There's another way," Melnik said. "He may be dead. Grass is either working for him or he's killed him. The one thing we know for sure is that Grass is the enemy."

"The one thing we don't know for sure is where the hell he is. So all we can do is sit and wait to hear from someone. They've all got photos of Naman and Grass—"

"Which isn't going to help. Naman and Grass know we're after them, so they'll know their description is out, so they'll either have decent disguises or they won't show up anywhere near any of your cops."

"I also told them to let us know if anything at all queer goes down, anything they don't understand, anything unusual."

"Right," Melnik said, "a lot of good that's going to do. How are they going to recognize what might be important? How are—"

A sudden ringing cut him off, and Horner reached into his pocket and took out his beeper. He shut it off and looked around. "There was a phone back at the corner," Melnik said, pointing at Seventh Street, "outside the Space Museum."

He and Wintre stood waiting while Horner made the call. He didn't say much while he was talking, just an occasional "Yeah" or "uh-huh," and finally he hung up.

"Anything?" Melnik asked.

"Something." Horner nodded. "Palm Beach. A young woman was found dead in her apartment this morning. She was naked, tied spread-eagled to the bed, had been raped, and was left with a rubber dildo jammed into her mouth, probably to stifle her screams."

"And what else is new?" Wintre asked. "I hate to say this, gentlemen, but that is *not* unusual. Maybe they don't know much about things like that in Palm Beach, but if your friends in New York or Washington called up with every incident like that, your beeper battery would be worn out in an hour.''

''There's one more thing,'' Horner went on. ''The rheostat from a mechanical vibrator had been spliced into a cord ripped off the TV, and the bare ends had been connected to one nipple and to her vagina. She had been tortured and electrocuted.''

Melnik slapped his hands together. ''That's our man,'' he said. ''That's Grass. Let's go.''

''Long time,'' Detective Holloway said.

Horner nodded. ''How you been?''

Holloway nodded. ''Getting by. You?''

Horner nodded. ''How's the wife?''

''Sara's doin' just fine,'' Holloway said.

Horner's mouth was dry. ''And how's your daughter?''

Holloway stared hard for a second. ''Just fine,'' he said. ''Away at college.'' He turned to Melnik and Wintre. ''So what do you want, the good news or the bad?''

Horner wanted both, he wanted to ask what college, what's she studying, what's she like, does she—?

He shut up.

''It's been a long time since we've had any good news,'' Melnik said. ''Let's go for it.''

''It's your man,'' Holloway replied.

''How do you know?''

''Positive make.''

''Tell me about it.''

''They all know the girl at this bar, the Happy Fella. She goes there like two, three times a week. She picks up some guy and takes him home. Different guy each time. Sometimes when she don't connect she takes home one of the guys works there behind the bar, you know? There's this one kid, works there cleaning up, he's got a real crush on her. So she tells him, a week or so ago, next time she don't connect he can come home with her. The bartender, he says she's just foolin'; no way she'd take the kid. But he don't know that, and like I say he's got a crush on her, and so every night since then he's got his eyes on her all night, hoping nobody will show up, you know what I mean? So last night nobody *does* show up. And it gets past eleven, it gets past midnight, and the kid starts thinking it's maybe gonna happen tonight, and then about one-thirty this big guy shows up and that's it.''

''She goes home with the big guy?''

"You got it. The point being that soon as the guy walks in the bar, the kid has his eye on him, thinking Oh, shit, and hoping maybe not, you know?"

"I know. So the kid makes him? How?"

"From the photos you sent."

"I don't want to be a buttinsky," Horner said, "but you know and I know there's photo makes and there's photo makes, am I right?"

Holloway held up both hands, palms outward, fingers pointing up, as if to show he had nothing up his sleeves or stuffed between the fingers. "Hey, I been around long enough to know there's no point stiffing yourself. It's all clean. We showed the kid a dozen phonies first, and then a bunch of locals, and he sits there shaking his head no, no, no, and then we drop your guy on him and his face lights up. That's the guy she left with, no doubt about it."

"What's the bad news?" Melnik asked.

Holloway spread his palms wide again, this time fingers pointed down, palms up, helplessly. "That's all there is. There ain't no more. Nobody else saw him, nobody saw him at her place or, better yet, after he left her place. No one saw his car—"

"You checked the neighbors? No one heard her screaming and looked out the window?" Melnik asked. Holloway gave him a look, and he apologized. "Sorry. You know your business."

"Damn right. Nobody heard nothing, probably because he shoved that rubber cock halfway down her throat. Sorry, miss," he said to Wintre. "But that's what he done." He turned back to Horner and Melnik. "Doc says it was there before she died, so no way she was doing any loud screaming. Her car was left at the Fella, so they drove back to her place in his car. Or maybe they took hers and then he drove it back to the Fella and picked up his own. Either way, nobody at neither place noticed nothing. So like the man says, that's all there is, there ain't no more."

2

ON THE twentieth day of July, 1944, Count Claus von Stauffenberg walked into the Wolf's Lair, Hitler's staff headquarters in East Prussia, carrying with him a briefcase filled with explosive and a timing device. Slowly he worked his way through the crowded meeting until he was standing next to Hitler. He put the briefcase on the floor, practically at Hitler's feet, as he leaned intently over the map and studied the

Führer's words. After a minute or two he backed away from the table, casually made his way through the crowd back to the door, and left. He hurried to the nearby grass airfield, where a small plane was waiting to carry him back to Berlin to announce the death of the tyrant.

Sometime during the next few minutes, while Stauffenberg was racing along the country roads toward the aerodrome, another staff officer wanted to get closer to the map over which Hitler was gesticulating. He picked up the briefcase and moved it out of his way, dropping it on the other side of the heavy oaken planking on which the map table rested. When the bomb went off, those officers not shielded by the planking were killed; Hitler, though hurt and badly shaken, survived the blast. Count von Stauffenberg and the rest of the conspirators did not. Hitler had them hung by the throat with piano wire, and personally watched as they died.

Some fifty years later, Carlos Grass was not about to make the same mistake. On the other hand, he had to admit to himself, he had it a lot easier than Stauffenberg. To get into the Wolf's Lair Stauffenberg had had to pass the scrutiny of several tiers of armed guards, all primed to high levels of suspicion by Hitler's paranoia. He had to bluff his way into the Lair without opening his briefcase, for the explosives within would have been easily identifiable. Today, at six o'clock in the morning, at the entrance to the Grand Ballroom of the Breakers Hotel in Palm Beach, there were no armed guards. The door stood open and the group within consisted of janitorial staff mopping and polishing the floor, vacuuming the drapes, readying the place for the reception for the German chancellor that would take place tomorrow. None of them would have recognized the small package of white plastic in Grass's pocket as an explosive, nor would they have dreamed of asking him to empty his pockets to show them the contents.

He wandered casually through the room. They took no notice. The Grand Ballroom is a room unlike any most Americans have ever seen, and the staff were used to guests walking through it and gaping at the high ceilings, tall mirrors, deep draperies, and polished floor. To enter the ballroom was to travel back in time and across oceans of space, to the Great Hall of Versailles or the fabled and misty banquet halls of Xanadu and Camelot. Or to the Wolf's Lair in East Prussia.

In one corner stood the audio equipment. It was in use nearly every day, moved from one meeting room to another depending on whether the event was a wedding, a business or committee meeting, a charity dinner, or the ceremonial visit of a foreign head of state. Grass passed it by with a sharp glance and continued on his way. From his pocket he selected a small Phillips screwdriver, paused and surveyed the room admiringly, noticed that no one was paying any attention to him, and wandered back toward the audio setup. Quickly he unscrewed the microphone head and slipped it into his pocket. It took no more than fifteen seconds. He continued on, out of the ballroom.

He turned right and headed down the hall toward the large French doors opening out onto the beach, which was deserted at this hour of the day. The sun was just rising out of the ocean, casting bright light and long shadows behind the palm trees on the sand. He sat down on a chaise lounge and took the microphone head out of his pocket. He loosened the two small screws holding the mesh topping in place and carefully removed the speaker. He took off the wires and connected them to the tiny device the bearded man at HardSoft had provided, and he connected this in turn to the speaker. There were now two small wires left, extending from the solenoid. He took the package of plastic out of his pocket and scooped out a teaspoonful. He kneaded it into a small ball, considered a moment, then added another dollop just to be sure. He pressed this down into the microphone case, inserted the two loose wires into it, then carefully fit the entire device back into the case. It was a tight fit but a good one. Finally he screwed the mesh topping back in place.

He walked back through the French doors, carefully brushing the sand from his shoes, and wandered back into the Grand Ballroom. He took his time walking through it, admiring the fine murals on the rectangular pillars, until finally he reached the audio equipment. He screwed the microphone head back in place. He turned the volume down low and switched the mike on and tapped it gently. He heard the amplified click clearly, and he switched the mike off again. Then he walked out.

There was nothing else to be done. He yawned. He had had only a few hours' sleep after a long day and a busy night. He smiled at the recollection, smiled again at his vision of the future when Chancellor Waldner would step up to the microphone in the Grand Ballroom and begin his speech, and decided he deserved a rest. As he walked through the lobby toward the elevators he noticed that the newsstand was just opening. It had been two days since his little escapade at the Happy Fella; he wondered if the girl had been discovered yet. He bought a local paper, took the elevator up to the room, and slipped back into bed without waking Walter Naman.

3

AT TEN O'CLOCK that morning Naman had a leisurely breakfast by himself in the domed dining room of the Breakers. Grass slept late in the mornings, and this suited Naman. He liked to have the time to himself. He liked to go over and over his plans, searching for a flaw and not finding one. For one more day he would do this, and then it would all be over.

He finished his coffee and wandered out into the long columned hall. What he would have liked to do next was go back up to the room and move his bowels, but his bowels didn't seem to be ready yet. He set off down the long corridor for a digestive stroll. One could walk for nearly a mile through the myriad halls of the Breakers without leaving the air-conditioning or repeating the scenery. Near the south wing he came upon a paneled reading room with high windows looking out onto the ocean and with upholstered chairs and a supply of newspapers from around the world. He took three of the papers and settled down.

The first, the *Frankfurter Allgemeine,* was full of stories about Waldner's American trip. Naman read them all, and found nothing to make him think of altering his plans. In fact, it was all perfect. Waldner was in Washington today, and would arrive this evening in Palm Beach. Naman hoped he would brush his teeth before going to bed, but even if he didn't he would certainly shave and brush tomorrow morning, and the job would be done.

Naman looked next at the London *Times,* which spent a bit less space on the German chancellor's trip and a lot more space on the rising spate of Nazi hate crimes in the German republic. Black-clad German skinheads were parading through the streets of Dresden to mourn their local hero, a Nazi named Rainer Sonntag, killed by a gang of pimps in a dispute over turf. A picture showed silent onlookers and fifteen hundred policemen watching impassively as the crowd of neo-Nazis, estimated at several thousand, raised their arms stiffly in the gesture familiar from fifty-year-old newsreels and shouted *"Sieg Heil!"* The black-and-white grainy quality of the newspaper picture captured perfectly the sense of déjà vu.

A separate article, bylined by the German correspondent, reported that within the last few days the heads of the German federal criminal-investigation division and counterintelligence service had pinpointed an ugly rise in popular sympathy for neo-Nazi attitudes not only in the East but in the West. The surprisingly rapid spread of the Nazi ugliness seems to be related, the correspondent reported, to the newest German official figures for unemployment, which had now reached three million.

An editorial lamented the fact that the current wave of neo-Nazi violence looked set to explode across Europe, at a time when thugs had embarked on a campaign of terror across the Continent and when violence and arson aimed at immigrants and Jewish groups was stirring chillingly familiar memories of the thirties. The neo-Nazis were back as roaming skinhead gangs who chant *"Heil Hitler."* And they were spearheading a new mood of right-wing extremism, which was taking hold of many working-class voters on the Continent. . . .

The *Times* wondered why nothing was being done to stop this rising wave of terror, and answered itself by going on to explain that a failing economy was touching a raw nerve that existed in every country: hatred and fear of foreigners and Jews.

The *Times* did not, of course, mention that the rising wave of Nazi terror was being fed from above, by the German chancellor himself. Naman folded the paper and put it down. He wondered if they suspected any such thing. It didn't matter; without proof they couldn't say anything.

Well, he thought, he would soon give them something better than proof. He would give them a dead Nazi chancellor, and we would see what would happen to the Nazi movement without his protection. He thought of all the children reading the papers today, skipping over these stories to go straight to the sports pages. He thought of himself in 1935 and 1936 and 1937; he never had the faintest notion of what was going on. He had had no idea of what the future was bringing.

He folded the paper and leaned back in his chair. Sufficient unto the day is the evil thereof. Today's evil was nothing worse than the recalcitrance of his bowels, and tomorrow's evil might well be averted by the death of the German chancellor. *We shall see,* Naman thought. *We will do what we can, and we shall see what we shall see.*

He glanced down at the paper in his lap and opened it again, turning it to the last page but one, to the personals. He hadn't bothered to check to see if Vorshage had tried to contact him, not for more than a week now. He had no need to—his plans were set and in place—but idly he opened the *Times* and glanced through the personals—

—and his eye was caught by a small announcement:

GILBERT, FRANÇOIS: Looking for survivors. 21863

Naman stared at it for several moments, then slowly lowered the paper. Someone had reached Gilbert? *Looking for survivors?* François was dead? He felt an overwhelming sadness, a weariness, settle over him. He gave it a minute or two, then shook it off and stood up. The reference would be to an English-language newspaper, and one that would be available to him in this country. The story probably wouldn't have been important enough to make the American papers, so it was the *Guardian* or the *Observer,* but most probably the *Times.* He walked down the high-ceilinged corridor to the front desk and asked in an English accent if the hotel kept old issues of the London *Times.*

"That depends. How old?"

"A couple of weeks or so, if you have them. I've rather lost touch since I've been traveling."

"Well, we'll have some of them. We keep them for pickup by a recycling plant."

The desk clerk took Naman down the hall and opened a storage room. "I'm afraid we don't keep them in order—"

"Not to worry. I'll just glance through them, if I may."

"Make yourself at home," the clerk said, and left him.

GILBERT, FRANCOIS: Looking for survivors. 21863 . . .

He leafed through the papers until he found the February 18 issue. He turned to page 63 and there it was. "François Gilbert, a French-born English citizen, was found tortured and murdered in his photography shop in the village of . . ."

He read it through once, and then again. Worse than he had thought. Gilbert was not only dead, he had been tortured. Just as he had been by the Gestapo fifty years ago. *Plus ça change, plus c'est la même chose.*

So they were after him, he thought, putting Gilbert aside. He felt a momentary twinge, but shook it away. No matter how Gilbert had suffered, he was safe now. Time enough to mourn him later. The question was, who had done it? Who was after him? And had Gilbert talked? What did who know?

Naman walked back down the corridor, thinking things out. He stopped by the chair in which he had been sitting when he saw the personals ad, and sat down again. Lost in thought, his bowels forgotten, he picked up the third newspaper, *The New York Times,* and glanced through the first page. Waldner would be addressing the United Nations this afternoon; it was not a terribly important story for that city. There was nothing about the rising tide of Nazism, beyond a few sentences in that story.

He leafed through the rest of the paper, put it down, stood up, and decided his bowels weren't quite ready to be moved yet. He walked down the long hallway and back again, with no improvement. He stopped by the chair with *The New York Times* lying on it, and sat down again to kill some more time. He picked up the paper and turned the pages again, looking for anything interesting to pass the time until his bowels decided to cooperate. There were the usual articles: A show had opened, bringing no glory to the American theatre; a business had closed, putting further strain on the city's tax base; a book had been published by a female professor of women's studies at a midwestern college, explaining how the Clarence Thomas confirmation hearings a couple of years ago had turned out to be a disaster for women; an Israeli tourist had been kidnapped and buried alive in an abandoned building in Manhattan—

Naman had nearly turned the page before it registered, and when it did he forgot his bowels. The tourist's name was David Melnik. He read the article through, and then went upstairs to have a talk with Carlos.

4

"NOT LIKELY they'd actually stay at this hotel, is it?" Holloway asked as they pulled up in front of the Breakers.

"Don't know about likely," Melnik said. "It's certainly possible."

"Seems to me they'd want to stay as far away as possible from any likely surveillance."

"On the other hand," Horner said, "if they're going to hit him in Palm Beach it's gotta be either in the hotel or on the road to and from the airport. Hard to set up a roadside ambush without a dozen men or so, and we don't have any evidence for such a large group. If he's going to hit him in the hotel he either has to be waiting for him, which means he's either checked in or gotten himself a job there, or he has to come in at just about the time when surveillance and security would be tightest. So I think it's a reasonably good bet."

"On the *other* hand," Wintre said, "he would do better not to be here at all when it happened. He could check in, plant a bomb, and leave before it goes off."

Melnik shook his head. "Tricky things, bombs. Trickier still to plant them ahead of time. You have to be worried that someone might find it, number one. And number two, how can you be sure Waldner will be exactly where he's supposed to be in two or three days' time? Schedules change, things happen."

"So what you're saying is," Holloway asked, "you think he's here?"

Melnik shook his head again. "I don't think anything. I just plain don't know. I don't even know who we're looking for, Naman or Grass."

"I'd settle for either one right now," Horner said. "I'd settle for just a whiff of their perfume."

5

GRASS WAS still asleep when Naman got back to the suite. Naman walked quietly into Grass's bedroom and began to go slowly but methodically through his suitcase, thinking he would have warning enough if the big man began to awaken: There would be a moving, a tossing, a clearing of the throat. But instead there was no sound at all until the words softly came: "Looking for something, *Väterchen?*"

Naman turned, and Grass was lying in bed, on his back as he had been when Naman first looked into the room; the only difference was that his eyes were open.

Grass sat up in bed and swung his legs over the side. He was naked, and the muscles in his arms and legs undulated as he moved. Naman looked without wavering into those cold blue eyes, a mongoose to the other man's cobra, he hoped, willing him not to move any further, not to advance, while his own fingers kept rifling through the suitcase. When Grass had first accosted Naman, outside the bank in Philadelphia, he had got his attention by pointing a gun at him. Naman hadn't seen the weapon since, but it wasn't likely that Grass had got rid of it. If he was the one who had done that to Melnik, he would certainly have had the gun with him. To carry it on the airplane from New York he would have had to ship it through in his suitcase, and there would have been no reason to take it out yet. Naman hoped.

But there were mongooses, and there were sheep, and Naman began to think he might be the latter as Grass stood up and pulled on his pants. "Bad manners, *Väterchen,*" Grass said, and walked across the room toward him.

Naman's fingers touched something hard. He had found it. His fingers clasped around it and brought it out, and both men stopped and looked at it. It was a Glock 25, with silencer attached, and it was pointed at Grass.

Grass smiled and shook his head. "Sorry," he said. "It's not loaded." And he advanced again across the room.

It occurred to Naman that if they had been staying in an ordinary hotel room Grass would already have been upon him. But in this over-sized suite he was still three steps away. There was something to be said for luxury. "Shall we find out?" he asked, and leveled the gun at Grass's midsection. "One more step and I pull the trigger."

Grass stopped. He spread his hands and cocked his head to one side. "What's wrong?" he asked. "You're too old for premenstrual syndrome."

"You lied to me about Melnik."

"Ah, you've seen the papers, then. *Was kann ich sagen?* He was on to you, old man. He was trying to stop you."

"So you buried him alive?"

Grass gestured dismissively. "Don't believe everything you read. I was trying to find out what he knew, how far he had got. You asked me to, remember?"

"I told you not to harm him."

"He's not harmed, I promise you. Scared a little, maybe. I was *trying* to scare him, put a little pressure on him."

Naman was not listening. He was looking beyond Grass, toward the bed. On the floor beside it, carefully folded, was a newspaper. Even from this distance Naman could see it was not the *Times*. It was probably today's local paper, and from the neat way it lay folded Naman guessed that Grass had been reading the latest account of his adventure. "Give me the paper," he said.

Grass turned and looked at it. He paused.

"Don't be bashful," Naman said. "And don't be stupid. Just slide it slowly across the floor with your foot."

Grass walked back to it and kicked it carelessly forward. Naman gestured with the Glock for him to back away, then stepped forward and picked it up. He saw Grass shift his weight forward to the balls of his feet as he bent toward the paper, but he kept the gun level and his eyes locked on Grass's, and the moment passed. He glanced at the headlines on the folded-back page, and experienced a moment of disappointment. It was the front page of the local section, and carried no mention of the New York episode. He glanced up at Grass, who was standing easy now, watching him.

"Just trying to learn about the local flora and fauna," Grass said. "You never know."

Naman stepped back as far as he could, putting as much space between the two of them as possible. He glanced at each of the articles in turn, flicking his eyes back to Grass between each story—

"Murder of Local Woman Is Work of Deviate," the page's bottom headline whispered. With a sinking feeling he read the article through. The resemblance to what had been done to Gilbert was unmistakable. "You killed Gilbert," he said.

Grass spread his hands wide in a caricature of an apology. "You gave me the slip in Berlin. I had to find you."

"You're not Lise's son."

"Bravo, *Väterchen*! I thought you'd never pull your head out of the sand." He stared at Naman with disdain. "Did you really, for even one single moment, think that I was the son of a Jewish whore, born of the sperm of a hundred misfit soldiers not fit to serve in the real war?"

Naman's eyes went cold and dead, and he raised the Glock.

Grass had been trying to rattle him, but now saw he had gone too far. He smiled and held out his hands ingratiatingly. "No offense intended," he said, "but I have to tell you, *Väterchen*, you're getting old. You're really going to kill me now? Without knowing who I am? Who sent me here?"

"All my life," Naman said sadly, "all I have ever wanted to do was die. To be left alone, to divest myself of this world, to go away. And all my life I have encountered people like you. Scum, vermin. The only pleasure I have ever had is killing such monstrosities."

Grass's smile never wavered; an aura of confidence was his only shield. "No curiosity?" he teased. "No thought that perhaps things aren't what they seem? It hasn't even occurred to you that the pleasure you feel in disposing of Waldner might be just the slightest bit misplaced? You don't wonder how I knew all about your little whore and her sick bastard?"

He was right, Naman acknowledged. Something was very wrong, and he had better find out what. "Go ahead, then," he said. "Tell me."

"No," Grass replied. "Why should I, since you'll shoot me anyhow? That is, if the gun is loaded. And if it isn't, why should I tell you anything at all?"

"You will tell me," Naman said, "because every moment you talk is another moment you are still alive, another moment you might turn to your advantage. It won't work, but you will try."

"Correct as always," Grass said. "Well then, it was Vorshage. Ah!"

he cried, detecting the smallest movement of Naman's eyelids. "You didn't expect that, did you? Not your old friend Vorshage! But why not? It hasn't been Waldner who's been protecting the Nazi movement in Germany, it's been Vorshage himself. Oh, such a shame," he said, making fun of Naman's reaction. "What a pity, when you can't trust your best friend."

"Why should I trust you instead?"

Grass shrugged. "As you said, I'm playing Scheherazade here. Trying to keep you interested because I stay alive only as long as you are interested. I could make up lies if they were more interesting than the truth, but I really don't have the imagination to do that. I'm concentrating all my energies on trying to figure out how to get that gun out of your hand, and so I stand here rattling off the truth while my mind races over other possibilities." He smiled. "You see how truthful I am? You believe that part at least, don't you?"

"Why should Vorshage be protecting the Nazis?"

"Why not?"

"Is he a Nazi himself?"

"*Aber natürlich!* Was it Freud or Marx who said, 'Give me a child until the age of six and he is mine forever'? Vorshage was six in 1942. His character was formed by Dr. Goebbels. Oh, I know you and he have worked together for many years against your common menace, the East Germans and the Russians. Well, of course. They *were* a common menace. Vorshage is a great patriot. He has spent his life fighting for Germany. What counts for him is not America or freedom, Israel or the Jews, but Germany. And Germany, he feels, would be best served by a resurgence of the Nazi state. Can you deny that he is right? Did Germany not reach its greatest power under Hitler? What German patriot would *not* want the emergence of the Fourth Reich? But you know what is really funny?" he went on. "It's that Vorshage himself is being used."

"By Schlanger?"

"Oh no, no. Schlanger is being manipulated by Vorshage, not the other way around. No, the really amusing thing is that both of them are being cuckolded—if I may used that term—by Herr Hauptmann."

"Hauptmann? Who is he?"

"Oh, *Väterchen,* do not destroy all the admiration for you that has been built up all my life. You don't know Gerhard Hauptmann? He is the, how shall I put it, the Iacocca of Germany. No, that is not correct. Iacocca is a public figurehead with little real power. Hauptmann is perhaps the converse of Iacocca. He stays behind the scenes but he actually runs several of the largest corporations in Germany. This whole affair is being directed by him. Vorshage and Schlanger think they are using him to bankroll their political movement, but actually they are doing exactly what he wants, just as if he had strings dangling from their wrists and feet. The purpose? Nothing but business. Sordid, mundane, commercial business. Waldner is influenced too much by the Greens, by the silly environmentalists. The increasing regulation of German commercial life is cutting into business profits. What is even worse than the regulations is that Waldner is beginning to enforce them. And so we get rid of Waldner. It's as simple as that. And if at the same time we can blame a Jew, what could be better?''

''How do you blame the Jew?''

''Your body will be found here, with a suicide note explaining how you have always hated the Germans for what they did to you at Auschwitz. The idea of seeing the hated chancellor of this most hated state here in America was too much for you, and so you killed him. Vorshage will issue a statement saying that Mendoza, the man you killed with the car bomb, was a German security agent assigned to track you down. I have left a paper trail behind us which the Americans will soon pick up, linking you to the bomb. The investigation will be closed as soon as it is begun.''

''What bomb?''

Grass waved the question away negligently. ''No one will suspect anything else, and everyone will go their way happily ever after. Except you, of course, I'm afraid.''

''You've got everything worked out perfectly, haven't you? Except for one little flaw. I'm the one holding the gun.''

''Yes, there is that problem,'' Grass admitted. ''But it's not quite so serious as all that. It's a Glock twenty-five-millimeter, *n'est-ce pas*? I am, what, five feet away from you? And you understand how the silencer works on the Glock?''

''Perfectly.''

''Ah, I don't think so. The normal noise of a gun, of course, comes from the sudden expansion of the gases inside the firing chamber. What the silencer does is trap those gases internally and then allow them to ooze out slowly, so that there is no sudden expansion and therefore no noise.''

''Thank you for the lesson in physics.''

''Ah, but there is more to the lesson. This entrapment of the gases slows down the firing mechanism of the Glock, or at least the repeater mechanism. The gun will not fire twice until the gases from the first shot have escaped the barrel. It all takes not much more than a second, but a second can be a long time in certain circumstances, *nicht wahr*? It is all very—how would you say?—inconvenient, if you need two bullets in a hurry."

"One will be sufficient. I'm an excellent shot."

"I don't think so," Grass said. "I think, yes, you are good enough to hit me at this range, even if I try to bounce around and evade you"— and as he said this he began to bounce around lightly on the balls of his feet, first to the left, then to the right—"but I don't think you are good enough to put it right between my eyes. And anywhere else will not be good enough to stop me from reaching you. I would prefer, of course, that you do not hit me at all. And so I offer you a deal. Hand the gun to me now, and you will die quickly and easily. The nozzle in the mouth, a bullet through the brain, *poof!* it is all over. All your pain, all your anguish, all gone. But if you force me to take it from you, I promise you will die very slowly. Very slowly indeed. With a pain you cannot even begin to imagine."

"And how would you explain to the police a man supposedly torturing himself to death?" Naman asked, and immediately realized his mistake. Grass had got him into an argument, and that was the beginning of the end.

So enough! He lifted the gun, but as he did so Grass jumped suddenly to the left. Naman turned the gun toward him, but he jerked back again. Naman realized he was overcorrecting, but it was too late; his finger pulled the trigger, and the Glock made a horribly empty sound as the hammer clicked down on an empty bullet chamber.

6

"WE'LL CIRCULATE the photographs, of course," the general manager, Mr. Lester, assured them, fingering the photos of Naman and Grass they had placed on his desk. "I'm sure if either of these gentlemen is staying here someone will recognize him."

"Well, that's the problem," Melnik said. "If they're here, they're probably disguised."

Mr. Lester shrugged slightly and shook his head. " 'Elderly white male,' " he read from the accompanying paper. " 'Possibly with dyed hair or a wig. Height, five feet eight inches. Weight, one hundred sixty. Possibly a German accent.' The accent will help," he admitted.

"I wouldn't count on it," Melnik said. "He had an accent when he spoke with me, but other people I've talked to say he can speak perfect English if he wants."

"We probably have a hundred guests that fit this description," Lester said. "The other one's slightly better," he went on. " 'Large white male, six feet tall, approximately two hundred pounds. Muscular and aggressive. Slight limp.' "

"But not so's you'd notice it," Horner interjected, "unless you're looking real close."

Lester nodded. "We'll see what we can do for you. I'll have these circulated to the staff immediately. Can I be of any further help?"

"I'd like to take a look around," Melnik said. "Where Waldner will be staying, the place the reception will be held, the dinner, the speech, every place he's likely to be."

Lester stood up. "If you'll follow me, gentlemen?"

7

THE BANQUET ROOM seemed about as good as could be expected. At least there were no windows to worry about. A half-dozen policemen in plainclothes, mingling with the guests, could be placed at scattered spots that among them would cover the entire room.

But the outdoor reception area was a nightmare. It was an enclosed plaza, surrounded on one side by the lobby, rising in a sheer wall to the eleventh floor. Melnik took the binoculars Holloway had brought along and raised them to his eyes, scanning slowly up the side of the hotel. The sun was still over the ocean, and it glittered painfully back at him from every window so that the inside of each room was invisible. Beyond any one of those windows a gunman could be waiting. The other three sides of the plaza were even worse, for the upper floors contained balconies with half walls. A sniper could set up unseen behind any one of those walls and have a clear view of nearly the entire plaza.

"We'll want to check each one of those rooms," Melnik said.

"We don't have the manpower," Holloway objected. "I bet there's more than two thousand rooms here."

"Two thousand seven hundred," Lester confirmed.

"We'll do what we can, room to room," Melnik insisted. "We'll check on as many of the occupants as we can and then make a map of the other rooms and keep an eye on them from here when Waldner comes."

"It ain't gonna help much," Horner said.

Melnik had a tight feeling in his stomach. "I know," he said. "Which room will be Waldner's?" he asked Holloway.

"Oh, none of those you can see from here. His will be right on the ocean." Lester led them through the plaza, back into the hotel through a corridor, and out again onto a walkway fronting on the ocean. The sun was blinding bright. They stood with their backs to it and gazed up at the hotel. The sunlight reflected from the windows was just as bright.

"Reflective film on the windows?" Melnik asked.

"Of course. Otherwise the air-conditioning bill would drive us out of business. When this place was built, back in the twenties, there wasn't any air-conditioning, but they closed up in the summertime. If we did that now we'd lose our work force. Sometimes I wonder who actually owns the hotel, them or us. That will be the chancellor's." He pointed to a corner room on the second floor. "It's unoccupied at the moment, if you'd like to take a look."

Melnik nodded and studied it through the binoculars. There was nothing to see.

Naman hadn't fallen for Grass's sucker advice to try to put a bullet between his eyes. He realized that was only an attempt to get him to aim for the head, which is a smaller target and harder to hit than the body. When Grass bounced right, then swiveled and came at him head on, Naman aimed the gun squarely at his midsection and pulled the trigger.

When the hammer clicked on the empty chamber Naman was paralyzed for just the tiniest fraction of a second—was the gun really empty?—and then he realized that Grass had probably kept an empty first round in the chamber to guard against accidents. He squeezed the trigger again. This time he got the lovely *poof* of the silenced gunshot, but that fraction of a second had allowed Grass to level out his body in a hurtling dive at Naman's feet, and the bullet shot over his head. As Grass's shoulder hit Naman just above the knee he saw a tiny hole appear in the window on the other side of the room, and then he was flying backward, smashing against the wall, trying to get off another shot. But the firing mechanism wouldn't repeat quickly enough, and Naman's shoulder hit the wall with a force sufficient to stun him. He felt his breath go; his arm went limp and lost all feeling, and the gun flew out of his hand as he dropped to the floor.

Melnik moved the binoculars up, scanning over the rooms above Waldner's suite and then to each side. Nothing to see. The group turned and walked to the end of the hotel property, then headed back inside. Wintre was in front with Lester; Melnik came next; Horner and Holloway brought up the rear. As they passed under the suite that was to be Waldner's, Wintre shook her head suddenly, and Lester glanced up.

He brushed something off his shoulder. "Damn sea gulls are a nuisance." Then he looked more closely at the stuff he was brushing, and gave a puzzled shrug. "No, not a bird."

Wintre was brushing the same stuff out of her hair. Melnik leaned forward to help. He caught some of the powdery stuff in his fingers and looked at it closely, then back up at the hotel windows. "You have hurricanes down here, don't you?" he asked.

"Not since 'sixty-six. Used to have one nearly every year before then. The Breakers is the safest place in Florida if one hits again. Most of these buildings you see on the beach have been built since 'sixty-six, and every year they take fewer and fewer precautions. I'm expecting to see them swept out to sea when the next one hits."

"The windows," Melnik said. "Do you tape them?"

"Not necessary anymore. They're shatterproof glass, and the reflective film holds them in place if they break."

Melnik nodded and held out his hand to Horner, with the powdery stuff from Wintre's hair still on his fingers. "Glass," he said.

Horner nodded. "Could be." He looked up at the side of the hotel. Melnik trained the binoculars on the windows of Waldner's suite. "Don't see anything," he muttered. He raised them to the level above, didn't see anything there—

—yes he did. Just as he was about to move on he saw it. He handed the glasses to Horner and pointed at the window. "That one there, just above Waldner's, lower right corner. Bullet hole."

"Could be," Horner admitted. "Didn't hear anything, though."

"When Grass took me in New York, he had a silencer on his gun. Let's go!"

Naman was still conscious; the gun skittered to a stop three feet from his hands. He wasn't even stunned. He was mentally quick, alert. He told his body to twist around and stretch out for the gun. But as if there had been a mixup in communications, he saw Grass twist and move instead. While Naman was still trying to communicate with his own lethargic body he saw Grass's hand flick out like a snake and grab the gun. He saw Grass stand up and smile, holding the Glock negligently.

Finally, he was able to move. When he did every bone in his body ached. Instead of beating Grass to the gun, the most his right arm could manage was to reach up painfully and wipe the blood from his cheek.

"Don't be upset, old man," Grass said. "Forty years ago I'm sure you would have killed me. Twenty years ago you would have had a chance. But today, what could you expect? You're probably not any good in bed anymore, either." He smiled. "Well, now for the good news. I lied again, *Väterchen*. I'm not going to torture you. You're not going to die a slow and painful death. You were quite right, of course. That would not be compatible with the scenario we wish to present to the American authorities. Just a quick bullet into the brain, and then you can rest. Won't that be lovely?"

Naman screwed all his working parts together, and just before Grass reached him he jumped up and darted into a far corner of the room.

"Why play games, *Väterchen*? You can't get away from me. And, unlike you, I won't miss." He raised his gun and aimed it steadily at Naman.

"You think you're dealing with an idiot? You can't shoot me from there. You've got to make it look as if I killed myself. The gun has to be right up against my head, or in my mouth. You've got to catch me first."

Grass laughed. "Right as usual. No, you're not an idiot. You're just an old man who got in my way. So then, let's get on with it."

Naman was crouching behind a writing table in the corner. Grass backed away toward the door and put on the chain lock. "Careless of you to leave this unlatched when you came in. We wouldn't want to be disturbed." He moved back into the room toward Naman, then suddenly jumped a few steps to his right. Naman darted to the left. "Like a chess game, isn't it?" Grass laughed.

Melnik and the others came running down the hall silently on the thick carpeting. They stopped outside the door to suite 3148 and Melnik put his ear against the door to listen. But the door was thick and tightly closed, and he heard nothing. He turned to Lester, who handed him the passkey, a magnetic card that would open all the doors in the hotel.

Of the four of them, only Holloway carried a gun. Melnik waited while he took it out and cocked it. Then Melnik slowly, quietly inserted the magnetic key into the lock. He pushed it all the way in, then slowly began to pull it out. There was a soft click and the green light came on. Melnik nodded to the others, took a deep breath, then in one motion twisted the knob, threw the door open, and hurled himself against it—and was bounced to a jarring halt when the chain lock held tight.

• • •

Grass was enjoying himself. There was just enough danger to make the game fun. The walls of this old building were solid enough that Naman wouldn't be heard if he shouted for help, but just to be sure Grass turned the radio on loud. What else? If Naman could reach the phone he could grab the receiver and shout into it for help. It wouldn't get here in time to save him but it would ruin the suicide story and Grass's whole plan. If he could throw a chair through the window it would have the same effect. He wasn't strong enough to throw a chair across the room, but if he could get to the window he might manage something. So there was enough of a challenge to raise the adrenaline.

Quietly Grass stalked him. With each motion around the room, with each jump behind a chair or table, he came inexorably closer.

He was still more than six feet away when the door suddenly banged open to a full three inches before the chain lock stopped it. He caught a quick glimpse of bodies banging against it; this was no chambermaid coming to clean the room. He was startled but not panicked. His reflexes took over. He raised the gun quickly and aimed it at Naman's huddled figure.

Melnik threw his body against the door, but the chain was a heavy one and held securely. He bounced off. He felt a hand on his shoulder pulling him out of the way. Horner lowered his shoulder like a bull and crashed into the door. The chain catch splintered loose and flew across the room. The door bounced open. Horner's momentum carried him into the room, where he stumbled and fell.

As the door broke open Grass pulled the trigger. Naman jerked once with the impact and fell back against the wall, hung there for a second as if pinioned, then fell to the floor.

Grass whirled to face the intruders. He saw the big black man sprawling on the floor; no danger for the moment from him. He saw Melnik charging in through the open doorway, and lifted his gun toward his face. But he had to wait a split second for the firing mechanism to reset, and in that moment he saw that Melnik was unarmed and that another man was flying in behind him holding a gun outstretched. Instinctively he moved his aim and fired at the immediate danger.

Holloway was moving too fast to allow for a head shot. The bullet caught him in the right shoulder. His gun fell from his useless hand and he sprawled backward.

Grass turned toward Melnik, ignoring the black man behind him. That was his only mistake of the day.

Horner pulled himself up off the floor. He saw Grass, his back to him, shoot Holloway and then turn toward Melnik. He sprang forward like a huge bear, wrapped his arms around Grass, lifted him off the ground, spun, and threw him with all his strength across the room.

Grass crashed through the drapes and into the huge window. It splintered under the impact. His foot caught on the edge, but it wasn't enough to stop his momentum; it was only enough to make his body spin topsy-turvy as he fell through the powdering glass, tangled in the drapes which ripped free under his weight. In the next moment he was gone and the room was deathly quiet.

Melnik ran to the window and leaned out through the broken opening. On the ground level, three floors below, there was a canvas canopy covering a concrete walkway. It was now ripped and flapping in the breeze. Through the tear in it he could see Grass's body sprawled on the stone. He thought for a moment the man was dead, and then Grass lifted his head.

Melnik didn't know what to do. He started to climb through the window to jump down after him, but it was too high. Yet he couldn't let him get away.

Then Grass tried to move, but his right leg hung helplessly and stubbornly behind. It looked as if he had cracked his hip in the fall. He wouldn't be going anywhere very fast.

Melnik turned back to the room. Holloway was sitting up, leaning against the sofa, cushioning his right arm with his left hand. Blood had soaked through, dark and wet; he was hurt and stunned, but he'd be okay. Wintre had come into the room and was bending over Naman's spread-eagled form. She looked up at Melnik and shook her head. Horner, continuing his spin after throwing Grass through the window, had fallen onto the sofa, where he now sprawled with a grimace of pain, both hands massaging his lumbar region. "Oh, my achin' back," he groaned.

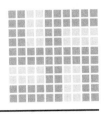

21

1

Melnik slept late the next morning. When he awoke he was alone in bed, and he sat suddenly upright. He heard the shower running, and he lay back down again, happy and relaxed, his hands clasped under his head, looking up at the ceiling and luxuriating in the realization of how lucky he was. Of how *stupid* he was, and of how that didn't matter if you were lucky enough.

He had resisted her from the first moment he saw her; he had seen only the pretty face and the lovely body, and he hadn't wanted to become involved. Hadn't the energy, really. Had had enough short affairs in his life, had slept around too much. He had wanted to find a real woman and settle down for life, and when she appeared he hadn't seen the woman for the flesh.

And yet, somehow, it had happened. Somehow she had claimed him, and now he lay comfortably in bed, all his worries over, looking at the ceiling and seeing his future spread out there. His last adventure was over and he was glad of it. He would settle down now. He would take the office job Mazor had been pressing on him, and he would sit behind a desk from eight-thirty till five every day, and then he would come home to his wife and family. He would have two boys and one girl, and they would laugh every day and sleep every night.

Would she want to come to Israel? She was still young, and properly ambitious; she might want to make her career here in Washington. He sighed. Could he live here in this city, in this country?

He nodded. He could. He could do anything, with her.

The shower stopped, the bathroom door opened, and Lisle Wintre came into the room with a towel wrapped around her. She came over to the bed and kissed him on the cheek, and he pulled the towel open. She clasped it shut again and stood up.

He didn't mind. He had found wisdom in his newly mature years. If she didn't want to play now, that was all right; he would respect her wishes. He would always be good to the mother of his children.

"We have to talk," she said.

"The words out of my mouth," he replied. "And that ain't sanitary," he added in a thick Jimmy Durante burlesque. The only thing that bothered him was that children always wanted to know where their father had proposed to their mother, and he didn't think it would sound right if it had been in bed.

While he was hesitating she began. "I know you've slept around all over the world." He sat bolt upright and opened his mouth, but she held up her hand. "No, it's all right, I'm not criticizing. I've known for quite some time. You have a reputation, you know." She laughed then, at the look on his face. *"Didn't* you know? I guess I was talking about you quite a bit with Randy, so he asked around and came back and told me that you have this, well, reputation."

"I don't want to lie to you," he said. "And I guess it's true but it certainly sounds exaggerated. I mean, I've been around quite a while, you know."

"It's all right." She smiled at him. "I just want you to know that I know and I don't mind."

He thought about that for a second, then nodded seriously and reached out for her. "This is different," he said. "I swear to you this is all very different. I've never felt like this before."

She laughed. "Of course not. We're all different."

"No, I mean that!"

"Shh," she said, putting her finger across his lips and disentangling herself from his grasp. "Don't say anything you'll regret later. Let me talk." She sat down on the chair on the other side of the room. "This has been the most wonderful fling and I will never forget it for the rest of my life. But I've been giving very serious thought to what I really want out of life."

This was not good. He did not like the turn this conversation was taking. His mind flipped through it from the beginning, searching for where it had begun to go wrong, and quickly he found it. "Who's Randy?" he asked.

"You say that every time I mention his name. *Randy.* My friend at the CIA. He's the one I wanted to talk to you about."

"You checked with the CIA about me? Those people haven't gotten anything right since the Bay of Pigs. Don't believe a word they say," Melnik implored.

"I'm going to marry him," she said. She waited for Melnik to reply but he couldn't, not a word. She got up and walked around the room. "I haven't told him yet, but I've made up my mind. He knows about us— Well, I haven't actually told him anything, but I'm sure he knows from the questions I asked him about you."

"I swear to you that's all in the past," he said, and again she laughed. "You're incorrigible." Then she sat down on the bed and kissed him on the cheek. "I mean it, darling. I am going to marry him. So thank you for everything, and good-bye."

"What if I said," he began, swallowed, and then said it again. "What if I said I wanted to marry you? I want to stop this nomad's life and settle down. Even here in Washington if you like."

"If you said that I'd give you two aspirin and a cup of hot tea, and if you didn't feel better by tomorrow morning I'd call a doctor."

"I mean it," he said. "I'm not joking. This is not a Noël Coward play. I love you, I want to marry you."

She gave that one a long pause, then slowly shook her head.

He didn't know what to say. He was bewildered by this turn of events. She was going to marry *whom*? Irritated, agitated, he asked again, "Who is this guy Randy? You never mentioned him before."

She shook her head, gently smiling at him. "Where is your head this morning? He's the one who got us the radio when you pretended to be in the coffin, and he took care of me when I came back from Germany." She bent down and kissed him on the nose. He reached up to pull her down but she slipped sideways and evaded him, and he suddenly deflated and sank back down on the bed. He wanted to hold her, to argue her out of it, but he realized that you can't argue with a kiss on the nose.

She felt a sudden, almost overwhelming flash of uncertainty. Was she throwing away the best thing that had ever happened to her? And then she realized that no, she was right, he was wrong. David was an exotic, exciting creature; almost an alien life strain from another planet. It was the killing that had given her the first clue, almost without her realizing it: the way he had learned to kill without remorse, had accepted the necessity. It took a terribly strong man to do that, it took a man who was *too* strong. A man who had never learned to compromise with the complexities of this world, with the demands of conflicting necessities.

She understood why he was the way he was and she forgave him for it; she was no longer angry when he spoke of eliminating Grass. She understood, but she couldn't live with such a man. A phrase from Sunday school came back to her: "Whither thou goest, I will go." That was the problem: She couldn't go with him into that world, she couldn't live in the harsh glare of his sun. The imperatives of his life had made him too strong, too intense for her; he was inhabited by forces beyond his control, and ultimately they frightened her.

"You're too strong for me," she explained finally. "Too domineering. I couldn't live with you for the rest of my life."

"What are you talking about? I let you be on top, didn't I?"

"No," she said, smiling but serious, because in his joking he had put his finger on it. The forces of his professional life were too strong to be held in check; they swept over into the most intimate areas. Even in sex he was too strong. "*Letting* someone be on top implies a consideration of their wishes, it even implies *asking* them. You simply *put* me on top. It was what you wanted, you never asked. And it was all very lovely," she went on before he could interrupt, "but I couldn't live with domination all my life."

"You want a man *you* can dominate," he said.

"Don't be bitter; it's not attractive. I want someone with whom that word never even enters the discussion. I do love you, David, I suppose I always will in a way, but you're the wrong man for me."

2

In Los Angeles, Norma Middler lit a single candle and sat *shivah* for Walter Naman. "Is he really dead this time?" was all she had asked when Melnik called.

"He's really dead. He was shot in front of our eyes. We were just a moment too late."

So she was now the new owner of Mr. Naman's business, World Security Consultants. "You don't want to leave everything to me," she had protested two years ago when he told her he was making a will.

"To whom else?" he had replied. "You and me, who else have we got?"

Which was true. She had always thought—no, not *thought;* perhaps *pretended*—that someday he would retire and the two of them might marry. . . . She shook her head quickly to disabuse it of such notions. So not that, but just that they would live out their days together, not much differently than they did in the office.

But he was dead, so it was not to be. She had never really expected it. And instead of a pension she had a business that was worth nothing without Naman. And she had his little condominium off the Boulevard. She was walking around in it now, searching for some sign of his presence, but there was none. No sign, even, that he had ever lived here. It might have been a model apartment, open to the public. Once she had closed up the office, and the landlord had scraped the name off the door, Naman would have left no sign behind anywhere, no indication that he had been on this earth at all.

She had put all his mail on the coffee table, and now she picked up the envelopes and looked through them. Bills, advertisements, more bills, nothing else. Not one letter, nothing personal in all the pile, she thought as she leafed among them. One envelope caught her attention briefly; it was from the Banco Real of Eleuthera, Bahamas. She wondered what Mr. Naman could have had to do with them. The thought passed from her mind, and she dropped the envelopes and wandered off. She would open them all tomorrow, pay whatever bills there were, close out his estate.

She sat down at the kitchen table, and lit the candle, and sat a lonely *shivah.*

3

"What a fucking cock-up," Holloway said morosely. "Next time you guys come barging in here, bring a program. Can't tell the good guys from the bad guys without a goddamn program. Better still, next time you guys come barging in here, don't." He focused his gaze on Horner. "Minute I saw you walk in that door," he said, "I knew I didn't want to see you. You were bad news the last time I saw you, and you're bad news now. Goddamn, I don't know which was worse: humping my old lady, nearly getting me killed, or making me the laughingstock of the East Coast."

"We brought you flowers," Horner said.

"You know what you can do with your flowers."

"They're long-stem," Horner said.

"Good. I hope they've got thorns, 'cause I'm personally gonna shove them up your—"

"We brought them to the hospital," Melnik said. "But they told us you checked yourself out." He shook his head. "Bad idea. You shouldn't be at work. You should be in bed."

"I should have my goddamn head examined, is what I should have. For ever listening to you two creeps."

"You should be in the hospital with that shoulder," Horner insisted.

"What I should do is shoot you. Minute you walked in that door two days ago, I should have shot you. I'd be in a hell of a lot less trouble than I am now."

"What's the problem?" Melnik asked. "What's going on?"

"It loses something in translation. You had to be there."

"Where?"

"In the hospital. In that guy Grass's room when we interrogated him."

"You talked to him already?" Melnik asked. "They told me he'd be out for twenty-four hours with the shot they gave him for his hip."

Holloway shook his head. "He brought himself out of it. He's a tough son of a bitch. He had to talk to us right away, make sure the old guy didn't kill your German president or ambassador—"

"Chancellor."

"Whatever. Had to make sure we got the stuff—"

"Wait a minute," Horner said. "He told you Naman was trying to kill the chancellor?"

"The old guy, yeah, Naman. He's been on his trail—"

"Who's been on whose trail?"

"Grass! He's been on Naman's trail, for chrissake. He had just caught him when we came barging in—"

"Wait a minute, you're going too fast," Melnik said. "Start from the beginning." He put the flowers down on the desk and sat down. "Why has Grass been chasing Naman? Who is he? Who does he work for?"

"The Krauts. He's German secret service."

"And Naman?"

"A nut. He was trying to kill the German president."

"Chancellor."

"Yeah, yeah."

"Grass told you this?"

"Right."

"And you believe him?"

Holloway sighed. He motioned for Horner to get them each a cup of coffee from the percolator in the corner, and he told them the whole story.

It was a simple story, as Grass had told it the previous night from his hospital bed. He was an agent of the German secret service. He was on the trail of a man, Walter Naman, who was planning to assassinate Gottfried Waldner during his American trip. Naman, according to Grass's information, was either operating on his own or had been hired by Israeli agents for the task; Grass hadn't been able to confirm either possibility. He had caught one Israeli making contact with Naman, so he was sure there was at least some connection, but the Israeli had escaped before he could interrogate him.

"He didn't mention burying the Israeli alive?" Melnik asked.

"Didn't mention it. I did. I told him the story you told me. He denies it. His word against yours. Claims he met you once in Philadelphia, later got word that you had been locked in a coffin. He went to investigate, found the coffin empty and somebody shooting at him. He escaped. You want to stop interrupting and let me get on with it?"

"Sorry."

"So okay. He gets onto Naman's trail and follows him down here, to make a long story short. Catches up with him in the hotel, has him dead to rights when the door is broken open and three men charge in waving guns. What's the poor guy to think? He figures it's more perpetrators, so he shoots Naman and then some asshole throws him out the window. He's thinking of suing Palm Beach County."

"The girl he killed in the motel?"

"What girl? He knows nothing about it. We got any proof? Yeah, sure," he said as Melnik started to interrupt. "I know what you're gonna say. So yeah, there was semen in the lady's vagina, and we can have it DNA-analyzed. But the courts're throwing out DNA convictions all over the place, 'cause the scientists themselves are saying it's not certain proof. You wanta argue with them? No? So what else we got? We found some hairs in the bathroom, looks like he took a shower there. And while he was unconscious we took the liberty of snatching a hair or two from his body, and I'm willing to bet they'll match, but so what? Again, it's an indication, not a positive identification, not like a fingerprint. And he left no fingerprints. So what've we got? We got some indications. What we don't have is convictable evidence." He leaned back sadly. "The fact of the matter is, the way things are these days you can't convince a DA to go to trial without a couple of witnesses or a confession or at least a good fingerprint or two."

Melnik shook his head. "He'll never get away with his cock-and-bull story. He's got to come up with some sort of corroboration—"

"He has. He asked us to call the German ambassador in Washington, and he put through a call back to Germany. Early this morning we got a wire from the ambassador confirming. He is an agent of the German government, and was assigned to prevent an assassination attempt. Walter Naman was the suspected perpetrator."

"Whom did he call in Germany?" Melnik asked.

"Whom?" Holloway smiled. "Keep forgetting you're a foreigner. Man named . . ." Holloway looked at his notes. "Gerhard Haupt-mann."

Horner looked at Melnik. Melnik shook his head. He had never heard the name before.

"Naman was going to kill Waldner with some sort of heart attack weapon," Holloway continued. "We sent a crew over to the hotel and they found it disconnected."

Melnik nodded. "After they took you and Grass and Naman away yesterday, we looked around the place and found it. We pulled the plug."

"So it's all over. The only problem is you threw the wrong guy out the window."

"That's all bullshit," Horner said.

"Yeah, tell me about it. —No, don't." He held up his hand. "I don't want to hear anything more, I just want you guys out of here."

"So you're going to let him get away with it?"

"Get away with what?"

Melnik began to answer, but Holloway held up his hand for silence again. "No, let *me* tell *you*." He began to tick off the answers on his fingers. "One: killing the old guy in England. That's England's prob-lem, not ours. You think England is going to want to extradite? You got any proof that would even begin to satisfy the extradition procedures? That this guy Grass is the guy that did it?" He paused. "No? Okay, then, let's go on. Number two: burying you alive in New York. The way I see it"—he looked directly at Melnik—"you're the man. You willing to go to trial on this one? Get up there and testify? 'Cause you know as well as I do what the defense is goin' to do, they're gonna cross-examine the shit out of you. 'Goes to reliability of the witness,' they'll say, and you'll be under oath and they're gonna ask you every damn thing they can think of about your duties as a secret agent of a foreign power. You want to get up there under oath and lie about it? Or tell them all your secrets?"

"No," Melnik said.

"No. I didn't think so. So what are we up to? Number three, right? He killed the girl here. That's our problem. You give me some proof that it was Grass and we'll act on it. Number four: He killed Naman. We got witnesses to that, right. We got him dead to rights on that. But if we go to court he tells his story about catching the purported assassin and then a bunch of guys burst in with guns. So he reacted in what any jury would think is a reasonable way. He's not a crook, he's a fucking hero. Don't forget, he's got the heart-failure equipment to show the jury, the stuff that Naman had set up to kill Waldner."

"How do you know Naman set it up? What if it was Grass who set it up, and Naman was trying to stop him?"

"What if? *What ifs* ain't proof. And this particular *what if* ain't even sensible. It's stupid. Look, the stuff was in Naman's room, right? The most you could go for is they were working together, and that don't fit with what we found when we broke in. So what I'm suggesting is, you guys came down here to stop the assassination, and you did it. So relax and go home."

"You're going to let him get away with everything?"

Holloway sighed and held up his hand again. He thrust out one finger. "One: He's not getting away with the main thing. He came down here to kill the guy, right? And he didn't do it, right? We stopped that, and he's buried in a hospital bed safe and sound. Tell me if I'm not right. Number two: He's not going anywhere. With that broken hip he's going to be in that bed for quite a while. So you've got time to come up with something we can book him with. If you can, we do; if you can't, we don't. Number three: If you're so all-fired hot on bringing bad guys to justice like in the comic books, what about his bosses back in Germany? If you're right and he was trying to kill the German whatever, then the guys fronting for him now are just as guilty. A lot more guilty, 'cause they're his bosses. So what are you going to do to bring them in? Go ahead, don't be bashful, tell me your plans."

"They're too big," Melnik admitted. "We don't have any proof against them. Even if we could bring charges against Grass they could claim that they were fooled by him, they didn't know what he was doing."

"Oh, good. So you understand the concept of proof. Well, that's the way it works in this country too, buddy. You got no proof, we don't do nothing."

Horner said, "He killed a guy in a hospital back in New York. Killed a cop, too."

"Great! You got proof, let's book him. You got fingerprints, witnesses?"

"We got a nurse who saw him there."

"Saw him there? Am I picking up on something? 'Saw him there' means saw him at the hospital, am I right?"

"Right," Horner admitted.

"It doesn't mean 'saw him with the gun in his hand,' or 'saw him in the guy's room' or 'saw him shoot the guy,' am I right?"

Horner nodded. "Right."

"So what are you jerking me around for? What have you got on this guy? You got *bubkes* on him is what you got. The son of a bitch nearly killed me and I'm going to have to let him go because you don't have anything. So get the fuck out of here, go back to New York or Tel Aviv or wherever and leave me alone, all right?"

What could they say? They got up and walked to the door. As they reached it Holloway called out softly, "Horner?"

"What?"

He looked down at his desk and mumbled, "Sara sends her regards."

4

HORNER SAID his back was killing him and he had to go back to the room and rest. Melnik decided to go talk to Grass. As soon as he walked in the hospital-room door Grass opened his eyes and smiled. "Guard," he called loudly, and the uniformed policeman sitting outside in the corridor came in. "You will notice I am alive and well," Grass said. The guard looked puzzled and nodded. "Please check to see if I am in the same condition when this man leaves." He turned to Melnik as the guard went out again. "Well, long time no see, as they say here in America."

"Refresh my memory," Melnik said. "When *was* the last time we saw each other?"

"New York. We had a long talk about Herr Naman, remember?"

"I'll never forget it. You'll no doubt be pleased to hear that I will remember being in that coffin as long as I live."

"I don't know what you're talking about. Did someone actually bury you alive, as I am told? Then perhaps the effects are still with you and you are hallucinating when you think it was me."

"There's nobody here. It's just you and me. I thought we could have a little chat and be honest with each other."

"I may have been thrown out of a third-story window, but I landed on my hip. Not on my head."

"I mean, since it turns out we're both on the same side—"

"Are we indeed?"

"Aren't we? It seems that we were both trying to stop Naman from killing Waldner."

"As to that, I have no knowledge. It was my impression that you were working with Naman. But you will deny that. Of course the Jews have always been great friends of Germany."

"Actually, that's true, aside from that dozen years' hiatus beginning in 1933."

"As you wish," Grass said complacently.

"My friend says you killed a man in a hospital in New York."

"Your friend? You mean the big black one who threw me out the window? Obviously a homicidal maniac. But why should he think a thing like that? It was told to me that the man who was killed was smuggling in arms for Waldner's murder. But he had already been caught and the arms intercepted. I would have no further interest in him, except perhaps to question him."

"Of course. Since you were trying to stop the Waldner assassination."

"Precisely."

"What my friend thinks," Melnik went on, "is that the man was killed *because* he was caught, to stop him from being questioned."

Grass nodded. "That makes sense."

"But it wasn't you who did it?"

"No."

"Then if I were you, and I were telling the truth, I would be very fearful for my own life. The people who killed him would want to kill you, for the same reason."

"You still haven't got it straight, my *meshuggeneh* friend. And they always tell us that Jews are so smart. I suppose it's a myth, like German efficiency and American know-how. I shall tell you once more, and then I am very tired so perhaps you will leave me alone. No one is going to kill me to prevent me from talking because I have already talked. I have told the Americans all I know. I have nothing to conceal because I am not one of those trying to murder Waldner. I was the one who stopped the assassination. You thought I was the enemy, but you had the wrong man." He closed his eyes and waved Melnik negligently away.

5

MELNIK DROVE disconsolately back to the hotel room he shared with Horner, whom he found lying on his back on the floor with a pillow under his knees. "Back's really bad?" he asked.

"It ain't good. My own damn fault. They told me not to lift heavy objects."

"Probably never mentioned anything about not throwing them out of hotel rooms," Melnik sympathized as he slouched down on the couch and took his shoes and wig off.

"Get anything out of Grass?"

"Oh, certainly. A smirk, a bit of effrontery, a dollop of sarcasm, even a touch of wit." He leaned back and closed his eyes. "Our Miss Wintre says she's getting married."

"Oh? Congratulations."

"Not to me."

"Sorry, my mistake. I thought that was where you spent last night."

"She's marrying Randy."

Horner noticed that Melnik didn't correct the assumption that he had spent the night with her, but he didn't press the point. The world had certainly changed since he had been a young and randy buck. "Who's Randy?" he asked.

"My point exactly. They're all crazy."

"Women?"

Melnik nodded.

"Not crazy," Horner said. "Different. Very different. Forget 'em. Where do we stand with Grass?"

Melnik shook his head tiredly. "I don't know. You tell me."

"Okay, I will. I've been lying here thinking. The way I see it, there are three possibilities, and one of them is impossible. One, that he's telling the truth—"

"Yes, that's impossible," Melnik agreed.

"No, that's not the impossible one. It's the one you don't like, but it's not impossible."

"Horner," Melnik said solemnly. "I swear to you on my word of honor that he is the one who locked me in that coffin. I did not catch merely a fast glimpse of him, I could not possibly be mistaken. We were walking together, talking together. I *know* it was him."

"That's not the point. The point is you're making a hidden assumption."

"Which is?"

"That we're the good guys and they're the bad guys. And all the good guys are good and all the bad guys are wicked." He shook his head. "Like my people say in one of their songs, it ain't necessarily so."

"That song was written by two Jews, you know," Melnik said.

"Right. They're my people. Anyone who can write music like that is my people. Jews got a great sense of rhythm, you know?"

"Horner"—Melnik sighed in exasperation—"get on with it."

"Your hidden assumption that all the good guys are necessarily good is just wrong. Look man, I was in Nam. I saw what some of my true-blue American GI Joes did to women and children and babies. Yeah, sometimes there were excuses: We didn't know who was the enemy and who was hiding behind who, but I saw guys doing it just for the fun of it, too."

"Doing what?"

"In the First World War, before we got into it, my daddy used to tell me, there were propaganda stories about the German soldiers. They called them Huns, to emphasize their cruelty. The stories told how these guys would toss Belgian infants on their bayonets, from one to the other. My daddy didn't go for that. He said it was just for the stupid masses. I believed him. But I saw it in Nam. I saw the same thing there, and it wasn't no Huns doing it. I saw one of our guys shove a bayonet through a crying baby and toss her across the room, like he was playing lacrosse. There are shits like that in every country in the world, so you can't say you know that Grass is working for the Nazis just because he's a sadistic psycho. And if you tell me you don't have people like that in Israel too, I'm telling you you don't know what the fuck you're talking about. So one possibility is that Grass is telling the truth. Not about the coffin, he's lying about that, but that he was trying to stop Naman and thought you were working with him and that's why he tried to kill you."

"So okay, you can be a psycho and still work on the side of the angels. That doesn't prove it's so in this case."

"What I'm saying is because he's a sadistic prick that don't prove he's the bad guy. What is proven is the impossibility of number two: that Naman was trying to stop Grass and Grass set up the equipment to kill Waldner, because the equipment was set up from Naman's room.

It is just not possible for Grass to have done that without Naman knowing about it. So what we're left with is possibilities number one and three," he went on. "Number three is that they were working together to kill Waldner. They had some kind of falling-out, some argument that we'll never know about, and we broke in at just that point. In which case the people he called are part of it, including the German ambassador to Washington. Which to my mind is kind of unlikely. And that's all there is, there ain't no more. So I think we have to go with number one: Naman was the villain, Grass the hero, and we go home."

Melnik thought about that in silence, then slowly nodded his head. "You're right. So okay. If Naman was the assassin and Grass was trying to stop him, he succeeded and the threat is now over."

Horner agreed. "You can put Grass on your list for revenge sometime in the future for what he did to you, but that's a personal thing between you and him. This case is over."

"Assuming possibility number one is correct. How about number three? They're working together, something goes wrong, Grass pulls out a gun, we break in, and *boom*! it's over. That doesn't necessarily mean the ambassador's involved; he's just passing on the message he gets from home. It does implicate this guy Hauptmann, whom we'll have to find out about. And Vorshage, but we knew he had to be in on it anyhow from what happened to Wintre."

Horner shook his head. "That doesn't hold up."

"Why not?"

"Grass's behavior. You were just down there talking to him and what did you say? He's calm, happy, smug. If they were both trying to kill Waldner and we break in and so they failed, what is Grass's position? We've got no proof against him but we've foiled the assassination. So what does he do? He calls up his bosses in Germany and says he has to break cover and they have to bring him home. And they say, 'Sure'? They say, 'That's okay, Grass old boy, you didn't carry out your assignment, you didn't kill the man, but we don't care as long as you're safe and happy'? Is that the way things work in this world? You tell me, you're the bigshot spy."

Melnik agreed. "He wouldn't dare call them to tell them he had failed."

"Right. So we're back to number one: He really does work for the German secret service and was trying to stop the assassination. He succeeded."

Melnik shook his head stubbornly. "I just can't buy that. The son of a bitch is no good. How about," he said slowly, feeling his way, "how about a slight modification to number three? He was hired to kill Waldner, either with or without Naman, I don't know, and when he's caught he calls his bosses to tell them he succeeded."

"But he hasn't succeeded."

"Maybe he tells them he has."

"What's the point of that? They'd find out soon enough that he hasn't."

"And he'd be worried about that," Melnik had to agree, "he'd be desperately trying to figure a way out of his situation. Instead of which, he's lying there in bed laughing at me." He shook his head disconsolately. "I don't know, I just don't know."

"Let's go see Wintre. Maybe she's come up with something."

6

HAGAN HAD spent the night at the Sheraton Park, but now he was coming home. He hadn't decided what to do; he was just coming home. He hadn't decided either to kill her or to forgive her. He found that he couldn't do either; nor could he live with this anger eating away at him. So he buried it. He didn't think about it. He knew it was there, like a ravenous beast deep within the cavity of his chest where his heart ought to be, but he pushed it down there out of sight and kept one hand on its head, and didn't look down to see it.

He didn't know what else he could do. He didn't want to spend another night like the last one, alone in a hotel room, alternately cursing and weeping like a broken child, threatening to kill her, begging her to stop. When the dawn came he greeted it as his salvation, but the long day that followed was worse than the night. In the daytime life returned: Outside his window, far below on the street, he saw people walking and driving, going to work, shopping, getting on with their lives while he huddled helplessly alone. He had to get a grip on himself, he said. But he didn't.

When the second night began to fall he left the room and checked out. He couldn't spend another night there, he could not. And so he buried the beast and went home.

His thoughts were still tumbling around without any conscious plan in mind as he reached his street, and without conscious thought the habits of the last few months took over as he reached his house. He automatically dimmed his lights and cut the engine as he turned the corner, so that he glided silently and invisibly down the slight incline into his drive. Without thinking, he did as he always did these days: Instead of pressing the button on the infrared activator and opening the garage doors he left the car sitting there and quietly got out.

He entered through the walk-in door to the garage, and saw with chagrin that there were two cars there, Charlotte's and one other, and a cold chill clamped down over his neck and sped down his spine as the beast in his chest tumbled around and tried to clamber out. He couldn't believe it. It wasn't true. She wasn't up there with—

No, he thought. She wouldn't be expecting him home this evening; his note had said he'd be out of town for a few days. She hated to dine alone, and so she had asked some people over for dinner. He took a deep breath and pretended to be upset about that. He would have to go upstairs and smile and make polite conversation. Why did the bitch always manage to do everything at the wrong time? He wondered if he could perhaps slide upstairs without being seen and slip straight into his own bedroom. He could later claim he had come home with a migraine and didn't want to interrupt the party; and that wouldn't be far wrong.

But when he climbed the steps and silently opened the door to the kitchen, hoping they would all be in the dining room and he could slip around it unseen, he saw that the house was empty. There was no conversation from the other rooms, no sounds of a party, and nothing in the kitchen gave indication of any preparations. He came quietly into the house, peeking into the dining room and the living room; it was all empty, no one was there.

Two groups of people must have come, he told himself, holding the beast at bay. They had had drinks, and then gone out to a restaurant for dinner, traveling in one car. That was why Charlotte's car was still there in the garage along with the other. But why were there no dirty glasses in the living room? Charlotte would never clean up while her guests were still there. And if they hadn't had drinks, why had they come here before the restaurant? And most of all, the beast shouted, why was the car in the garage, as if to shield it from the neighbors' eyes, instead of simply being parked outside?

He felt the heat rising from his gorge, nearly choking him. He found it difficult to breathe. No, no, his mind was saying; it isn't like this at all.

But he knew it was. She thought he was out of town for a couple of days and so she had brought her lover home. Home, to their bed! And suddenly it was all too much, it was too much for a man to bear, and the beast slipped its shackles and came tumbling out. He ran up the stairs to his den, went to the desk, and took out his gun. Then, calm on the outside, bubbling over with helpless rage inside, he walked down the hall toward the closed door of Charlotte's bedroom.

7

THEY HAD LEFT Wintre on the phone to the FBI, giving them the numbers on each of the credit cards found in Naman's and Grass's possession. The Bureau would check out where and when they had been used in the past couple of weeks, in an effort to trace the conspirators' movements and the history of the enterprise.

It was early evening when they reached the Palm Beach County sheriff's building, and took the elevator up to the office Holloway had lent them. "So," Melnik said without preamble, "how did things go with the FBI? Are they going to check all that for us as soon as they fill out the necessary forms in triplicate?"

"They've already checked it out," Wintre said. "I've got the data sheet right here."

Melnik made that peculiar expression which on a normal face would have been a lifting of the eyebrows. Without the eyebrows it produced a comical wrinkling of his forehead that made him look even more like a space alien. "Things have changed since I last worked with them," he said.

"Sometimes you sound like a dinosaur who forgot to go extinct," she said, but not unkindly. "Anyway, do you want to take a look? It all hangs together except for one little thing."

"Tell me about the one little thing," Melnik said. He would check the records himself in detail, but that could wait till later. He had respect for her intelligent sifting of information.

"The dates and places on the charges indicate clearly where and when they came into this country. They came separately, but on the same day. Naman went to New York, Grass to Los Angeles but he almost immediately flew from there to New York."

"What is it that doesn't fit?"

"An American Express card. It was a replacement for one that was stolen in New York the day Naman arrived there. Grass didn't get there till early the following morning, so it was definitely Naman who stole it. He used it to check into the Pierre Hotel, and used the replacement card to check out a few days later. But the card was found in Grass's pocket."

"That's it, then," Horner broke in. "It fits perfectly: Naman must have given him the card to buy something with. It's proof that they were working together. I think we can get him on this. The only other possibility is that he caught up with Naman just before we got there and took his AmEx card and put it in his own wallet without touching anything else of Naman's, and that don't make sense. We can hang him on this."

Melnik looked skeptical. "Reasonable doubt. A good defense lawyer could magnify reasonable doubt to argue that your scenario doesn't actually prove anything."

"That's not what I meant when I said it didn't fit. The card was used for just one other purchase," Wintre said with a triumphant look in her eye, and then she stopped.

"You're not going to tell us," Melnik said.

"You want us to guess?" Horner guessed.

She smiled and nodded.

"You are an irritating woman," Melnik said. "I begin to have sympathy with Mr. Hagan, and God help randy Randy. I wonder why I ever thought I loved you," he said, trying to turn it into a joke. But it didn't work, it wasn't funny. "Tell me about the card," he said.

"You remember the telegram to Naman's secretary? Asking her to get a tape recording of—"

"Waldner's voice! My God, I forgot all about that!"

"Yes, so did we all. What was it about, do you think?"

"It had to be for identification, somehow . . ."

"Exactly. Yet the whole idea behind the heart-attack machine was that it would go off when anyone at all came close, but it wouldn't affect anyone except Waldner because of his pacemaker."

Melnik nodded. "Puzzling," he agreed. "Tell me about the AmEx card."

"At first it didn't make sense to me. When he tried to pay with the card, the clerk ran it through and found it had been reported as stolen."

"Has the clerk been interviewed yet?"

"He's in no condition to describe anything. He's dead. Evidently when he confronted the customer with the fact that the card had been reported stolen, he was shot. The bullet came from a Glock 25, and nobody else in the store saw or heard anything, which means it must have had a silencer."

"That's Grass's gun, then."

"Except he'll certainly say he took it away from Naman moments before we broke into the room."

"What happened at the shooting?"

"Another clerk came in a few minutes later and found the man dead. The computer was still keyed to the incomplete transaction, which showed the stolen card."

"What kind of a store was it where he tried to pass the card?"

"Computer-technology stuff. The customer had brought in a digitized recording of a voice and asked that a detection or recognition apparatus be designed around it. The story was that it should operate to open a closed door at the sound of that particular voice. The order form in the firm's files specifies miniaturized electronic circuitry that would open or close a circuit when Waldner spoke into it."

"How do you know it was the tape of Waldner's voice he brought in?"

"The customer, after he shot the clerk, took the equipment when he fled. But he left the recording behind. They haven't yet identified it positively, but it's certainly a voice speaking English with a German accent. It has to be the Waldner tape that Naman's secretary provided, and he wanted it as an identification device. Maybe something he planned to use on the heart-attack machine but found it didn't work. But was it Naman or Grass who sent the telegram and arranged it?"

"It was Grass," Melnik said. "It had to be."

"There you go again," Horner said, "as one of our presidents used to say. It's your prejudice talking; you can't be sure it was Grass."

"It's experience talking. Naman's been around a long time, he's got a track record of how he works. He wouldn't react by pulling out a gun and shooting a man, and even more important, he wouldn't be careless enough to get into that situation: He'd never use a card that had to have been reported missing by the time he tried to use it. What obviously happened was that he stole the AmEx card and then arranged to have the replacement sent to him instead of to the original owner. That would give him a few extra days to play with, and it shows how careful he was about time. But we're talking about using it again a week later; he'd never do that. He'd have known it would have been reported stolen. Grass, on the other hand, would react in precisely that manner. He's cruel enough to pick up the gun at a moment's notice and shoot anyone who crosses him."

"Is he also stupid enough to use a card a week after it's been stolen?"

"No," Melnik admitted. "But he might not have known its history.

Or he might have used it on purpose." Yes, he liked this idea as he talked it out. "He may have been planning to use Naman as the fall guy all along, and he was leaving a trail that would connect back to him. After all, if the German chancellor is murdered, what better scapegoat to give the people than a Jew?" He turned to Wintre. "But it wasn't attached to the heart-attack machine. Why not?"

"They didn't have time?" Horner suggested.

Melnik shook his head. "Wintre said it: It wasn't necessary. The heart-attack machine would zero in on Waldner because of his pacemaker. It must have been," he said slowly, "intended for something else . . ."

"There's another apparatus around? And we haven't found it yet!"

"What time is it?" Melnik asked urgently.

"Seven o'clock."

"Jesus Christ! We've got trouble. The banquet is starting right now."

"What are you thinking?"

"No time to explain!" But then he realized he'd have to, since he didn't know what to do next. He took a deep breath. "Yes. Okay. That piece of equipment will trip a solenoid valve when it hears Waldner speaking. It could open a door, sure. It could also complete any electronic circuit—"

"—and set off a bomb," Horner interjected.

"Damn right. That's why Grass is lying there so fat and happy. He *hasn't* failed. This device obviates the problem of setting a bomb in advance; he doesn't have to know where Waldner will be at a particular time in the future. Whenever Waldner gets to the bomb and talks to it, it'll blow in his face."

Horner picked up the telephone and dialed through to Holloway's office. "This is Horner," he said, wasting no time and getting right to the point. "There's a bomb set to explode at any moment in the Breakers."

"Tell me about it," Holloway said just as quickly.

"We don't know that much and we don't have time to explain—"

"Try," Holloway ordered succinctly.

Horner quickly rattled off the facts they knew about the digitized tape and the recognition software and the dead man in the audio-technology store.

"That's it?" Holloway asked. "That's all you've got?"

"That's it," Horner confirmed. "It may not be enough to convict somebody at trial, but it sure as hell ought to be enough to empty out the goddamn hotel before a hundred people get blown to bits."

"Yeah," Holloway said, but somewhat doubtfully.

"You're not worried about getting into more trouble?"

"It sort of entered my mind."

"Well we're *not* wrong about this; Grass planted this bomb. And even if you think we might be, the choice comes down to you getting your ass chewed or all those people getting theirs blown off. Are you hearing me?"

"Yeah. I tell you what. I'll bump this upstairs right away."

"Holloway, we don't have time to fuck around, man. This thing could go off any minute."

"I'll have it on the boss's desk in forty-five seconds."

"That's not good enough!" Horner shouted. "Take the goddamn authority yourself—"

But the phone had already gone dead in his hands. He turned to Melnik and Wintre. "You heard?" He glanced again at his watch. "If you're right . . ."

The hors d'oeuvre table was set up in the spacious hallway outside the banquet room, flanked by tables holding white and red wines. The crowd was already gathered, and the noise level was pleasantly muted but vivacious. The Miami crowd was still gathered together in a group, looking around edgily, irritated that a social event of this magnitude had been scheduled for Palm Beach instead. But already some of them were beginning to drift off into the general mêlée; others would follow as the wine flowed.

The St. Petersburg contingent was pleasantly self-confident; the mere prospect of landing a major-league baseball team had done wonders for their collective psyche. Orlando looked a bit dowdy, as usual. Jacksonville had already dispersed; they lacked a collective consciousness. And the Palm Beachites moved sociably through the crowd, graciously welcoming.

A glass was tinkled loudly, and those closest to it stopped talking and turned to look. It was tinkled again, and the circle of comparative silence widened step by step, until the hotel manager felt enough people were listening. "Would you step into the dining room, please, ladies and gentlemen?"

The tall, wide doors opened at this announcement, and the crowd began to percolate in.

"If you're right, we better not wait for Holloway to come through. We better get over there ourselves. That bomb could go off any minute."

"We're at least fifteen minutes away," Wintre said. "Plus five minutes to go down the stairs and get into the car—"

Melnik was looking through the yellow pages of the telephone directory. "Give me the phone," he said, holding out his hand as he scanned the page he had finally found.

"What are you going to do?" Horner asked, but realized there wasn't time for explanations; he handed the phone over.

Melnik dialed. It was picked up on the first ring. "Ah wanta speak t' th' manageh," he said in a husky Southern accent.

"I'm sorry sir, the manager isn't in his office just now. I'll connect you with the front desk."

Melnik started to protest, but before he could say anything the operator had cut him off. He bounced his fingers irritably against the table until the phone was picked up again at the other end.

"Breakers, front desk."

"Is th' manageh theah, son?" Melnik asked.

"No sir, but I'll try to help you if I can."

"Well, Ah sure's hell hope you can," Melnik said, speaking slowly with a drawl he had learned from watching old Robert Mitchum movies. "For youah sake, that is, son. This is Grand Wizard Sheldon of the Florida Klan of the United Ku Klux Klans of America speakin' to you, boy. Now you hearin' me loud and clear?"

"Yes sir," the voice answered nervously.

"You a white boy, son?"

"Yes sir."

"A Christian boy?"

There was a slight pause and then the voice said, "Yes sir. Can—can I help you?"

"You just shut your mouth 'bout helping me, you hear that, boy? You just stand there to 'tention and listen to what I'm tellin' you. The Grand Konklave of the United Klans of the United States of America is not happy with your Jew bosses throwin' a big banquet for a bunch of foreigners while our own chillun can't get no bread to eat, you hear what I'm sayin', boy?"

"Ahh, yes sir. But the Breakers is not owned by Jewish—"

"Son, you heah to talk or to listen? The Jews own *ever*thin' in this heah country, don't you know that? So to rectify the situation, what we have done is put a bomb in youah big ol' banquet hall. You hear that?"

"A bomb?"

"Tha's what ah said, boy. It is now"—Melnik glanced at his watch—"oh seven twenty-two hours. That ol' bomb is goin' blow youah place sky-high sometime between seven twenty-five and seven thirty." He laughed, just like Mitchum in *Cape Fear* and *Night of the Hunter*. "We put a li'l uncertainty in it so as to give y'all a bit of excitement, y'hear what I'm sayin'? So you bettah get youah white Christian ass out of that theah hotel, but don't y' go tellin' any of them foreigners, y'heah me?"

He hung up. "Now," he said, "let's get over there."

Waldner had not mingled with the crowd before dinner. He had been ushered into the dining room quietly, and sat at the head table talking to his hosts as the people flowed in and began to fill up the tables. When they were all seated the master of ceremonies approached the microphone, tapped it with his fingernail, and asked for their kind attention. He went on to give a thumbnail sketch of recent German-American relations. The sketch bore little resemblance to the real world.

"... and it is my honor to present to you now the chancellor of the Federal Republic of Germany, the Honorable Gottfried Waldner."

Harold Blumen hung up the phone and stood for a moment panic-stricken and white-faced, unsure of what to do. A guest had come up to the front desk while he was talking and had waited patiently; now, however, he began to show signs of impatience. Blumen didn't even see him. He hung up and just stood there, staring straight ahead and beginning to shake. Nobody had taught him anything about this back at the Cornell School of Hotel Administration.

Gottfried Waldner acknowledged the applause and stood up. There was a lot he didn't like about his job, but he did enjoy the public appearances. He milked the applause unmercifully as he patted his pockets, apparently looking for his glasses. Finally he judged he had taken it as far as he could; he had a fine instinct for such things, and before the applause began to die down he had moved out of his seat and advanced to the speaker's lectern.

Harold Blumen came out of his shock to find an angry man shouting in his face, demanding to know something about service and respect and what had happened when even the Breakers was no better than the Plaza and—

Harold didn't even see him. What he did see was Joyce Galya walking down the corridor. He ducked around the desk and grabbed hold of her arm. "Come on," he said urgently.

"Don't be stupid," she whispered angrily. "If I knew you were going to behave like this I would never have—"

"Come *on*," he said.

"I am *not* going up to the bedroom with you in the middle of the day! Now let go—"

"It's not that!" he nearly screamed. Then he took a deep breath and told her quickly about the call.

"What are you going to do?" she asked.

"I'm getting the hell out of here!"

"You can't do that! You've got to tell them!"

"How? What—"

"I'll set off the fire alarm," she said, running back to the front desk. "You go to the banquet room and make sure they get out right away."

"But—"

"Hurry! I'll be right along to help you."

She turned her back on him and hurried off. The man who had been demanding service came up to Harold. "Just what is going on here?" he asked angrily.

Harold still didn't see him. He turned and ran down the corridor as the fire alarm bell began to ring throughout the hotel.

Herr Waldner took his place at the lectern and carefully arranged his notes. He put on his glasses and glanced at them, took his glasses off and looked out at his audience. He tapped his fingernail on the microphone and heard the reassuring amplified click. He leaned forward on both hands and opened his mouth to begin, when a bell began ringing loudly. He looked around inquiringly, but no one seemed to know what it meant. And then the doors at the rear of the hall banged open and a young man came running in. "It's a fire drill," he called out. He came running up to the lectern and stepped in front of Waldner. "I'm sorry to disturb you folks, but I'm afraid we're having a slight emergency here. I apologize, but I'm afraid I'll have to ask all of you to leave the banquet hall immediately."

Joyce Galya had come into the room by now and was throwing open the other doors. "If you would just file quietly out the doors," Harold said, "and, uh, just walk around outside and wait on the beach under the umbrellas and, uh, we'll get you back in here just as soon as we can."

The people simply looked at him dumbfounded.

"It's sort of like a fire drill," he explained.

Someone whispered loudly, "Oh my God, the hotel's on fire!" People began to get up, slowly at first, but within a few seconds everyone began to jump up and then they saw others in front of them and they began to run to the exits, and suddenly the room was in a panic as chairs were overturned and shouts became curses.

Harold turned to the people at the head table. "We'd better get out, too. We can leave through this door right here." As he ushered them out Waldner turned and saw that the banquet hall had erupted in pandemonium. The rush had swelled into a stampede before the girl had been able to get all the doors open, and now the guests were knocking each other down in an effort to get out.

Waldner felt a responsibility, an obligation to help. Pushing aside the young man's clutching hands he went back into the room and returned to the microphone, determined to soothe the madding crowd. "Ladies and gentlemen," he tried to say. "Please, there's no cause for alarm. If we stay calm, all will be well. . . ."

That was what he tried to say, but he was caught up in the atmosphere of panic and without realizing it he lapsed into his native tongue: *"Meine Damen und Herren! Ich bitte sie . . ."*

Inside the microphone, the computer program "heard" Waldner's voice and compared it to the digitized version stored in its memory chip. It didn't know the difference between the German and English languages, but it had been programmed in English and it decided that although the sounds were similar they were not identical. So it did not send the signal that would close the solenoid valve and complete the electronic circuit, and a moment later Waldner's bodyguards managed to break through the crowd. They urged him away from the microphone, nearly lifting him bodily, and carried him out of the room, down the hallway, and out into the safety of the Florida beach and the warmth of the setting sun.

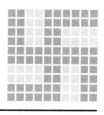

22

1

"Herr Hauptmann was in a tough spot," Melnik said, sipping his gin and tonic with equanimity. "My heart bleeds for him."

"I'm sure it does," Horner said, and Wintre chimed in: "We all feel for him."

They were sitting in the bar at the Palms Lounge in the Breakers, where a grateful management had insisted that all drinks were on the house, looking out through the darkly tinted glass at the sun setting over the palm trees. "He was in a tough spot," Melnik repeated. "That telephone call from Grass was probably the most unwelcome one he ever got in his life."

"He could have hedged his bets," Horner said.

"Not once he picked up the phone," Melnik answered. "His big mistake was in ever picking it up at all. It should have gone to a secretary, who would have told Grass that Herr Hauptmann was out of town at the moment and would get back to him as soon as he could. But he hadn't set it up that way. Hauptmann didn't trust anybody to know what was going on. He liked to keep his own finger on the pulse of the project, and so Grass had a number that rang directly in Hauptmann's office, bypassing all his secretaries. Like the hot line Bobby Kennedy had installed between him and Hoover. J. Edgar hated that line with a passion, and I'll bet Hauptmann feels the same way now."

Horner nodded. "Once Grass had him on the phone he had to either fish or cut bait."

"Poop or get off the potty," Wintre added.

"Come or go," Horner responded, "as our New York hookers say." He chuckled softly to himself and took another swig of his gin and tonic. They were all feeling pretty good, pretty happy with themselves.

"Right, but what could he do?" Melnik asked rhetorically. "Grass calls him up and says the project is completed. But he's been watching television and he hasn't seen anything there about Waldner's assassination. And yet here's Grass on the phone saying he's been caught by the police and it's all a big mistake and the project is complete. If he believes that Grass is telling the truth and Waldner is dead he has to back him up. With his own man as the new chancellor he has the power to cover up anything from their side, so all he has to do is get Grass out of our hands and back to Germany. If he believes that Grass is lying and the project isn't complete, and so he says, 'No, we will not back up your story, you're on your own,' then he's a dead man because in that case the project has failed and Grass is obviously going to spill his guts in return for a lighter sentence. So he really had no choice: He had to hope that Grass was telling the truth and back him up all the way."

"And if we hadn't caught that bomb in time Grass would have been telling the truth," Wintre said.

"Right," Melnik agreed, "and then everything would have been fine for him. With Vorshage backing Hauptmann's order to bring Grass home we wouldn't have had a chance to prove it was he and not Naman who had set the bomb, we wouldn't have had enough to hold him against that kind of diplomatic pressure. They would have brought him home, congratulated him and paid him off, and he would have disappeared. Hauptmann's boy Schlanger would have been the new chancellor and could have hushed up any attempt at follow-up."

"Pardoned everyone, the way Ford pardoned Nixon."

"Absolutely. But now we've got Grass dead to rights."

Horner's chuckle broke out into a deep-throated laugh. "I'll never forget the sight of his face when we told him." He described it again for the other two even though they had all been there. "We walk into that man's hospital room and we say, 'Hey there, man, guess what we got?' And he don't answer, he's just lying there looking at us, waiting for us to tell him Waldner's been blown away. But instead we say, 'Man, we got your fingerprints—' And before we even get a chance to finish the sentence he starts telling us how he was in the banquet room the day before and had been wandering around and had touched the microphone out of curiosity. 'Like people do,' he says, 'to see if it's working, to hear your own voice.' " Horner laughed again. "The son of a bitch had his story down pat, all right. But then Melnik here says, 'Not on the microphone, Mr. G. We found your prints on the plastic explosive inside the microphone.' " Horner laughed and slapped his thigh with exuberance, spilling his drink as he did so.

"It must have been too complicated hooking that up to do it with gloves, fitting those tiny wires into place with the gadget and the solenoid inside the thin mike. So he had his story all ready about how his prints were on the outside, in case any fragments of the microphone were found. But that plastic explosive takes prints better than anything I can think of, and there just isn't any way for him to explain those prints away."

"And the beauty part is that he can't give us a phony story," Wintre chimed in, "because he's already implicated Hauptmann by his earlier telephone call."

"The only problem is," Horner said, "that Grass is now spilling his guts so fast it's keeping ten stenographers busy writing everything down. He'll blow that whole organization wide open and Waldner will be able to throw them all in jail for the rest of their lives. But Grass is going to get off pretty damn light, for turning state's witness. That must bother you."

Melnik shook his head. "No. It doesn't bother me. In fact, the shorter the better. Because when he comes out I'm going to be waiting for him."

Wintre looked at him, thinking: *That's why I could never live with him.* "You're going to kill him."

"Erase him." He looked at her. "Won't the world be better off without him?"

"That's not the point."

"It's my point. The man is a psychopathic sadist and murderer. Do you think a few years in prison is going to change him? Teach him the error of his ways? Make him repent so that when he comes out he'll be a credit to society and a boon to mankind? Or even that he'll be neutral, will spend the rest of his life pumping gasoline or serving McDonald's hamburgers without bothering anybody? The only thing he knows how to do, the only thing he *likes* to do, is inflict pain and death. And when he comes out that's exactly what he's going to do again. Except that I'll get to him first."

"But don't you see what that does to *you*? It makes you a murderer."

Melnik was silent for a while; then he said, "Yes, I suppose that's true: He does what he does because that's what he is. And that's what I am because I do what I do. Not much difference there. But what would you have me do? Use the fire God gave me to burn incense all day long under a nose of wood and stone? No thank you! Scratch the backs of such swine instead of disposing of them? No, I thank you. . . ."

"Shakespeare?" Wintre asked.

He shook his head. "Cyrano, with a bit of license. A man who died for unrequited love."

She smiled, entirely without remorse or pity. "Your love was requited quite sufficiently," she reminded him.

He looked at her for a long moment, then turned and gestured to the hovering waiter for another drink.

"You'll get over it," Wintre said. "From what I hear, you always have. What bothers me is that Hagan will take credit for everything, telling the papers that he had 'his assistant' in charge of the operation."

Horner shrugged. "Can't win 'em all," he said.

Melnik raised his glass. "Live and let live."

Wintre nodded. "Come and go," she said.

2

RANDOLPH BURROUGHS took a cab from the airport to the hotel, and now came up to the front desk asking if they would ring Miss Lisle Wintre's room. The clerk said he thought Miss Wintre was now in the Palms Lounge. Randy thanked him and walked down the hallway, impressed with the service, which was not the sort of thing you got in Washington unless you were at least of senatorial rank. He saw her in the corner, at the table overlooking the ocean, with the two men whom he thought must be Horner and Melnik, and he very nearly turned around and walked out. But where would he go, he thought? Back to the airport and straight back to Washington with his tail between his legs? All his life it seemed he had been in this kind of situation: staring like a kid through the candy-store window at a group of in people who were complete without him, who didn't necessarily dislike him but who certainly didn't need him. Who particularly didn't dislike him, he thought, because they never even realized he existed.

When Wintre came back from Germany she had stayed in his apartment for a couple of days, and although, on the one hand, nothing had happened—they hadn't gone to bed together or anything like that—on the other hand, something had definitely happened: They had talked, and had become friends. He didn't want to ruin that now by making an ass of himself. But he wanted more from her than just friendship and— Goddamnit. He walked across the room to her table.

Her back was to him, and Melnik saw him first. He looked up as Randy approached the table, so that Lisle turned around and saw him. She smiled and jumped up and hugged him, so everything was just great. She introduced him and Horner pulled over a chair and they all sat down again. "What are you doing here?" she asked.

Well, that was the obvious question. He had known she was going to ask it, and all the way down on the plane he had been thinking of what he would say, but he had never come up with a decent answer. So he just shrugged, as if to say it wasn't very important, and mumbled the truth. "I came down to get you."

Which wasn't the whole truth, of course. She hadn't exactly told him what her relationship with Melnik was, but he had been able to sort of read between the lines. And the thought of her down here sleeping with him was just impossible to bear. When she had left his apartment to come down to Florida to help them guard against the assassination, that was one thing. But as soon as he heard that the killing had failed and the perp had been arrested, it had turned into something else altogether. It had turned into her just staying down here with this guy Melnik.

Of course, he didn't know if she was actually going to do that. But he couldn't sit home in Washington, calling her apartment and her office every hour to see if she had returned. He might miss her on the way down—she might be flying back up to Washington, and they might have to just wave at each other as they passed at thirty thousand feet— but that was better than sitting there waiting for her day after day after day.

"You came to *get* me?" she asked.

"To bring you back," he muttered, knowing that she was going to be pissed off, knowing that he had no right to talk that way.

But she just smiled and said, "Randy! That was very sweet of you." And she put her hand in his, and he thought he would never understand women no matter how long he lived. But that was okay, because he could see from the look on Melnik's face that he felt exactly the same way.

3

ON THE PLANE back to Washington, Randy told Lisle the latest development. "It's becoming a real pissing contest between Vorshage and Hauptmann," he said. "Begging your pardon for the language, little lady. They're each trying to write faster and tell the mostest the quickest, and the German feds are running back and forth trying to decide which one to use as witness and which one to throw the book at."

"I thought Vorshage would still be in a position to deny everything."

Randy shook his head. "Caught like a bear in a honey trap, honey, and all because of you and your poor friend. What happened is, when you came back from Berlin and told me what happened I had our boys check out the situation, and there was no murder reported there."

"What? But—"

"Right: There was a bloody body in the hotel room when you left." He shook his head. "Uh-uh. Both girls checked out and were gone."

"Are you trying to tell me I imagined it? Because if you are—"

"Hold on! Let me explain. It all fits the pattern perfectly. Vorshage must have had a cleanup squad sent."

"Oh." She pondered the implications.

"Right!" he said. "So it couldn't possibly have been a casual robbery and rape. They did a good job, but they couldn't hide all the blood. They had poured wine over it and turned the mattress over so it wouldn't be noticed. My guess is they probably intended to have a little accidental fire there after a few days, to completely get rid of everything. But when we reported what happened, the local police came in too soon.

"So it couldn't have been a casual murder; it was definitely planned. Now, Vorshage might could have denied any part in it; he could have said someone in his office overheard your conversation with him and done the dastardly deed. And maybe he could have denied Hauptmann's allegations that he was the point man, could have claimed Hauptmann is lying. But when you put your story together with Hauptmann's, it becomes just too damn much. So even as we speak, he and Hauptmann are trying to outdo each other with details, names, and places."

Burroughs leaned back in his seat and smiled happily.

"Almost makes you believe in God," Wintre said.

"Don't it just? And speaking of God, have you heard about your Mr. Hagan?" He shook his head in mock sadness.

"What happened?"

"A terrible tragedy," he said. "They'll try to keep it out of the papers, but I don't see how they're going to keep this stuff quiet."

"What stuff?"

"Well, it seems his wife's been having an affair with some guy. And this guy called her and they talked on the phone in an incriminating way, you know? So she erased it—or thought she did—and went off and slept with the guy yesterday afternoon. Then she comes home and she takes a look at the answering machine to see if there's been any messages, and she sees the lid is up and there's no tape in there. Now she *knows* she left the machine on, she had erased the call from her lover just before she left, so what the hell happened? She thinks there must have been a burglary, but she looks around and nothing else has been touched. So she wonders, where could the tape be? And the only place is in the tape deck in the living room, so she looks and there it is. She still doesn't understand what's going on but she hits the button to play it, and there is this guy's voice and the conversation they had, right there on the tape. It turns out what she must have done is just pushed the rewind button, which doesn't erase it but just rewinds back to the beginning. She doesn't understand this at the time, but there it is, so she knows that somehow she screwed up erasing it. And not only that but Hagan must have heard it because who else could have taken the tape out and put it in the deck?

"Then she finds a very terse note from him: He's been called out of town for a few days. So she calls his office right away, and his secretary says no, she doesn't know anything about him going out of town. So she knows right away what's happened, and she figures he's going to leave her and she's all upset. She breaks down, because I figure she's having this affair but she really loves him. How could anybody love that son of a bitch?"

"Never mind. Go on."

"So she doesn't know what to do, and she's kind of—not hysterical, I guess, but all upset. And so she calls this old friend of hers and he comes over—"

"Not the man she was sleeping with?"

"No. Like I said, she evidently really loves Hagan, and the thought of losing him—which would drive you and me mad with joy—frightens the hell out of her. She like never wants to see that guy again, and she calls up this old friend. Very platonic-type friend. And evidently by the time he gets there she really is kind of hysterical. So he talks her into taking a couple of sleeping pills, and he sits by her side until finally she falls asleep. And then he lies down on the chaise in her bedroom, in case she wakes up and became suicidal or—well, he probably didn't know what.

"In the middle of the night he wakes up: He hears sounds downstairs, someone's moving around. So he doesn't know what it is, he figures maybe it's Hagan come home but maybe it isn't, and so he picks up a poker from the fireplace and he opens the bedroom door. And right there at that moment, there's Hagan. And he has a gun in his hand. . . ."

"What happened?"

"What happened? He shot the guy."

"Oh my God, did he kill him?"

Randy laughed. "No, he missed. Well, he hit him in the foot. With a .22 that's not much worse than a bee sting."

"Hagan thought he was the man she was sleeping with?"

"I guess. What his story is, he came home and heard somebody moving around up there and it didn't sound like his wife. He didn't know, so he went to his room and got out his gun just to see, and he comes down the hall and the door opens and there's this guy standing there with a poker in his hand. So what does he think? He shoots him."

"He thought it was a burglar?"

"Well, that's gonna be his story. I'd guess what he really thought was he surprised his wife with her fancy man."

"You think he'll get away with it?"

"In court? Probably. But whether he does or not, he's finished in D.C. People are always going to be asking, what was this guy doing there in his wife's bedroom in the middle of the night? The only thing worse in politics than being caught in some woman's room is some other guy being caught in your wife's room. Every time he walks into a meeting, people are going to be smiling. Especially since the topper is, when he tried to shoot the guy he missed! I mean, that is funny." He shook his head in half-mocking commiseration. "His career is finished. And the *really* funny thing is, it was the wrong man."

Epilogue

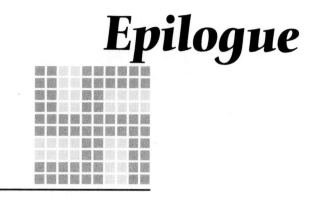

A FOGGY NIGHT in London town. Melnik felt as if he were walking through an old movie, the feeling enhanced by the total lack of color. An old, black-and-white movie about Sherlock Holmes or Jack the Ripper. Traffic noises muted by the dripping drizzle, even footsteps muffled and soft. In the cobblestoned mews through which he walked the only light came from dim lampposts. The only color was a dim yellow halo around the light bulbs; it barely reached the end of the alley, where a wooden sign dangled from one nail, announcing the Green Lord.

He thought for a moment of Horner, the Jolly Green Giant, and that reminded him of Wintre, his long-lost love. Great, he thought. Perfect thoughts for a night like this. He pushed open the door to the Lord, and entered into a thick warmth emanating from an open fire and a dozen tired bodies. He found an empty table in the corner, fetched a pint, and sat down.

It would never end, he thought. He would spend the rest of his nights like this, wet and lonely, sipping a beer and trying not to remember. Sipping a beer and waiting for someone.

The chair beside him scraped back across the floor, and a heavy figure dropped into it with a grunt. The man took off his hat and dropped it wetly onto the table, wiped his arm across his beard, and shook the raindrops loose onto the floor. "I hate this town," he said. "Couldn't you have found a table nearer the fire?"

Melnik gave no answer. The man expected none. He took a notebook out of his pocket and laid it on the table beside his hat. Melnik picked it up. In 1985 the Mossad had found concrete evidence that Saddam Hussein was building a nuclear reactor capable of providing plutonium for a nuclear bomb, and the Israeli air force had then bombed it out of existence. That danger had been averted, but it would never end. . . .

"No question about it," the man said, "it all checked out."

Melnik nodded. Gerhard Hauptmann, implicated by Grass's testimony, had extricated himself from the threat of a lifetime in jail by providing testimony of his own. He had provided details of the work he had done for several Middle Eastern nations, providing them with plans and materials for biological warfare. Part of the agreement had been that the testimony remain secret. The German government wanted it kept secret for obvious reasons: The Germans did not need the embarrassment it would provide. Hauptmann wanted everything kept secret; under the agreement he would simply disappear. The Israelis wanted it secret, so they would have the opportunity of finding the factories and destroying them before the Iraqis, Syrians, and Iranians knew they were at risk.

Melnik finished reading the notebook and nodded. Within the week there would be a series of simultaneous explosions across the Middle East. Accusations would fly far and fast, but no one would admit responsibility, and eventually the furor would die down. And the world would be a bit safer, as it was after Iraq's Tammuz 17 reactor was destroyed. For a few years, until a new threat emerged.

It would never end.

He sat there after the other man left, and allowed his thoughts to wander. If it would never end, didn't that free him from responsibility rather than tying him down? Couldn't he retire and take the desk job Mazor continued to press upon him, begin to live a normal life, leave the cloaks and daggers to younger men? Get married, raise a family. . . .

Yes, he thought, he could do that. He really could. He finished the beer, buttoned up his coat, and stepped out into the cold.

All he needed was the right woman.

As a general rule, people, even the wicked, are much more naïve and simple-hearted than we suppose. And we ourselves are, too.

—Fyodor Dostoyevsky, *The Brothers Karamazov*

ABOUT THE AUTHOR

DAVID E. FISHER holds a Ph.D. in nuclear chemistry from the Oak Ridge Institute of Nuclear Studies and the University of Florida. He has been a playwright and actor, and is currently professor of cosmochemistry and director of the Environmental Science Program at the University of Miami. His dozen previous books include both novels and works about science and politics. His last book, *Across the Top of the World,* told the history of polar exploration in the context of his journey to the North Pole aboard a Soviet nuclear-powered icebreaker; his next examines the science of hurricanes in the context of Andrew, which he endured. He is married and has three children.

ABOUT THE TYPE

This book was set in Meridien, a classic roman typeface designed in 1957 by the Swiss-born Adrian Frutiger for the French typefoundry Deberny et Peignot. Frutiger also designed the famous and much-used typeface Univers.